STONER'S CROSSING

Judith Pella

Judith Pella

BETHANY HOUSE PUBLISHERS
MINNEAPOLIS, MINNESOTA 55438

"Border Ballad" song from *Cowboy and Western Songs* by Austin E. and Alta S. Fife, Clarkson N. Potter Inc. Publishers, New York, 1969.

Cover illustration by Joe Nordstrom

Published by Bethany House Publishers
A Ministry of Bethany Fellowship, Inc.
11300 Hampshire Avenue South
Minneapolis, Minnesota 55438

Printed in the United States of America

Library of Congress Cataloging-in-Publication Data

Pella, Judith.
   Stoner's crossing / Judith Pella
      p.   cm. — (Lone star legacy : bk. 2)
   Sequel to: Frontier lady.
    1. Frontier and pioneer life—Texas—Fiction. 2. Mothers and daughters—Texas—Fiction. 3. Women pioneers—Texas—Fiction. I. Title.
II. Series: Pella, Judith. Lone star legacy ; bk. 2.
PS3566.E415S76   1994
813'.54—dc20   94-4891
ISBN 1–55661–294–X   CIP

To my son Jon, whose good-natured spirit is the model
for the character, Jonathan Barnum.
"Blessed are the pure in heart: for they shall see God."
Matthew 5:8, KJV

Books by Judith Pella

Lone Star Legacy

Frontier Lady
Stoner's Crossing

The Russians (with Michael Phillips)

The Crown and the Crucible
A House Divided
Travail and Triumph
Heirs of the Motherland (Judith Pella only)

The Stonewycke Trilogy (with Michael Phillips)

The Heather Hills of Stonewycke
Flight from Stonewycke
Lady of Stonewycke

The Stonewycke Legacy (with Michael Phillips)

Stranger at Stonewycke
Shadows over Stonewycke
Treasure of Stonewycke

The Highland Collection (with Michael Phillips)

Jamie MacLeod: Highland Lass
Robbie Taggart: Highland Sailor

The Journals of Corrie Belle Hollister (with Michael Phillips)

My Father's World
Daughter of Grace
On the Trail of the Truth*
A Place in the Sun*
Sea to Shining Sea*
Into the Long Dark Night*
Land of the Brave and the Free*
Grayfox*

*Michael Phillips only

Acknowledgments

I'd like to take a moment to offer thanks to some folks who had a special part in this book. First, to my friend, attorney William Barnum, who initially suggested that Deborah needed a good lawyer; he also gave me many helpful tips. Also, I'd like to mention the invaluable assistance of Angela A. Dorau, Assistant Archivist of the State Bar of Texas; she gave me much information on the legal history of Texas. Finally, some very special thanks to my friends, Don and Ame Cook, and their children, Beth, Mike, and Ben, for their wonderful hospitality—in the true Texas style!—while I visited that grand state in which this book is set.

JUDITH PELLA is the author of five major fiction series for the Christian market, co-written with Michael Phillips. An avid reader and researcher in historical, adventure, and geographical venues, her skill as a writer is exceptional. She and her family make their home in California.

CONTENTS

PART 1

PURSUIT OF THE PAST

1

The high plains stretched out before the tall rider like an endless horizon of searing death. And it was only May, not even summer yet.

The palomino mare picked her way across the rocky, broken ground with as much care as her anxious rider would allow. The rider had to force himself not to drive the animal faster, to push her to keep pace with the pounding of his own heart. He glanced back several times but saw only the undulating heat waves that dogged him as relentlessly as any human pursuer.

If only he had checked his water supply before he had been forced to take flight! That had been purely stupid, like a greenhorn kid or one of those city dandies who had lately been trying their hand at ranching. *He* knew better. He had been riding this wild country for more years than he cared to admit.

He reached for his canteen just to see if . . . maybe . . .

One quick heft told him it was only half full and would never be enough to see him across the Llaño Estacado. But he hoped to heaven he wouldn't have to go that far.

Perhaps a prayer or two wouldn't hurt right now, but that wasn't exactly his style. *Now, if the preacher were here,* the rider thought, *I sure wouldn't stand in his way if he wanted to send a word heavenward.*

The rider had to admit to himself that he might not be in this fix if he had listened more to the preacher in the first place, walked the straight and narrow, and all that. But he was more apt to act first and think about the consequences later—if he ever did. Usually the thrill of some wild and dangerous challenge far exceeded any retribution that might happen as a result. In the old days, being wanted by the law—with a noose ever dangling in his future—had never stopped him; in fact, that had only heightened the thrill. Sure, he had settled down some since then. What man doesn't as he begins to feel his age and his mortality?

But, unfortunately, Griff McCulloch was no saint. He doubted he ever would be.

Griff twisted in his saddle once more to view the ground he had just traversed. Nothing. Only heat following him, and heat in front of him—heat, and no prospects of water for miles. His mouth tasted like dirt and tumbleweed, but he couldn't afford to indulge himself. He'd need water a lot more later on.

He was about to swing his gaze forward once more when he saw what he had been both dreading and anticipating for hours. It was faint, but there was definitely a cloud of dust southeast of him, some five miles off. Griff had been almost certain he had lost him, but that Pollard was a better man, at least a better tracker, than Griff had given him credit for.

Well, it was probably best this way. They had been destined for a showdown ever since that day nineteen years ago when they had first crossed paths. And then again, some ten years ago when he had seen the fellow at Fort Griffin, Griff thought it was going to blow up in his face. But nothing had come of it. Griff had managed to get himself and Deborah away without being seen. He had been ready to kill Pollard that day, but the ex-sheriff had disappeared, not to turn up again until last night in the Double Eagle Saloon in Danville.

Griff dug his heels into the palomino's flanks. This was no time to ruminate over past mistakes. Pollard was on his tail and closing fast. If there was going to be a showdown, Griff would just as soon be the one to choose the battleground. In the distance ahead, about a mile away, he could make out a pile of big boulders that would give him some cover in a gunfight.

He had no doubt this was about to turn into a fight. He had sworn ten years ago to kill Pollard if he brought danger to Deborah, and he hadn't changed his mind since.

"Geeiup!" Griff urged the mare. She held back a little, for she had enough good sense to know this wasn't the kind of terrain you raced over carelessly. Griff was no fool either; he knew—

It happened quicker than thought, faster than he could berate his foolish panic. The palomino went down, a hoof caught in a crevice in the dry, cracked earth. Griff rolled away from the animal as it fell, but escaping personal injury would hardly matter if his horse was hurt. She was a fine beast—better, even, than the palomino he had lost years ago in the battle with the Comanche.

It didn't take him long to see that he had another score to settle with Pollard.

The horse would have been back up on her feet if she were

uninjured. When Griff came up to her, she lifted her head and shook her golden mane a bit as if in affectionate response. But she made no attempt to stand.

"You okay, girl?" Griff murmured as he examined each of her legs. He groaned inwardly as he felt the bones grind unnaturally in her right foreleg. She gave a pathetic whinny, and he gently eased the leg back to the ground.

Griff cursed bitterly. He wanted to blame Pollard, but he knew it was his own fault. If he hadn't panicked . . . if he hadn't let that drifter rile him last night . . . if he hadn't been drinking . . .

But there had been a celebration. A cowhand friend of his from another ranch was getting married and having his last fling before tying the knot. And Slim, off selling horses in Fort Worth, hadn't been there to keep Griff from the bottle. Griff knew he ought to be careful, but one thing just led to another, and before he knew it, he was drunk. The problem was, liquor always made him ornery as a polecat. When that drifter accused him of cheating at cards, he just got horn-mad.

"You take that back, you low-down sidewinder!" Griff had slurred.

"Make me!" challenged the drifter.

"You calling me out?"

"You bet I am!"

Everyone in the Double Eagle had scattered, and someone had gone after the sheriff.

Griff and the drifter faced off, and even though Griff had easily twenty years on the kid, he still outdrew him without so much as losing his breath.

When Pollard showed up, Griff was still drunk—but not too drunk to immediately recognize the man who had officiated at the attempted hanging of Deborah Stoner, now Deborah Killion. When the saloon doors burst open and Pollard appeared, Griff was still standing over the dead drifter holding his smoking gun. Both men exchanged shocked looks. Griff didn't wait to find out if Pollard recognized him or made the connection to Deborah. He holstered his Colt and bolted.

He *had* been too drunk to think straight. He probably should have hid out somewhere close by, but, instead, he lit out west, figuring to draw Pollard out on the barren plains and kill him there so no one would be the wiser.

For all these years—it was 1884 now—he and Deborah had managed to keep a low profile and not cross the path of anyone who had been involved in those proceedings at Stoner's Crossing. They stayed away from town as much as possible, Deborah hardly ever going in, and he only when necessary for business and the occasional evening of recreation. A man couldn't live like a hermit, no matter what. Deborah seemed to prefer the solitude of the ranch, but Griff had to have some action, even if just three or four times a year.

There was no reason why they couldn't have gone on like that forever. Who would have thought Pollard would find a sheriffing job in Danville, a little more than a day's ride from the ranch?

It occurred to him that Pollard might have told someone in town about him and Deborah, but Griff couldn't worry about that now. For the present, he just had to concentrate on Pollard. Get him . . . or die trying. And dying was becoming a strong possibility, for without a horse he had little chance of surviving.

He had to quit thinking that way, or he'd give up entirely. "Your not dead yet, you old buzzard!" he told himself crossly. "Now get moving."

He loosened his saddlebag and rifle from the palomino. He still had a chance of eliminating Pollard. Last night he had not been planning on a shoot-out, any more than he had planned on a long trek across the Staked Plains. But a quick examination of the contents of his saddlebags turned up enough ammunition for his rifle and Colt to give that sheriff a good fight. There was a rock about two hundred yards away. It was barely two feet high and only a little wider, but it was the best cover that was readily available to serve him for protection. He loaded his Sharps buffalo gun, which he had no doubt would be a sure defense against anything the sheriff had.

He had one thing to do, however, before he moved his gear and prepared for the battle.

Griff drew his Colt from his holster and spun the chamber around to make sure it was full, though he'd only need one bullet for what he must do. He licked his dry lips. All the water in the world wouldn't have helped him just then.

He stood over his injured palomino. "You were a fine horse," he said, his voice choked with emotion. "If I ever get another one like you, I'll treat her more decently."

He pulled the trigger, and the shot reverberated in his ears. He wiped a sleeve across his eyes but would never admit the moisture there was anything more than sweat.

Then he gathered up his gear and went to the rock to wait.

Pollard would have heard the shot. If the sheriff had any doubt at all as to the position of his quarry, that uncertainty would now be erased. He'd be within rifle range in a matter of minutes.

Griff was as ready as he'd ever be.

2

It wasn't long before that distant cloud of dust took the shape of a man on horseback. Griff peered over the edge of the rock and watched the rider approach. It was Pollard all right, heading straight for him.

Pollard stopped and, squinting against the glare of the sun, spent a moment apparently studying the place where the horse had fallen. Then his gaze swept the surrounding area, resting occasionally on a scattering of rocks similar to the one where Griff had found refuge.

Griff smiled to himself and set the muzzle of his rifle on the rock, taking careful aim. The sheriff obviously wouldn't be expecting this, no doubt thinking he was out of range of most rifles. But the Sharps had a range of almost double a Winchester. Griff could pick off Pollard like a duck in a pond. Still, even in his outlaw days, Griff hadn't been one to kill needlessly. Best give the sheriff a chance to state his purpose first. Griff might just learn if Pollard had revealed his discovery to anyone else in town.

"If you're on foot," Pollard shouted, "you ain't got a chance. Give it up now and it'll go easier for you."

"You ain't got nothing on me, Sheriff. That gunfight in Danville was fair and square."

"So why are you running?"

"Who says I'm running?"

"I'm taking you in, McCulloch. I reckon after nineteen years it's about time I caught up with you."

Griff stared down the sights of the buffalo gun and fired, blasting a hole in the parched earth two yards beyond where the sheriff stood. Pollard jumped in surprise, then dropped to his knees. But when Griff tried to fire again, his rifle jammed, giving Pollard a chance to scramble to the cover of a small boulder about fifty yards away, placing Griff well within range of the sheriff's Winchester. But Pollard didn't fire.

"Hey, what're you shooting, man? A feller don't stand a chance against a cannon like that."

"You figure I oughta give you a chance?"

"I'm just doing my job."

"Which is?"

"I don't think I gotta explain that to you. I'm taking you in for past crimes, McCulloch, and I'm getting even for you rescuing Caleb Stoner's daughter-in-law."

"Past crimes are one thing, Pollard; Deborah Stoner is quite another. She's innocent, and you know it."

"She was convicted of murder by a proper trial and everything."

"What's it to you, Pollard? You think to make a name for yourself by hanging a woman?"

"That would go a long way to making up for all the trouble that woman brought me. I spent three years in prison because Caleb convinced the court that I was in cahoots with you. Caleb made sure I was disgraced as a lawman after that. I spent years sweeping saloons to pay for enough drinks to keep me going. This here badge I'm wearing is only a deputy star that I got because no one else would take it. I reckon to get paid back now. The five thousand dollar reward Caleb is still offering will sure help."

Griff had never heard about the reward, but then he had never made any inquiries for fear of stirring up a hornet's nest. At least he now knew why Pollard had set out after him alone. He thought Griff could lead him to Deborah, and he sure wouldn't be willing to share the reward money with anyone else in town. So, it was pretty certain that Pollard had told no one about his suspicions.

"Now, you just take me to the Stoner woman," Pollard went on, "and maybe I'll cut a deal with you."

"You don't know where she is?" prompted Griff.

"I got a pretty good idea," said Pollard. "I asked about you in town last night. Fellers said you worked for a woman named Deborah Killion. I don't reckon that's just a coincidence of names. But I figure she'll come along a lot more peaceably if I got you with me. So I suggest you cooperate. Otherwise, you're just gonna die out here, and I'll still bring her in."

"Yeah, I'll cooperate all right," sneered Griff, drawing his pistol. "Like this—" He punctuated his words with gunfire.

This time he wasn't aiming for the dirt. But Pollard ducked in time, and the bullet whizzed over him, inches from his head.

Pollard returned fire, his bullet taking a chunk out of Griff's boulder. Bits of rock flew in Griff's face, one large piece leaving a bloody gash in his left cheek.

Griff fired again, raising his head a little higher from his hiding place in order to take better aim. That was just the mistake Pollard was waiting for. His shot tore into Griff's left shoulder with painful force. Griff choked back a yell and ground his teeth together; he didn't want his adversary to know he was wounded. The bullet had only grazed him, but the pain seared his arm like a fire. At least it was only his left arm. Griff took off the kerchief from around his neck and stuffed it into the wound; then he fired again.

They exchanged several more rounds of gunfire, but it soon became clear to Griff that in their present positions, they were engaged in a classic Mexican stand-off. It was entirely possible for them to hold each other off until one or the other ran out of ammunition— or died of thirst. Griff had no idea how much ammo or water Pollard had, but even the washed-up deputy would have had more time to prepare for this confrontation than Griff had last night. Griff figured *he'd* have to be the one to break the draw. The best way would be to keep out of range of Pollard's Winchester and still stay close enough to make the best use of the Sharps' range. But even if his Sharps didn't jam again, there was simply no cover to make that possible.

The next best thing was to get *Pollard* out in the open. That still meant Griff would have to expose himself, but at least then they'd both be at a disadvantage. It was the only way.

Griff flexed his wounded arm to assure himself that he could hold out in a hand-to-hand fight if it came to that. The arm was sore and weak, but he could make a fist that he thought, from the looks of the aging Pollard, could hold its own.

Griff quietly emptied his Colt, the remaining bullets dropping into his hand. Then he aimed and fired over the top of the rock toward the deputy. The empty *click* was loud enough to carry over the distance between the two hiding places. He hoped his feigned message was clear to Pollard.

"Okay, Pollard, I'm ready to deal," Griff yelled, covertly reloading his Colt as he spoke.

Pollard chuckled. "That's real smart of you, McCulloch, 'cause I got enough ammo to hold out for days—and water, too."

"All right! You don't have to rub it in. Are you gonna deal, or not?"

"You bet. Just throw your weapons out where I can see 'em, then come out with your hands high."

"And what's in it for me?"

"Like I said, you can go free; all I want is the woman."

Griff hesitated long enough to slip out all the spare bullets from his holster belt, stashing them in his saddlebag in order to further the impression that he was out of ammo. Hopefully he'd be able to come back later for the bag and his saddle. Then he tossed his Sharps rifle out into the dirt, followed by his Colt. He aimed them to land just a few feet left of center so when he made his move they'd not be too far away.

"Okay, now you, McCulloch," ordered Pollard.

"Yeah. Just remember, I'm worth more to you alive than dead."

"You ain't got nothing to worry about. Now, move it."

Griff stretched his hands above his head, wincing slightly as he lifted his left one; then he stood and made his way slowly out into the open. He stopped with the weapons in the dirt far enough away not to look suspicious, but close enough for comfort.

Pollard took a moment before he also rose from his hiding place, obviously taking time to check Griff over to insure he was unarmed and safe.

Griff read the sheriff's motives. *I'm unarmed,* he thought, *but I hope to blazes I ain't safe.*

Pollard was looking rather satisfied with himself. This was, after all, a big day for him; not only was he about to pocket five thousand dollars, but he was going to settle a score that had been on his personal books for nearly two decades. Griff saw that the years had not been overly generous with Pollard. The toll of drink showed in his face, with its reddish cheeks and nose and bleary eyes. The Vigilante Committee at Danville that did the hiring and firing of lawmen must have been pretty desperate to hire this old drunk as deputy. The newly arrived Houston and Texas Central Railroad was slowly civilizing the town, but Danville was still one of the wilder towns in Texas, and lawmen didn't have a very long life span there. If Griff could help it, that would also be the case with Pollard.

The old deputy immediately made a stupid mistake—he headed directly for Griff's weapons before securing his prisoner. He did, however, keep his six-gun trained on Griff as he bent over and picked up the Sharps. He kicked the Colt about ten feet away, much to Griff's dismay.

"This is some weapon you got here," Pollard said with admiration. "I don't reckon you'll miss it." He ran his hand over the polished wood butt; Griff himself had made it out of walnut.

There wasn't going to be another opportunity like this—at least Griff wasn't going to count on it. While Pollard's attention was momentarily focused on the Sharps, Griff made his move.

18

With speed born of desperation, he ducked and dove for Pollard's legs. Pollard dropped the rifle, shock registering clearly on his face. And before the man could discharge his six-gun, Griff had tackled him to the ground. His shot went wild.

Pollard cursed.

They rolled around in the dirt, Pollard trying to get another round off from his pistol. Griff grabbed Pollard's gun hand but found that the has-been lawman was stronger than he appeared. His weight was like a millstone as he straddled Griff. Griff would have managed better if his left arm had been at full strength, but as it was, he had to put all his efforts into keeping that six-gun at bay.

During one slack instant, Griff managed to free his right hand long enough to slug Pollard in the chin, landing a blow that should have loosened the man's teeth. But the old drunk hung on tenaciously. It couldn't be pure physical strength driving the deputy now, but rather some other force impelling him. Hate, vengeance, greed—whatever it was, Pollard fought with the viciousness of a wounded coyote.

Risking imminent danger from the gun, Griff shifted his attention for an instant, rallying his efforts for a new strategy. He didn't have much time, for he had to be faster than Pollard could squeeze off a shot. But in that split-second time frame, Griff gave a mighty bodily thrust. He was almost as surprised as Pollard that he was able to throw the sheriff off; but Pollard's strength must surely be ebbing. Griff now rolled on top, gaining a slight advantage. At least he was in a better position to do something about that pistol. He whacked Pollard's hand against the dirt as hard as he could.

Pollard held firm. He had too much at stake to succumb easily. "I ain't letting you go," Pollard gasped.

The stress of that futile attempt to dislodge the gun sent pain shooting up and down Griff's arm, along with a trickle of fresh blood. Pollard had surely noticed the blood from the start and realized the wounded ex-outlaw could not hold out for long. He, too, was just waiting for the right moment.

And it came too soon for Griff.

Pollard jerked his hand forward. He didn't quite free it from Griff's grip, but he only needed one more twist and then—

Suddenly the six-gun exploded!

The force of the shot jolted the two men apart. Pollard still held the gun, and he quickly leveled it at Griff, not wanting to make any more mistakes.

"You just don't know when to quit, do you, McCulloch?" said

Pollard, surprised, despite his bravado, that he still held the advantage. It was another moment before he realized just how much of an advantage he did in fact hold.

Griff lay sprawled out in the dirt, not moving.

"Hey, McCulloch! You ain't dead, are you?"

Pollard would probably be able to bring in the Stoner woman without Griff, but it would be a long sight easier *with* him. Pollard scrambled to his feet, still aiming the gun. He kicked Griff's leg.

Griff groaned and lifted his head, but everything before his eyes was blurry, and the man standing over him aiming that gun appeared to be swaying curiously. He then realized he had blacked out, and from the looks of Pollard, it had to have been only for a few seconds. If he could bring Pollard down again, he might still have a chance.

But when Griff tried to move, pain like he had never known before coursed through his entire body. It couldn't be the arm . . .

Instinctively his hand went to what seemed the source of this new and terrible ache. Near his right side his hand felt a huge bloody rent. He fell back again in agony.

Oh, Deborah! I failed you. I'm so sorry . . .

Then everything went black.

PART 2

CAPTURE

3

Stride for stride, the skewbald mare could not hope to keep pace with the mighty white stallion. He was obviously a thoroughbred, not of natural mustang stock. Perhaps he was a fugitive from the stable of some wealthy Spanish *caballero,* or perhaps he had been sired by such a fugitive and foaled on the open range, a free-born creature from birth. Whatever his bloodline, he was sixteen hands high and easily dwarfed his mares. The stallion's power was evident in his rippling muscles and the long legs that sped him effortlessly across the prairie.

Deborah Killion, atop the skewbald, marveled at the stallion's form, realizing at once that this ride was not so much a race as an exhibition of the stallion's grandeur. They had been running this herd of mustangs for three days now, from early morning until dusk, attempting to tire the wild horses and lure them into a specially built corral. Deborah and her cowhands had the advantage of taking turns and getting fresh mounts two or three times during the day. The stallion had not had the benefit of such rest except at night.

The herd of mustangs splashed across a buffalo wallow, and mud flecked the stallion's white flanks. The mares in his herd were close to exhaustion, but the stallion ran at their rear—prodding them, bringing up stragglers, pushing them to and well beyond their limit. Yet he himself showed no indication at all of tiring. There was untapped strength yet in that grand animal, Deborah thought. She remembered Broken Wing's gray and wished he were still alive to challenge the white. That would have been a race to make history, indeed.

Deborah gulped a lungful of air as she, too, splashed across the wallow. Then she laughed. She was getting too old for this kind of race!

She reined in her mare. It was late, and the sun was already dipping low in the west. Obviously, this wild herd would need another day or two of running before they were ready for capture. Deborah shook her head in awe. Usually two or three days was enough to get control of a herd and head them in the direction of the corral.

Wiping a sweat-soaked strand of blond hair from her eyes, Deborah watched the stallion turn his herd back toward familiar range. He had slowed, sensing that for the time being, at least, the chase was over. In a few minutes the herd stopped to graze while the stallion stood above them on a small rise, as if both to protect them and lord over them. He stamped his hoof and swung his long, sleek neck around toward where Deborah and her mare stood observing them.

"Another time, fine brother!" Deborah murmured.

Even from a distance of two hundred yards, she could see the untamed arrogance in the stallion's black eyes. He would not be caught easily, that was certain. And, to tell the truth, Deborah was not really eager to do so. She sympathized with his desperate desire for freedom. She herself had once been restrained and hobbled, and she had yearned for freedom. That might have been a long time ago, twenty-some years, but part of her would never forget what that kind of captivity was like.

Yet Deborah had also learned the truth of divine paradox: surrender to God brought freedom—not just the physical freedom afforded by the open range, but liberty of the spirit.

Those years at Stoner's Crossing had finally taken their proper place in life's perspective. They represented only two of the thirty-nine years of Deborah's life. Undeniably, because of the terrible nature of those particular years, they had made a strong impact on her life and her future. But still, it had been only two years. Certainly the following nineteen of fulfillment and happiness must balance those out.

The stallion loped down the hill, probably to gather his mares and find some shelter for the night. Deborah reined her own skewbald mare around. It was time to get back to camp.

She had no desire to ruminate long over the past years, except to recall the fond memories they carried. "It's the future that really counts," she whispered softly into the breeze. "The future always brings improvement and growth, and even its share of happiness."

She thought of Sam and what a joy their marriage was. After five years, they were still like a couple of kids in love. Even if her children were almost grown adults—Carolyn was eighteen, and Sky was sixteen—she was not yet an old woman. The beauty that others had found so stunning at eighteen had not entirely vanished from the

24

long years on the harsh plains. Sam said her eyes still reflected the endless prairie sky in springtime, and her golden hair camouflaged what gray the years had brought. Only her skin showed the passage of time—brown from hours of working outdoors, with crow's-feet edging the corners of her eyes, and lines framing her gentle, expressive mouth. Sometimes she thought she looked more like her Cheyenne sisters now than when she had lived among the Indians and worn buckskin garb.

But life was too good *now* to dwell long on the past, and she didn't intend to. She had a ranch to run, horses to catch and break, and a family to tend to.

"You've no time to daydream, Deborah," she said to herself. She nudged her horse into motion and rode toward camp at a gentle canter.

When the camp came in sight a quarter of a mile away, she saw a rider galloping toward it from the other direction. She sensed immediately that something was wrong, and she dug her heels into her mount's flanks and urged the mare to a gallop. Deborah reached the camp just a few moments after the rider.

It was Jasper, one of the young stable hands, all in a sweat and wild-eyed.

"Miz Killion, you got to come quick!"

By now most of the camp had gathered. Longjim ran a hand along Jasper's horse and shook his head derisively at the youth. "This better be important! You got this poor animal all in a lather. Get on down so we can cool him off."

"Yessir, Longjim," Jasper said obediently. Longjim Sands, the top hand of the Wind Rider outfit, was not a man that anyone argued with, much less a mere kid. Jasper swung off his horse, but added with the same urgency, "Miz Killion, this is important."

Deborah dismounted and was about to urge Jasper to state the problem when her daughter Carolyn joined the group.

"What is it, Ma?" she asked. "What's wrong?"

By now Deborah was growing impatient. "We'll all find out if we just give the poor boy a chance to speak," she snapped. Then, more gently, she added to the stable hand, "Go on, Jasper. What's happened?"

"It's the law, ma'am. He's come to the ranch and he's got Griff, but Griff is in bad shape—real bad."

"Bad shape?" Deborah repeated, trying to make sense out of the lad's incomplete words. "What do you mean?"

"He's shot, ma'am, shot bad. But the deputy, he's still holding a gun on him. Told me to bring you back—and for you not to think of escaping like you did before, if you cared what happens to Griff. Ma'am, what does he mean, 'not to think of escaping'? As if you had to run from the law."

Deborah turned pale as the full impact of the youth's words hit her. She didn't know how it had happened, but somehow her secret had been revealed. And Griff was wounded, perhaps dying.

Without another thought, Deborah swung back toward her mare and was about to slip a foot in the stirrup when Longjim laid a restraining hand on her shoulder.

"Deborah, don't you act rashly!" he said. "You don't have to go back there. Me and the boys'll help Griff. You just get outta here, far away."

"No, Longjim, I'm too old to start running now." Her voice was strained. All she could think of was her dear friend, Griff McCulloch, hurt and dying. He had probably been shot trying to protect her. Never in their long friendship had he let her down, and she wasn't about to run out on him.

Carolyn shouldered her way into the center of the group. "What are y'all talking about? What'd you have to run from?"

Deborah looked at her daughter, and her heart twisted inside her. Then Sky stepped forward, a look of confusion on his face.

"I will explain it all to both of you soon," she said. "But first we must see about Griff." To Longjim she added, "Get me a fresh mount. Come with me if you wish. But no shooting."

"There's enough of us, Deborah," argued Longjim. "There ain't a man here that wouldn't fight, even the law, for you. We could take 'em."

Several voices agreed with Longjim, and Deborah was touched, especially since no one but Longjim had any idea what they were consenting to.

She shook her head firmly.

"I think it's time it ended, Longjim. It had to happen sometime." She paused, now calmed somewhat since the initial shock of Jasper's news. "Sky," she said to her son, "would you ride out to Beaumont and see if you can find Sam? You know his circuit better than anyone."

Sky hesitated, then asked, "You . . . you will be here when we get home. . . ?"

"I hope so. If not, you will know where to find me."

"Ma!" Carolyn looked at her mother frantically. "You can't go—not without me."

Deborah wished she could think of some errand to send Carolyn on to prevent her from witnessing her mother's arrest. But nothing came immediately to mind. And Carolyn would not have readily accepted an obvious distraction. She had too much of a mind of her own for that.

"Let's go, Longjim," Deborah said. She turned to her daughter. "Carolyn, I'd prefer you stay here—"

"What for? What can I do for you here?" Carolyn set her jaw and stared at her mother. "I'm going."

Weighing the futility of argument against the urgency of leaving, Deborah shrugged. "All right. But when we get there, you do as I say."

Carolyn raced to saddle her horse.

Deborah hurriedly gave some last minute instructions. "The rest of you boys stay here and finish rounding up those horses. I don't want anyone coming after us." She turned back to Jasper. "Did someone fetch a doctor for Griff?"

"Yeah, ma'am, but it ain't likely one'll get here before tomorrow."

In five minutes, Deborah, Longjim, and Carolyn were on their way. Sky rode with them for a few miles, then headed south. The three remaining riders continued toward the east and whatever was waiting for them there.

4
_____

As the three riders paused on a rise overlooking the ranch, Longjim slipped his six-gun from its holster and spun the bullet chamber to make sure it was loaded.

Deborah glanced over at him and gave a slight shake of her head.

"We don't have to walk in like sheep going to the slaughter, Deborah," he said.

"Don't worry, Longjim," said Deborah confidently, "we're not." She had been praying during the whole two-hour ride. She knew they were not alone; they had more protection in her Lord than from Longjim's Colt.

He shrugged, then reluctantly holstered his gun.

Deborah surveyed the ranch for a moment. It looked quiet and peaceful in the twilight. A light burned in the bunkhouse and a couple in the main house, but otherwise it was dim and still. Despite her confidence a moment ago, a part of her held back, wanting desperately to avoid this confrontation. Was her whole life about to crash in on her? Would she have to relinquish her freedom, be forced to face a gallows for the second time? Had she been foolish all these years to think that her life could continue in contentment forever?

But above all, could she face what must surely lie ahead? How could she give up the ranch she loved, the life she loved? And her family. . . ? *Dear God, how can I give them up?* She and Sam had only just begun their life together. How could she part from the man she loved so dearly? And Sky and Carolyn—

Deborah glanced covertly at her daughter. Carolyn had been looking at her mother all along, perhaps seeing the sudden fear and distress that etched her face. Their eyes met and held for a moment. Carolyn's large, expressive eyes probed hers, questioning, even silently *demanding* an answer. Carolyn had remained silent during the ride, but she was not the type to remain passive for long.

In a sudden flash of memory, Deborah recalled the day Carolyn had been born. Broken Wing, in his gentle, simple way, had helped her accept the child she had been so fearful of bearing. Over the years, Carolyn *had* often been a challenge to raise, but Deborah's love and acceptance of her capricious and headstrong daughter, apart from the tragic circumstances of her conception, had been unfailing and genuine. And it was that very love—misguided, perhaps—that had prevented her from revealing the past to Carolyn. Sam had always favored complete honesty with Carolyn, but he had never forced Deborah to follow his way of thinking. Deborah wanted to be honest, but every time she thought of the torment her existence with Carolyn's father had been, the circumstances of his death, and the fact that she herself still stood convicted of his murder, she could not find the courage to tell her daughter.

At last Deborah's cowardice was about to catch up with her. By postponing the inevitable, she had only created a worse situation. Now Carolyn would not only have to face the truth about her parentage, but would have to do so without her mother's present comfort.

But this was not the time for those revelations. Griff was dying; perhaps . . . he was already dead. Deborah could only deal with one crisis at a time.

Her grip tightened around the reins, and she pressed her knees against her mount's flanks, urging him forward. Over and over she reminded herself that she was not alone, that God was riding into this crisis with her.

Still, she felt her heart wrench as they rode down the hill.

5

Griff figured he didn't have long. He lay sprawled out on the nice couch Deborah had bought last year and had shipped all the way from Boston. Even in his pain and distress, he couldn't help thinking that he was getting blood all over the fabric. Yolanda had attempted to bandage the wound, but it wasn't doing much good. His blood was soaking the bandages faster than she could change them. Griff had tried to get Pollard to take him to a bed in one of the back rooms, but Pollard wanted to watch the front door. He wasn't about to let Griff out of his sight.

Griff thought about trying to attack the man, but every time he moved the pain nearly made him faint.

"You know, Pollard," Griff said, "you're a fool if you think she's gonna walk right in here. Those cowhands that work for her will move heaven and earth to protect her."

"We'll see."

"Why, she probably ain't even gonna come back at all. She's probably halfway to Mexico by now."

"You better hope that ain't true, McCulloch, 'cause if it is, you're a dead man."

Unfortunately, Griff knew Deborah well enough to be pretty certain that she'd never run out on him—the fool woman! She wouldn't even think of going to Mexico.

"What're you gonna do if I die before she gets here?" Griff asked.

"I'll figure that out when she comes."

"*If* she comes."

"I don't take her for the kind to turn her back on a friend—and if you've been with her for all these years, I bet you're that, and maybe more, eh?" Pollard gave a leering wink.

"Why, you dirty—" Griff yelled and tried to lunge at Pollard, but everything went black and he fell back against the couch. He felt a fresh trickle of warm blood in his side.

Pollard smiled at Griff and shook his head without much pity. He then licked his dry lips. "Hey!" he called toward the kitchen door. "You, woman in there, what you got to drink?"

Yolanda, looking pale and frightened, appeared with a pot of coffee.

"I mean something stronger than that," Pollard sneered.

"We keep no spirits in this house, señor," she said in a shaky voice.

"All right, gimme more coffee then."

Yolanda refilled his cup, then set down the pot and turned to Griff. "Señor Griff, are you . . . all right? His eyes were closed and his breathing was so shallow she could not be sure if he was, in fact, still alive. She bent close and felt a weak stream of breath from his mouth. She gently dabbed his forehead with a cloth, then lifted the blanket covering him to inspect the bandage. She shook her head dismally. The bandage she had changed only fifteen minutes ago was soaked.

"He still alive?" asked Pollard, sipping his coffee as if he really didn't care.

"He will die if he doesn't get proper care." In her deep concern, Yolanda found the courage to speak firmly. "If you are a lawman, you cannot allow—"

Before she could finish her thought, the front door opened. Yolanda jumped up and ran to the door. Upon sight of Deborah, relief filled Yolanda's face as if Deborah had the power by her very presence to fix everything—to make Griff live, to make this awful deputy sheriff leave their home. Sobbing, Yolanda ran to Deborah and embraced her.

"Oh, Deborah, I . . . I . . ." Weeping overcame her, and she sank into Deborah's arms.

Deborah held Yolanda tenderly, this dear woman who had been a faithful servant, friend, and family member for so many years. While she held her, Deborah took in the situation. She recognized Pollard, even though he had aged beyond the toll of the years. He had been somewhat sympathetic toward her during her trial and at the time of her near-execution. There was no sympathy now on that hardened and worn face.

"I was right," Pollard said in a voice that sounded like a dry desert wind.

The sound of his voice seemed to steady Yolanda; at any rate, she straightened and, with determination, stepped aside so Deborah could fix things and make all return to normal.

Deborah ignored Pollard and headed directly for Griff. But Pollard tensed and swung his gun toward her, forcing her to stop halfway there.

"Not so fast, ma'am," Pollard warned. He nodded toward Longjim and Carolyn. "I want all of you to get outta here now."

"You can't—" Longjim began to protest.

"Don't tell me what I can and can't do," snapped Pollard sharply. He might be close to victory, but that only seemed to make him more jumpy and nervous.

"Do as he says," said Deborah.

Carolyn, stoic that she usually was, seemed near to tears. She loved Griff like the father she never had, and she was obviously distressed not knowing if he was alive or dead. "I don't care what happens," she said stubbornly, "I'm not leaving Griff here like that—"

"You listen to your ma," came a weak voice from the couch.

"Griff!" exclaimed three voices at once.

"Go on!" yelled Pollard. "Get out now. And don't try nothing like sneaking in the back way, 'cause I'll shoot McCulloch first and ask what you want later."

Longjim, Carolyn, and Yolanda slowly retreated, closing the door behind them. Pollard seemed to relax a little. He hadn't liked the look of Longjim, whom he judged to be a dangerous man. He could handle a mere woman and a dying man.

"Well, Mrs. Stoner—but I forgot, it's Mrs. Killion, now, ain't it? I reckon, as they say, you are through running," Pollard said.

"Please," pleaded Deborah, "let me help Griff."

"Ain't this touching? Why, I begin to regret siding with you nineteen years ago," Pollard went on in a less-than-sympathetic tone. "They were probably right about you back then; I bet you and McCulloch had something going on together all along. That's why he rescued you and why he's still around."

"I swear, Pollard," Griff said, somehow managing to infuse his weak voice with menace, "I'll kill you before this is all over!"

"If you last that long."

Ignoring Pollard, Deborah went to Griff and knelt down on the floor beside him. She took the cloth that Yolanda had left on a nearby table and blotted the sweat from Griff's forehead.

31

"Why'd you come back, Deborah?" he asked.

"Do you really need to ask, Griff?"

"Naw . . . I just wish you hadn't. It was blame crazy of you . . . blame—" He stopped, gasping as a sharp pain assailed him.

Deborah paused a moment to study his condition. She needed no medical degree to see he was in a bad way. His normally ruddy complexion was ashen, even beneath a two-day growth of beard. The bandage at his side was soaked with blood. She well knew that men with wounds such as his, especially this far out on the frontier, did not usually survive. Deborah wanted to weep. She had never before seen Griff down like this, so helpless, so vulnerable. She realized how much she had always counted on his strength, his protection. Now she must protect him.

Deborah looked at Pollard. "Griff needs a doctor and some fresh bandages."

"All right," said Pollard. "Get that Mexican woman in here to help, but no one else, you hear? They can call a doctor after we leave."

"Leave? Where are we going?"

"I'm taking you in to Danville tonight."

"That'll take all night!" protested Deborah. "It's dark out there, and dangerous. And when will we sleep?"

"I got a couple hours of shut-eye before you got here," answered Pollard. "You can sleep in the saddle if you want. I ain't taking no chances staying around here any longer than I have to."

Deborah called to Yolanda, but when she appeared Pollard had another task for her first. He tossed a length of heavy rope at her.

"Tie up Mrs. Killion," Pollard instructed. "Make it tight, 'cause I'm watching."

When Yolanda hesitated, he put his gun to Griff's head. Deborah nodded to her and gave her hand an affectionate squeeze. "It's okay, Yolanda. Do what he says."

"Oh, but Deborah! How can he do this thing. . . ?"

"It's going to come out all right." Deborah tried to back her words with a encouraging smile. "We just have to trust the One who is really in control."

"Sí, señora."

"When I'm gone, Yolanda, do everything you can for Griff. Concentrate on him, and don't worry about me."

Yolanda nodded again, tears once more filling her eyes. As she tied the rope, following Pollard's instructions, each knot, each tightening pull, seemed to bring more pain to Yolanda than to Deborah. But in the end the job was done to Pollard's satisfaction. The rope bound Deborah's hands firmly in front of her, with two strong lengths going up from her hands to wrap around her neck. It gave her very limited movement, exactly the effect her captor wanted.

From his bed, Griff groaned when he saw her trussed up like a wild beast. Fury surged across his face, but he was so weak he could do nothing but curse himself for his own helplessness.

"Okay, you," Pollard said to Yolanda, "go tell someone to saddle up two fresh horses."

"What about Griff?" asked Deborah.

"There'll be plenty of time for that after we're on our way."

Five minutes later, the horses were waiting out front. Deborah felt hollow inside and a little shaky. Being tied up as she was reminded her of that terrible day when she had made her way to the gallows in Stoner's Crossing. Again she was a prisoner, and again beside the same man who had been with her then. Once more a gallows loomed in her future, but there would be no Griff McCulloch to rescue her.

There was, however, an important difference between then and now. This time she had more than a human deliverer to depend upon. And for that reason, she did not want her friends to risk their lives for her. When Griff mustered the strength to threaten Pollard, she silenced him.

"Griff, you just worry about getting better. I'll be fine." But when she took a final look at him, all the stoicism in the world could not have kept her tears at bay. She had seen enough death and dying to know Griff was as close to death as a man could get. She might never see this dear friend again. "Oh, Griff!" she cried. One last time she dropped down beside him, and unable to embrace him as she wanted, she kissed his cheek instead. "You know I love you, Griff. You are my dearest friend."

"I know that, Deborah. And I know you can be strong now, just like always."

When Yolanda opened the front door, Longjim thrust his way forward. His expression clearly indicated that he wanted to attack Pollard, but the deputy held his gun close to Deborah. An abrupt move would place her at too much risk.

"Longjim, don't try to come after us," Deborah said. "I don't want anyone else in danger. We will leave this in the hands of justice. Mr. Pollard is taking me to Danville until I can be transported back to Stoner's Crossing."

"I ain't gonna let 'em hang you, Deborah!"

"Longjim, please!" said Deborah, with a sidelong glance at Carolyn who was close by and listening anxiously.

"Ma, what does he mean?"

"Carolyn, when Sam gets to the ranch, I'd like you and Sky to come with him to Danville. I'll explain everything then."

"Let's get moving," said Pollard.

He grasped Deborah's arm and led her outside, just as he had done nineteen years before.

6

Sam wasted no time in getting to Danville. At that, nearly three days had already passed since Deborah's arrest. But it had taken Sky all the first night and part of the next day to locate Sam, so they didn't even arrive at the ranch until sundown the next day. They stopped long enough to change horses, hear a more complete explanation of events, and check on Griff.

McCulloch was finally under the care of a doctor, who had arrived only moments before Sam and Sky. The man couldn't give them encouraging news. The patient had lost a lot of blood and it appeared as if an infection was setting in. The one hopeful sign was that the bullet had gone clean through and no surgery would be required.

"Time will tell," sighed the doctor.

But Sam was not inclined to leave it in time's hands. He knelt beside Griff, who was by now only semiconscious, and prayed over him, pleading to God for a miracle.

Then they were off—Sam, Carolyn, and Sky. Another long, hard ride lay before them. They pushed their horses to the limit and rode into the night, stopping only for a couple of hours of sleep when Carolyn nearly fell out of her saddle with fatigue. But none of them wished to loiter along the way, for they had no idea how long Pollard would keep Deborah in the Danville jail.

Bone-weary and anxious, they rode into the dusty Texas town that afternoon.

They found Deborah in the Danville jail. A sick lump rose in Sam's throat and tears welled in his eyes to see her so, but he was proud of how strong and peaceful she looked. She was no longer a helpless pawn, at the mercy of circumstance or the whims of others. Only when Pollard let Sam into the cell and Deborah rushed into his arms did she break a little. She was, after all, only human—and in a frightening and dangerous situation. He rubbed a hand over her silky hair and murmured soothing words in her ear. In a few moments, she seemed to calm down.

"Well, Sam," she said, motioning for him to sit with her on the low cot that served as a bed, "my father used to talk about the chickens coming home to roost. I guess this must be what he was talking about."

"I don't doubt for one minute that you're gonna get out of this, Deborah. I won't rest until you do."

"The sheriff says a conviction for murder never runs out. It still stands today, as does the sentence."

"Listen here, Deborah, the *legal* authorities ain't never executed a woman in Texas yet, and they ain't about to start with you; I don't care what Caleb Stoner does."

"He's more powerful today than he was twenty years ago."

"So are you, and don't you forget it! You got friends now, and you're not alone against his manipulations. That's the only way he was able to do what he did then. You were isolated. He called all the shots. It's different now."

Neither of them mentioned the fact that hanging wasn't the only fear weighing upon them. Imprisonment could be even worse than death, especially for a woman. They silently clung to each other as if that closeness could banish such fears away.

After a few moments, Deborah said, "Sam, something is eating at me even more than all that. It's Carolyn. I never wanted her to find out like this. I never wanted her to know at all, but to have it all thrown so suddenly at her . . . I should have told her long ago. And Sky also, but I don't worry as much about his reaction as hers."

"Do you want me to have them come in?"

"Yes, but I'll talk to Sky first. I think it's best if I tell Carolyn alone."

Sam nodded his agreement.

"Before we discuss anything else, Sam, I must know . . . how is Griff?"

"There's a doctor tending him now, and he don't look real good. But you know Griff—he's a tough old cowboy. I reckon he's got a few more years left in him."

"I hope so. Tell him when you see him that I'm praying for him. Maybe God will use this to have an effect on his heart."

"That's what I'm praying, too, Deborah."

They paused for a few moments to get a sense of God's peace in the matter; then Sam went on. "Pollard said there'll be a Texas Ranger here tomorrow to transport you to Stoner's Crossing. He said he didn't want to risk taking you alone."

"I reckon I'm a mighty dangerous hombre," she responded in an unsuccessful attempt at humor. It brought only a forced twitch to Sam's lips.

"He just better not treat you like some common criminal."

"But I am a convicted murderer, Sam. They know no differently."

"One look oughta tell 'em you're innocent!"

Deborah sighed. "I have a feeling it will take more than that."

Sam responded only with silence. For all his simplistic answers about faith and trust and not being alone, he knew they were up against tough odds. Faith in God would be the ultimate victor, but they could not be passive partakers of the faith. God was as much a being of action as was Sam.

"Maybe they ought to bring along a whole company of Rangers for you," said Sam defiantly.

"Sam, I know you're just joking, but I am afraid that Pollard has a very real concern. I'm going to count on you, Sam, to make sure Longjim and the boys don't try anything. I could see it in Longjim's eyes; he not only wants to rescue me, but he wants revenge for Griff. My problem must be settled in a court of law. I want to be cleared of this—for me, and for Carolyn."

"I agree, and I'll keep a rein on Longjim. But I don't care what happens, I ain't letting no one hang or imprison you! I'll strap a gun back on if I have to!" There was no levity in Sam's voice; he was deadly serious.

"Oh, dear Sam!" Weeping, Deborah embraced him again and held him tight. She hated to let him go; she loved him so much. She needed him, too, not so much for his manly protection, but for the strength of his spirit and the deep love he had for her. Somehow these bolstered her more than any shows of physical heroism.

Before Sam left, he gave her a Bible, the same plain book she had gotten from old Hardee Smith's store in Fort Dodge. Now it was quite worn and used.

Then Sam kissed Deborah and sent in Sky.

36

7

Half an hour later it was Carolyn's turn. As the girl came up to the cell door and waited while Pollard unlocked it, Deborah gave her a studied appraisal, as if seeing her for the first time. She fully realized that after this day, Carolyn might never be the same again, nor would their relationship be the same.

Carolyn was still wearing her work clothes. A dusty brimmed hat covered her dark hair, which was pulled back in a single braid. A faded gingham shirt, once red but now faded to a dull pink, topped a long split skirt with a patched hole over the left knee. Carolyn bemoaned the fact that she couldn't wear the more practical Levi's that the boys wore. But, of course, they didn't make them small enough for most women, who even on the range were expected to wear silly skirts. Deborah and Carolyn compromised by splitting their skirts down the middle and sewing in wide, roomy legs.

There could be no doubt that this young woman was a product of the West, a female who knew her way around a ranch as well as any man. She walked with a slight swagger, and Deborah was ever fearful that one day she'd find her daughter hunched over a poker table, a cheroot clenched between her teeth. Deborah had raised Carolyn to be independent, certainly, able to take care of herself. This was no land for the weak and helpless. If that's what men wanted— and Deborah seriously doubted it—there were plenty of weak women to be found elsewhere, but seldom on the plains and prairies. Deborah wanted her daughter to be respected by men, not dominated or even pampered by them.

Carolyn's characteristic petulance and swagger, however, were noticeably absent now. Deborah went immediately to embrace and comfort her. Was it possible Carolyn sensed that her secure world was about to cave in? There was something in the fearful expression in her eyes that went beyond the shock of seeing her mother in jail.

They sat on the cot and Deborah took Carolyn's hands in hers, as much for her own sake as for her daughter's.

"Forgive me for making you wait," Deborah said, feeling an explanation was necessary. "But I wanted to see you alone, and I wanted us to have as much time as we needed."

"It's okay, Ma . . . but what's going on? Are you gonna tell me?" Carolyn could speak proper English as well as her mother, but she preferred what she called the "cowhand's talk."

Deborah didn't bother to correct her as she normally might have. It didn't seem so important now. In spite of the rough clothing and less-than-feminine manners, Carolyn was a lovely girl, and Deborah was proud of her. Yes, the Stoner blood in her could not be denied. It was plain to see in her height—perhaps five feet nine inches, and already towering over Deborah by several inches—and in her wiry frame, though, with maturity, the curves of her figure had filled out somewhat. Her father's mark could also be discerned in her dark hair, which had changed dramatically from the light hair of her baby years that had in the Cheyenne camp often brought danger of her being mistaken for a captive. Her eyes, though brown like her father's, were most like Deborah's in shape and expression. Depending on her mood, they could be warm as a summer day or as icy as a winter Norther—a true mirror into the innermost parts of her enigmatic personality.

Deborah and her daughter might clash more frequently than she'd like, but the real truth was that Deborah could find little fault with the girl in things that mattered. If she was moody and demanding, and at times self-centered, Carolyn could just as easily be kind and generous and sensitive. Griff had often commented that she might be ornery and spirited, but there wasn't a bad bone in her. All Deborah's fears when Carolyn had been conceived and first born had been for nothing. More than blood was needed to pass on the vindictive, violent, and harsh traits of her father. Only the Stoner arrogance sometimes revealed itself in Carolyn, but that was tempered most of the time by the girl's faith in God.

Deborah forced her mind back to the question still lingering, unanswered, in the stale air of the cell. She could avoid it no longer.

"Yes, Carolyn," she said slowly but with determination, "it is time I told you what this is all about. I should have done that long ago, and now I regret that I didn't. But I want you to know I didn't tell you because I wanted to spare you, as much as myself. These things are very painful, and I thought knowing might cause you to think less of yourself—and less of me. My reasoning seems rather illogical now. I suppose it was all just too awful to tell to a child—"

"I ain't a child anymore, Ma."

Deborah sighed heavily. "No, you're not. Will you hear me out before saying anything? Will you try to understand that I kept the truth from you because I love you?"

"I'll try," replied Carolyn with the same determination in her voice her mother had shown.

Deborah unveiled the tragic story of her ill-fated marriage, omitting only graphic details. She told of Leonard's death and of Caleb's obsession with seeing Deborah punished for the crime. When she finished fifteen minutes later, a dreadful silence filled the jail cell. Deborah tried to read her daughter's expressive eyes, but they were shadowed, purposefully veiled. She wanted to say something to Carolyn, something to make it all right, but the motherly words that could soothe a skinned knee or a little girl's hurt feelings were woefully inadequate for this. All at one time, Carolyn had learned that her father had been an abusive monster, and that her mother had been convicted of his murder. There were no simple words to fix such hurts.

As much as she wanted to beg and plead for some response, some sign of vindication from her daughter, Deborah just held Carolyn close as they sat together in the long and heavy silence. Deborah felt her daughter's tears dampen the fabric of her blouse, and Carolyn was not one to cry readily. Deborah realized just how deeply this revelation must have wounded Carolyn. But still neither spoke.

Five minutes passed before Carolyn pushed away from her mother's embrace. With some embarrassment, she wiped away her tears with a sleeve.

"What now, Ma?" Carolyn said in a voice resolved to be strong.

"I hope we will be able to go on from here," was all Deborah could think to say. She hadn't expected such a nebulous, impersonal question.

"But you're in jail, and this Pollard plans on seeing that your sentence is carried out."

"I'm not worried about that right now, Carolyn. I'm in God's hands." Deborah paused and looked directly at her daughter. "I *am* worried about you."

"I reckon I'm in God's hands, too." Carolyn was being stoic—too stoic.

"Carolyn!" Suddenly frustrated, Deborah could restrain herself no longer. She wanted to give Carolyn time, but she also feared the girl might bottle it all up within. "Can't you tell me how you *feel* about all this?"

"Feel. . . ?" Carolyn said the word almost as if such a notion had never occurred to her. "That ain't important. What's important is getting you outta here."

Deborah sadly shook her head and said quietly, "Not to me, it isn't."

"Well . . . I . . ." Carolyn hesitated, then tried again. "I'll talk to you later, Ma. I better . . . I better go and see . . . how Sky is. This must be hard on him, too."

Without another word, Carolyn called for Pollard, who quickly came and let her out. Her eyes were glistening, and she was chewing on a trembling lip.

Deborah watched her go, sadly, regretfully, wondering what she could have done to make it easier on Carolyn. More than the iron bars of her prison cell separated them now.

PART 3

LEONARD'S DAUGHTER

8

An hour before dawn Carolyn awoke, and, unable to lie still, she crept from her bed in the boardinghouse in Danville where she and Sam and Sky were staying. She dressed quickly and quietly and stole from her room like a thief, her destination the town livery stable. No one was around at that hour, but Carolyn needed no help to saddle her speckled gray stallion, Patch, a son of Broken Wing's fine gray. She then rode northwest from town until she was far away from all signs of civilization.

Carolyn loved the lonely, barren stretches of grass and mesquite, and the rugged buttes and deep canyons that scarred the dry earth of the High Plains. These plains could be treacherous to the inexperienced, but Carolyn by no means considered herself *inexperienced*. She could ride and shoot as well as any man on the ranch—well, almost any. She supposed no one would ever come close to the expertise of Griff and Longjim, and she'd heard stories about Sam, too, though he had never demonstrated his talents. Regardless, Carolyn did not lack confidence in her own abilities; she was always the first to respond to a dare, to try a new adventure, to enter a contest. Perhaps within herself she felt she had more to prove than most others, not only because of the so-called handicap of being a female, but also from some much deeper drive. Could it be that her cocky confidence arose from a basic insecurity, rooted in a nagging fear that she *was* somehow inferior because of the shroud that had always hung about her beginnings, the partial explanations, the veiled comments about the past?

Now that veil had been lifted. The reasons for all the secrets had been revealed. And her worst fears had been realized.

She thought back to her childhood, how she had put so much effort into building a fantasy world around her dead father, of whom so little was ever said. She had wanted him to match up to Sky's father. There had been no end to the wonderful stories about Broken

43

Wing, the great Cheyenne warrior. Once, all alone, he had raided a Pawnee camp and brought back fifteen war ponies. Once he and Sam had driven a dangerous whiskey peddler from the Cheyenne camp. Once he had killed two huge bull buffaloes in one day and then given one to a family who needed it.

Carolyn loved her brother, but she envied him, even if she had a clearer memory of his father than he had. Broken Wing was *his* father no matter how much they said he considered her his true child also. And no one ever shied away from telling stories about him.

But the life of her own father had been summed up in a few brief sentences: *We were married for a short time, Carolyn. I hardly knew him. He was a rancher, a good man. He was killed in the war.* Even as a child she had been able to see past the mere words. The hesitation when her mother said "a . . . good man" might have been slight, but its lack of conviction was obvious. But Carolyn had, if only subconsciously, avoided probing and questioning the vague disquiet she always felt when her father was spoken of. On some level, she had always feared the truth might be a terrible thing. Now there could be no more denying it.

Her father was a monster.

Her mother was a convicted murderer.

Yes, both her mother and Sam said she was innocent, but when her mother had spoken of the day of the murder, her voice had lacked complete assurance. She said everything had been such a nightmare she sometimes couldn't tell the dream from the terrible reality.

"But I couldn't have killed him. I didn't kill him!" Deborah had said. "I saw someone . . . at least, a shadow or something . . . at the window. I thought about killing him; for weeks toward the end, not a day went by that I didn't think of it. I feared it would drive me insane. Maybe . . . it did for a time."

No wonder they had convicted her if she had appealed to the court with testimony like that, thought Carolyn. Even she, Deborah's own daughter, wasn't sure what to believe.

But what if she *had* killed him? Hadn't he deserved it? No one had a right to treat another person the way he had her mother. And Carolyn was in no way fooled; her mother had told only a watered-down version of the story. He had treated her worse than an animal.

But he was Carolyn's father!

How could she believe such things about her own father? She recalled the little fantasies she used to spin about him, the glorious war hero. He rivaled even Broken Wing in the wonders of his exploits. She had cast him as the beloved commander leading his loyal

44

troops into battle, killed while rescuing his comrades, mourned in his death by private and general alike. As Carolyn had grown older and her needs more complicated, she sometimes imagined that her father was not really dead at all, but rather had been accused of some crime for which he was innocent—not unlike Robin Hood—and, for the safety of his family, had been forced to flee. But one day he would return to claim his daughter whom he had, of course, never stopped loving. No wonder she had never questioned her mother, in her usually tenacious manner, about him. The truth could never rival the tales of her imagination. However, that particular fantasy about a Robin Hood father had ended by her mother's marriage to Sam Killion; even a naive thirteen-year-old girl knew her mother wouldn't marry another if her husband still lived. Naturally, Carolyn had never been practical enough to fit Broken Wing into this equation. But at the age of fourteen her private fantasies had stopped and she just tried to forget about her father.

Now she wished she could retreat to the safety those imaginings had provided.

Still, it had never been Carolyn's way to shy away from a challenge, except in the case of her father, and it was about time she faced this one squarely. Even if she wanted to pretend it didn't exist, she couldn't. She could not hide from the fact that her mother was sitting in jail with a sentence of death looming over her head.

There was only one thing she had to come to terms with now. What should *she* do about it all?

Most urgently, they had to clear her mother's name and get her out of jail. . . .

Suddenly Carolyn realized there was something even more important than her mother's release that had to be dealt with first. Her mother had hinted at it in jail, but Carolyn had adroitly avoided the issue and probably hurt her mother in the process. Carolyn had to decide how she *felt* about all this, and then she had to apologize to her mother.

How did she feel?

Was she angry at her mother for keeping those secrets? She wanted to be, and at first, when she ran out of the jail, she was . . . a little. But she was almost a woman herself now, an adult, and she could begin to understand a woman's urge to protect her children. More than that, Carolyn knew her mother well enough to know she was not selfish or cruel. She would never hurt Carolyn on purpose. And Carolyn knew she must assure her mother of this before anything else.

What about her father? Did she hate him? She didn't even know him, yet he had hurt her mother whom she did know and love. Shouldn't she hate him for that? But maybe he would have loved Carolyn and treated her with kindness. Maybe . . .

Maybe I am just building fairy tales again, she thought dismally. *But how can I hate a man I never knew, whom for the last eighteen years I have tried so desperately to protect and love?*

It was so much easier to think of actions instead of feelings. But what of her actions, anyway? What should she do about it all? Get her mother out of jail, of course, but then what?

Did it matter? Why should she *do* anything? Why shouldn't life just go on as it always had? She had to admit she had a good life, one that she was not eager to change. Most of the time she was happy, even content. At times, especially when her fears were worst, she could be moody and irascible. Yet she loved her life on the ranch. She loved her brother, who was her best and perhaps only real friend near her own age. They had great times riding and racing and working together. And she loved Griff, who had taught her so much about surviving in the hard and sometimes unrelenting country that was their home. The other ranch hands accepted her and treated her with the respect of an equal. She dearly loved Sam, her stepfather. He had taught her about the spiritual aspect of life and led her to a personal faith in God, and had, thus, given her a purpose in her life beyond that nebulous, fearful abyss of her past.

She loved her mother, too, though Carolyn realized she sometimes didn't show it as a daughter should. The lies about the past had affected their relationship, but they hadn't dominated it. Mother and daughter had their share of good times together, though their strong wills were apt to clash frequently. Still, it was not so bad that Carolyn was ready to destroy it all—

But did she have a choice? Wasn't it already destroyed? How could anything be the same again? How could *she* be the same person now? Whatever Leonard Stoner was, whatever he had done, one thing was certain—he'd had an unalterable effect on his daughter's life. And, according to her mother, Carolyn had a grandfather out there somewhere. From her mother's viewpoint, he didn't appear to be the most noble of men, but should Carolyn then forget all about him? *Could* she? What was he to her, anyway? Didn't he hate her mother and wish her dead? Carolyn had no doubt where her loyalty should lie. Yet, he was . . . her own grandfather.

Carolyn reined Patch to a stop. The sun had fully risen now, its scorching rays beating down on her. All was still and quiet as if she and her horse were the only living things for miles—as well they might be. But the raging storm of Carolyn's emotions made up for the peace surrounding her.

What was going to happen now?

What was she supposed to do?

"I don't know . . . I just don't know."

She leaned over Patch and stroked his charcoal mane. His nearness somehow comforted her.

"Dear Lord, what should I do? I don't want to hurt my mother . . . I don't want to hurt anyone. I don't want my life to change, but it's going to. Show me, God. Show me!"

9

When Carolyn rode back into town about midmorning, she wasn't really in the mood to see anyone. She wanted to talk to Sky, though not just yet. Right now she wanted solitude.

But she was not going to get her wish. A small knot of people had gathered near the boardinghouse where she was staying. Shouting and yells rose from the group.

"Atta boy!"

"You get him, Billy!"

"Take that, half-breed!"

The sheriff—not Pollard, but the regular sheriff who had been out of town for the last week and just returned—quickly dispersed the spectators with his own shouts. When the area had cleared of most of the by-standers, Carolyn saw two figures fighting in the dirt. One was her brother; the other was Billy Yates.

Whenever Billy was around Sky, he found some reason to pick a fight with him. Billy was three years older than Sky, and in the past his natural size had always given him the clear advantage over Sky. But at sixteen, Sky had already outgrown the Yates boy by two or three inches. Billy still out-weighed Sky, but years of ranch work had given Sky muscles, strength, and endurance far beyond his years. This was the first time in a couple of years that the two had tangled, and Carolyn noted proudly that her brother was giving the bully a run for his money.

The sheriff, on the other hand, was not in the least impressed. It was hard enough keeping peace in this wild town with all the real desperados that passed through. He didn't need to waste his time on punk kids. He had trouble pulling the two youths apart, but finally he was able to get a good grip on Billy and lug him to his feet, giving the young man a violent shake and standing him erect.

"Can't you leave this poor Injun kid alone?" the sheriff asked.

"I don't like the looks of him, an' I don't like to breathe the same air as him," snarled the Yates boy. He was nineteen now, but in no way mellowed by age.

Sky, who had started to rise, took another lunge at Billy. The sheriff shoved him back to the ground where Sky stayed, panting and tense.

"Okay, Billy," said the sheriff, "you get outta here, and if you can't come to town without starting trouble, I'm gonna bar you from here altogether, you hear?"

Billy shrugged in an attempt to show he was unimpressed by the sheriff's threats. But he complied with his order and marched away, not without a final scowl toward Sky.

The sheriff yanked Sky to his feet. "Well, boy," he said in a gruff but not entirely unfriendly tone, "you're almost as bad as that Yates boy. You can't seem to come to town without getting into trouble."

"I didn't start it," protested Sky.

"Well, you ain't the first Injun to make *that* claim, but it still don't matter. Trouble is trouble, and you best learn how to control that hot head of yours."

By now Carolyn had arrived on the scene and was listening to the conversation. She could not keep quiet. "My brother don't have no 'hot head,' Sheriff!" she retorted angrily. "But a man has to defend himself against scum like that—" She jerked her head toward the retreating figure of Billy Yates. "Especially when the law ain't gonna do nothing about it!"

"Lookee here, girl!" the sheriff replied, no trace of friendliness in his voice now. "I think your family's got enough trouble around here without you starting more. Now, both of you, skedaddle before I put you in jail with your ma!"

Carolyn took a threatening step toward the sheriff, but Sky put a hand on her shoulder and held her back. "Let's go," he said firmly. He had to nudge her once or twice to get her to move.

"Someone ought to shoot that Billy Yates!" she blurted when they were well away.

"Maybe someone will one day," replied Sky, "but it ain't gonna be me."

"A kind word don't always turn away wrath, Sky, no matter what Sam says."

"I think the things Sam tells us are right, but not everyone is called or able to live like he does. That's not why I try to avoid trouble. I'm afraid that once I got started really fighting people like Billy, I might not be able to stop." He paused and shook his head, his muscles still taut with repressed fury, his hands clenched into fists. "But when they speak ill of my father, I *could* kill!"

"Well, if it's any comfort to you, Sky, at least the things they say about *your* father ain't true." She was immediately sorry for the bitterness that crept into her tone.

"I'm sorry," Sky replied with compassion. "I forgot for a minute."

No matter how angry Carolyn might at times be at the world in general, she would always have a tender place in her closely guarded heart for her brother, her best friend.

She softened her tone as she replied, "That's okay, Sky. I wish we could all just forget."

"It's too late for that. As long as Ma is in danger, we gotta do what we can to help her."

"I know, but it might mean digging more into the past. Who knows what else we'll find out."

"We'll find enough to prove our mother's innocence!" declared Sky firmly.

"I suppose . . ."

Sky's eyebrows shot up and he gave his sister a rare hard look. "You sound as if you don't believe what Ma said."

"I believe her, but . . . Sky, like you are afraid to start fighting, I'm afraid to find out any more, that's all. I'm not sure I want to know."

"Learning these things about your father is hard, Lynnie, but if I know you, you will be too stubborn to let it go."

She made an attempt at a smile and nodded in agreement. "You're probably right, doggone it! I never did know how to leave well enough alone."

They parted at the livery stable where Carolyn left her horse. Sky returned to the boardinghouse to clean up a bit before visiting his mother. As Carolyn watched him walk away, she could not help wishing, despite all the pain his mixed blood caused him, that she could be him. He had a heritage and a history to be proud of, no matter how much people like Billy Yates tried to belittle it.

But she could not change who she was, or her parentage. She just had to accept it and go on. It would help no one, especially her mother, if she moped around filled with self-pity, making life miserable for herself and everyone else. Maybe she would have to turn over a few more painful rocks in her parents' past; maybe she would find out that her mother did indeed kill her father; maybe she would meet her grandfather and be faced with his hatred.

Whatever happened, she would just have to take things as they came, put a little more trust in God, and be strong. That was the only way she would be of use to anyone.

10

When it came time to transport her mother to Stoner's Crossing, Carolyn resisted the suggestion that she stay behind. Deborah practically begged her to stay at home, and Carolyn noted a desperation in her mother's tone that seemed to far exceed the surface dangers of the trip. Still, Carolyn remained obdurate until Sam drew her aside and sternly asked his stepdaughter to give some consideration to the added burden of worry her presence would place on Deborah. Carolyn accepted the rebuke contritely.

She was also swayed by the reasoning that with Sky busy running the ranch, there ought to be some member of the family besides Yolanda, who had her hands full under the best of conditions, available to care for Griff. Carolyn had a soft spot in her heart for Griff, so she agreed to stay. But she told herself that the minute Griff was well, if things were not already cleared up, she would go south.

Those first couple of weeks after Sam and Deborah departed were bitterly lonely for Carolyn. Sky was gone all the time, as were Longjim and most of the other hands, working at spring roundup. Yolanda offered company, but most of her conversation revolved around house and hearth, which completely bored Carolyn. She wanted to be out working with the boys, riding, drinking in the countryside she so loved. She didn't exactly begrudge Griff her time. She loved him, too, and as long as he needed her she would not leave him. But that didn't prevent her from gazing longingly out the window or pacing restlessly.

And Griff was in no position to entertain her or relieve her boredom. He remained in critical condition. The doctor, when he made his biweekly visits, was amazed he stayed alive at all, especially after the infection set in. Griff was either comatose or delirious the entire time, and Carolyn was terribly afraid for him. One cowhand who stopped by to visit mentioned that he'd never known anyone who'd been gut-shot to survive. Carolyn tried to reassure herself that Griff's wound wasn't exactly a gut-shot, but was nearer to his side. It was a futile reassurance at best.

Griff looked so pathetic that she wanted to cry. And maybe that was another reason for her restlessness; she was simply uncomfortable with the vulnerability her teetering emotions caused in her.

One particular day, he seemed his worst. His skin was ashen, and he had dropped thirty pounds from his hefty frame. His eyes, which had always danced with mischievous humor, were sunk deep in black-ringed sockets. He literally looked like death. Carolyn suddenly knew with an intensity she had not previously felt that Griff could die. Then she began to weep in earnest.

As much as she tried to fight it, she knew she must accept the fact that soon Griff would be taken from her.

"Lord, am I really gonna have to say goodbye?" she murmured. "It just don't seem right. Griff's not that old; he's got a lot more still to give."

She paused and let the silence, broken only by Griff's labored breathing, close in around her. She wasn't really looking for some miraculous answer to her prayer. She found that God usually didn't work that way with her. The answers to her prayers most often came in quiet, subtle ways. Sometimes answers didn't come at all, or as Sam would say, God was just deliberating or telling her to wait a while. Often when she prayed, she just hoped for the best, trusting that God had heard and would answer in His time.

Thus Carolyn was not fully prepared for the sense of security that suddenly enveloped her. She could not believe the peace she felt all at once as she gazed at Griff's wracked body. She almost felt guilty for it. But a voice inside her—in her heart, or mind, or deep within her soul, she did not know—assured her clearly and persistently:

Griff will live.

There was no more to it than that, really. A quiet impression that could not have come from her anguished, fearful soul. God himself had seen fit to bless her with this assurance.

Her tears gave way to excitement, not only for Griff's sake but also because it showed her all over again how much God loved her. When it really mattered, at one of the lowest points in her life, He chose to bolster her with such a miracle, with undeniably heaven-sent peace. She realized anew that God was truly there for her when she needed Him. And He was there for Griff, too.

After that day she had a completely different attitude toward the time spent nursing Griff. She no longer felt lonely and forsaken, and she realized that her previous reaction had in large part been her way of subtly separating herself from Griff, protecting herself by severing her emotional ties to Griff. Now, she talked to him all the time, even though he never made any response. She'd babble on and on about all the news she heard from roundup activities, or about the new horses, or she'd pass on funny stories the hands told her.

Yolanda acted worried about this at first, afraid, perhaps, that all the recent stress had finally gotten to the poor girl. It just wasn't normal for the child to sit there talking to the unconscious figure. But when it soon became obvious that Carolyn was in much better spirits than she had been in a long time, Yolanda stopped fretting.

One day, two weeks later, Carolyn was trying to feed Griff some broth. The doctor said that as long as he could swallow without choking, they had to try to get some nourishment into the patient. A good portion of Yolanda's excellent chicken broth was dribbling down Griff's chin, but Carolyn thought enough was being consumed to keep him alive, anyway.

As was her habit, Carolyn kept up a constant flow of one-sided conversation with his unresponsive form. "My goodness, Griff! If you could only see yourself. I don't reckon a baby could do worse. Whoops! There goes some more. I'm gonna have to get you one of them baby bibs."

"Watch your English, girl," came an unexpected and barely audible reply. "Your ma don't want you talking like the cowhands."

"Aw, she don't really—"

Suddenly Carolyn stopped. The voice was coming from her patient, who had not spoken a coherent word in two weeks!

"Griff? Did you say something, or was I hearing things?"

"'Course it's me. Who else did you expect?"

"Oh, Griff, you're awake!" She set down the spoon and bowl and jumped up.

"Where're you going?"

"To get Yolanda. She'll want to know."

"What about the rest of that there soup? It was mighty tasty."

Carolyn laughed, then bent down and joyfully kissed Griff's cheek.

The next time the doctor came by, he was more than a little surprised at his patient's progress. He had fully expected to come to the ranch only to find a freshly dug grave. Not only was Griff not dead, he was getting back some of his color and, though he still couldn't tolerate solid foods, he was feasting on Yolanda's beef and chicken broth.

"Let him eat what he wants," the doctor instructed. "Change that bandage two or three times a day and keep using that cleaning solution I left. And most of all, he's got to stay in bed two more weeks— no exceptions! After that, he can get up once or twice a day, no more! Build him up gradually." To Griff's protests, the doctor added, "You aren't to even look at a horse for another month after that. Then— and only then—we'll see how you're doing."

"A month! You gotta be kidding! I shoulda just kicked the bucket if I have to stay cooped up for over a month."

The doctor addressed his next statement to Carolyn. "It's up to you, young lady, to see that he follows my orders. If he gets up too soon and breaks open that wound, he's liable to go right back to where he started."

"Don't worry, Doc," Carolyn said with a stern warning glance toward Griff. "I'll keep him in bed if I have to tie him there."

Griff proved to be a terrible patient. He hated being in bed and made no bones about telling anyone who happened to be within earshot. What was worse, he couldn't do anything about it even if he tried. And he did try, but most of the time all he could do was gather enough strength to sit up and eat. Once, when he felt particularly strong, he swung his legs out of bed when no one was watching. He only fainted for his efforts.

"Fainting!" he lamented when he came to. "Just like a woman! What's gonna become of me, Lynnie? I'm a has-been. May as well put me out to pasture. I'm finished!"

Carolyn tried to cheer him up, and finally managed to lift his depression by losing several games of poker to him.

11

Upon regaining consciousness, the first thing Griff wanted
to know was what happened to Deborah. His last clear memory was
of Deborah's hands being bound together. When Carolyn filled him
in on all that had gone on afterward, he cursed Pollard vehemently
and swore to get even with him.

He knew better than anyone what a return trip to Stoner's Crossing could mean for Deborah—not only the possibility of execution,
but also having to face the wrath of Caleb Stoner. Unfortunately Griff
didn't have his wits about him enough to hide his fears in front of
Carolyn.

"Not there!" he exclaimed when Carolyn informed him of Deborah's transfer. "That's worse than Daniel stepping into the lion's
den. She ain't never gonna get no fair treatment there."

"What do you mean, Griff?"

Griff quickly tried to repair his error. "Aw, nothing. You know
how I feel about the law."

"Griff!" Carolyn demanded hotly. "You better tell me straight, you
hear! Everyone's been lying to me all these years, and I ain't gonna
put up with it no more. I want to know *everything*."

Griff groaned and laid a weak hand over his forehead. "Later,
Lynnie, honey. I better rest now—"

"Oh no, you don't! You been sleeping all day. Now out with it!"

Griff smiled in spite of himself. He and Carolyn had always had
a special friendship. He never could figure out why she seemed to
adore him so, but had he been more intuitive he might have seen
that the reason was, in part at least, because he had never *tried* to
win her love or respect. She was a natural rebel, that girl, always
trying to march to a different drummer, as her mother often said.
Griff supposed he and Carolyn were kindred spirits in that sense.
They understood each other and gave each other plenty of room to
be themselves. Griff never expected Carolyn to measure up to some

standard that simply didn't suit her basic nature, even if her parents might have done so out of love.

That same mutual understanding, however, prevented them from being able to bamboozle each other. She'd know if he tried to humor her with some white-washed story now, and she wouldn't let him get away with it. But he wondered just how much Deborah had told her daughter of the events of nineteen years ago. He did have a certain loyalty to Deborah, too.

Well, he thought resignedly, Carolyn was going to keep asking questions and she was going to demand answers, so he might just as well give it to her straight rather than wait until she drove him to distraction.

"Did your ma tell you how I came to be involved in all that happened to her?" asked Griff.

"She said you rescued her from hanging, and she hid out with you until the law came and found you out, and y'all had to run away. I guess Sam was sort of involved in all that, too, but I'm not real clear about that."

"I reckon it's clear enough. Sit down a minute, Lynnie." He motioned her to the chair beside the bed. As she sat, he carefully shifted his position in the bed, wincing a little. "Your ma probably didn't want to bore you with all the details and maybe she figured to spare some of us from losing face before you. Anyway, I figure you're near a grown woman and can make your own fair judgments without any help from us. Leastways, that's what you're gonna have to do now. But I got confidence in you."

"It's about time someone started treating me like an adult!"

"Well, don't let it go to your head, Lynnie. You still got some growing to do."

"Okay, but what is it you're gonna tell me?"

Griff sighed and rubbed his chin thoughtfully. "I'm gonna stick to the facts I know personally, 'cause I don't ever want it to be known that I bad-mouthed a man unfairly. You know that in the old days I used to do some things that wasn't exactly law-abiding." Carolyn nodded, and Griff continued. "Me and a half dozen men rode together, robbed a bank or payroll, or did some rustling. What we did was wrong, and we all deserved to be punished for it. And I don't doubt that in some places we'd have hung for what we done. Where there wasn't no organized law, some folks just took the law into their own hands; not that that ain't understandable in this frontier. Still and all, a feller deserves a fair hearing, even if it's right out on the range, and I'd say most folks gave a man that much, at least. There was one exception—a man who would act first and never ask a single question; a man who strung up suspects so regular that most rustlers just left his herd alone out of sheer fear. That man's name is Caleb Stoner, your grandfather.

"I know this is true, 'cause Stoner caught a couple of my boys crossing his range and accused them of rustling his cattle. Without turning 'em in to the law or even giving them a chance to defend themselves, he took 'em to the nearest tree and hung 'em. It ain't as if Stoner's place is out on the frontier where there ain't no law; he's got his own town within a few miles and at least some form of law. Regardless, I know for a fact that my boys was innocent, 'cause they was with me and never touched no Stoner cattle."

Carolyn listened attentively, thoughtfully, but her verbal response caught Griff by surprise. "Griff, like you said, that's pretty common in this country. You know the saying that the noose is the only law around sometimes."

It almost sounded as if she were defending Caleb Stoner. Such an idea was unthinkable to Griff. He forgot for a moment who the Stoners were to Carolyn.

"Girl!" he exclaimed, the exertion bringing on a brief coughing attack. When he recovered he continued without missing a beat. "That's just *one* story I'm telling you—there's more. Them Stoners had a reputation for being the most ruthless cusses around. You tell me what kind of man it is that his own wife is forced to kill him? And then her father-in-law bribes and threatens an entire town to do that poor woman in? I'm being generous in describing them as wild lions."

"Griff, my ma said she didn't kill my father," Carolyn said.

"Well, what I meant is that it's a crime that a woman would even be accused of doing such a thing." Even as Griff spoke, he knew Carolyn wouldn't accept his hasty correction.

"When she told me, it didn't sound completely true—I mean, not that she was lying, but more like she wasn't even sure herself."

For a brief moment such vulnerability flickered across her countenance that Griff's heart constricted with sympathy for her. He reached for her hand and held it tightly in his—a gesture that normally would have been awkward for both of them, but now was right and necessary.

She lifted plaintive eyes toward him. "Did she kill him, Griff?"

The touching look in her eyes, followed by such a beseeching question, pulled at his heart, but at the same time it also exasperated him. While he wanted to hug her tight and protect her, he also gave a brief thought to throwing her over his knee and spanking her for her infuriating persistence. But, whatever he did, he knew he had to tell her the truth.

"That's what I always thought," he said. "I guess she never came right out and said so, one way or another. But that ain't the point, Lynnie. If she did, she was completely within her rights, or so I believe."

"Can you prove that?"

"What in tarnation are you talking about?"

"Well, if it could be proven, then she would have been freed."

"That's what I've been trying to say; Caleb bought the court. Innocent, or guilty by reason of self-defense, your ma never got proper justice."

"Then someone had better prove that," she said with an unbending finality.

Griff was glad they had somewhat moved away from the subject of the characters of Caleb and Leonard Stoner. As much as he despised them, he was reluctant to denounce them before Carolyn. She was, after all, related to the Stoners, had their blood flowing in her veins.

"I think that's exactly what Sam is going to try to do," Griff replied.

"Do you think he will be able to, Griff?"

"If anyone can, he can. He knows the law, and he's almost as stubborn as you are."

PART 4

SAM'S QUEST

12

Deborah had always been afraid of stirring up trouble, but now that trouble had found them without any help, Sam was not going to hold back. He intended to hit Stoner's Crossing like a Texas tornado if he had to.

Unfortunately, that human tornado met with more resistance than he could have dreamed possible. When he tried to talk with those citizens who had been around twenty years ago, he encountered not only reluctance, but, in some cases, outright belligerence. He butted against these attitudes for two days, against folks with suddenly failing memories, or people who plainly told him he'd be sorry if he tried to mess in what was none of his business.

It finally became clear that the only person from whom he might hope to get straight answers was Caleb Stoner. Since Deborah's arrival, Caleb had maintained his distance. He didn't even come by the jail once to gloat. But if Caleb wasn't planning a confrontation with his former daughter-in-law, Sam determined that he'd just have to confront Stoner.

Sam rode boldly up to the gates of the Stoner ranch and was stopped immediately under the coarse wooden archway that announced "Stoner Bar S Ranch." He must have been expected, because Sam didn't know of ranchers who routinely kept a guard at their gates. He could see the house in the distance, but he was blocked from getting any closer by three heavily armed cowboys.

"What's your business here?" The man was a big, tough-looking fellow with a six-gun on each hip and a buffalo gun slipped loosely in his saddle, but his accent was strangely musical, like British mixed with a Texas drawl.

"Name's Sam Killion. I'm here to see Caleb Stoner."

"He's expecting you, is he?"

"I'd be surprised if he wasn't." Sam held the man's hard gaze steadily. This was certainly not the most dangerous man he had ever confronted.

"What's that supposed to mean?"

"You just tell him he's gonna have to face me sooner or later, so why put it off? I just want to talk."

"Well, he doesn't want to talk to you. Mr. Stoner says he'll do his talking in court if he has to—or maybe at the hanging of that murdering woman."

Sam rankled, and it took all his self-control not to jump down the man's throat. "And who are you that I gotta listen to you?"

"I'm the foreman, Toliver, and what I say goes."

"One way or another, I'm gonna see him." Sam's flat statement was uttered through clenched teeth.

"Not today, you're not."

Sam momentarily debated his next move. He knew he'd get nowhere trying to rush this brick wall of men. So, reluctantly, he reined his mount around and rode away.

Sam's uncle always used to tell him that the squeaky wheel got oiled. Sam thought that sage philosophy might work with Stoner, so he rode out to the ranch every day for the next three days. Deborah tried to stop him, tried to impress upon him what a ruthless, violent man Stoner was. But Sam had to do something; it just wasn't in him to sit idly by while someone he loved was in danger.

Each day the same trio of armed cowboys stopped him. Caleb was not going to be cajoled or convinced. On the fourth day, however, the wheel finally did get some attention—but Sam didn't think it was quite what his uncle'd had in mind.

When Sam reached the gate that fourth day, the three guards were nowhere in sight. Sam thought he'd finally made it. However, as soon as he spurred his horse to cross the threshold, he was met by a barrage of gunfire. None of the shots were aimed directly at him, so he held his ground at the gate, though it took some doing to keep his skittish horse under control.

"Stoner!" Sam yelled when there was a lull in the shooting. He knew Caleb would not be nearby, but someone was close enough to hear and carry back a message. "You won't help your case by killing me. All I want to do is talk. Maybe if we help each other, we can figure out who really did kill your son. It wasn't Deborah, and that's a fact; so the real killer is just walking around free."

The only response he received was another flurry of gunfire. Sam had no choice but to turn around and leave before some stray bullet did manage to find him.

Discouraged, he returned to town. But he was not ready to give up. If he couldn't make a frontal assault, he'd have to be a bit more subtle. That's when he conceived of the idea of sneaking up on the house. If he could just get close to Caleb, he'd be able to make the man talk to him. He didn't much like having to resort to breaking and entering, but he was certainly not above such extremes to save Deborah.

When he questioned Deborah about the layout of the Stoner ranch and other possible approaches that might be secluded, she reluctantly told him of a trail she had discovered while she lived at the ranch. It had been ideal for her purposes—she could get to it from behind the stable, and it took her some distance from the ranch without anyone seeing her from the house. It was a long trail, and though she had only followed it for a mile or two, she had always wondered if it might eventually curve around and lead back to town. It could well have been a means of escape for her, but before she had the chance to find out, she had been made a virtual prisoner in the house.

With this information as a guide, Sam went in search of the trail the next morning, leaving town at dawn. It was not an easy undertaking because he would have to find the trail from the opposite end, where it might possibly come out near town. He spent most of the morning following dead ends, but the skills he had learned during his days as a Ranger finally paid off when he struck upon a little-used path some distance north of town that did not end abruptly in a pile of rocks. It seemed to be heading in the right direction, so he followed it, praying it wasn't another wild-goose chase. Before long he realized it was just an old dried-up ravine; but that was no reason why it couldn't be a bona-fide trail. There hadn't been water in that ravine for a hundred years, so it seemed likely he wasn't the first man to ride this way. Even after he estimated he was on Stoner land, he was still fairly obscured by the steep, rocky walls of the old riverbed.

The ravine took him several miles, and the sun had reached its zenith and was already arching toward the west when the ravine walls became low and the rocky riverbed gave way to a smoother, pebbly area that finally opened up into grassland. The trail was extremely circuitous, taking several more hours to get to the ranch from town than the regular road would have done. He estimated he was still miles from the Stoner house. His suspicions were confirmed when he discovered an old dead tree that Deborah had described as a landmark. That had been as far as her own explorations of the trail had taken her.

He was more exposed now and kept a sharp lookout. But at this distance from the house he didn't expect anyone to be watching for him, if they were watching at all. Nevertheless, he didn't want to be accidentally discovered by some cowhand. He rode for another half hour, encountering no signs of human life and no resistance. Maybe he would finally get in to see Caleb Stoner today.

According to Deborah's description, the house could not be far. It was likely over the next rise, Sam decided. He dismounted, wanting to approach with utmost caution. His feet had no sooner touched the ground when riders topped the crest of the rise, guns blazing.

Sam was an excellent horseman and in no time had swung back up on his mount. Keeping his head low, he raced back down the hill in the direction from which he had come. These gunmen were not aiming over his head. One bullet sliced past him less than an inch from his scalp, whipping his hat off. Had he been sitting upright, it would have pierced his heart.

His pursuers dogged him for a quarter of a mile, firing at frequent intervals. He managed to keep out of range most of the way. His six-gun was in his saddlebag, a weapon he carried as protection against snakes and wild animals on the trail, but he was not yet desperate enough to use it against human enemies. These men *were* his enemies, and they knew full well who he was—and were determined to stop him at any cost. More than likely, they figured they could do away with him on this back trail and Caleb would never be suspected.

As Sam approached Deborah's dead tree, one of the bullets at last hit its mark, penetrating the back of Sam's shoulder like a fiery poker. He had been wounded before and knew how to keep his head in such circumstances, if only the pain and bleeding didn't make him pass out. In any case, he didn't know how long he could keep riding at this breakneck pace.

When Sam passed the dead tree, his pursuers backed off. Perhaps that was the boundary of the Stoner range and they knew better than to risk killing him anywhere else. In these parts, trespassing was a valid cause for shooting a fellow.

Sam responded to the easing of the pursuit by slowing to a brisk trot until he reached the ravine and knew he'd be safe enough for the time being. There he paused, wadded up his neckerchief, and pressed it into his wound before heading back to Stoner's Crossing.

13

It was dark by the time Sam reached town. He rode past the jail because he didn't want Deborah to see him like this. She'd be worrying about him, he knew, but he best get himself patched up first.

During his earlier excursions about town, Sam had noticed a sign over a second-story window for a "Doctor R. Barrows, M.D., D.D.S., Undertaker and Minister of the Gospel." Interested in meeting the local cleric, Sam had stopped by the upstairs office, but the doctor had been out. Now Sam prayed fervently the man would be there. A light from the window gave him hope. He also prayed that the "M.D." was legitimate, because at the moment he needed medical, not spiritual, attention.

By now, his weakened condition made it difficult to climb the long, rickety flight of stairs on the outside of the building. Finally reaching the top, he leaned against the wall and knocked on the door, then waited.

When the door was flung open, Sam said, "I need a doctor."

"That's a fact," the man said, giving him a quick survey. Doctor Barrows was of average height and build. He did not have the kind of countenance that inspired confidence in a wounded man. His face had not seen a razor in two days, and his teeth were yellow and rotting—a poor advertisement for a man bearing the letters "D.D.S." by his name. His eyes were red and rheumy as if he had spent too many hours staring into a whiskey glass. And though he appeared to be no older than fifty, there was a slight tremor in his hands.

"Looks like you stopped an unfriendly bullet," he went on. "Well, you came to the right place." His voice was strong in comparison to the rest of his broken-down appearance. Whatever his medical expertise, he was a man with fine verbal skills, and, in fact, Doc Barrows preferred preaching to practicing medicine. However, he was not a man to turn away a paying customer. "Come in and I'll see if I can fix you up—that is to say, if I can't fix you up, then there isn't much hope anyone can."

At least Sam could not fault the man with false modesty. He walked in and sat on the examination table. When Sam stripped off his shirt, Barrows poked and prodded around the wound.

"It isn't a mortal wound," he said at last. The doctor seemed almost disappointed, but he was, after all, also the town undertaker. "Where'd you pick up this hunk of lead?"

"I guess I got to admit I was trespassing," Sam answered, "but I hoped I would have received a better reception than this."

"Around here folks like their privacy—" The doctor stopped short, distracted by another thought. "What is your name, anyway?"

"Sam Killion."

"Ah, I see now. You are the Stoner woman's man, are you not?"

"That's right." Sam refrained from quibbling about his wife's proper name.

"And you were nosing around the Stoner place?"

"Trying to find some answers, the truth about what happened to Leonard Stoner. Were you around then?"

"Yes," Barrows answered curtly, then went on before Sam could respond. "I've got to get that bullet out. I want you to lie on your stomach on the table, but before you do, you better have some of this."

Barrows held out a bottle of whiskey.

"That the only anesthetic you have?" asked Sam.

"Nothing works better, and it's a long sight cheaper than those fancy ones they've come along with lately."

Having no other choice, Sam drank the two large glasses offered. Long years of abstinence combined with his empty stomach and recent loss of blood caused the liquor to have an immediate and most stunning effect. The room was spinning as he lay down, and he prayed that the pain would be numbed as effectively as his sense of equilibrium.

This only distracted Sam momentarily from his initial excitement over the doctor's admission that he had been in Stoner's Crossing at the time of Leonard Stoner's murder. This was the best thing to happen to Sam all day, especially since the doctor was the first person to respond in a less than hostile fashion.

"As a doctor," Sam said as Barrows cleansed the wound by pouring whiskey into it, "you must have treated Leonard Stoner." Sam's words came out slow and labored, punctuated by several winces as the whiskey stung his wound. His tongue felt thick and unwieldy.

"Can't treat a dead man," Barrows replied. "But I did tend the body." Barrows picked up a long, pointed instrument and began probing into Sam's wound.

The pain exploded through Sam's entire back and down his arm, but he was determined to continue this promising conversation.

"They said it was a . . . gun—I mean, a . . . a Colt that killed Leonard. Is that true?" Sam was having great difficulty forming a coherent thought.

"True enough. But you'll find that in the official court records."

"No records . . . no one knows where. . . . they are." Sam grunted as the probe dug deeper.

"That so?"

"Perhaps . . . you . . . can tell . . ." For a moment Sam forgot what he was going to ask, and only his inner determination forced him to focus. ". . . From your . . . medical findings . . . how. . . ?" With each passing moment Sam felt his head become lighter and lighter as his vision grew darker and darker.

"He wasn't lucky like you, Killion," said the doctor almost too buoyantly. "Young Leonard took his bullet right in the heart. That's where I found it at the autopsy, lodged in the heart. Kind of ironic, isn't it? I mean, considering everything."

"Did . . . did . . . it enter from the front or back. . . ?" But Sam did not hear the answer, if there was an answer, to that most important question.

Faintly, as if from a long distance away, he heard, "There it is! I knew I'd find that bugger."

Then Sam blacked out.

He awoke no more than half an hour later according to the clock on Barrows' mantel. Sam was still lying on his stomach and the doctor was still working on him, putting a bandage on.

"There you go," said Barrows, "all fixed up. You can stay here for a couple of hours, unless you feel up to going back to where you are staying."

Sam rolled over. "Just give me a hand and I'll see." With the doctor's help he got into a sitting position. The room spun for only a few minutes. When he felt steady, he said, "How much do I owe you?"

"Well, seeing as how you are new in town and I've heard you are also a fellow man of the cloth, I'll give you a discount." He rubbed his unkempt chin. "Fifteen dollars ought to do it."

Even as drugged and tired as he was, Sam's eyebrows shot up at the doctor's so-called discount.

Barrows added, "If you want to stay here for the night, I'll only charge you another dollar."

"Thanks," said Sam, "but I think I can make it back to the hotel." Sam scooted off the table and found that, though his knees were weak, he could stand on his own. He slipped his shirt on, and Barrows placed a sling around Sam's arm. Then he paid the doctor and started for the door. But before he reached for the doorknob, he paused as an unfinished thought, which had been nagging at him since the surgery, finally clarified in his mind. He turned back to Barrows. "I didn't hear you too clearly before, Dr. Barrows, but did you say that bullet that killed Leonard Stoner came from the front?"

"I don't believe I said, either way." Barrows was washing his hands in a basin. He stopped and leveled a direct gaze at Sam. "I just can't remember that far back."

Something in the man's steady look indicated that he remembered all too well. Like everyone else in town, he wasn't about to reveal any information to the husband of the woman who murdered Caleb Stoner's son.

"I will give you a bit of friendly advice, though," said the doctor, wiping his hands on a none-too-clean cloth. "Caleb Stoner is going to do everything he can to see that your wife hangs for what she did. Your best hope is to get a good lawyer."

Sam left, more discouraged than he had been in a long time. He had been so hopeful—first about that trail, then about the doctor who had seemed a lot more talkative than the other townsfolk. Maybe if he hadn't passed out and had been able to pursue his questioning . . .

Well, he would never know what might have happened then.

To compound this failure, it looked as if he would never get close to Caleb Stoner. This last encounter made it fairly certain that next time, Stoner's boys would not miss. Stoner's message was clear: *Give up, or you are a dead man.*

Sam was not one to give up easily, but he simply had no other tricks up his sleeve.

Returning to the hotel, he sent the manager's son to the jail with a message for Deborah. He desperately wanted to see her himself, but he knew that in his present state he would only cause her unnecessary anxiety. It took all his remaining strength to get up to his room to his bed. He did remember to pray but fell asleep long before he finished.

14

Sam slept late the next morning. He woke with such a dismayed start that it sent pain coursing all through his body. The bright, hot sunlight streaming into his room told him just how late it was. He jumped out of bed—at least, he had intended on jumping, but it was more of a lunge and a stumble. He skipped breakfast, pausing only long enough to gulp a cup of coffee before going to visit Deborah.

If he had hoped to spare her needless concern by waiting until morning to see her, he was totally unsuccessful.

"Sam! What happened to you?" she exclaimed the moment the sheriff let him into her cell.

Not only the presence of his sling, but also his pale face was enough to arouse Deborah's worst fears. There was nothing else for Sam to do but tell her everything that had occurred.

"I don't want you going back there again, Sam."

"I reckon I'd be downright foolish to try it again."

"Caleb will never budge in this matter. He'll die before he'd do anything to help me."

"It's almost as if..." Sam began, but the idea was so farfetched that he could hardly voice it.

"As if what?"

"Well, I was thinking that maybe he don't want the truth to come out because he's protecting himself, or someone close to him. Maybe he killed Leonard, or even his young son, what was his name...? Laban, wasn't it?"

"Caleb could never have killed Leonard unless it was some kind of freak accident." Deborah shook her head at the incredible notion. "As for Laban, I have thought of him, but ... I just don't know. Regardless, even if he did, there is no way we can prove it with Caleb obstructing our every move."

"The answers are on that ranch, Deborah—"

"Promise me you won't go back there, Sam. I couldn't bear any of this if something were to happen to you."

"Don't you worry about me, Deborah. Just remember that God helps us to bear all things."

Deborah opened her mouth to protest his adept sidestepping of her plea. Instead, she said nothing and just held him close.

They were quiet for several minutes; then Sam said earnestly, "I ain't gonna do nothing foolhardy, Deborah. But I feel that if we could just get to Caleb . . . if we could just talk to him, get some response from him, we'd be able to get to the bottom of all of this."

Deborah nodded. There were so many *ifs* but nothing solid. It sometimes seemed as if they were fighting shadows.

Two days later, they did get a response from Caleb, but it wasn't quite what Sam would have wished for. He was having lunch with Deborah in her cell when the sheriff entered the back room where the jail's two cells were located. He was holding a piece of paper and appeared none too pleased to be the one to disclose its contents.

"I got a court order here," he said.

"Is the circuit judge in town now?" asked Sam. He had been anxious to speak to a judge.

"Nope. Someone rode all the way to Austin to get this," answered the sheriff. "Anyways, this says that you, Mrs. Killion, are to be transferred to the county prison."

Sam jumped to his feet in protest. "What! You can't do that. Why, it's—it's illegal! My wife has rights—"

"It's perfectly legal," said the sheriff, "especially if there is some reason to believe this jail facility ain't secure enough for the prisoner."

"Secure! I can't believe—"

"Sam," put in Deborah, laying a calming hand on her husband's arm, "I think this is just another of Caleb's obstacles." To the sheriff she added, "It *was* Caleb who instigated the court order?"

"I reckon that ain't no secret. He was worried about the way your husband was poking his nose around, and he'd heard about his exploits as a Texas Ranger. He also was worried about other associates who have helped you in the past. The authorities in Austin thought his request was valid. And they also believed that because of your unpopularity in his town that it'd be for your own good, your safety, that is, to be removed."

"When will this happen?" Deborah asked calmly.

"Soon as they can send someone up here for you. Maybe tomorrow."

"All right," said Deborah. "Can my husband and I have a few more moments alone?"

"Don't see why not."

The sheriff exited and Deborah turned back to Sam. "Come on, Sam, let's sit down and discuss this."

Sam's jaw twitched with anger, but he took a breath and made a conscious effort to let go of it. He sat back on the bunk.

Deborah continued. "It's not so bad, really. That sheriff is right, in a way. I mean, in that there is no telling what Caleb might do to me. He could easily incite this town to a lynching. That sheriff isn't exactly hostile to me, but like everyone else around here, I doubt he'd stand up to Caleb." She paused for a moment. "By the way, I haven't heard from Pollard lately. Is he still around?"

"I ain't seen him, but I heard he's spending a lot of time at the saloon and cantina. I don't think it was enough for him just to arrest you; he's bent on seeing this all the way through to the . . . end." Sam faltered on the word *end,* and his and Deborah's eyes met.

A brief instant of fear tried to intrude upon Deborah's calm, but she shook it away. This was no time to fall apart. She had God, she had Sam, and she still had an abundance of hope. When she lifted her eyes again toward Sam, they reflected a great deal of determination.

"Sam, I was thinking about what Dr. Barrows told you about getting a lawyer. Maybe it's time we did that."

"I want to see you cleared of this thing." Sam was agitated, frustrated, and angry, but he was doing his best to stay calm. "Yet, if it takes getting some fancy lawyer to wrangle around the law a little to get you off, then that's what we'll do. We gotta find the real killer, but you're right, the first thing to do is get you out from under this conviction. No one's gonna put a rope around your neck or keep you in prison."

"Believe me, I don't want that either!" Deborah's hand went unconsciously to her neck. Even if the state had never "legally" hanged a woman, Caleb might take the law into his own hands. He had almost gotten away with that nineteen years ago.

Sam took her in his arms and tenderly kissed her lovely, precious neck. She was more important to him than his own life, and he was quite willing to sacrifice himself to save her. The problem was that he was practical-minded enough to realize that *willingness* just might

71

not be enough. In his lowest moments—and he was almost there now—he had pictured himself standing by a gallows watching her execution, unable to ride in, like Griff McCulloch, guns ablaze, to rescue her. He wondered often how far he would let her friends go to protect her, how far he would go to save her. Would he throw all his Christian principles out? Would he lie, steal, kill? He had prayed he'd not be tested to this point; but if he was, he asked that God would fortify him where he was weak. It was all he could do.

"Deborah," he said quietly, as if this resolve was one of great consequence, "I'll go to Austin when they take you, and I'll find a lawyer."

He was still discouraged when he left the jail that day. The idea of his Deborah sitting in a county prison was as demoralizing as anything that had yet occurred. He had been to such prisons on business as a Ranger, and he knew what kind of despicable pits they were. Not only were there filth and disease, but there were also other prisoners, many of the worst kind, even among the women.

Such knowledge plagued his thoughts as he sent his first telegram back home to inform the children of their mother's status. He would have preferred to have said nothing since he had no good news to report, but he knew that to Deborah's anxious loved ones silence was as cruel as bad news.

15

Caleb Stoner's influence in the state capital was one thing Sam had not taken into account. He had tried to believe that once away from the center of Caleb's power in Stoner's Crossing, he'd have no difficulty in obtaining justice for Deborah. That, however, was not to be. Stoner had apparently preceded Sam to Austin and, anticipating Sam's course of action, had set several extremely disheartening obstacles in place.

Sam had reluctantly left Deborah at the county prison some thirty miles south of Stoner's Crossing and about fifty miles west of Austin.

They both knew he could do her more good in the capital than sitting around the county seat awaiting each day's visiting hours.

Upon arriving in Austin, Sam discovered Stoner was going to make it difficult, if not impossible, for him to do Deborah any good at all. First, Sam learned Stoner was a close friend of the governor, so any immediate hope of intercession from that quarter was well dampened. Then there was the problem with judges. Even the most sympathetic men were wary of a case that was fast becoming infamous and easily a political anathema. One judge suggested Sam get a good attorney. That, however, was not easy advice to follow.

The reputable attorneys, mindful of their careers and future standing in the state hierarchy, would not touch a case that could possibly place them at odds with the governor himself. One man was eager to defend Deborah, but Sam didn't like the look or sound of him. He seemed more interested in the novelty of defending a woman accused of murder, and cared nothing about her innocence. He said Deborah's best bet, if they were about to file for an appeal, was to plead guilty by reason of insanity and throw herself upon the mercy of the court. He took a particular relish in the words "throw herself."

There didn't seem to be a lawyer in town who really believed in Deborah's innocence. Either they had been brainwashed by Caleb, or they believed she killed Leonard by reason of self-defense. Sam thought he'd be willing to accept that plea if it saved Deborah, but he knew that, at least for Carolyn's sake, Deborah desired her innocence to be proven beyond all doubt.

So after several weary days of interviewing lawyers, Sam returned one day to his hotel for dinner as discouraged as ever. While waiting for his meal he idly picked up a newspaper left behind by the previous occupant of his table. The front page was dominated by the results of the Presidential Nominating Conventions in which Grover Cleveland and James G. Blaine had become the nominees of their respective parties. Another article reported on problems in Africa as various nations battled for control of that continent. Sam realized how out of touch he was lately with world events. But when he felt as if his own world was collapsing, it was all he could do to focus on other events.

He turned the pages absently while he waited for his meal, catching a key word or two here and there, not really comprehending most of what passed before his eyes. The story that finally did jump out at him was small and unpretentious, buried on the fifth page. The word *Attorney* caught his attention, and when he paused and backtracked, it said *Famous Philadelphia Attorney Announces Retirement*.

The article went on to tell about the life and accomplishments of the man who not only had had a successful private practice for thirty years, but had also served two terms as a U.S. Senator immediately following the Civil War, and had once been considered for the presidency. After returning to private practice a few years ago, he had again made headlines by defending a man accused of the slaying of three women. This extremely unpopular move on his part had garnered much criticism for him until he proved beyond all doubt the man's innocence by tracking down the true killer.

Sam had heard of Jonathan Barnum and vaguely recalled reading in Texas newspapers accounts of that Philadelphia trial. But he knew little of the man himself. The article said he was a tenacious fighter who enjoyed defending the underdog and espousing seemingly lost causes.

Sam immediately thought of Deborah's cause. He did not want to believe it was a *lost* cause, but even he had to admit it was becoming successively more difficult.

He scanned the article one more time to see if there was an address for the attorney, but there was none. Forgetting all about his dinner, Sam folded up the newspaper, tucked it under his arm, and hurried from the hotel, where he caught a cab and instructed the driver to take him to the offices of the Austin *Globe*.

For the first time that week, he felt a surge of hope. On the surface it might appear a harebrained idea. What famous eastern attorney would want to get involved with some obscure residents of Texas, especially considering that the man had just begun a well-earned retirement? Even if by some miracle—and Sam had by no means given up on miracles!—the man sympathized with Deborah's plight, how could they expect an elderly gentleman to make an arduous trip west to handle the case? It seemed unlikely, even impossible.

But as his coach pulled up in front of the *Globe*, Sam recalled something that propelled him from the vehicle with a light, confident step.

"With God nothing shall be impossible!"

Even at that late hour, the place was still open. He obtained Barnum's office address, then rushed over to the telegraph office where he dashed off a lengthy signal to Philadelphia.

The reply came two days later, informing him that Mr. Barnum could not be reached because he was vacationing. It was from Barnum's secretary, a Chester Duncan, who went on to tell Sam that Barnum was no longer accepting cases. He suggested Sam seek other legal counsel and politely offered his best wishes.

Oddly, this negative response in no way dampened Sam's rising spirits. He doubted his request had ever actually reached Barnum. More than likely the secretary was fielding correspondence and would not bother the attorney with such a message. Moreover, Sam had not really expected a positive response in written form. From the beginning he had suspected it was going to take personal contact to convince a man of Barnum's stature to consider Deborah's case. Perhaps it had been a waste of precious time to send the telegraph, but he had felt it necessary to try that avenue before rushing off on a trip that could turn out to be a wild-goose chase. Still, Sam had a sense inside that he was being directed by the hand of God, that seeing that newspaper article in the first place had not been a mere coincidence.

This spiritual assurance, however, made it no easier for him to leave Deborah. He could be away two or three weeks. He had only managed to get a six-week grace period in which to put together an appeal. And that time was steadily slipping away.

He did not even spare the time to visit Deborah in prison before leaving for Philadelphia. Instead, he wrote a letter explaining everything and posted it on the way to the stage depot where he would begin the fifteen hundred mile journey. He also paused long enough to send one more telegram, this to the Wind Rider Ranch.

16

Sam's two telegrams to the ranch proved to be somewhat ill-timed. The first one had arrived shortly after Griff regained consciousness and had begun to improve.

DEBORAH TRANSFERRED TO COUNTY PRISON STOP STONER AFRAID OF ANOTHER ESCAPE ATTEMPT STOP HAVE MET WITH HOSTILITY HERE SO WILL GO TO AUSTIN TO TRY TO FIND A LAWYER WILLING TO TAKE HER CASE STOP STONER A POWERFUL MAN IN THIS PART OF THE STATE AND HE BLOCKS OUR EVERY MOVE STOP WILL KEEP YOU INFORMED STOP PRAY FOR US END SAM.

Everyone in the family was appalled at the thought of Deborah in some horrible prison. What was even worse, Sam sounded as if he were beaten.

Carolyn broke the stunned silence after the telegram was read. "That does it! I'm going south, and no one's gonna stop me!"

She had been hinting at this since Griff's recovery and, so far, had been ignored. Now Griff saw she was through with subtle hints, and he responded with equal force. "You're plumb crazy, girl!"

"You'd do the same thing if you could, Griff."

"I ain't no eighteen-year-old kid, either."

"Sky, you understand, don't you?"

Carolyn's brother had been standing quietly by, observing the explosion between his sister and their foreman. He had no doubt in his mind who would win the debate. He also believed that there was more involved in his sister's decision than simply supporting their mother. And he, for one, could not dispute any aspect of her reasoning.

Sky nodded and answered in his quiet, thoughtful way. "Griff, you and I are both bound here to the ranch. I promised my mother I would run things, and you are stuck in that bed. Now, if I thought I could do her more good down south, I'd go in a minute. As it is, I think it's right for Lynnie to go. Besides, we both knew she'd have to go there sooner or later to meet up with those Stoner people. They are her family, too."

Griff rolled his eyes and shook his head. "There ain't no use fighting both of you."

Carolyn smiled triumphantly. "I'll take two horses so I can travel faster—"

"You ain't thinking of going alone, are you?" demanded Griff.

"With you down and Slim still in Fort Worth, we sure can't spare anyone to accompany me. It's better if I go alone, anyway. If I do get to the Stoner ranch, I'll be less threatening by myself."

"More like a sitting duck!"

"You can't really believe any harm would come to me, Griff. Caleb Stoner is my grandfather. He wouldn't . . . well, I think he might actually be pleased to see me. He lost his son nineteen years ago; maybe I'll be able to make up for that loss a little. Maybe I'll even be able to soften that heart of his that you seem to think is so hard."

"All right! But there ain't no way you are gonna ride all that way alone."

"You can't do nothing about it, Griff."

"Why, if I could get outta this here bed, I'd blister your bottom so's you couldn't sit a horse for a week."

Carolyn suddenly repented of her disrespect. "I'm sorry, Griff. I'm just so worried about Ma, and I feel like I'll burst if I don't do something."

"I know, girl. I feel the same way."

When Yolanda reproved Carolyn for her foolhardy plan of riding through hundreds of miles of frontier alone, Carolyn finally relented. "That is no way for a lady to travel, señorita. What would your poor mama think? I could never face her if I permitted this thing."

So Carolyn conceded by booking passage on the train out of Danville. It was going to take longer, but it was better than having everyone hounding her.

Griff stopped his arguing and even began to feel that Carolyn's decision might be the best way after all. Besides, Sam would be there to help keep the girl in tow.

———————

After Carolyn's departure, Sam's second ill-timed telegram arrived, informing them of his intention of traveling to Philadelphia to speak to a lawyer.

Griff groaned when he read it. "Now what's Lynnie gonna do down there all alone! There's no way to tell Sam."

"Carolyn can take care of herself," Sky said.

"You kids think you're so durned independent!"

"You taught us nearly everything there is to know, Griff."

"Well, it ain't enough." Griff ranted and raved for several more minutes, until suddenly he stopped, a look of satisfaction replacing his earlier chagrin. "I shoulda thought of this before Carolyn left. Staying in bed is killing my brain."

"Thought of what?"

"I got me a friend at the Stoner place—that is, if he's still there."

"That's incredible, Griff. How could you have managed such a thing since you've been trying so hard to keep anonymous?"

"It was a fella Sam and I had a run-in with a couple of years ago. He was on his way to Stoner's ranch to take a job." Griff smiled to himself as he recalled the encounter. "He didn't think nothing of it when Sam asked that he keep mum about our meeting when he got to the ranch. He just figured it had to do with keeping silent about good deeds and all that. Anyway, it was as much to his advantage as to ours."

"Good deeds?" asked Sky, curiosity piqued.

"It's a long story. Suffice it to say that I think he'd be more than willing to look out for Carolyn."

"I doubt Lynnie will like that."

"Well, she don't have to know! Now, you just gimmie a pencil and paper. I got a telegram to send. And I want you to get it to Danville as quick as you can."

17

Carolyn was not in the most pleasant mood after three days on a train that took her east through Fort Worth and south to Waco, followed by a two-day stage ride south and west through Austin. She had been miserable and uncomfortable the entire way. And, to make matters worse, Yolanda had insisted Carolyn wear a dress and look like a lady for the trip. The stage had been especially tedious, packed with several cigar-smoking men who blew smoke in her face and talked incessantly.

In Austin, she spent half a day looking for Sam before she finally learned he had checked out of his hotel with the intent of traveling east. This puzzled her, but instead of wasting more time on that mystery, she decided to go to the county prison to see her mother.

The prison was most of another day's ride from Austin. She secured a ride on a freighter's wagon, and for the hundredth time on this long, arduous journey, she regretted not having ridden Patch from the ranch.

Nevertheless, Carolyn was excited to see her mother. Despite their clashes, during the weeks of their separation she had come to realize just how much she needed her mother's love and wisdom. And then she chided herself for thinking of her own needs now when her mother was in prison and fighting for her very life.

As Carolyn passed into the visitor's receiving area of the prison, she determined to do all she could to comfort and uplift her mother.

But when the guard led Carolyn into the locked visiting room and Carolyn first set eyes upon Deborah, all her good intentions fled.

She burst into tears and started to run to embrace her.

But the ever-present guard stepped between them and directed Carolyn to a chair on the opposite side of the table from Deborah. Crushed and deflated, Carolyn sat down. She sniffed and tried to wipe away her tears, making a brave attempt to regain her lost resolve.

"It's all right, Carolyn, dear," said Deborah in a gentle tone, not revealing any shock at seeing her daughter in this most unlikely place. She reached her hands across the table and Carolyn, with only one hasty glance toward the guard, took them. That contact helped to strengthen her. She took a breath and began to feel calm.

"I had to come," Carolyn blurted out an answer to the unasked question. "When I heard they'd taken you to a place like this, I just couldn't sit by idly anymore. Sky would be here, too, but he knew you'd worry about the ranch if he left."

Carolyn paused to take a dismayed appraisal of her mother. She was looking pale, even after only a couple of weeks in prison. The drab gray prison shift she was wearing didn't help her color at all. And the way it hung in limp folds around her body—how much weight had she lost since this whole ordeal began? Still there could be no mistaking the essential serenity in Deborah's eyes, such as Carolyn desperately wanted to find within her own self now.

"You shouldn't have come," said Deborah.

"I had to."

"Well, then let's leave it at that. I suppose I might have done the same thing in your place." Deborah paused a moment before asking the question uppermost on her mind. "How's Griff?"

"He's as ornery as a mule. The doc says he's gotta stay in bed a month, but every day he tries to get out. I nearly had to tie him down to keep him from coming with me."

"I'm so glad to hear that. He'll be all right then?"

"Oh, sure. Griff's too tough for anything else."

Deborah smiled. Her daughter was trying to sound just as tough as Griff.

"And Sky?" asked Deborah.

"You'd be proud of him, Ma, at how well he's taking care of the ranch. Like I said, he woulda come with me except for his duty to the ranch. Besides, we felt it was more my place."

"Your place. . . ?"

"Being the oldest and all."

"And that's all?"

Carolyn looked away. She had wanted to wait to get into her deepest reasons for coming south. She knew her mother would hurl the same protests at her that Griff had used. Yet, now that she thought of it, how long could she wait? Carolyn had only been able to see her mother today because she had begged and pleaded with the warden on the grounds that she had traveled so far. Normal visitations were once a week, on Sunday, and that was three days away. Carolyn could not afford to waste time that was getting more precious with each passing day. If it meant that she must proceed with her plans like a herd of stampeding cattle, so be it.

She took a breath, then said bluntly, "I'm gonna go to Stoner's Crossing, Ma, and I'm gonna get to the bottom of all this." Carolyn did not ask, neither did she insist, but rather she spoke with implacable finality.

Deborah replied with exactly the same tone. "You are not."

"Don't make me defy you, Ma, not now. This is something I gotta do, and whether you believe it or not, you need it, too. I think I'll be able to find out things where no one else—"

"They tried to kill Sam the last time he went to the ranch," Deborah interjected.

"Ma! Is he all right? Is that why I couldn't find him in Austin?"

"Yes, he's all right now." Deborah briefly explained what had happened to Sam at the ranch, and about his trip to Philadelphia. "Do you see now why you must stay away from Caleb Stoner?"

"I can do this, Ma, I can!" Was she trying to convince herself as well as her mother? "Once they learn who I am—"

"And what makes you think they will believe you?" reasoned Deborah.

That problem had not occurred to Carolyn, but she had an answer for it. "I'll make them believe. And I *will* learn the truth."

Deborah sighed. At that moment Carolyn looked and sounded as much like her father as she ever had. Perhaps she could do this thing, after all.

"Carolyn, they don't want the truth to come out. That's why they shot Sam. What do you think will happen to you if they learn you are trying to prove my innocence?"

"I refuse to believe that anyone's gonna hurt me. Sam was a stranger. I'm . . . I'm Caleb Stoner's granddaughter. But if it'll make you feel any better, I don't need to tell anyone I'm trying to get you free. I don't even have to tell them who I really am. Maybe I can just get a job on the ranch and be free to poke around."

"Carolyn, you don't understand how it is there." It was the only argument, lame as it was, that Deborah could use. How could she find words to describe the vindictive and hateful way in which Caleb

Stoner had treated her twenty years ago? And even if she made the attempt, would Carolyn believe her? Deborah had felt from the first moment she told her daughter the truth that Carolyn needed to believe the best about her father's family. Thus, she had watered down the story as much as possible. Maybe the best thing Deborah could do for Carolyn, and for their relationship, was to let Carolyn find out for herself. Besides, how could she stop her? She was locked up in prison, and Carolyn was a headstrong, independent girl. If Deborah forbade her to go, Carolyn would be forced to defy her mother, and Deborah did not want to place her daughter in that position. Moreover, she knew if that happened, it would produce a wall between them that neither of them could afford now.

So, fully realizing she was possibly sending her daughter into danger, she nodded her head in ascent. "All right, Carolyn, I won't stand in your way. But will you take some advice from me?"

"Oh yes, Ma!"

"Don't try to deceive Caleb. It will go better for you if you tell him the truth. If he wants proof of your parentage, show him the birthmark on the back of your arm. Your father had one just like it. Of course, that's not conclusive evidence, but, with everything else, I think he will have to accept who you are. But Carolyn, above all, be careful. There still may be a murderer somewhere out there who will do anything to keep from being discovered. Sam's not here for you, so please take care!" Her final words were the closest Deborah came to revealing the awful fear in her heart.

"I will, Ma, and I won't give up until I've found the truth and you're out of here."

Then she sent a defiant glance toward the guard, and before the woman could do anything to stop her, Carolyn jumped up and ran into her mother's arms.

"I love you so much, Ma!"

"I love you, dear Carolyn! And I will pray for you every day."

Mother and daughter kissed and hugged each other one final time before the guard stepped forward and parted them.

PART 5

CAROLYN'S LEGACY

18

The Crystal Hotel in Stoner's Crossing was not exactly the kind of place a respectable young lady would choose to stay. But it was the only hotel in town, and the first floor wasn't a saloon. Like the rest of the town, it was run down and threadbare, as if its proprietor had little pride of ownership, but at least it was a real hotel with a lobby and front desk.

Carolyn had expected more of the town named after her grandfather. She had heard he was a wealthy rancher and had assumed that with wealth would come a certain opulence. Rich Texas ranchers were by no means noted for their modesty. But this was a town as rough and coarse as any on the Texas frontier where Carolyn had grown up. Stoner's Crossing sported one long main street that was the center of activity, but there were also a couple of side streets on which were located several frame houses of residents and two or three shops. The main street was lined on both sides with an uneven and ramshackle assortment of buildings.

In a town of about five hundred citizens, including those residents on outlying ranches, there were four saloons and one that was called a cantina. These were rather quiet in the middle of the afternoon when Carolyn arrived by stage, but she had no doubt they'd be lively enough at night. She studiously stayed away from them.

Besides the saloons and the hotel on the main street, there was a general store, a doctor's office above the store, a Land and Title office, a Cattlemen's Association Hall at the far end of town, a bank, and a sheriff's office. These were in connecting buildings on either side of the street, fronted by a foot-high plank sidewalk.

Carolyn took special note of the sheriff's office and tried to imagine that day long ago when her mother had been led from there to a hastily built gallows. The gallows no longer remained, its wood no doubt finding a place in other construction over the years.

After entering the hotel, Carolyn requested a room. The clerk, a

85

young man of about twenty-five with a pasty complexion and wire spectacles, pushed the register toward her. She hesitated only a moment before she signed: *Carolyn Stoner.*

The clerk responded with a perfect double take when he turned the book and glanced at the signature. But Carolyn gave him no chance for a verbal response. She paid him an extra dollar for a much needed bath and asked, "Where's my room?"

"Uh . . . up the stairs, down the hall, and third door to the right."

The room held only a rusted iron-rail bed and lumpy horsehair mattress, a wobbly wooden chair, a washbasin with a stand, and a bureau with one of its drawers missing. She shrugged all this off in her hurry to get a bath. She might not be here very long, anyway.

She deposited her two carpetbags, then took out a change of clothes. She was grateful Yolanda had made her take a towel and soap, for none was provided at the hotel. With these items, she headed directly for the room down the hall where the clerk had told her the bathing facilities were.

Taking a bath, however, proved no easy matter. Though there was a pump for water in the bathing room, Carolyn had to heat it over the stove, which in turn required her to first build a fire. It was a long time before she finally slipped her tired body into a bathtub only half filled with tepid water. But it was water, and it did feel good. Besides, with the heat from the stove and the summer heat outside, she was glad the water was no warmer.

She used the time spent preparing the bath and soaking in the tub to meditate on her plan of action now that she was in Stoner's Crossing. Should she send a message out to the ranch, telling Caleb Stoner she was here and invite him to the hotel to meet her? Griff always said it was best to meet an adversary on your own territory, not his. But was Caleb Stoner an adversary? Her mother was obviously afraid of the man, and Griff hated him. Yet shouldn't she make her own appraisal of the man, draw her own conclusions? If he truly believed her mother killed his son, then naturally he'd have no love for Deborah, but that didn't necessarily mean he was always a hateful, spiteful man.

It might be better if she went to the ranch to meet him, to set him at ease, to show her good faith. She must avoid presenting herself as hostile. If it meant a little deception, despite her mother's advice, then so be it. But why should she be deceptive? She wasn't hostile. Or was she?

It was still as confusing as ever!

She felt as if she were in the middle of a feud. She loved her mother and desperately wanted to see her vindicated and freed. Yet now she had a new family she wanted just as desperately to perceive in a positive light. And this new family apparently was committed to insuring that her mother remained where she was, at least until she could be executed. Suddenly everything in Carolyn's life was at odds with everything else. The only thing she was sure about was that no matter what happened, someone would lose—and *she* was going to lose, regardless of who won.

Carolyn stepped out of the tub, toweled herself dry, and dressed. She wore a split skirt, a red flannel shirt, boots, and her old plainsman wide-brimmed hat. Even as she cinched the leather belt at her waist, she realized she was readying herself for riding. Perhaps she had made her decision, then. She would meet Caleb Stoner on his ground and hopefully prove to him that she had only the best of intentions.

Carolyn gathered her belongings, exited the bathing room, and walked down the hall to her room. She put her key in the lock and was about to turn it when she heard the sound of heavy boots climbing the stairs.

Three men strode toward her, one clearly the leader of the group. He was dressed in an expensive black broadcloth suit, with fine leather boots and a black sombrero that hung by a cord at his back. On each hip was a gleaming pearl-handled Colt, in exquisite holsters. Except for a fine layer of recent dust clinging to his clothes, he was meticulously groomed. In his mid-thirties, he still had jet black hair and moustache with no trace of gray. His swarthy skin indicated he was of Mexican or Indian blood—probably Mexican, judging by his clothes. His face was arranged in what seemed to be a perpetual scowl. His lips, thin and nearly obscured by the moustache, were twisted in either irony or ire, Carolyn could not quite tell which.

The two other men were cowboys. They also were armed with six-guns and looked as if they'd have no qualms about using them.

"What is your name?" the first man asked in an abrupt, demanding tone.

"Carolyn . . . Stoner."

"You hesitate. Why?"

Carolyn put a hand on her hip and faced him squarely. She wasn't armed, but she confronted these strangers with challenge. "Who are *you,* and why are you asking me these questions?"

"I am Laban Stoner, and I have no relative by your name."

"Who says I'm your relative?"

Laban's twisted lips twitched in a momentary affectation of a smile. He paused for a moment as if pondering a distant memory.

"You come into a place called Stoner's Crossing," he said at last, "and sign your name as Carolyn Stoner, and you expect us to believe this is just a coincidence? And this just weeks after a woman from the past, whose name was also once Stoner, was arrested. Tell me this is mere chance."

"I didn't say it was a coincidence. I just questioned that I'm *your* relative. I am a relative of someone named Caleb Stoner. I happen to be his granddaughter. I never heard of anyone named Laban."

Laban's scowl deepened and darkened at hearing this, as if it were a worse affront to be overlooked entirely. Carolyn decided she didn't like the looks of this man at all. She liked his next words even less.

"You will come with us."

"What?"

"Come."

"I will not! Do you think I'm crazy to go off with a bunch of strangers who are armed to their yellow teeth? Forget it."

"In this town when a Stoner gives an order, it is obeyed!" If Laban Stoner could possibly look darker, he did so at that moment.

Carolyn found herself trembling a bit, but she didn't flinch.

"Well, my name's Stoner, too, mister! And I say I ain't going unless I feel like it!"

The two cowboys exchanged shocked and slightly amused looks at her impudence—looks which were immediately dampened by a rabid glance from Laban.

Laban's next words were even, measured, suppressing his rising anger. "You do not wish to see Caleb Stoner, whose granddaughter you claim to be?"

"Well, you didn't say you were taking me to see him. I reckon I'll go, in that case."

And so it was that before her first day in Stoner's Crossing had drawn to a close, Carolyn was riding out to the place where her mother had once lived and where her father had been murdered.

19

Laban Stoner seemed as reluctant to enter the ranch house as Carolyn. He had even knocked on the door first. She had belatedly realized this must be one of the half-Mexican sons of Caleb Stoner that her mother had briefly mentioned in her account of her years with the Stoners. But Deborah had not mentioned their names, and Carolyn had not given them another thought until, riding out to the ranch with this Laban and the two cowboys, she wondered who this unpleasant man was and how he was related to Stoner. He had informed her that he was Caleb's son, yet for a son, she thought his behavior at the house was unusual.

But hadn't Carolyn's mother mentioned something about the mistreatment of the younger sons? Carolyn wished she had asked her mother more questions, probed deeper into the history of this enigmatic family. *Her family.*

Carolyn was led into the parlor by an elderly Mexican woman, while Laban—her uncle?—went to find Caleb.

On the ride out, Laban had said little, but Carolyn had managed to learn that he had been visiting the cantina in town when she checked into the hotel. The clerk, not wanting to be derelict in his duty to the town father, thought the Stoners ought to be informed immediately of the arrival of another Stoner so soon after the other woman. He had gone to the saloons hoping to find someone from the ranch who could carry a message back. It was pure luck that Laban himself happened to be there. He chose to act immediately on the information rather than go back to the ranch. Thus, Caleb was only this minute learning that someone claiming to be his granddaughter was sitting in his parlor.

What would he think? Deborah said he had known nothing of her pregnancy. Would he be furious? Incredulous? Perhaps both.

In an attempt to still her growing nervousness, Carolyn strolled around the room. If she had hoped to discover more about Caleb

Stoner and his family from the contents of the parlor, she was disappointed. Perhaps its very sparse and impersonal appearance was a statement in itself. There were furnishings of rather good quality, if somewhat old and worn, and two or three original paintings that must have been of some value. But the room was void of any family photographs, books, or even an odd bit of nick-a-brick that might be of sentimental value. Perhaps the male domination of this household explained that. Perhaps—

The opening of the door startled her, and she jerked around with less poise than she would have liked.

The man who stepped into the room, closing the door behind him, seemed not in the least concerned that his entry had disturbed her. He made no attempt to apologize, gave no welcoming words of greeting. He studied her with an intensity that made Carolyn squirm in spite of herself. She stood silent, her mouth ajar, her eyes wide.

The man was probably in his early seventies, tall and lean and gray. His dark eyes were clear and penetrating but set deeply in dark sockets; his mouth, a nearly exact duplicate of Laban's—except that, since his moustache was thinner, the twisted quality of ire mixed with mockery was more pronounced. His features were sharp, astute, and most definitely intimidating, but as Carolyn looked more closely, she could see that the years had greatly marked him. Besides a slight stoop in his shoulders, his lean face was deeply creased with lines, his skin discolored with freckles and spidery blood vessels. Yet he carried himself as straight as his bent shoulders could and appeared to be openly fighting the ravages of time.

"I am not in the habit of entertaining women who dress like men," he said, his voice breaking the brittle silence like a hammer shattering against an anvil.

Carolyn opened her mouth, then quickly clamped it shut again, the ready reply on her lips having been intended for a different greeting. But Carolyn was no innocent Southern Belle. She was well used to the rough and sometimes insensitive world of men and had learned early to hold her own in that world.

"Well," she rejoined as smoothly as she could under the circumstances, "you ain't *entertained* me yet! Nor have you properly introduced yourself, but I assume you are Mr. Caleb Stoner. I'm Carolyn, as you probably already know."

Only a flicker of surprise at this young woman's boldness flashed across his well-controlled countenance.

"Carolyn Stoner, I believe you said," Caleb replied.

"Yes."

"You know I had three sons, all of whom could have sired a child of about your age."

"My mother is Deborah, and my father was Leonard."

"You are certain of this?"

"That is what my mother told me, and her word is as good as gospel."

Caleb grimaced at this, making it clear that he was of a different opinion on that subject.

"I reckon the real question, Mr. Stoner, isn't my certainty, but yours. I know this is coming at you unexpectedly. It hit me between the eyes, too, when I found out."

"When was that?"

"Just after my mother was arrested a few weeks ago."

"You were never told before that?"

"No." Carolyn purposefully left her reply ambiguous, leaving open the possibility of gaining Caleb's sympathy by implying dissatisfaction in never having been told about her father.

"Why are you here now?"

"I don't really know. I guess when I found out about you, I just had to see you for myself. If my mother hangs, you will be the only family I have left."

"You know I have been supportive of her arrest?" When Carolyn nodded, he continued. "And that doesn't bother you?"

"It does, it truly does. I gotta admit I don't understand it. I wish there could be peace between you, and maybe I hope I can be something like a bridge that can bring you together."

"She killed my son."

"I don't think she did."

He met her words with another silent appraisal. She immediately regretted so quickly refuting him. But deception did not come easily to Carolyn.

"Of course. She is your mother; what else would you think?" His tone was still not gentle, and far from kindly, but Carolyn sensed he was allowing her some latitude. If he had some ulterior motive for this, Carolyn could not see it. He went on. "But returning to your previous question, that is, regarding my acceptance of your story. It supersedes any further discussion about your mother's guilt or innocence."

"Maybe we won't have to discuss that part of it at all. I mean, deciding a person's innocence is really up to a court of law, ain't it?"

"A court of law already decided that nineteen years ago."

That statement stung at Carolyn's heart as much as any words yet spoken. In essence Caleb was right.

"But we digress again," said Stoner. If he noticed the discomfiture that had suddenly shaken Carolyn, he said nothing. "Can you prove your identity?"

"What would happen if I could? Would I be among friends or enemies?"

He made no immediate reply. Instead, he strode to a small window in the room and gazed out at the blue sky and the dirt yard that surrounded the house. In his obvious reluctance to answer the question, Carolyn felt an odd connection with this man. As she was torn between her mother and grandfather, he, too, was in a quandary. Carolyn might well be the daughter of the son he loved, the son in whom Caleb had placed his hopes for the future. But she was also the daughter of the woman he believed murdered that son. He would want to love her and spurn her all at the same time.

"It's hard, isn't it?" Carolyn said quietly, full of empathy. "I think I have felt the same way. You are my grandfather—I've never had a grandfather before—and I want so much for us to care about each other. Yet I know how you must hate my mother. I just don't know how to feel about you. Couldn't we just put aside the past? I never hated my father. I never wanted him to die. I—" But Carolyn stopped abruptly as unexpected tears rose to her eyes. She tried to blink them away, hating herself for this silly show of emotion. She already sensed that this man had a low enough opinion of women, considering them helpless, mindless creatures. She did not wish him to think that of her. She desperately wanted his respect. And obviously, Caleb Stoner only respected strength.

"So, what do you want of me, Miss Stoner?" asked Caleb stonily, turning to face her. "Do you wish to win my sympathy in order to gain your mother's freedom? Or is there something else you want?"

"I told you, I don't want anything except to know you. I was hoping you'd want the same. But maybe—"

"What I want is proof."

Without another word, Carolyn slipped off her buckskin jacket and rolled up the right sleeve of her flannel shirt. Still silent, she turned her bare arm so he could see the birthmark on the back of her upper arm. Caleb studied it for a long time. Because Carolyn was turned away from him, she could not see his expression.

He finally said, "It is not what I'd call conclusive evidence."

"No, it ain't," said Carolyn. "But why would I lie about this?"

"Come now, Miss Stoner, don't tell me you have given no thought to the kind of inheritance that could be yours as my grandchild?"

If her words did not convince him, then her stunned expression should have. Carolyn had, in fact, given this no thought at all. Now, of course, she saw there was more reason than mere vengeance for Caleb to reject her, and she suddenly felt very helpless. If he thought she was some kind of fortune hunter, then her motives would always be in question. How could she ever convince him otherwise?

But apparently Caleb was no fool when it came to reading others. He turned to face Carolyn squarely. His countenance was hard, so terribly, terribly hard. Yet there was just barely discernible a small fissure in the man's granite expression. Perhaps in spite of himself, he did indeed see in her a resemblance to his eldest son, the son he had loved. Carolyn chose to read that revelation as a kind of reluctant tenderness. No matter who her mother was, he could not reject that part of Carolyn that was his dear son's.

"Until we get all this sorted out," Caleb said, his cool voice indicating none of the emotion Carolyn thought she observed, "I think you ought to stay at the ranch . . . as my guest." He added this last, Carolyn guessed, as a response to her earlier question about being a friend or enemy.

Carolyn knew this didn't answer her question entirely, but she figured she had better take what concessions she could get from Caleb Stoner. He was not a man to give away anything readily, especially in regard to his emotions.

Carolyn was at least glad to be able to write a note to her mother that evening, reassuring her that the meeting with Caleb was progressing well.

20

Laban could not believe what his father was saying. The man was actually accepting this girl into his home and, by all appearances, accepting her story that she was his granddaughter. Laban would never have taken his father for such a sentimental old fool.

But even Laban had no choice but to admit—though he'd never

do so to his father—that the girl did bear an uncanny resemblance to both Leonard and Deborah. He had seen it the moment he set eyes upon her in the hotel, that arrogant glint he had known so well in Leonard. Still, it galled Laban to see his father accept her so readily and on such congenial terms.

Will I never escape the insidious ghost of my brother, Leonard? Laban thought bitterly.

He wondered again if his hopes would always be dashed under the white heels of his so-called betters. He seemed doomed to be nothing more than the half-caste son. Caleb would do almost anything to keep him from inheriting his fortune, but to go so far as to accept the child of his son's murderer?

Laban wasn't going to stand for it. He had worked too hard, *slaved* too long under Caleb's degrading and demeaning hand to give it up easily.

He cast a hard, cold look at his father now as they sat alone in the study. "You are making a grave mistake in allowing her to remain here."

"I never asked for your opinion in the matter," Caleb said with a sneer. "I felt you ought to be apprised of the situation, that is all."

"You have always regretted accepting her mother—it will be the same with the daughter, mark my words!"

"I only have one son now to lose." Caleb left no doubt as to how little the loss of Laban would affect him.

"She will not take my place, do you hear?" Laban's voice rose with passion.

Caleb laughed. "Believe me, I doubt she would want to. If she is a true Stoner, her ambitions are sure to be *higher* than that."

His inflection on the word *higher* incensed Laban.

"Why you—!" he blustered threateningly.

"Don't you dare speak so to me!" snapped Caleb, effectively cutting the younger man off. "I am still your father."

"And may God have mercy on me!"

"Get out of here. I don't want to see you until you can be civil to me."

Laban snorted derisively. "I won't put up with much more of this, *Father.*" He spat out the final word with contempt. "Just make certain that girl watches her step around me." He lurched to his feet and strode to the door.

Caleb's voice stopped him as his hand poised on the doorknob. "If anything happens to her, you will pay, Laban. Mark *my* words!"

Laban flung open the door with a vengeance and, stalking from the room, slammed it behind him. His fury mottled his face to a livid red.

How dare they try to rob me of my due!

At that moment, Laban Stoner could have killed them all—his father, the girl, anyone who stood in his way. But he refused to succumb to his passions. In the end that would get him nothing but a noose around his neck. Instead, he stormed outside and vented his anger in bullying the ranch hands, taking much pleasure in boxing the ears of the young Mexican stableboy.

Let Caleb have his way now. It wasn't going to last. Laban had known for years that his inheritance was on shaky ground. Caleb avoided discussing his will with Laban and was forever threatening him that he'd not get a cent. Thus, in the last couple of years Laban had been working toward a more certain way of insuring he'd get what was rightfully his. Now, with the appearance of the girl, he'd have to accelerate those plans. One way or another, the Stoner Bar S Ranch would be his!

21

Caleb gave his son's retreating figure a final smirk before leaning back in his chair and ruminating upon the recent turn of events.

For some sweetly malicious reason it delighted him to see Laban so agitated. It was a small recompense to Caleb for all the years he'd had to spend guarding his backside from Laban's greed. Not that Caleb seriously believed that his skulking, no-good half-breed of a son really had the guts to kill him; but as long as there was even a slim possibility of it, Caleb had to be alert.

And for that reason, Caleb was not at all adverse toward the arrival of this granddaughter out of the past. He did not doubt for a minute the validity of her claims. The birthmark she had which was identical to Leonard's, and also to one Leonard's mother had had, was only the beginning of the basis for his accepting her. She definitely had his son's eyes, especially evident when they flashed with that haughty passion he remembered so well in Leonard.

Oh, Leonard! Why were you taken from me in the prime of your life, when I had so many plans for your future?

Is it truly possible that part of you lives on? That your loss is not nearly as complete, as deadly final, as I had believed? Ah, but why couldn't you have sired a son, a man I could have poured my life into as I did you? If I didn't know such things were beyond the schemes of men, I would blame that murdering wife of yours. But I'll bet she delighted in the fact that she gave birth to a mere girl, knowing how it would gall me to pass my legacy on to her. If, indeed, I choose to do so.

Female or not, she is of my blood—and my son's blood. And Deborah knows that I'd sooner pass what I have along to a female than to that misbegotten greaser whelp who despises the very air I breathe.

Caleb expelled a heavy sigh. He picked up the daguerreotype of his son he kept on his desk. The pain of Leonard's loss clutched again at Caleb, as fresh as if it had occurred only yesterday instead of nineteen years ago. Caleb was a cold, ruthless man, yet it was possible, even for such a man as he, to possess feelings. Laban might describe these emotions as his father's "fatal flaw," and attempt to use them to bring the powerful old man to his knees. Carolyn, on the other hand, might see them as Caleb's "soft spot," a vulnerable side that could be nurtured and expanded until love and mercy balanced his arrogance and ruthlessness. But regardless of how Caleb's deepest emotions were defined, they existed, and they centered on his dead son, whom, in his own way, he had loved.

And now there was Carolyn, Leonard's own daughter. Could he possibly come to love her also?

Yet Carolyn was clearly Deborah's daughter as well as Leonard's, especially in that impudence and willfulness of hers. She acted like a swaggering cowboy and spoke to him with all the respect and deference one would use toward a stableboy. Still, Caleb had to admit, that's also when she most resembled Leonard.

In many ways Caleb was as disturbed as Laban. He was not quite ready to accept the girl, but neither was he prepared to reject her out-of-hand. She would take some taming, to be sure. That feisty spirit of hers would have to be broken as he might break a green colt. But in the end she could mean the fulfillment of his dream that his empire go to Leonard's progeny. That was surely a better outlook than he'd had before today. He'd been fretting over this very thing for months now, ever since—

No, he mustn't dwell on that! He must only keep his sights on the fact that his future was looking brighter by the minute. Not only was Deborah back in jail, but Caleb now had an acceptable heir.

Laban, of course, might prove to be a problem in the matter of the inheritance. He might not have had the nerve to kill Caleb, but where a young, albeit gritty, young girl was concerned, Laban would bear close watching. It wouldn't hurt if Caleb assigned someone to look out for the girl, too—someone he could trust. He already sensed that, like her mother, she would not be one to be easily housebound. The moment he had left her earlier, she had gone out to the stable to see to the care of the horse she'd brought from town. She was still out there. What more could he expect of a girl who refused to wear a proper dress to meet her grandfather for the first time.

Caleb rubbed his bony chin. There was really only one man to whom he could entrust this delicate matter.

Half an hour later, Caleb's foreman, Sean Toliver, stood before him. Toliver was barely thirty years old, but in spite of his youth, he was extremely capable. He had come west from England years ago, a mere lad of fifteen, but he had filled those ensuing years with enough adventures to quickly make him a seasoned frontiersman. He had been on several cattle drives in the early days when Indians were still a menace. He had ridden as a scout with Ranald Mackenzie, fighting Comanche. In '75 he joined the buffalo hunters in the wild and dangerous hunt that had all but exterminated the bison. When he had come to the Bar S Ranch two years ago, he had quickly made himself indispensable. Toliver was a real man in Caleb's estimation, and he had often considered leaving the ranch to him. They looked at life in much the same way, with no-nonsense, canny eyes.

"Thanks for coming, Toliver," Caleb said, as if his foreman really had a choice in the matter. "Have a seat."

Caleb left the confines of his desk and moved to a leather chair next to a table that held a selection of alcoholic beverages. Toliver took the seat opposite Caleb, his brawny frame filling the chair. He appeared to be completely at ease in the presence of his stern, often daunting employer. That was something else Caleb liked about the man—he had guts.

"What can I do for you, Boss?" Toliver spoke in a British accent tempered curiously with a Texas twang.

"I suppose by now you have noticed my new houseguest?"

"It's hard not to; she's quite the looker. Where did you find a filly like that, Mr. Stoner?" He gave Caleb a meaningful wink.

"She happens to be my granddaughter," Caleb replied in a tone that clearly indicated Toliver might be getting a bit *too* relaxed.

"Sorry about the misunderstanding, Mr. Stoner. I didn't mean any disrespect."

"Never mind. I have something far more important to discuss." Caleb paused, leaned toward the table, and lifted a decanter. "Whiskey, Toliver?"

"Don't mind if I do."

Caleb poured two glasses, handing one to Toliver before leaning back comfortably in his chair.

"I'd like to talk about a very delicate matter with you, Toliver, and I'd like to be certain it never leaves this room." Toliver nodded in assent, and they sealed the agreement by sipping their whiskey. "Up until today," Caleb continued, "I had no idea I even had a grandchild, the daughter of my eldest son who was killed nineteen years ago."

"And you are certain she is who she claims to be?"

"As sure as I need to be for the present."

"What's the problem, then?"

"I am most favorably disposed toward the idea of a child of my son, Leonard, carrying on after me. I would have preferred if it had been a boy, of course, but I could learn to live with it as it is. Unfortunately, there is someone who stands to lose much because of this turn of events."

"Laban, I presume?"

"Yes. The girl has not even been here a full day, and he is already highly resentful of her, although nothing has even been mentioned about the state of his inheritance. I think he might try to make things difficult for Carolyn while she is staying here at the ranch."

"I can see why you'd think that."

"That's where you come in, Toliver. I'd like you to keep an eye on the young lady. I have a feeling you'll be seeing as much of her as I will."

"She did look as if she knew her way around a ranch."

Caleb raised an eyebrow, silently stating his disapproval of such unladylike behavior. "Her mother allowed her to become wild and impudent."

"Would you like me to tame her while I'm at it?"

Caleb's thin lips curved into a humorless smile. "I don't care what else you do with her as long as you keep her safe."

"Oh, she'll be safe with me, Boss, you can count on it!"

"Thanks, Toliver."

"I think I ought to be thanking you. This is one job that's going to be a pleasure!"

"Just see to it that you don't forget it *is* a job, and I expect it to be done well."

"Don't worry about that, Boss. Your granddaughter will be as safe as a babe in its mother's arms." Toliver paused, sipped his whiskey, let it roll around pleasantly on his tongue a moment before swallowing, then said, "What about my other work? It's roundup time, you know."

"I know you can't be her shadow, but try to keep tabs on her and on Laban, too."

Caleb was certain this was going to work out perfectly. Perhaps Sean Toliver and Carolyn Stoner would one day be a romantic match to boot. Nothing would please Caleb more than to see his ranch go to Leonard's child *and* a man like Toliver.

Only one other thing would be necessary to complete his life and allow him to die a happy man—he wanted the chance to watch his son's murderer hang by the neck until she was dead.

That consuming desire had not changed one degree since the day nineteen years ago when she had been snatched from the gallows by that thieving outlaw. Caleb had nearly given up hope of vindication and could hardly believe his good fortune when that no-account Pollard had appeared in town with her last month. He had wanted nothing more than to ride to town immediately, just for the pleasure of seeing her once more behind bars. But he had restrained himself for a very practical reason. Things in these parts were different twenty years ago. The town had been smaller and more isolated, and Caleb had had a firmer grip on its citizens. He was still confident of his influence, which had spread even to the capital. But these days people were apt to be more scrupulous about the law. It was hard enough to get a court to hang a man, much less a woman. There might be another trial, and Caleb was concerned about protecting his image. He didn't want to risk garnering sympathy for Deborah by letting his desire for vengeance be so obvious. He had to play this with more finesse than he had before. Deborah had more in her favor now than she had back then. It was entirely possible that her sentence could be commuted to imprisonment instead of hanging.

But Caleb Stoner would be satisfied with nothing less than seeing Deborah hang.

It didn't bother him that his granddaughter was also her child and the girl might mourn her mother. He felt confident he'd be able to manage the girl, just as he'd done with the town and his friends in the state capital. Why, once Carolyn was convinced of her mother's guilt, she might have little sympathy for the woman who murdered the girl's father.

Yes, in no time, he ought to have that girl tamed and looking at things his way. In no time at all.

PART 6

PURSUIT OF HOPE

22

The dirty glass allowed only a dull shaft of light to penetrate into the dank, gray room, and that was deflected and broken by the iron bars in the window casement.

Sitting on her bed, her Bible open in her lap, Deborah purposely ignored the unnatural gloom of the early morning. She made a concerted effort not to focus too closely on her surroundings, trying not to see the filth and ugliness, trying not to think that outside the drab and foreboding prison walls was the wide open land. Sometimes it seemed to take all her strength to avoid thinking of the hillsides dotted now with a few late-blooming wild flowers, or the grassy prairies she so loved—all open and free and beautiful.

She was successful most of the time in keeping the eyes of her heart on the Lord, finding hope and succor in God alone. But there were difficult moments when her mind wandered toward thoughts of home, of riding her favorite horse, flying with carefree speed over the grass, the wind stinging her face, blowing her hair. In those times, she felt her imprisonment, the closeness of the walls, the oppression of captivity, far too acutely.

Deborah had been struggling with this feeling since yesterday when a stray thought had brought it all crashing in upon her. Depression had begun to overwhelm her, and she lay upon her bed after lights out, praying until she fell asleep. At dawn she awoke, still heavy-hearted, and sought consolation in her Bible. Passages from the Psalms had lifted her spirits, and she had begun to sense, at last, a release from her oppression.

She simply could not become self-absorbed; of all her loved ones, she was at the moment the safest.

Sam was traveling thousands of miles away on the slim chance that he could convince a famous eastern lawyer to champion her cause. She had to keep praying that his spirits and hope would be buoyed, that he would not become discouraged.

She also prayed for Griff who, though apparently improving, was not yet fully recovered. Any small setback could prove disastrous, even fatal.

Sky was also shouldering a huge burden for a boy of only sixteen. Yes, he had good help in Slim and Longjim, but she knew Sky well enough to know he would take his responsibility seriously and expect more of himself than anyone else would.

And Carolyn ... Deborah was afraid to even consider what she had allowed her daughter to get involved in. The brief note she had received from Carolyn yesterday was somewhat reassuring, but still Deborah found it impossible to trust Caleb Stoner. She wondered now if she should have forbidden her to go to the Stoner ranch. Perhaps Carolyn would have obeyed.

At that outrageous thought, a smile invaded Deborah's gloom. Carolyn had been determined; nothing would have stopped her. Now she had entered the most dangerous place of all, and Deborah could do nothing about it.

Nothing but pray.

And that she must faithfully do. She was not helpless as long as she had that one weapon. Perhaps God had her in this very place to keep her still long enough so she could devote her whole self to that one important effort.

In this place, where she was surrounded by the obvious needs of others, she could spend hours in prayer just for them. In fact, theoretically, she shouldn't have any time at all for self-pity.

Deborah thought of her two cell mates. Nell James was about Deborah's age and had been a hardened criminal almost from childhood. She was now in the middle of a six-year prison term for horse stealing and attempted murder. Nell admitted she was "guilty as sin" for the thieving part, but the man she had tried to shoot deserved it because he had been roughing her up and trying to horn in on her rustling operation. He had walked away scot-free, claiming he had been attempting to bring her to justice.

The other woman was a twenty-seven-year-old red-headed saloon girl named Lucy Reeves. She had come west five years ago from Boston as a mail-order bride, but her prospective bridegroom had been killed in a gunfight. Alone and desperate, she married another man, who turned out to be a brute. She left him after a year, and while he was riding after her to bring her back, he was killed in a thunderstorm, struck down by lightning.

Lucy didn't mourn his loss, but she ended up in the same position as when she had first come west. She needed to make a living—

which was almost impossible for a woman to do alone and with no money . . . a *respectable* living, that is. She had no trouble at all getting a job in a saloon. She told herself she'd work long enough to make train fare in order to return home to Boston. Then she committed her terrible crime: she stole fifty dollars from her boss. She claimed the money was rightfully hers and that he had withheld it from her. No one believed her word against a man who was rather influential in the town. She was sentenced to two years in prison, and now had only a few more days of that term to serve.

Deborah heard such stories all the time here in prison. Some of the women were victims like Lucy; others were perhaps more deserving of their punishments. But they all were needy. For the most part, their hope had been pretty well destroyed by the realities of life. And any shred of hope left in tact was being steadily wiped out by their sojourn in prison.

Deborah thought there could be no lower existence possible than prison life. Although the two dozen women were kept entirely separate from the hundred men in the prison, their standard of life was no better. The food and conditions were far worse than when Deborah had been imprisoned with the Cheyenne women at Fort Dodge. At least then there had been a camaraderie and kinship among the women that had been uplifting and positive. Here, each woman seemed isolated within personal barriers. The strong tried to dominate the weak, making everyone defensive and suspicious. The women guarded themselves against becoming too friendly, perhaps because they wanted no ties to this nightmarish existence.

Deborah's thoughts were interrupted by the sounds of stirring in the bunk opposite hers. Lucy Reeves was waking. She let out a miserable-sounding groan as she raised up on one elbow, rubbing her sleepy eyes with her other hand.

"Morning already?" she said with a thick voice.

"Just after sunup," Deborah replied.

"That's what I hate most about this place; there's no chance to sleep late. Where I lived before, because we used to work late, there was nice heavy curtains over the windows. That's the first thing I'm going to do when I get out—sleep till noon."

"Sounds nice, Lucy. The first thing I'm going to do is ride a horse as far and as fast as I can—that is, after I hug my children and kiss my husband."

"So you think you really are going to get out someday, Deborah?"

Lucy was the only person who had been open and friendly to Deborah. They had exchanged their stories and talked on a personal level. Perhaps because Lucy knew her release was near, she wished to start living again as a civilized person, not a caged animal.

"I have to hope, Lucy. My only other choice is despair, and I refuse to give in to that."

"There are other choices, Deborah. And if I was in your spot, I'd think about them."

"What do you mean?"

Lucy sat up, dangling her feet over the side of the bed. Then she glanced furtively over her shoulder toward the bars that formed the front of their cell. Apparently satisfied there were no listeners, she ambled over to Deborah's bed and sat on the edge. She was a pretty woman, with her freckled face washed free of the heavy makeup she was accustomed to wearing as a saloon girl. Prison life had made her pale, with dark circles under her green eyes, but even so, Deborah thought the girl probably looked better now. Lucy complained that prison also had made her lose her figure, which before had been buxom and curvy and appealing to men. She was thin, and the drab gray prison dress didn't help.

Lucy leaned toward Deborah with a confidential air. "I've been talking to Nedra, you know, in the third cell down. I'll let you in on something, Deborah, because I like you and I think you can keep things to yourself." She glanced again at the cell door. "Nedra's planning to escape. She asked me to come with her."

"How can you think of escaping, Lucy, when you have so little time left to serve?"

"I may be crazy, but not that crazy. It's you I'm thinking of."

"Me?"

"Sure. You don't plan on spending the rest of your life here, do you?"

"No, I don't. But I had hoped to leave by the front door, not the back."

"Sounded like they had an open and shut case against you. Didn't you say you'd already been convicted?"

"Yes, but my husband is on his way east right now to speak with a lawyer—"

"Lawyers! Don't trust them, Deborah. Through most of my trial, my lawyer was half drunk—and he was *all* drunk the rest of the time. You'll have better luck with Nedra. She's got a good plan, but she can't do it alone. She wants someone with a good head on her shoulders; that's why she asked me. She thought you'd work out, too."

"Thanks for the thought, Lucy, but I'm not ready to take that kind of risk yet. I tried that route and—"

106

Nell, in the bunk over Deborah's bed, began to stir. Lucy quickly placed a finger over her lips and jerked her head toward their cell mate.

"Don't let her in on it," Lucy said in a whisper. "Nedra absolutely doesn't want her because of her violent temper."

"I won't say a word," assured Deborah.

"And I'm serious about that lawyer business. You'll be better off escaping."

"What's that 'bout escaping?" Nell asked in a groggy voice.

"I said there was no escaping this stinking sunlight," answered Lucy quickly.

"That's for sure. They gotta get somethin' on these windows." Nell rolled over and was soon snoring again.

Lucy returned to her own bed, sat for a few minutes, then rose and began pacing idly about. Her restlessness soon began to affect Deborah, who tried to focus on her reading but found it more and more difficult. She wanted to get up and pace also.

She thought about what Lucy had said. Deborah had already tried escaping once and here she was locked up again. True, she'd had nineteen wonderful years of freedom, raised two fine children, married two remarkable men, acquired a productive ranch, and most especially, discovered a real faith in God. She could not deny that God had given much to her and made the most of those years, but she was still right back in the same—

Deborah silently rebuked herself. She was *not* in the same place. Nineteen years ago she had been alone, helpless, and without hope. All that was changed now. People who loved and cared for her were out there right now working and striving to free her. Poor Griff had nearly given his life for her, not to mention all the hands at the ranch who had been willing to risk unknown danger on her behalf. That was a far cry from the young Deborah Stoner who had not a friend in the world, and had not even had a lawyer to defend her at the trial.

She could not let herself forget how fortunate she was now, how much hope she had.

She remembered the excitement Sam had injected into the letter he had written her before leaving for Philadelphia. He said he truly believed God was guiding him in this direction. He didn't want to promise what might come of it, but he knew that if God was behind it, something good would spring from his efforts.

She had to believe that, too, and to banish all thoughts of escape.

The idea of running gave in to hopelessness and despair. And she still had hope.

23

Sam was discouraged.

He had arrived in Philadelphia on Thursday and gone directly to the law office of Jonathan Barnum. There he had met with an obstinate clerk named Chester Duncan, the same man who had sent Sam the telegram in Austin.

Mr. Duncan had been superficially polite; actually, he had been rather condescending to this provincial dressed in rather coarse clothes who spoke with a rural accent. Sam had worn his best suit for his arrival, but it did look somewhat rumpled after sitting in his carpetbag for over a week. He was out of his element here, in this big city, in a fancy office, standing before a man of education and culture. But Sam was on a mission, and he would not be so easily daunted.

"Look here, Mr. Duncan," Sam said respectfully but firmly, "I've come a long way to see Mr. Barnum—"

"I had hoped to save such an ordeal with my telegram."

"And I appreciate that. But you see my wife is in a lot of trouble, not of her own making, and she needs some powerful help. Now, we got lawyers in Texas, but she needs the best, and I just sense Mr. Barnum is the man for us."

"But as I explained in my telegram, Mr. Barnum has retired— why, he's not even in town at the moment."

"Is he sickly or something?"

"Of course not! I never saw a more robust man for his age."

"There you go!" Sam said triumphantly. "I'll bet he don't even care to be put out to pasture then. He's probably just itching to be back to work."

"A month ago all he was talking about was getting away to do some fishing. He has worked hard all his life and has earned a comfortable retirement."

"I don't dispute that. All I ask is a chance to talk to him, to tell him about my wife, and to let *him* decide if he'd like to take this case or not."

Duncan shook his head obdurately. "I have been entrusted with the responsibility of closing up this office, disseminating Mr. Barnum's caseload—not taking on new cases. My responsibility is to Mr. Barnum alone. I am sorry, Mr. Killion."

Sam scratched his head and thought a moment. "Maybe you could get hold of—"

"Impossible."

"Could you tell me where—?"

"I'm sorry."

Sam sighed, a bit abashed but still not discouraged. He bade the protective clerk good-day and returned to his hotel. After a good meal and a night's rest, he was ready to begin his quest anew.

He went back to the office, hoping someone new might be there, only to find Mr. Duncan hovering over the office like a hen over her brood. Sam tried once more to prod the man into helping him, but without success. He'd had better luck converting drunken cowboys.

At that point his confidence had begun to ebb. Back at his hotel, the desk clerk asked him how much longer he would want the room. Sam could give the man no certain answer. It was now Friday afternoon; he had an entire weekend to endure before he could approach other businesses for information. Perhaps some of Barnum's colleagues might know his whereabouts. But he'd not be able to find out until Monday.

He made the most of Saturday and Sunday. He visited Independence Hall and saw where the founding fathers had signed the Declaration of Independence. He spent several hours watching the ships in the harbor. On Sunday, he found a little church to attend. But he couldn't fully enjoy these experiences knowing that Deborah was sitting in that dismal prison. Every day he was idle meant another day of captivity for his wife.

Early Monday morning he began to walk the streets of Philadelphia. He visited several law offices near Barnum's, hoping someone might know where the lawyer was. Everyone knew Jonathan Barnum because he was something of a legend among his colleagues. But Sam spoke only to clerks and junior partners. None of the senior lawyers would see him without an appointment, and the earliest one he could get was Wednesday, two days away. He went ahead and made the appointments with a heavy sense of defeat.

Had this whole trip been a waste? Should he have stayed in Texas and continued to pursue Caleb Stoner?

Oh, God! he silently prayed as he walked down the street with tired feet and a pounding headache. *I was so certain you were directing me in this. Was I wrong? Show me your will, God. Maybe I've been working too much on my own power, maybe I haven't given you a chance. Well, I give up! I just don't have what it takes to fight this battle. I gotta have you, Lord! I can't do it myself!*

By one o'clock in the afternoon, most of the offices were closed for lunch. Sam wasn't really hungry, but he needed a distraction from his hopeless mood so he stopped at a little cafe near one of the law offices he had just visited. He ordered a sandwich and coffee and was about to sit back and read the newspaper when a man from another table rose and approached him.

Sam remembered him as a clerk he had spoken with an hour ago. He was about twenty-five years old, and Sam remembered him especially because he had been of a somewhat different disposition than many of the other brash young city men he had thus far met. He had appeared quieter, more sincere, and had shown true sympathy with Sam's plight.

"Mr. Killion, I don't know if you recall who I am—"

"I spoke to you in—well, I can't remember whose office—but I do recall you, Mr.—" Sam smiled sheepishly. "Except for your name."

"I'm Robert Allen." He offered his hand and grasped Sam's with a firm hold. "I don't wish to interrupt your lunch, but I'd consider it an honor if you'd care to join me."

Sam was grateful for the prospect of friendly conversation and was quick to accept the invitation. He carried his meal over to Allen's table.

"I haven't been able to stop thinking of your problem, Mr. Killion," said the young man in a soft, earnest tone after they had engaged in several minutes of small talk.

"Please call me Sam."

"Thank you, Sam. It must be terribly hard dealing with, having your wife in prison. I am a married man myself, and I can imagine what a burden that would be."

"Sometimes I wonder what I'd do if anything were to happen to her. But I really believe God is gonna get her out of this—well, most of the time I believe that. There are times when I get a twinge of fear."

"That's only normal, I suppose. At least you have your faith to carry the lion's share of the burden."

"Thank God for that! Are you a believing man, then, Robert?"

"I surely am. But I must say that it doesn't always make life easy for me, especially in the legal profession. I have to deal with matters of integrity and scruples almost daily. Your situation is a prime example."

"How's that?"

"Well, when I spoke with you in Mr. Thomson's office today, I wasn't entirely forthcoming with you. In my defense, I felt rather constrained to protect the interests of others. I mean, you were a complete stranger, and though I sympathized with your plight, I felt it would be unfair of me to involve others without their prior permission. I have been wrestling with that decision ever since. I have prayed for wisdom also, and that God would show me if I am to act upon this in any way. You can imagine my incredulity when I saw you come into my favorite restaurant after I thought I'd never see you again."

Sam smiled. "I reckon that is pretty remarkable. Are you thinking this might in some way be an answer to your prayer?"

"It very well might be. At least, now I feel more certain than ever that I ought to pursue this matter further."

"Can you tell me what you're thinking?"

"I see no harm in that. I feel as if you are no longer a stranger. But I must add that my only reluctance now is that I might instill in you false hope. What I have to offer is extremely remote, a 'shot in the dark,' so to speak."

"I've had so many ups and downs, Robert, that one more ain't gonna do me no harm."

"Well, then, it is simply this: my wife went to school with Jonathan Barnum's daughter. They are not close friends, because they now travel in rather different social circles. But they have maintained a casual connection through the years as mutual friends. Thus, it is possible my wife could speak to Miss Barnum. Perhaps upon our recommendation she might be willing to tell you where Mr. Barnum is vacationing."

Sam wanted to jump up and hug the young law clerk. Instead, he gave him a huge, beaming grin. He could find no words to express his gratitude—and his relief.

24

Sam lost two more days trying to see Jonathan Barnum's daughter. She was understandably dubious when Robert Allen's wife told her about Sam. Upon meeting Sam and talking with him, however, she came to sympathize with his cause and agreed to tell him how to reach her father.

Unfortunately, Barnum was staying at his fishing lodge in New Jersey, and there was no way to reach him except by mail. Sam figured he could travel faster than the mail, and Miss Barnum gave her blessing for him to go there in person. It would still consume another couple of days at the very least.

First, he had to take the steamer down the Delaware River to a town called Salem. This took most of the day, so he was forced to spend another night in a strange hotel. At first light he mounted a rented horse and, following directions given him by Barnum's daughter and reinforced again by the man at the livery stable, set out on what he hoped was the last leg of his tedious journey.

The stableman's directions served him for about an hour. Then he had to make his way by stopping passersby along the road, or pausing at occasional farmhouses. Putnam Creek was simply not the easiest place to find, and perhaps that was exactly why Barnum had chosen it as his retirement retreat. It was a good thirty miles from Salem, and Sam should have been able to reach it in one day; but he had been forced to take many byways to get directions and then had made too many wrong turns. As a Texas Ranger he had successfully tracked Indians in a snowstorm and bandits on a trail several days old and caught his quarry. But finding a city lawyer was proving to be his undoing.

He had to admit, though, that the country in these parts was lovely. Rolling green hills, grassy meadows, woods of oak and maple and elm and other deciduous trees. It was far different from the plains on which he had spent his entire life. There wasn't a sprig of mesquite to be seen, and everything was so lush and alive. Still, he couldn't wait to get back home. He missed that dry, prickly mesquite, the yellow grass, and the perpetual clouds of dust. And he missed Deborah and Carolyn and Sky—even that ornery old cowboy, Griff McCulloch. He wanted them all to be together again where they belonged, and for life to resume its delightful monotony. But for that to happen he had to keep on his present lonely path, spending another night in a strange place, and another day—many days, if he had to—searching for the elusive Jonathan Barnum.

A night under the stars, with sweet forest smells all around him, helped to revive Sam's sagging spirits. He decided that part of his slumping mood had been from staying too many nights in stuffy city hotels, and eating too much fancy restaurant food. Coffee over a campfire, hard biscuits, and fresh fish caught in a nearby stream was feast enough to lift anyone.

By the next morning he was ready to continue his quest. After traveling for about two hours, Sam met an old farmer driving a load of hay to town. The man had lived in the area all his life and knew Putnam Creek well. He also knew the best fishing holes along the creek.

"If that there city lawyer knows anything," said the man to Sam after he waved him down on the road, "he'll be fishing about half a mile up from the big bend in the creek. There'll be Falstead's Hole, or Buzzard's Quay. Else, he'll be on the Little Fork."

Elated, Sam replied that the Little Fork was exactly where he needed to go. The farmer described in detail how to reach this place. Sam decided that if an ex-Texas Ranger couldn't find Barnum with those directions, he had no right to be let out alone.

Half an hour later he found Putnam Creek, and in another hour he located the Little Fork. From there he had directions given him by Barnum's daughter to get to the cabin. At the Little Fork he had to dismount and walk his horse because the woods and undergrowth were too thick for riding. It was past noon when he finally came upon the cabin.

It was a log cabin, very rustic but solid, with a warm and homey air. An encouraging stream of smoke rose from the stone chimney and, hitching his horse to a nearby tree branch, Sam approached eagerly, not only anticipating the end of his search but perhaps lunch as well. Several knocks on the door, however, produced only silence in response.

Sam walked around back and, finding no one, explored in a wider circle around the cabin, soon making his way back toward the creek.

He was still hiking through the woods when he heard the sound of a voice.

"I'm going to get you one of these days, you ornery critter, just you wait!"

Though a bit alarmed by the unfriendly tone and words, Sam was not about to back down. If the speaker wasn't Jonathan Barnum, it might well be someone who knew how to find him; but even if it was a grizzly, Sam was determined to confront him. Before drawing closer, Sam, accustomed to the ways of the West, where a man coming upon a camp unannounced could well expect a bullet for a welcome, called out a greeting.

"Hello! Anyone out there?" he called.

"Ho! Who's that?" came a startled but not unfriendly reply.

A couple minutes later Sam broke out from the thick woods into an open grassy slope that led down a low embankment to the creek. There, sitting on a rock at the edge of the water was a man of about sixty years of age holding a fishing rod, its line extended far out into the middle of the water.

The man turned, put a finger to his lips and said quietly, "Step lightly, lad, or there'll be a poor lunch today."

Sam obeyed, and with the practiced stealth of a Comanche warrior he moved slowly toward the water's edge. He wanted desperately to speak to this intense fisherman, to find out who he was and if his quest had at last come to an end, but he held his tongue, though it took every bit of self-control he had left.

It seemed to take forever, but perhaps only five minutes elapsed before the fishing line began to tug. With expert swiftness, the fisherman jerked his rod back to set the hook, then began to reel in his catch. This was no small feat. The fish, obviously a big one, put up a formidable battle, pulling out many feet of line before the tenacious fisherman finally overpowered it and began reeling it in. The man was now on his feet, sweating in the noonday sun but clearly enjoying himself.

He laughed when the fish, a largemouth bass, was flopping around on the sandy bank. "Look at this fellow! Ten pounds if he's an ounce."

"It's a mighty fine catch," agreed Sam, peering over the man's shoulder at the floundering creature.

The man talked as he removed the hook from the fish and deposited him in a gunny sack. "Yes, sir, but you should have seen the one that got away!" He gave Sam a sly grin. "This one's granddaddy, he was, and twice his size. I've been trying to nab him for years, and

I almost had him—just before you called out, in fact."

"Sorry if I was the cause of your losing him." Sam now understood the strange words he had first heard in the woods.

"Not your fault at all. That fellow is just a fighter. You've got to admire such a creature."

"Might not be right eating a fellow like that, anyway."

"Heavens no! It'd be the taxidermists for that one." The man tied off his fish bag that contained three other smaller fish, then straightened up and faced Sam. "Don't think I've seen you around here before." He extended his hand to Sam. "I'm Jonathan Barnum."

He looked like a strongman in a carnival, big, tall, and thick all over but not fat. He was dressed like a farmer—frayed overalls, faded chambray shirt, scuffed boots, and a tattered straw hat. Sam would never have taken him for an educated—and famous—eastern lawyer. His drooping eyes, slightly puffy, and the sagging folds of skin around his mouth gave him the appearance of an old hound dog. The hand he offered to Sam was as thick as a ham and bore the calloused marks of a man accustomed to physical labor.

Sam's wide grin and exuberant greeting must have puzzled the man. "Boy, am I glad to make your acquaintance! My name's Sam Killion. I've come from Texas to see you, Mr. Barnum."

"Have you? Well, you'll have to tell me all about it. But not on an empty stomach. I don't know about you, but I am overdue for lunch."

"If that bass fits into the menu, you'll get no argument from me, Mr. Barnum."

"One other thing," the lawyer said as Sam helped him gather up his gear. "Here in the woods we don't stand on formality. You call me Jonathan and, if I may, I'll call you Sam."

"Gladly, Mr.—that is, Jonathan!" Sam picked up the lawyer's fishing rod, pausing a moment to admire the fine equipment. "I've seen fishing reels like this in stores, but I ain't never used one. Must be a dream."

"I always say good gear is half the battle."

"Well, this is the finest I've seen." Sam turned the handle on the reel that was made of expertly carved wood, and it responded smoothly. "This ain't store-bought, is it?"

"Actually, I made it myself. Woodwork is sort of an avocation of mine."

That explained the calloused hands. When they entered the cabin, Sam saw other examples of Jonathan Barnum's talent in the furnishings of the cabin, all resplendent with such detail and magnificent workmanship that Sam was in complete awe. He had no doubt that

Barnum had built the sturdy cabin as well. Somehow all this gave Sam more confidence in the man than his educational credentials or even his presidential qualifications.

While Jonathan set about cleaning the catch, Sam built up the fire in the stone hearth. They talked as they worked.

"Now, Sam, what's brought you all the way from Texas just to see me? It must be something important, because I haven't made myself all that available."

"That's the truth, Jonathan! And, by the way, that fellow in your office deserves a raise. He protects you better than a she bear does her cubs."

"Oh, Chester!" Jonathan chuckled affectionately. "He does take his job seriously. But he's a good man, been with me for twenty years."

"I reckon I could understand that, and I didn't feel real good about hounding him like I did. I mean, you are retired and deserving to be left alone, and all."

"How did you finally get him to break down?"

"I never did. I happened to meet someone who knew your daughter. She finally told me how to find you."

Jonathan smiled. "That doesn't surprise me at all. She never thought I should retire in the first place; said it'd drive me crazy. I've been trying this retirement business for a month now—fishing every day, working on my wood projects whenever I like, hiking in the woods—and you know, she was right!"

"Are you saying you'd like to get back to work?"

"I wouldn't be opposed to the idea." Barnum paused, giving Sam a significant glance. "You wouldn't have a bit of work for me now, would you, Sam?"

"I do indeed, Jonathan . . . I do indeed!"

PART 7

INTO THE FRAY

25

Everything was new and the people were all unfamiliar, but aside from that, it was still a ranch like many other ranches in Texas . . . not unlike the Wind Rider Ranch itself. At least, that's what Carolyn kept telling herself.

The main difference, however, was that at home she would never have become this bored or idle. There was never a time in the year when there wasn't hard work, and a lot of it, to do. Carolyn had never played the owner's pampered daughter, or—heaven forbid!—the housemaid to the men. She and her mother worked elbow to elbow with the men out on the range or in the corral. Yolanda took care of the housework and cooking. Sometimes Deborah and Carolyn helped out when there was time, but more often than not, they proved to be a nuisance to Yolanda because neither mother nor daughter was very adept at household tasks.

There was plenty of work on the Stoner Bar S Ranch. Even as Carolyn stood on the porch of the house gazing upon the sunlit morning, nearly every Bar S hand was out on the range busily engaged in spring roundup. Only a couple of stable hands remained behind.

And Carolyn.

Caleb had not exactly given his blessing for her to go out and join the men. He had been scandalized enough by her riding apparel on her arrival, and, thus, she felt it expedient that she try to appease him somewhat. So, for the next two days she had worn a proper skirt and dawdled about the house, getting in Maria's way and going absolutely crazy with boredom. She had seen little of Caleb during this time, mainly at meals, and she had begun to wonder what was the use of it, anyway. Perhaps he was avoiding her, though when she did see him, he seemed congenial enough. More than likely he was just going about his business and figured she'd fend for herself.

Maybe it was time she did just that. At least that was what she had in mind when she rose that morning and dressed in her work clothes—the scandalous split skirt and a cotton shirt with high riding boots. Maybe she was reading too much into Caleb Stoner's expectations because of things her mother had said. And if not, perhaps it was time he realized she couldn't be poured into a mold of his making.

She placed her wide-brimmed hat on her head. Her dark hair was braided into a single braid that reached to the middle of her back. She liked it best that way, practical and simple. She walked over to the stable, hoping she'd be free to use a horse. The one she had rented in town to ride out to the ranch on her first day had been returned to the livery stable by one of the hands who had also picked up her baggage at the hotel.

She poked her head through the crack in the partially open door but saw no one in the dim light.

"Can I help you, señorita?"

The voice startled her because it came from behind. She gave a little gasp, then turned.

"I'm sorry if I frightened you."

"Oh, it's nothing. I just thought I was alone. Don't worry about it," she replied. "You're one of the stableboys, ain't you?"

He was about Carolyn's age, and just slightly taller than she, but sturdily built, and clearly accustomed to hard work. His swarthy complexion came only partly from his Mexican heritage; most was courtesy of the Texas sun. She thought she saw some Anglo in the set of his jaw and the light brown of his eyes. His sombrero cast his handsome though boyish features in shadow, but he seemed friendly even if he didn't wear a ready smile.

He nodded to her question as he pushed open the door to allow more light into the stable as they entered. "If you're looking for the Patrón, he went to town early this morning."

"No, I wasn't looking for him." She paused in a brief moment of uncharacteristic hesitation, then plunged ahead. He could only tell her no, whereupon she'd do what she wanted anyway—and worry about consequences later. "Actually," she said, "I'd like to saddle up a horse. I don't suppose anyone'd mind."

"The Patrón left no instructions, señorita—"

"Oh, please, call me Carolyn. And what's your name?"

"Ramón."

"Well, Ramón, I'm sure Mr. Stoner won't mind." She threw off any remaining hesitations and walked boldly into the stable. "What'd y'all have here?"

Ramón explained that most of the stock, the thoroughbreds Caleb Stoner was famous for, the carriage horses, and most of the saddle mounts not used for roundup, had already been taken out to pasture. Only three saddle mounts remained for use by the hands working in the ranch compound. This wasn't much of a choice for Carolyn, who was used to the pick of the corral at home. A bay mare looked the best of the lot and she gave the animal a friendly pat and cooed soothingly in her ear.

"This one'll do," she said briskly. "I can saddle her up if you tell me where to find the gear."

Ramón had heard that this girl was the Patrón's granddaughter, but he had not been given permission to let her have the run of the stable. It was a well-known fact that Caleb Stoner had no use for women outside the ranch house parlor. Now here was his own grand-daughter making herself at home in the stable, and dressed—of all things!—in trousers. He'd had his ears boxed too many times by the Patrón and his son to relish a repeat. Yet, what could he do to stop this girl short of holding a gun on her? She obviously was not going to accept no from a mere stableboy as a deterrent.

When the bay was saddled, the girl mounted with all the skill and grace of one to whom such a task is second nature.

"If the Patrón should ask, where should I say you are going?"

"Oh, just out for a ride . . . which direction is the roundup chuck wagon?"

He gave her a concerned glance. "Señorita Carolyn, I don't think—"

"Come on, Ramón. I'm bored silly. I work roundup every year at home and no one gives it a thought."

"It would be different around here, I think."

"I can take care of myself. Just tell me where the wagon is."

"North of here, ten or fifteen miles by now."

Carolyn gave him an appreciative smile before turning the bay and trotting away.

Ramón shrugged. When the Patrón found out, the girl would be in so much trouble that Señor Stoner would forget all about boxing the stableboy's ears.

At home, usually four or five spreads participated in spring roundup, with the Wind Rider Ranch and the Flying Y outfit fielding the chuck wagons. Often spreads as far away as the XIT in the Panhandle and even a couple in New Mexico would send representatives to be on hand should any of their stock have strayed that far. It was still mostly open range out by the Wind Rider Ranch, and everyone's cattle mingled freely during the fall and winter. Thus it took weeks of hard work for the cowhands to gather in the stock that had wintered on the open range, cutting out each particular ranch's cattle, sorting and branding calves, and sorting the herd according to those ready for market and those to be fattened another season. It was the busiest season of the year—and, needless to say, Carolyn's favorite. She had left just as roundup was getting underway at home, so she felt fortunate to get in on the Bar S action. There would be less open range in these parts, and thus the operation would no doubt be on a smaller scale, but at least it was something to do.

The sun was arching high in the sky, and she had traversed many miles surrounded by the solitude of the prairie, meeting no one, encountering only a couple of jack rabbits. There was more open range than she had estimated, but now that she thought of it, she should have judged Caleb to be a man to shun modern ways, especially that evil modern invention called barbed wire.

An approaching rider interrupted her thoughts. She urged her bay into a canter to meet him. It was Sean Toliver, Caleb Stoner's foreman. Carolyn had met him her first day at the ranch; he had been a friendly fellow, and handsome to boot.

"Well, hello!" he said, reining his sorrel mount to a stop. "Are you lost, Miss Stoner? You've wandered somewhat astray." She had forgotten about that interesting accent of his, kind of foreign with a dose of Texas drawl mixed in.

"Not if that's the roundup camp up ahead." The closer she had come, the more she could hear the distant bawling of cattle.

"It is, but what would you be wanting way out here?"

"Just some relief from my boredom, I reckon. You know, I grew up on a ranch. I ain't cut out for the domestic life."

Sean gave her a studied appraisal, his eyes boldly scanning her form from head to toe. "No, I don't suppose you were." He smiled, a frank, very personal smile that would have made a more worldly-wise woman uncomfortable. Carolyn just blushed a little, hating herself for it, and decided that Sean Toliver was even more handsome than she had at first thought.

To compensate for what she felt was an immature response, she took on a swaggering air and said, "Well, are we just gonna sit here, or are you gonna ride with me to camp? It must be chow time."

Laughing, Sean gave his mount a gentle prod with his spurs, and they rode into camp together at a brisk trot.

26

The last thing Carolyn wanted to do was make a grand entrance into the roundup camp. That, however, was the unfortunate effect of a woman riding into camp at mealtime when all work had ceased and the men were hanging around the chuck wagon eating.

Heads turned and the men took definite notice. A female on the ranch was rare enough, but at roundup it was unheard of. The cook gave a low whistle as he ladled a mess of beans onto a plate, but the recipient, holding his plate out for seconds, turned his head at just the wrong moment, jerking his plate away, causing the beans to plop with a *splat* to the ground. The cook leveled a mild verbal harangue at the hapless cowboy, accompanied by a chorus of mocking guffaws from those nearby. However, for the most part, the incident was lost on the arrival of this pretty young woman dressed in a split skirt and not even riding side-saddle, but sitting *astride* her mount.

"Look what you've done, Carolyn! I'm not going to get any work out of these boys today," Sean said.

"Don't blame me for their foolishness," Carolyn replied tartly. "Put *me* to work if you have to—in fact, put me to work whether you have to or not."

"You?"

"Like I said before, I've worked a ranch all my life—"

"Hey, Mr. Toliver!" cut in one of the hands. "You gonna do it? We are shorthanded."

"That'll be the day!" shouted another.

"Hey, wait a minute," protested another; "my ma worked our ranch during the war and dang-near turned a profit when no one else could."

"There just ain't no way a woman is gonna do the same work that I—"

"Now, don't be so narrow-minded," another voice said. "If a gal *can* do the same work, then she oughta be allowed to."

There was something in this new voice that forced Carolyn to swing her gaze around toward where it was coming from. The speaker was leaning laconically against the chuck wagon, hands jammed into his pockets, chewing on a piece of prairie grass. The man's tone, which had arrested Carolyn's attention, was sarcastic, hinting of challenge. His eyes, though squinting against the glare of the sun, were obviously laughing at her. Carolyn rankled. She had been protected against such old-fashioned oafs on the Wind Rider Ranch, but had encountered the occasional new hand who had to be convinced that the owner's daughter could hold her own. It always made her furious. And it did so now.

"I can do the work, and I'll go up against any one of you blowhards that thinks he's man enough to take me on!" She glared at the men, particularly the one by the chuck wagon.

"Hey, Gentry, I think she's challenging you!" shouted one of the cowboys to the fellow by the wagon.

Gentry spit out his grass and chuckled dryly, patronizingly. "Listen here, girl, this ain't no wild west show, or rodeo; we got real work to do."

"That it, Gentry? You chicken?" said someone.

"I'm afraid of losing my pay for foolishness," said Gentry. "But, Stanton, you're welcome to take the gal on."

The cowboy named Stanton sputtered, then said, "Why should I? I never said nothing against the girl."

"Neither did I, now did I?" Gentry aimed his comment at Carolyn.

She was about to retort when Toliver broke in. "Okay, it's time to get back to work. Like Gentry says, I'm not paying you for foolishness."

While Toliver's attention was momentarily diverted, Carolyn dug her heels into her mount's flanks and rode toward the placidly grazing herd. She pulled up on the fringes and took a moment to survey the cattle. A catch rope and a couple of other lengths of rope were attached to her saddle, so her mount probably had some range experience. She was tired of these arrogant men making sport of her. She would put their doubts to rest once and for all by roping one of the calves.

Spying out an unbranded mid-sized calf nibbling grass beside his mother, Carolyn attached the catch rope to her saddlehorn, took up the coiled end of the catch rope in her hand, and spurred her mount into motion. The cattle cleared out of her way, and the calf tried to do the same. Carolyn kept him in her sights, and he must have realized that he was the object of the chase, for he made a more concerted effort to escape. Carolyn kept on him as he picked up speed, not letting him get more than a twenty- or thirty-foot lead. She let him run only long enough to allow her to lift her rope into position, swing it over her head, and pitch it at and over the calf's neck. The whole procedure took only a few seconds. Carolyn sighed with relief when she saw it was performed flawlessly. Yes, she knew what she was doing, but even the strongest and most seasoned cowboys had their lapses.

Now, she prayed that her horse knew what it was doing, for the mare would have to hold the rope taut while Carolyn tripped and tied the calf.

"Okay you—I don't even know your name," she said to the bay, "don't let me down now."

Carolyn leaped from the horse and jogged to the calf, who was prancing about, testing the soundness of the rope. In one swift motion she grabbed the calf's opposite foreleg, pulled it toward her so the calf fell onto its back, then slipped the loop of another rope around that leg, under the hind legs and back again several times around all three legs. The whole procedure took well under sixty seconds and, though she was satisfied with the time, she would have been even faster had she had familiar equipment and her own horse. Griff could do it in under twenty seconds.

Carolyn stood, avoiding the eyes of the watching men. She wanted nothing more than to witness their incredulous stares, but she refused to let them see that it mattered to her. She had barely straightened her back when she heard footsteps jog up behind her.

"Let's not waste your effort. Stretch out that hind leg so's I can get him branded." It was the fellow named Gentry, holding a hot branding iron in his hand. Apparently while Carolyn had been busy roping the animal, he had noted the brand on the calf's mother and made ready the appropriate iron.

Carolyn promptly obeyed. In a few seconds the job was done, the calf was untied and loping back to its mother. Carolyn stood again, shook the kinks out of her ropes, and coiled them as she returned to her horse. She pointedly did not wait for any further comments from Gentry. But he followed after her.

"So, now what?" he asked in a quiet Texas drawl.

"I guess I can do the work," she replied, unable to keep the smugness from her tone.

"You think Mr. Toliver's gonna hire you then?"

"What's it to you?"

"Nothing really, just curious." He started to walk away but stopped and turned back toward her. "By the way, you do pretty fair work . . . for a girl." Then he strode off.

Carolyn stood gaping, furious at his back-handed compliment, even if he had sounded sincere. *For a girl* . . . of all the nerve!

The arrival of a new rider arrested her attention. It was Laban Stoner. Carolyn groaned inwardly, whether because of her fear of repercussions for her unladylike behavior, or simply because of Laban's foreboding presence, she didn't know. Of one thing she was certain, the Stoners did not have the kind of hold on her that they had on her mother. She could walk away at any time, but she wasn't going to leave easily. A single dark look from Laban—Uncle Laban!— wasn't going to break her. Because her mother's life was at stake, Carolyn had a strong motivation to remain at the ranch as long as necessary. And that in itself might be enough for the Stoners to hold over her. She did not want to think in those terms, though. She wanted to believe the best about her grandfather, and even her uncle, as long as possible.

She strode over to where Laban had dismounted and was speaking to Toliver. Laban leveled his brooding gaze at her.

"Who said you could come out here?" he asked flatly.

"Didn't think I needed permission," she replied.

"That was your first mistake."

Carolyn smiled at the man's preposterous attitude.

"Don't laugh at me, girl," he said sharply. "Others have made that mistake, and it was their *last* mistake."

"Don't let one mistake breed another by threatening me, Mr. Stoner," said Carolyn hotly. "And, as far as my being here, this is open range and I have as much right to be riding on it as you. But I guess I can understand if you don't like a stranger interfering with your roundup, even if I ain't some greenhorn. I'll clear out for now, but I'm gonna speak with my grandfather—so if I *do* need permission, I'll get it."

Her words might as well have been spoken to a wall for all the effect they seemed to have on Laban's stony countenance.

"Toliver," Laban said to the foreman, "see to it that she has an escort back to the ranch."

"I don't need no escort," Carolyn protested.

"You heard me, Toliver."

The foreman shrugged somewhat apologetically to Carolyn. "I'll take you back."

"Not you," said Laban. "I have to talk to you."

With a barely concealed roll of the eyes, Toliver turned toward the men. Most of them had already gone back to work and were busy roping and branding, but a small knot of men were still milling around the chuck wagon finishing their meal. It was to these, and one in particular, that Toliver directed his next order. "Gentry, mount up and take the girl back home."

"Aw, Boss!" Gentry complained.

"Move it!"

Gentry dumped his plate and cup into a washtub. "That's what I get for standing around instead of working," he muttered.

27

It was a disgruntled pair that rode away from the roundup camp that afternoon. Carolyn was fuming, not only at the insulting treatment she had received from her uncle, but also at the added affront of being escorted away, as if they couldn't trust her to either obey or make it back safely.

Then, for Toliver to choose Gentry, of all people, to be that escort! It was simply infuriating. And it only made it worse that Gentry was none too pleased with the assignment.

She rode at a brisk trot until she was out of sight of the camp. Gentry kept pace with her, though he pointedly remained about a length or two behind her. When she slowed to a walk, she turned in her saddle. "Look, if you don't like my company, you can go back to camp. I can take care of myself."

"I got my orders."

"Hang your orders!"

"Wish I could." Gentry rode up next to her. They were silent for a few minutes; then he continued. "So who in blazes are you, that you can talk to Mr. Stoner that way?"

"I'm his niece. Caleb Stoner's granddaughter."

"You don't say! Even so, the way I was brought up we couldn't talk to our elders that way."

"Well, I don't usually," she said defensively. "But that man has a way of making a body mad as a hornet!"

"You're right there."

They rode farther in silence. Carolyn's anger began to cool, but she hadn't forgotten Gentry's demeaning attitude toward her. Still, it was nice to have someone agree with her about Laban, so for the time being she was willing to let Gentry's other faults slide.

"What's your name?" Gentry asked. "Mine's Matt Gentry."

"Carolyn."

"Where you from?"

"North of here, near the Big Bend of the Brazos."

"That's mighty rough country up there. Your pa got a ranch?"

"My pa is dead. My *ma* has a ranch. The Wind Rider outfit."

"Oh, I heard of 'em. A big spread. So, your ma is that lady rancher. No wonder . . ."

"No wonder what?"

"Oh, nothing."

Carolyn reined her mount to an abrupt stop. "I don't know what you think about women ranchers and women cowhands, but let me tell you, my mother built that ranch from nothing into one of the finest outfits in the northwest of Texas. She could ride rings around you, and has forgotten more about cattle and horses than you'll ever learn. And on top of that, she's one of the grandest *ladies* you'll ever meet. Now, I may not be much in that department, but you ain't got no right to judge us by obsolete and twisted standards."

Gentry had stopped also and was now facing her. "I'm sorry," he said simply.

His complete sincerity caught her off guard. "Huh?"

"I said I'm sorry. You are absolutely right, you know. But if you can try to understand that I—and most of the boys—just ain't used to seeing female ranchers, especially them that can work almost as good as us."

"Almost—?"

"Aw, come on, Carolyn! Give me a little slack, will you? This is all new to me."

Carolyn urged her horse back into motion, a small, coy smile slipping across her lips. Gentry rode next to her.

"I guess I'm a mite touchy," she said.

"I reckon I'd be, too, in your place. You get this kind of treatment a lot?"

"Everyone's kinda used to me on my ma's place."

"Well, I'd say most of the boys on the Stoner spread ain't even heard of a cowgirl, much less seen one. We're a real backward bunch around here."

"I suppose I oughta go easier then, huh?"

He nodded and smiled, but said no more.

She returned the smile and they rode for a while in a more relaxed silence. Now that she had subdued her anger, she was able to make a more objective appraisal of her companion, Matt Gentry. He was in his early twenties, but he had an unaffected air of being quite seasoned and experienced. His soft gray eyes, as well as his narrow lips and wide mouth, were already amply lined at the corners as evidence of a life spent under the unforgiving western sun. All this was crowned with a mop of sandy, sun-bleached hair that curled around the band of his hat. A two-day's growth of sandy beard clung to his square jaw, emphasizing the ruddy, sun-burnt aspect of his face. Though he was not nearly as handsome as Sean Toliver, Carolyn thought he was not at all hard to look at.

She supposed she shouldn't hold Gentry's narrow-minded attitude against him. Many men were that way, at least where women were concerned. She had been uncommonly lucky to have been raised in an atmosphere where she was judged for who she was and what she could do, not for her gender. She wondered what it would have been like if her mother had never left Caleb Stoner's ranch. Carolyn shuddered to think how she might have turned out growing up under the shadow of Laban Stoner's scowl and Caleb's austerity. What would her father have been like? More of the same, according to her mother.

Her thoughts were interrupted as Gentry reined his mount. She followed the direction of his gaze and saw several riders heading toward the roundup camp. They were moving at a good pace.

"Who are they?" asked Carolyn.

"Looks like that shotgun outfit from the Bonnell place."

Sometimes during a general roundup, a big outfit like the Bar S would blackball a smaller ranch suspected of shady activities. This could work a great hardship on the smaller outfit, which couldn't afford to run its own chuck wagon, and thus often forced the ranch out of business. The small ranch might fight back by getting other small outfits on their side and teaming up to run their own wagon. This was called a shotgun outfit. Carolyn had never really seen this happen, but she'd heard of it.

"Did the Stoners blackball them?" she asked.

"The Bar S has been losing cattle lately, and about a month ago Toliver found one of our steers on Bonnell range with a tampered brand. He didn't have enough evidence to get Jim Bonnell arrested for rustling, but it was enough for Caleb Stoner to ostracize him. A couple of the other small outfits around here think Caleb is trying to run Bonnell, along with all the small fellows, out of business. This is their answer to Caleb."

"You think there'll be trouble?"

"Not unless Bonnell asks for it. But I've seen range wars start with less cause."

The shotgun outfit could just go about their business, round up their cows and be glad they were able to do at least that. But no doubt the wronged ranchers would be touchy and tempers would be hot. Carolyn couldn't imagine Laban Stoner or Sean Toliver backing down from a fight for the sake of peace.

"You want to go back?" she asked.

"Naw. The others can handle it. Anyhow, I'd really be in trouble if I got you in the middle of a shoot-out."

Carolyn rankled slightly at this, but she tried to understand Gentry's position. She also had to be practical. She had other important matters to attend to without getting mixed up in a feud.

"Well," she said, "I ain't afraid of a fight, but I'd just as soon not get in the middle of it if I can avoid it. I got enough troubles of my own."

"Aw, what kind of troubles could a kid like you have?"

"Ain't none of your business," Carolyn snapped.

Gentry smiled sheepishly. "There I go again, huh? Being a narrow-minded man. Sorry."

"Okay, you're forgiven." She paused, wondering what would be wrong with her sharing her problem with someone. Gentry might be able to help; he might know things about the ranch that could guide her search for her father's murderer. But Toliver would really be the better choice of a confidant, because as foreman he'd know a lot more than a mere cowhand. The fact that Toliver was so handsome and charming only had a little to do with this reasoning. Since she didn't want to tell her business to everyone, she said nothing more about this to Gentry. He probably didn't want to be saddled with her burdens anyway.

28

Carolyn saw her grandfather a couple of hours later at dinner. Maria served a spicy and tasty soup, not like anything Yolanda had ever made. But Carolyn's mind was not on the food; it was on what she had done that day and what Caleb might think of it.

When he asked, "What have you been doing today?" she toyed with the idea of lying to him—or, at least, softening the truth. But she decided with firm resolve that she was not going to cower before this man as her mother had.

"I rode out to the roundup camp," she said, an unmistakable challenge lacing her words.

"We are not accustomed to having females out on the range."

"I ain't accustomed to having it otherwise." No matter how hard she tried, she could not mask the disrespect in her words—and even *she* hated the sound of it. Repentant, she said, "I'm sorry, Mr. Stoner. My ma really didn't raise me to be rude. But sometimes I just don't think before I speak." She paused and met Caleb's eyes for a moment. Was he really the monster her mother painted him to be? He had thus far given no indication of anything beyond a stern and austere bearing. But why should he be treating her differently?

"How did she raise you?"

"I guess she raised me to take care of myself, at least as much as I could without forgetting that God is really the one in charge. She also taught me to speak my mind—and sometimes that gets me into more trouble than I care to admit."

"I come from a different school." Caleb held her gaze and seemed to study her as he spoke. "I learned that women were to be taken care of, protected from the harsh realities of this world. And that they are to be obedient and meek—and compliant."

"Times have changed, you know."

"For some."

"Well, I'd think you men would be glad to be rid of that respon-

131

sibility. It should be a welcome change. But even so, men and women still need each other. I may know a lot about ranching, but there are some things I just can't do because I'm not big enough or strong enough."

"We are not speaking of strong backs, Carolyn." He set down his spoon and glanced up at her. He seemed a little bewildered that they were having this conversation at all. She wondered when was the last time he'd had a debate with a woman, or if he ever had. "This is a matter of moral expediency."

"Huh?"

"The Scriptures command that women are to be submissive to men," he said curtly.

"Well, Sam—that's my mother's husband now, and he's a minister—he says that God formed Eve from Adam's rib 'cause He intended man and woman to walk through life side by side like equals."

"That's absolute heresy. No wonder you have turned out as you have if that is the kind of rubbish you've been fed."

"Sounds like this is one of those places in the Bible where God doesn't make himself real clear."

"It is clear enough to me," Caleb replied adamantly.

"All I know is that I am the way I am, and God accepts me that way, and I really wish you would, too."

"As I said, I am from a different school."

"I reckon this is gonna be hard for both of us, then, ain't it?" She paused and smiled. "I have a feeling we're both too stubborn to change—we have too much Stoner blood in us! But can't we just accept each other the way we are?"

"That is the crux of it, isn't it? That Stoner blood." Then all at once he looked at her, and she had the feeling he was seeing her for the first time. For good or ill, she *was* truly Leonard's daughter.

She nodded in response to his thoughtful query; then for no apparent reason, tears welled up in her eyes. Suddenly she, too, saw Caleb Stoner anew, as no one else in the world had ever seen him before. *Her grandfather.* Before the sudden impulse fled, she jumped up and hurried to where he sat at the head of the table, put her arms around his neck, and kissed his cheek.

Caleb Stoner had never been more shocked in his entire life.

Surprised herself, for she was not one to be overly generous with physical shows of affection, Carolyn backed away from him, slightly embarrassed, and straightened up.

"Forgive me, Mr. Stoner. I . . . I don't know what came over me. I—"

132

"Grandfather will do."

"What?"

"You may call me Grandfather."

She nodded dumbly. "Th—thank you. I'd like that."

"Eat your dinner now. Maria does not take it kindly when her food is left over."

29

The next morning Carolyn was just finishing breakfast with her grandfather when Sean Toliver poked his head into the dining room.

"I hope I'm not interrupting your morning meal," he said, though it was obvious he was doing just that.

"What is it?" asked Caleb.

"I'm here about the matter we discussed last night. You know, the horse."

"Oh yes. Well, we are finished eating, anyway." Caleb looked at Carolyn. "Mr. Toliver has an errand to do, and he'd like you to join him, Carolyn."

"Me?"

"If it's not an inconvenience."

"I reckon it ain't . . . that is, if you don't need me, Grandfather."

"No, you have my permission."

Carolyn opened her mouth to protest the fact that she really hadn't *asked* his permission, but just in time, she decided to keep silent. After all, Caleb seemed to be making a real effort toward conciliation. Since their surprising interaction the evening before, he had been especially considerate toward her. It truly amazed her that things were progressing between them so quickly. She began to wonder if her mother was, as Griff sometimes declared, more stubborn than Carolyn. If Deborah had struck a mulish, inflexible attitude toward Caleb, it was no wonder the two clashed.

"Do I need to change my clothes?" Carolyn asked Sean. She had donned a blue calico skirt and white blouse that morning just to show Caleb she could be conciliatory, too.

Sean gave Carolyn one of his penetrating appraisals, then said with a wry slant to his mouth, "No, Miss Stoner, you look just fine!"

Pink suffused Carolyn's cheeks. *Someday,* she swore to herself, *I'm gonna receive that man's looks and compliments without blushing!*

But he had a way about him that made her tingle, feel warm all over, and just a little light-headed. She supposed it was because this was the first time a man, a *real* man, had ever looked at her in quite that way. At home, the men were so much like family that no one would dare ever give her that kind of attention. When a new man came, he quickly learned what was expected in this area. One kid who had hired on recently had played up to her in the barn, and she had even let him kiss her. But that had meant nothing really, and even so, he was just a boy. When Griff had found out what had happened he nearly fired the kid; and, to be sure, nothing like that ever happened again.

Oddly, Carolyn was almost as innocent about men as her mother had been at that age, even though Carolyn was perpetually surrounded by them. She was at least ignorant of *romance.* If Sean Toliver had any romantic notions about Carolyn, he would soon find that she was as unspoiled as a newborn colt, with neither scar nor bruise upon her innocent heart.

They left the house together and crossed the dirt yard heading toward the stable. But they continued on around the back to the big corral where the horse breaking was usually done. There were about thirty horses prancing about the big area now. Carolyn's natural eye scanned the herd and found them to be a fine assemblage of animals without a plug or a jughead among them. Of course, Carolyn knew enough about horses not to judge solely on appearance.

"So, what do you think?" Sean asked.

"They're nice."

"That's all?"

"You want my professional opinion or something?"

"Last night Mr. Stoner told me to round up a couple dozen of his best saddle horses and let you have your pick."

"He did?" When Sean nodded, she continued. "He's kind of a funny man, ain't he? I mean, I never thought he would wear down so fast."

"Maybe he just decided, 'If you can't beat 'em, join 'em.' "

"Still, from what I heard about him . . ." She paused thoughtfully,

134

then looked at Sean frankly. "What kind of man is my grandfather, Sean? What do you think?"

"He's a hard, ruthless man. I wouldn't want to get on his bad side because he's an enemy to be extremely wary of. But I think if he likes a fellow, that man—or woman—will go far. Unfortunately, he doesn't *like* too many people . . . that is, really respect or admire them. He'll be friendly to people he wants to use, but that's not the same thing."

"Does he like you, Sean?"

"I suppose he does, as long as I'm useful to him. We tend to look at things in much the same way."

"How's that?"

"We know what we want, and we make sure we get it." He was suddenly looking at Carolyn with such an incisive gaze that she began to squirm.

"Well, about those horses—" she began in a thin voice as she tried to duck under the corral rail.

Sean placed a strong hand on her shoulder and moved close to her. His face was inches from hers.

"Your grandfather doesn't want you slipping through his fingers," Sean said. "I feel the same way. I want you, Carolyn."

"Sean, I—I—" Her heart was pounding like a herd of galloping mustangs. She was afraid he was going to kiss her—afraid, because she wasn't sure she knew how to kiss a man like Sean.

He seemed to read her trepidation. "You don't have to say anything at all. You just leave it to me, Carolyn. I know just how to make a girl like you feel good."

His lips sought her neck and began to move up and down her soft skin until she thought she'd die of ecstasy. Then he moved slowly toward her lips—*too* slowly, she thought. She wanted him to kiss her, but he was taking his time about it, kissing her cheeks and ears, and her neck again, while his large, warm hands roved over her body.

"Oh, Sean!" she murmured.

He continued to touch her and kiss her, yet still avoiding her lips. She never thought she'd want a man's lips to touch hers so much. She tried to move her head so her lips would be more accessible. But he seemed more interested in her neck. Then, just as he was drawing close again—

"Señor Toliver!"

It was Ramón. Sean cursed. Carolyn fell back limply against the wood rail as Sean backed off and swung around toward where Ramón was rounding the corner of the stable and coming into sight.

135

"That blasted greaser," he grumbled softly. Then out loud, "What do you want? I'm busy."

"Señor Laban is looking for you. He's up at the house and said you were to go there as soon as I found you."

"What's the matter?"

"Didn't say, but he looked like something was wrong."

"All right! You get back to work; I'll be along in a minute." When Ramón disappeared, Sean turned back to Carolyn. He ran a finger along her smooth cheek, then kissed it lightly. "I guess I'll have to give you a rain check, love."

"Oh . . . okay." Carolyn swallowed.

He smiled and she didn't even notice how patronizing his expression was. The only thing she was aware of was the memory of his warm lips on her neck and the unfulfilled hunger in her own lips.

"You go ahead and pick a horse."

"Huh?" She had forgotten all about the horses and Caleb's offer.

Sean smiled again. "Don't you worry, I'll be back."

She nodded dumbly, then watched him go with deep regret.

It took several minutes for her to regain her composure. And in that time, she began to feel like an utter fool. What kind of girl was she, anyway, that with hardly more than a look, she should become a silly lump of clay in a man's hands, allowing him to have his way with her? What would have happened if Ramón hadn't come along? She never thought she was the kind of girl who would practically enslave herself to the first man to show her attention.

But what a man!

How could a girl resist such a man as Sean Toliver? Even now as she was trying to rebuke her behavior, all she could really think of was that she wanted him to kiss her lips, long and passionately. She could almost taste his lips on hers. The thought alone was delicious.

And this man said he wanted her! That was almost too much for her to imagine. Her! A smudged-faced, gangly cowgirl!

"Señorita Carolyn," Ramón said, coming up behind her, "Señor Toliver said for me to help you with a horse. Have you chosen one?"

Carolyn was a lot happier for Ramón's intrusion now than she had been a few moments ago. It was best to try not to think about Sean Toliver right now. She had other important things to attend to at the ranch, and she couldn't be sidetracked. A romance with Sean wasn't going to free her mother; a horse of her own, on the other hand, could give Carolyn more freedom to roam about the ranch. She *had* to keep her mind clear!

"No, I haven't, Ramón." She studied the horses in the corral once more. It only took a minute for her to decide on a mare that was all black except for three white socks and a white blaze on her face. Not only was she unusually marked, but she had a lively step and a straight, proud neck. "I'll take that one," Carolyn said as she slipped under the rail into the corral.

Ramón handed her a rope and she went among the herd. They were tame animals, already broken, accustomed to the presence of humans. Though some backed away, others nuzzled her as she passed. She patted them and spoke to them, feeling more comfortable here than she had a few minutes ago in Sean's arms. When she reached the black mare, she placed the rope around the animal's neck and received no resistance at all. She led the horse to the gate Ramón was holding open.

"Come into the stable, and I'll fix you up with a saddle," said Ramón.

"Do you know if this horse has a name?"

"Señor Stoner doesn't name the horses, but I have names for all that don't belong to the cowhands. I suppose it's not really my place, but . . . I don't know, it seems like the horses ought to have names."

"I feel the same way. They seem almost human, don't they?" She gave the black an affectionate pat, already feeling a camaraderie with the mare. "So, what have you named her?"

"Tres Zapatos."

"Three Shoes . . . that's good."

Ramón went to a large rack in the stable where several saddles hung from hooks. He lifted one down and carried it over to the black mare.

"This is a good saddle," he said as he placed it on the horse and began cinching it down with Carolyn's help. "Perhaps the Patrón will want better for you, but this is the best available now."

"It's just fine."

Ramón glanced at Carolyn over the top of the saddle. "Are you really the Patrón's granddaughter?"

"Yes, I sure am."

"His dead son Leonard's daughter?"

Carolyn nodded.

"Maybe I'm too curious. You know how rumors spread around a ranch. They're saying Señor Stoner didn't even know about you until you came—there I go again. Curiosity! My mother says it will get me into trouble someday."

"Oh, that's okay, Ramón. It's all true, anyway. I only just found out about it myself, too."

"Is it connected with the woman they had in jail in town?"

"That's my mother."

"I'm sorry. I will say no more."

"It's all very complicated," Carolyn said. "I suppose I don't know the half of it all. But I'm gonna find out."

"If I can help you, let me know."

"That's nice of you. How long have you been here, Ramón?"

"At the ranch? About three years. But I grew up in Stoner's Crossing."

"But you were probably a baby when my father died, maybe not even born yet. I need to talk to people who were adults back then. The tricky part is that I don't think that would please my grandfather."

"Perhaps I can ask around."

"I wouldn't want you to get into trouble."

"I could be careful."

She studied him for a long moment, both puzzled and wary. "Why would you want to help me, especially if you might have to go against your boss?"

Ramón shrugged. "There aren't many people around here my age, and I'd like to be friendly." After a moment's thought, he added quickly, "Not friendly like Sean Toliver means."

Carolyn blushed. "You saw?" she managed to say.

"I didn't mean to. I'm sorry."

"Oh, forget it." Carolyn swung up on the horse. "I'm going riding."

"Carolyn," Ramón said as she started to move, "you should be careful around Toliver."

"I can take care of myself," she said haughtily, then rode out of the stable.

30

Carolyn did not see Sean Toliver again for three days. Apparently there had been trouble at the roundup camp. Shots had been exchanged with some of the hands from the Bonnell outfit, and though no one had been hurt, tensions were thick and Caleb wanted Toliver to stay at camp.

That was just as well, Carolyn supposed. She just did not know what to think of Sean and what had happened at the corral. It was confusing and a little scary, and she had enough confusing and scary things to deal with at the moment. She didn't need a romance to further complicate her life. Nor did she need something like that to distract her from her purpose. Thinking of Sean's touch and his kisses made her tingle all over, but she just had to stay on track. Her mother's life depended on her.

Perhaps part of her problem was that she didn't know how to help her mother now that she was here at the Stoner Ranch. When she had first made the decision to come, it had seemed everything would fall into place once she arrived. But that wasn't happening. The two people who could help her the most were the ones she was most afraid to approach—Caleb and Laban. Things were going so well with her grandfather that she was reluctant to spoil it, and she knew almost for certain that questioning him about her mother and father would do just that. As for Laban, he was about as approachable as a rattler.

"Well, I'm just gonna have to start taking some risks, that's all!" she told herself one morning after she had been at the ranch almost five days.

Then she had a brainstorm when Maria came to her bedroom door.

"I have fresh laundry, señorita."

"Come in," Carolyn said. She had just dressed and was sitting on her bed thinking.

Maria came in and set the clean clothes on a dresser, then began to put them in drawers. She was an old woman, probably in her seventies, and very round and wrinkled. But Carolyn was amazed at Maria's energy. She did all the cleaning and cooking and serving. And even though only Caleb and Carolyn were in the house now, it was a demanding job for such an elderly lady.

"How long have you been with my grandfather?" Carolyn asked as Maria worked.

"Many years! I came to him not long after he came to Texas."

"Thirty years, then."

"Oh, no—over forty years."

Carolyn did some quick figuring in her head. She thought her mother had mentioned that Caleb had bought his ranch with money he'd made during the California Gold Rush. "Didn't he come here after the gold rush?"

"No, no. I remember well that I came to work for him right after my own husband died—in 1843, it was. His first wife had passed on at that same time, too. It was a very sad time; it helped me to have a little one to care for, and I think it helped them too."

"You mean my father, Leonard?"

"Sí. He was—oh, let me see—four years old then."

"What was he like, Maria?"

Maria smiled, then quickly put away the last of the clothes and shuffled over to sit in the chair next to the bed.

"You are much like him, señorita, you know. I saw it when you first came here. He was a very smart little boy. You could never fool that one. Sometimes I would hide a candy in my hands and try to make him guess which hand. But he would just walk around me and take the candy. And so handsome! Any woman should have been proud to have one such as he for her husband—" She stopped abruptly as she realized the implication of her words. Flustered, she added, "Maybe he wasn't perfect—what man or woman is? But he had looks and an important name and a secure future."

"Maria, tell me about him and my mother."

"Oh, señorita, I don't know . . ."

"Please! I have a right to know, but no one will be honest with me."

The kind housekeeper gave Carolyn a sympathetic look; after all, this child was her dear Señor Leonard's daughter. How could she refuse her?

"It was not a happy time," said the servant. "There were arguments, you know, and the señora would try to lock her husband out

140

of her room. Once he had to kick down the door—but you are too young to understand these things, señorita."

"Did he . . . did he ever strike her?"

"It was said so in the trial, but I never saw."

"Are you sure?"

"Why do you question me?" Maria's voice rose slightly. "And does that give a wife the right to kill her husband? I do not wish to speak ill of your mother, Carolyn, but my dear Leonard did not deserve to die like that. It was very, very bad." She paused and dabbed the corners of her eyes with the edge of her apron. "I know she was unhappy, too—in fact, I was surprised she did not take her own life like the other one. Leonard should not have died, it wasn't right."

" 'The other one'? What do you mean, Maria?"

The woman looked up sharply, startled and a little afraid. "Nada!" she said quickly.

"No, Maria! You meant something. What?"

"It is not good to ask so many questions. I must get breakfast." She started to rise, but Carolyn laid a gentle restraining hand on the woman's arm.

"I'm sorry, Maria," Carolyn said contritely. Even Carolyn knew when she had pressed too hard, and rather than lose the rich source of information, she decided to try a subtler tactic. "I only want to know about my father. What was he like before all that?"

"Like I said," Maria's voice had lost some of its warmth, "he was handsome and smart."

"You were very close to him?"

"I practically raised him. His mama had just died when I came."

"Then you didn't know her."

"I know only that she was very beautiful."

"There are photographs?"

"I remember one in the parlor. But they are all put away now."

"Where?" Carolyn asked eagerly.

"It is not for me to say. Ask your grandfather, Señorita Carolyn, that is best. He would like to tell you about her, I think. He loved her very much and suffered great when she died."

"Oh, why bother him? If you just tell me—"

"It is late. You may not be hungry for your morning meal, but your grandfather will be."

"Maria." Carolyn jumped up and grabbed the housekeeper's arm as she rose from her chair. "Please, help me! My grandfather isn't going to help, not if he thinks it'll do my ma any good."

"And why should I? What your mother did was terrible, a sin—I don't care what may have been done to her."

"But what if she is innocent? What if your knowledge could save an innocent person? And what if your keeping silent will allow the real murderer to walk away free? Could you live with that, Maria?"

"It is not so . . . I was there and I do not believe it."

"But what would it hurt for me to look at pictures of my grandmother? That couldn't possibly help my mother—"

"The past is buried, señorita. Leave it that way, for everyone's sake."

"But, Maria—"

"I am sorry, señorita. I . . . I cannot help you . . ."

Maria hurried from the room, and Carolyn watched her go with some disappointment. She felt as if she had wasted the whole interview and not found a single thing of any value.

Her father was handsome and smart. But that didn't tell her anything about who he was as a person, or if he could have done the things her mother claimed. Maria, of course, thought he was a saint, but she was clearly prejudiced. And even she could not deny that there had been a lot of strife between him and Carolyn's mother. She had become especially defensive when Carolyn had mentioned physical attacks. Could she be hiding something?

And what had she meant by Deborah taking her own life? Was Maria implying that things were so bad as to drive Deborah to the point of suicide? And then there was that strange comment about "the other one." Whatever could that have meant? Maria was certainly not going to say any more about that, for she had seemed very distraught that she had mentioned anything at all. But what harm would it do for Carolyn to at least look at old photographs?

"Where is this all getting me?" Carolyn murmured to the empty room. "In deeper confusion, that's all."

And supposing Carolyn could prove Deborah had been abused? That might get her mother off on a self-defense plea, but Carolyn knew her mother wanted to be completely exonerated. Carolyn wanted it also. She did not want to think her mother had actually killed her father, in self-defense or otherwise.

Was that asking too much? Was she looking for the impossible? Where were the answers?

"Oh, God! Help me to solve this mystery. Help me to set things right. You know the truth, Lord; you know what happened nineteen years ago. And Sam always says that the truth will prevail. Let it be so now." Carolyn paused in her prayer as a new thought came to her; then she added with some trepidation, "And, Lord, please give me the courage to accept the truth, whatever it is."

142

31

Carolyn was quiet during breakfast. After her talk with Maria, she knew she had to speak with Caleb. But she was a little afraid. She wasn't the most tactful person in the world. And now she had to find a way to get her grandfather to talk about sensitive subjects without alienating him. She didn't expect it to be easy.

As they were finishing their meal and having a last cup of coffee, Carolyn mustered her nerve and broke the silence.

"I was wondering, Grandfather, if you could tell me what it was like when you first came to Texas. That must have been an exciting time."

"It was. You had to be a real frontiersman to live here then. It was no place for the fainthearted."

"But you came with a wife and child. Or was my father born in Texas?" Carolyn paused. "I guess it's kind of funny, isn't it? I mean, I don't even know where my own father was born."

"He was not born in Texas, but rather in Virginia. He was two years old when we came to Texas, before Texas became a state. Where we are now was considered the far frontier."

"That must have been hard."

"It wasn't easy. My wife—"

"That would be my grandmother?"

"Yes, she would be. She was from one of the very best families in Virginia and knew nothing of the kind of life that confronted us in Texas."

"Why did you come?"

"I suppose I had what they call 'itchy feet' in my youth. The confines of life in Richmond were too dull for me."

"Is that why you went to California for the gold rush?"

"Where'd you get an idea like that? I was never in California."

"I heard that's how you got the ranch, from discovering gold."

"I wanted to go to California, but at that time I . . . I couldn't leave

Texas. So I financed a friend's expedition in exchange for receiving half of whatever he found. He struck gold and made me a wealthy man. Unfortunately, the money came too late to make my Elizabeth's life any easier."

"She had already died."

"Yes."

"You don't blame yourself for her death, do you?"

His head jerked up with a sudden sharp look. "Why should I?"

"Some people might blame themselves, that's all."

"Well, that's nonsense. A man must do what he must do, and it is a woman's duty to follow her man, no matter what."

Carolyn sensed her grandfather was growing agitated. She was afraid she'd lose him as she had Maria, so she quickly changed the subject.

"Do you have photographs, Grandfather? I would give anything to know what they looked like."

Caleb pushed back his plate and rose. "Come with me."

Leaving her coffee, she jumped up eagerly. It had been so easy. Perhaps she was being too cautious around Caleb. Maybe he was just dying to tell her everything about his side of the family. Maybe he'd even be free with information about Deborah and those years, and Leonard's death. Perhaps all she had to do was ask.

They left the dining room and went to Caleb's study. He closed the door behind them, went to his desk, and picked up the framed daguerreotype. Without a word he handed it to Carolyn.

It was about five inches by seven inches; it was quite old and somewhat faded, and because it was a full-figure pose, it was not as clear as Carolyn would have liked. Her first impression was that this young man, who, at the time of the photo was about twenty-one, could have been Caleb in his youth. There were many similarities between father and son. As Maria had said, he was a handsome man, perhaps more handsome than Caleb would have been at that age. But his good looks were rather severe and dramatic, more like an imposing butte than a rolling valley. He was tall and sharp-featured, with eyes that even in the faded photograph appeared intense and striking. Carolyn immediately sensed she had seen those eyes before, and realized with a chill that Laban Stoner had the same eyes.

She shook away the pall that tried to overtake her and concentrated on other elements of the picture. She could tell he was a confident man, the way he stood so erect and proud, and held his head as if he defied anyone to challenge him. And that's when, with a bit of a start, she saw herself in her father. She could have told herself a thousand times that she was a Stoner, that he was her father, and this was her family; but *seeing* it in this way was more profound than any words.

Tears rose in her eyes.

She didn't care what kind of man her father was, it was still too unfair that she could not have known him. She lifted her moist eyes toward Caleb. And for a brief moment, as their eyes met, they understood each other's loss.

Then Caleb said something that shattered the growing tenderness in her heart, sending fragile fragments in many directions.

"Do you see now why she must be punished for what she did?"

"I—I—"

"She took him from us and she must pay."

"But, what if—" A sob broke in Carolyn's voice; tears streamed down her face. "What if . . . she didn't do it?"

"I know you want to believe that because she's your mother, but I saw her, Carolyn. I saw her standing over my son's body, his gun in her hand. I saw the terrible wound in his chest, his blood—"

He stopped suddenly and stepped toward Carolyn. There was something very cold and frightening in his aspect, and she retreated slightly. He grabbed her arm.

"Come with me," he said as he led her from the study.

Without a word, he led her past the parlor and dining room to the back of the house. She stumbled along behind him, weeping and afraid, but unwilling to resist him. They came to a small, sunlit room, a sitting room or drawing room, with large French doors that faced east and drew in the morning sun. But when Caleb opened the door, Carolyn had the impression from the musty odor that the room was seldom used.

Caleb continued to pull at Carolyn's arm, and she followed like a dumb sheep.

He led her around a dark green settee, then pointed with a trembling finger toward the Persian carpet. "There!" he said in a voice that was almost a growl. "His blood! My Leonard's blood. And she put it there."

Carolyn forced herself to look. It was a brown splotch on the carpet as large as a man's hand. It didn't look like much, and the sun had faded it over the years. Carolyn might not have even noticed it at all had it not been pointed out to her. But she trembled and her throat choked up when she realized it was her father's blood. She was standing in the very spot where he had been killed!

Was she also standing in the spot where her mother had shot him?

Caleb roughly yanked her around to face him. "You cannot love them both, Carolyn."

"Please! Don't do this to me!" Then she wrenched her arm from Caleb's grasp and fled for the stables. She had to get away—from him, from the ranch, from her own emotional turmoil—at least for a while.

32

The sun was arching toward the west when Carolyn rode back to the ranch.

She felt better now, at least not as emotional. She was still confused and sick over what had happened. But she thought she could face Caleb again. Whether she could face the ghosts of the past, she didn't know. Whatever had made her think she was strong enough for that kind of confrontation? She should never have come to Stoner's Crossing. This was no task for a confused eighteen-year-old girl—trying to solve a nineteen-year-old murder while mending the heart of a bitter old man.

But hadn't she always had a too high opinion of herself—just like that man in the daguerreotype?

Well, you have failed, Carolyn! she thought. *You are not a detective, nor are you some kind of bridge. The lines of hate and fear and bitterness that were drawn years ago cannot be wiped away so simply. The only thing you'll probably be successful at is bringing yourself down with everyone else.*

That was, perhaps, her greatest fear—that she'd come away from all this with the same hate that had destroyed so many other lives. Whether she'd end up hating Caleb, or her father, or her mother—it didn't much matter, because either way would kill her now. They all had become too much a part of her.

When she walked into the house that afternoon, she was ready to pack her things and leave Stoner's Crossing. It was just no use trying to win one family when in order to do so she must risk her other family. Caleb made that quite clear. But perhaps if she quit now, "cut her losses," as Griff would say, she could salvage something. And, if nothing else, she could return to the way it used to be. If she must choose between these warring families, then she had to choose her mother. She couldn't do anything else—*wouldn't* do anything else!

As far as finding her father's murderer . . . well, that was probably best left in the hands of professionals. Let the courts make that decision. That's the way her mother had wanted it.

Yet it was not in Carolyn's nature to let go so easily. She knew there was more to all of this than finding her father's murderer. And even more than freeing her mother.

The image of that enigmatic man in the daguerreotype rose up before her once more—her father. This was about him, about who he really was. Carolyn could no longer satisfy herself with the childish fantasies she had once spun. She was already sensing he could never be as noble a man as her fancies had created, but there had to be some praiseworthy qualities about the man who had fathered her, who had lent part of himself to her being.

Carolyn went to her room, took her carpetbag from the wardrobe and dropped it on the bed—then she stopped and flopped down next to the bag. No. She couldn't run from it. She had to go on, to dispel the myths so she could begin building her life, and who she was, on reality.

She thought of Maria. Yes, the old housekeeper had a slanted view of Leonard Stoner, but Carolyn had easily seen that the woman, try as she might to obscure it, knew there was a darker side to the man. Maria knew the family secrets, at least some of them. And she also knew where Caleb had hidden away all signs of the past.

Forgetting about her carpetbag, Carolyn hurried from her room in search of Maria.

At the stairway, she nearly collided with Caleb.

"What's your hurry, young lady?" he asked in his normally stern tone.

"I was looking for Maria."

"She is gone."

"Oh, well, I guess it can wait until this evening."

"She won't be back this evening. She has gone to Waco to visit her sister who has taken ill."

"That's rather sudden, isn't it? I mean, I just spoke to her this morning and she said nothing about it."

"Apparently a letter came from town after breakfast and she left immediately. Her niece, Juana, will be taking over her duties while she is gone. If you have a need, you will find her in the kitchen, I believe."

Why had Maria departed so suddenly without giving Carolyn a clearer explanation? Was it a coincidence that her sister had suddenly become ill, forcing Maria's departure before Carolyn could question her further?

If Maria knew the family's secrets, then the old servant must have left in order to protect not only herself but also the family she loved. But protect them from what . . . or whom? Carolyn? Caleb? Laban? Or simply from the truth?

Maybe Maria, having known Leonard, knew that his daughter was enough like him that she would not rest until she found those hidden secrets. And Maria was right. Carolyn could not leave the ranch now; she had to keep looking. In spite of the risks, in spite of the danger, she could not turn away from her chosen path.

She looked at her grandfather, as deeply into his eyes as she dared. He held many of the answers, locked within his iron will, not to be released easily. But now Carolyn was not totally dependent upon him for those answers. If Carolyn had read Maria correctly, it was possible there were more tangible things hidden somewhere in Caleb's house. Perhaps she would not need to loosen her grandfather's tongue, after all.

"Thank you, Grandfather, I don't need anything right away."

But as she walked away, why did she feel so vulnerable and as if she were being somehow deceptive. Why did Caleb Stoner's penetrating gaze seem to burn into her back?

PART 8

TWO NEW FRIENDS

33

The afternoon was gray. Clouds hung low in the sky, almost seeming to touch the prison walls. In the distance, perhaps five miles away, lightning flashed with brilliant regularity. Deborah had seen many summer storms such as this and knew instinctively that it was moving toward her, that its deluge of rain and wind would be released upon the prison before the hour was over.

The women were anxious to get their daily outdoor exercise before the rain struck. More than a dozen of them walked about the yard, or loitered alone or in small groups, several glancing up at the darkening sky periodically. There was a palpable tension in the prison yard; Deborah felt it as she completed her third lap around the perimeter of the yard, walking briskly, stretching her legs and feeling like a penned-up racehorse, hungrily assessing the height of the wall. But, of course, the idea of escape was nothing more than a whimsical fancy. She would never do it, and she had told Nedra so when the woman had approached her a week ago.

Sam had written from Philadelphia of his success. He'd found a good lawyer who was willing to take her case. They had left together for Texas and would arrive soon. Escape was only for the hopeless, and Deborah had renewed hope now.

Such was not the case with many of Deborah's inmates. As Deborah paused to catch her breath, Nell approached, giving her a hard look. Nell had never been very friendly to Deborah, ridiculing her faith when she could, constantly complaining about being locked up with Deborah and Lucy, the prison's two biggest "goody-two-shoes." She had even approached the guards and the warden about getting moved.

"Hey, would ya watch it?" Nell took a double step as if to catch herself from tripping. "Ya nearly knocked a body over stopping sudden like that."

"I'm sorry," Deborah replied, stepping aside.

"Yeah, well, next time you'll really be sorry."

Lucy came up to them. "Aw, Nell, you don't own the place, you know."

"Shut up," Nell said.

"Make me." Lucy placed her hands on her hips and stuck out her chin in gritty defiance.

Nell was taller, heavier, and far tougher than Lucy, but the Boston saloon girl did not shrink away even when Nell took a menacing step toward her. Deborah shouldered her way between the two.

"Listen," she said quickly, "it's going to rain soon and this'll be the last chance we have for outdoor exercise for a while, so let's make the most of it."

Nell glared at them. Lucy glared back.

"I don't like either of you," Nell said. "So you best just keep outta my way." She stalked off.

A few moments later the rain came. It gave no warning but fell in an immediate torrent, like an enormous bucket of water being dumped from the sky upon the prison yard. Deborah and Lucy were near the small overhang of roof that gave a very limited protection from the rain while they waited for the guard to open the doors. Nell, on the other hand, was across the yard and received a thorough drenching as she jogged toward protection. She glared at her two cell mates as if her plight were their fault. Deborah looked away, but, unfortunately, Lucy grinned at the woman with obvious delight.

Deborah knew there would be trouble. It had been brewing for days, and the incident in the yard, combined with the tensions accompanying the storm, proved all the catalysis it needed to erupt.

Right after dinner, after being escorted back to their cell following the meal, Nell was talking about having a nice smoke before turning in for the night. Deborah thought she was making an inordinately big deal out of it. Tobacco was a precious commodity in prison, even among the women, many of whom had taken up smoking out of sheer boredom. Favors were done for one another, or for guards, and payment was often made in tobacco. One such "favor" was that of protecting weaker inmates against bullies, or the bullies themselves agreeing not to harass others in return for tobacco. In this way Nell was able not only to smoke as freely as she pleased, but also to bribe guards for various privileges.

As soon as they were let into their cell, Nell went to the small footlocker where she kept her personal possessions. She took the key she wore on a chain around her neck and opened the locker and began rummaging through it. Suddenly her head jerked up.

"Hey! One of my tobacco pouches is missing!" she declared as she jumped up and leveled an accusing look at her cell mates.

"What're you looking at us for?" Lucy challenged.

" 'Cause there ain't no one else who coulda took it."

"Nell, that's impossible." Deborah tried to reason with her. "Your locker is locked and the key is around your neck. How—?"

"I don't care how, you two-faced, thieving—" She gave Deborah a fierce shove, pushing her against the wall with a painful thud.

Then she began tearing apart Deborah's bedding, ripping the thin mattress off the bedsprings and shaking out the blanket before she dumped out the contents of the small box where Deborah kept her few personal belongings because she didn't have enough to warrant a locker. Having no success, Nell turned toward Lucy's bed.

"Just you wait a minute!" Lucy stood before Nell with a warning glint in her eyes.

"Get outta my way!" Nell shouted. She pushed Lucy and went for her bed, stripping off bedding, flinging it across the room.

"You're crazier than a loon!" Lucy yelled.

"Don't you dare—" Nell swung around and lunged at Lucy.

By now the ruckus had alerted the guards, who had just locked up the last of their charges. One of them appeared at the cell door. "What's going on?" she asked.

"One of these lying thieves stole my tobacco."

"That's impossible," Deborah said. "You were in your locker this morning and nothing was missing. No one could have gotten into it since then."

"I was in a hurry this morning and didn't have time to notice. But one of you coulda took my key while I slept last night—"

"Aw, you're nuts," Lucy said.

Nell turned to the guard. "Make her open her locker," she said, pointing at Lucy.

"Go ahead, Reeves, open up," the guard said.

"I will not! She's loco—"

"Open it, now!" the guard demanded.

Lucy shrugged and obeyed. She unlocked the chest and flung open the lid. There was nothing besides half a dozen books, a couple of knitting projects, and a few other personal items.

"I tell you, I've been robbed, and these are the only ones that coulda done it," Nell insisted.

While attention was on Lucy's locker, Deborah noticed a pouch lying on the floor among the scattered bedding. Obviously, Nell had engineered this entire incident to get her and Lucy into trouble.

Deborah picked the pouch up with the intention of tucking it under Nell's pillow.

"What's that?" The guard turned slightly and saw Deborah's movement just as she pulled the pouch out from where it had been half hidden under a blanket. It was obvious the tobacco pouch had been among either hers or Lucy's things.

"That's it!" Nell declared triumphantly, seizing the pouch.

"Oh, how would you know it's yours? They all look alike—" Lucy was silenced as Nell displayed the side of the pouch that bore a large letter *N* stitched across it.

"What do you have to say for yourself, Killion?" the guard asked.

Deborah had no ready defense. She didn't want to see anyone get into trouble, but perhaps it was better that blame fell on her rather than Lucy, who was, she was certain, equally innocent and had the most to lose.

"I didn't take anything." But she doubted the guard would believe her.

"Nell's just trying to get us into trouble," Lucy said.

"I'll just have to take both of you to the warden."

"This is ridiculous," Deborah said. "Why would Lucy do something so stupid with only a few days left to her sentence?"

"I've seen crazier things," the guard said. "But if she didn't do it, then that just leaves you."

"Come on!" protested Lucy. "I keep trying to tell you, Nell's had it in for us for days."

"I only have the facts," said the guard. "And that pouch was found among yours or Killion's things." She then leveled a rebuking look at Nell. "And if you hadn't been so all-fired quick to take this into your own hands, I might have been able to discover exactly in whose things it was."

"Lucy is innocent," said Deborah.

"Then that means you must have done it."

Deborah said nothing. Let them think what they would.

"Well, it makes sense," the guard said. "It would be dumb for Lucy to do it." She grasped Deborah's arm.

Lucy hurried toward them. "Deborah couldn't have done it, either!"

"You don't have to defend me, Lucy," said Deborah. "Think about it. It's better this way."

Nell looked positively deflated as the guard led Deborah out of the cell. "What about Reeves?"

"It just doesn't make sense that she did it," answered the guard.

Nell clamped her mouth shut and said no more. This wasn't exactly turning out as she had planned and hoped, but there was a certain pleasure involved in seeing that sanctimonious Deborah Killion get into some trouble.

As the guard led Deborah away, Lucy caught her arm and quietly said, "Deborah, you don't have to do this."

"I know that," she said simply. Then she exited with the guard.

Lucy might have argued further had she realized what a harsh punishment Deborah would receive for her offense. Such volatile situations among the inmates were dangerous for the prison and had to be treated severely. Deborah would be locked in solitary confinement for a week. This was a tiny room no bigger than a horse stall, with no windows, no bed, not even hay on the hard, cold stone floor. Her food, consisting of gruel, hard bread, and water, was passed into the cell through a small locked grate; and thus, she saw no human the entire time, nor did anyone speak to her.

When they let her out she was paler and thinner than before, and her legs were weak and wobbly in spite of her attempts to exercise in the confined space. Returning to her old cell, she found it vacant. Lucy had been released and Nell had finally talked someone into moving her to another cell. Deborah was relieved.

That night as she was about to lie down to sleep, she found tucked between her mattress and blanket a folded note.

Dear Deborah,
   I'll never forget what you did for me. I don't know if I'll ever be able to repay you, but it won't be for want of trying. I'm beginning to think a lot more of that God of yours—He must be all right to have someone as fine as you believe in Him. I wish I could have gotten to know you and Him better.
   Sincerely,
   Lucy

Deborah refolded the paper and lay down, a smile on her lips. The misery of the last week was a small price to pay for the reward of Lucy's words. She reminded herself once more that God indeed brings good out of bad situations for believers. It was a truth she was going to have to continue to cling to if she was to survive this place.

Before she fell asleep she thanked God for the incident with the tobacco and for what had ultimately come of it. She also prayed for

155

Lucy. Being a free woman was not necessarily going to free her from her problems, nor was she likely to have any easier time making her way in the world than she'd had before prison. Deborah prayed that God would continue to pursue the feisty young woman and watch over her.

34

Two days after her release from solitary, Deborah was told she had visitors. She nearly skipped to the visitors' room. It must be Sam.

The guard opened the door and let her in, and to Deborah's surprise the guard waited outside and locked the door behind her. Deborah forgot to ponder this little irregularity the moment she laid eyes on Sam. She ran into his open arms, kissing him and holding him so tight it was a wonder he could still breathe. He returned her passionate greeting enthusiastically.

Only after a few moments did Deborah realize they were not alone in the room. Then she remembered that the guard had said *visitors*. A little self-conscious at her public display of affection, she slackened her hold on Sam, but even then she didn't let go entirely. She peered around Sam's shoulder and smiled at the stranger. He grinned back.

"Forgive us, Jonathan," Sam said, "but it's been a mighty long time!"

"Don't give it another thought, Sam. I haven't been a widower so long that I don't remember what it was like, especially after a lengthy absence."

"Deborah," Sam said to his wife, "this here is Jonathan Barnum from Philadelphia, our new lawyer."

"Mr. Barnum—" Deborah began, holding out her hand.

But Barnum quickly interjected, "Please, I don't stand on formality with my clients, and Sam tells me no one out West holds much with formality, so just call me Jonathan." He took her hand and shook it

156

firmly. "Now then," he went on, "I do hate to be a wet blanket when you two must have a lot of catching up to do, but I'm afraid our time here is limited. The guard said half an hour. And we have much to talk about."

"Yes, we do," Deborah said. "Why don't we sit down."

Three chairs had been placed around a table, and they settled themselves, Deborah and Sam sitting as close together as possible. "Before we start, Jonathan, I want to thank you for coming out here to help me," Deborah said.

"After everything your husband has told me about you, Deborah, I can honestly say it's my honor to do so. Well worth coming out of a very boring retirement for—and a chance to see the Wild West, to boot." He laid a leather satchel on the table and withdrew some papers. "Now, to business."

"What would you like to know?"

"Sam has filled me in on many of the particulars of the case, but I'd like to hear it all in your words, Deborah. I realize it may be hard for you to talk about it, and it is time-consuming, but I believe that's an aspect that can't be ignored."

Deborah nodded, then spent the next twenty minutes talking about her disastrous marriage to Leonard Stoner and all the events that led up to his death. Jonathan jotted down extensive notes, interrupting occasionally to ask questions or clarify something. Once or twice Sam interjected something Deborah had forgotten. In the end Jonathan had a pretty complete account of what had happened.

He looked up from his notes. "Well, well, this is all very interesting. Tell me, Deborah, do you believe you got a fair trial?"

Deborah smiled. "Of course not. What criminal does?"

"I see what you're getting at. No one would have believed you even if you had protested."

"Not then, and not in Caleb Stoner's town. But, to tell the truth, at the time I didn't think to protest. I was so disheartened and distressed by my life in Stoner's Crossing that I was glad to have it end—even on a gallows."

"Sam has implied that the whole trial was trumped up. What do you think?"

"I don't think anyone lied outright, but often testimony was so twisted and distorted that even the truth made me look bad. I don't know if Caleb actually bribed witnesses, but I think the townsfolk just knew what was expected of them."

"And you had no legal representation?"

"Oh no. We were lucky to have a circuit judge to conduct the

157

trial. That was nearly twenty years ago, Jonathan, and I'd say the nearest lawyer was in Austin. Even at that, it was just at the end of the War Between the States and so many men were still gone, including lawyers. It was amazing that I even had the benefit of a trial. Caleb was known to hang wrongdoers from the branches of a big oak tree on his land. But I suppose because I am a woman, he wanted to make certain my death was surrounded with at least the semblance of legality."

"His first mistake."

"How do you mean?"

"Well, had the execution been a success, of course, it wouldn't have mattered, but from our present perspective, we will be able to use his sham of a trial to our best advantage."

"You mean because the trial was no good, Deborah can go free?" Sam asked eagerly.

"Not quite," Jonathan answered. "Unless we can prove outright perjury or other illegal activity, the decision of the court must stand. However, we might be able to call for a new trial on a couple of different grounds. Because of the frontier status of the area at the time, you were denied your constitutional right to representation. Also, I believe we can easily prove that you were tried in a hostile town. Had you had proper representation, there is no doubt he would have asked for a change of venue—that is, asked for the trial to occur in a town where jurors had no foreknowledge of the case against you. I feel confident that on these grounds, we will be able to convince the court to reverse your conviction and remand for a new trial."

"That's as much as I could hope for," Deborah stated.

"I could hope for a few more things," Jonathan said. "For example, many of the previous witnesses will be gone now, and that may or may not work in our favor. Of course, we don't want hostile witnesses around; but, on the other hand, after so much time we may not be able to find any witnesses. Not to mention the fact that memories will be dulled with time, and evidence will be difficult to find. In that event, we will have a hard time making a case. If we get a new trial, it will do us little good if we can come up with no new evidence to present to the court. That's what I would most hope for, some new evidence—in your favor, of course! If we can throw enough doubt upon the prosecution's case nineteen years ago, the court may rule in our favor. In our justice system, the burden of proof still lies upon the state, not the defendant."

"That's all well and good," Deborah said. "But *my* deepest hope is to be proven innocent, to have all doubt removed. I have a daughter, my murdered husband's child, whose well-being may depend upon that."

"Then, Deborah, I suggest we build an aggressive defense," Jonathan said.

"We still need evidence," Sam said.

"That we do." Jonathan nodded. "Good, solid evidence. That means you, Deborah, must wrack your brain for anything you may have forgotten about the case, any detail, any point that you might have brushed aside, thinking it too trivial. You must clear away nineteen years of cobwebs, my dear, and inspect everything."

Sam shook his head. "It don't help that all the records of the trial were lost."

"No, that's unfortunate."

"It's real lucky for Caleb Stoner."

"Sam," Deborah said, "do you think he had something to do with that?"

"It was mighty convenient, that's all. And no one ever was able to say just how that fire got started. It happened just a year after your escape."

"We will be sure to subpoena Mr. Stoner," Jonathan said with relish.

"That's likely the only way we'll get a chance to talk with him. So far, he ain't let any of us get to him."

"Except Carolyn," Deborah said.

"What?" Sam gave her an incredulous look.

"She's gone to Stoner's Crossing, Sam. I couldn't stop her; she was determined to prove my innocence."

"That girl." Sam frowned, but there was more concern and affection in his gesture than reproof. "Has she been in touch with you since then?"

"I received a brief note some time ago and she said all was well, but I'd be lying if I said I still wasn't concerned."

"You want me to go fetch her back?"

"No, Sam. I doubt that she would come, anyway. We'll just have to trust that she'll be all right for now. Who knows, maybe something about her being Leonard's daughter will draw Caleb's sympathy."

"Maybe," Sam said with as much enthusiasm as he could muster. He refrained from reminding her that Carolyn was her daughter also. But stranger things had happened, and thus it was just possible Caleb did have a small heart beating within all that stone.

"If I may interject something," Jonathan interrupted. "Before long

159

Sam and I will have to go to Stoner's Crossing to do some investigating. We'll be able then to keep an eye on your daughter, even if from a distance."

"You will be careful, won't you?" Deborah said. "He may show Carolyn some patience, but no one can guarantee what he'll do to anyone else involved with me."

"Don't worry, Deborah, we will handle Mr. Stoner with the finesse of an eighteen-inch trout on a line—nice and easy, with a great deal of patience, and even more cunning."

PART 9

QUESTIONS, BUT FEW ANSWERS

35

For the next few days, Carolyn gave her conversation with Maria considerable thought. Short of prowling around the house like a common thief, she saw no way to find anything hidden away. She hoped that Maria would come back and help her, but the housekeeper didn't return. So Carolyn bided her time, thinking that if worse came to worst she would do some snooping; but first she would give herself some time to make discoveries in a more scrupulous fashion.

After her unsuccessful questioning of both Maria and Caleb, Carolyn should have thought twice about attempting to confront Laban. But he was the only other person around directly connected with her father's murder. And, in her mind, Laban was a prime suspect.

In fact, Carolyn did not approach him lightly. When she saw him in the stable rubbing down his favorite horse, her stomach constricted and her heart skipped a beat or two. But no one was around, and this seemed a perfect time to ask him a few questions. She seldom saw him and, whether she was avoiding him or the other way around, such an opportunity might not present itself again soon.

"Uncle Laban," she said, approaching him from behind.

He craned his head around to face her, his lips curled in a sneer. "The use of 'uncle' is rather presumptuous, don't you think?"

"Your father asked me to call him Grandfather."

"He's a doddering old man who doesn't know what's good for him."

"I can just call you 'Laban,' if that makes you feel better."

"It would make me feel better if you'd just leave this place. We don't need you around here stirring up trouble like your mother did."

"I don't reckon to leave unless my grandfather asks me to." Carolyn's stubbornness was obvious and, though she knew she was not putting him in a mood to be talkative, she couldn't help herself.

Laban turned back to his horse. Carolyn walked around to face him. "Listen, Laban, I don't understand why you should be so hostile toward my mother. I didn't think there was any brotherly love between you and Leonard."

"And so you think I should be glad she killed him and applaud her rather than resent her?"

"Something like that."

"It wasn't only Leonard she killed—that I could have forgiven. But she destroyed my brother Jacob, too."

"I don't understand."

"You know nothing about Jacob?"

"Only that he was your full brother and that he, too, wasn't treated very well by Caleb and Leonard. What happened to him?"

"She didn't tell you?" When Carolyn shook her head, Laban snorted and allowed his lips to twitch into the semblance of a smile. He seemed to enjoy his next words. "My brother was forced to leave Stoner's Crossing because Leonard caught him and your mother together. They were having an affair."

"What makes you think that?"

"They often went off together—alone. I testified to this in court, and I will do so again if I am asked."

"You've got to have proof before anyone will believe you." But even Carolyn was wondering if it could be true. Why hadn't her mother said anything about this to her? But why should she believe Laban? If he had murdered Leonard, wouldn't he do anything to take the attention off himself?

"I know what I saw, and what Leonard saw also. They might not have been caught in the act, but Leonard saw enough for him to nearly kill Jacob, forcing him to flee for his life. Little good that did him; he was probably killed by Indians out on the frontier—why else have I never heard from him since?"

"But you don't *know* any of this! In fact, just as good a case can be made indicating that you had the most to gain from implicating my mother in this way. And, after your brother left, you had the most to gain from murdering my father."

"So that's what you think. Well, no one believed that nineteen years ago, and no one will believe it now."

"Back then, everyone believed what Caleb wanted them to believe. It's different now; my ma isn't alone anymore. There are people on her side now who will ask the right questions and expect the truth, not Caleb's distortions. What will you do, then, Laban?"

"I will tell the truth."

"Did you do that when they asked you at my mother's trial what you were doing the night of my father's murder?"

He laughed. "No one asked, because it wasn't relevant."

That revelation shocked Carolyn. "Were there no other suspects in the murder?"

"Your mother was standing over the body holding the murder weapon. What other suspects did they need? No, Carolyn, your mother's cause was hopeless then, and remains so."

"No it's not, so be on your guard, Laban—the real murderer is going to be found."

"Is that a threat?" Laban laughed outright, a humorless, cutting sound.

"Take it however you wish." Carolyn caught his gaze and held it for a long, torturous moment.

Without warning, he grabbed her arm, twisting it painfully. "I could tear you in two easily. So take care about making threats."

"Let me go!" She wrenched her arm, and he loosened his grasp. She turned and started to walk away. But then she remembered the unanswered question she had raised. She was afraid of Laban, but she was also cocky enough to believe that he would never really harm her because of the trouble it would bring him. She decided to take a chance and push him just a little more.

"Laban, what were you doing the night Leonard was killed?"

"I am not a suspect."

"You weren't then, but don't count on that now."

"We shall see, my dear little *niece*."

"Yes, we will."

Laban turned his attention back to his work, and Carolyn knew she couldn't get another word from him.

36

On Saturday of Carolyn's second week at the ranch, she decided to accompany Ramón to town. Caleb gave his permission to this outing, but declined to go himself because he was feeling tired. He looked tired, too, and Carolyn wondered if he had been sleeping well.

They left in the early afternoon after Ramón finished his chores. It took a little under an hour to get there, and they arrived hot, sweaty, and thirsty.

"Come on," Ramón said, "we can get a drink at my mother's place."

Carolyn followed along eagerly until Ramón stopped at the cantina. When she hesitated, Ramón paused, puzzled. "A minute ago you said you were dying of thirst. What's wrong?"

"Well, Ramón, I ain't allowed to go in places like this," Carolyn answered, uncharacteristically abashed.

Ramón laughed. "The tough cowgirl does have her limits, eh?"

"Aw, come on! My ma would tan my hide if she heard I went into a saloon. I'm surprised your ma don't mind. Let's just go find your mother. She'll have something to drink, won't she?"

"Of course she will. That's her business—to quench the thirst of cowboys . . . and cowgirls. This cantina is her place."

"Really?"

Carolyn had heard all kinds of stories about women who worked in saloons, none of them very positive. Of course her mother and Sam had always stressed not judging people, but it was hard not to when everyone else had little good to say about such women. To think that her new friend's *mother* was a saloon girl added an entirely new dimension to the matter.

"Well, are you going to come? It's not such an evil place, really. After all, I grew up here, and I'm not such a bad person, am I? Besides, it's quiet inside now, and we can leave before the rowdy Saturday night crowd shows up."

Carolyn had been rather embarrassed by the silliness of her initial hesitation, so now she assumed her bravado and marched in. A slight smile on his face, Ramón followed.

The interior was dark after the brightness of the sunlit afternoon, and an unsavory odor of stale remains of tobacco, whiskey, and sweat, with a peculiarly unsettling fragrance of cheap perfume, permeated the place. When Carolyn's eyes adjusted to the dim light, she saw a typical saloon—she had once or twice *peeked* into the saloons in Danville. Besides the expected long bar and tables and chairs and piano, there were several woven Mexican blankets and sombreros hanging on the walls, giving added color and warmth that other saloons lacked. There were no customers in the cantina. A man stood behind the bar cleaning glasses.

Carolyn heard the music, something soft and dreamy, before she turned toward the sound and saw the woman seated at the piano. Ramón tugged at Carolyn's arm and put a finger to his lips.

The music was far different from the bawdy tunes Carolyn had heard coming from the saloons in Danville. She thought the woman was playing something classical, though Carolyn wasn't enough familiar with such music to be sure. It was beautiful, that much was certain. It made Carolyn think of a gentle breeze softly bending the heads of the prairie grass on a spring morning. She wanted to sway like the grass, and she closed her eyes and imagined a spot near the Wind Rider Ranch where she liked to go and lie in the grass on a warm day under one of the few big oaks on the land. When the music picked up tempo, she thought of a jack rabbit racing by. Then another series of notes made her think of the leaves of the oak rustling overhead.

She was wondering what Ramón was thinking and what images, if any, the music evoked in his mind, when the lovely music stopped. Apparently the woman finally realized she had an audience. She looked up at the two young people just as Carolyn opened her eyes. The woman seemed neither embarrassed nor annoyed, and though she didn't smile, there was a welcoming expression on her face.

"Ah, Ramón, mi muchacho!" she said with affection.

"Mamá, por favor! I'm not a little boy."

"Well, you are not 'mi hombre' either." The woman gave an affectionate wink at her son.

He shrugged and glanced at Carolyn as if she would understand how mothers were. Then he said, "Mamá, I have a guest from the ranch."

"I see," said the woman, giving Carolyn a careful appraisal with an arched eyebrow, which Carolyn couldn't tell meant disapproval or merely curiosity. "You are the Patrón's granddaughter?" To Carolyn's surprised response, she added, "It is hard to keep such news quiet in a small town."

"Well, it's no secret, anyway," Carolyn said, not knowing why her tone became slightly defensive. To make up for this, she held out her hand and said, "I'm Carolyn Stoner, señora..." Then she realized she didn't even know Ramón's surname.

"I am Eufemia Mendez." The woman took Carolyn's hand in a limp grasp, with cool fingers.

For the first time Carolyn took a close look at Ramón's mother. She was not old—perhaps in her early forties—and still had a rather youthful appearance, with smooth skin that was unlined except for fine spidery tracings at the corners of her eyes and mouth. Her eyes were wide-set, very dark and very beautiful. In fact, Eufemia Mendez was a beautiful woman in all respects except one: there was a sharp aspect to her beauty which, if it did not exactly detract from it, gave her a mysterious and somewhat cold look, in odd contradiction to the beautiful, gentle music she had just produced on the piano. Only when she addressed her son did she appear to soften. To others, she seemed to surround herself with a chilly north wind. The touch of her icy fingers combined with the chill in Eufemia's eyes made a shiver run through Carolyn's body, but she smiled in spite of it as she dropped her hand.

"So, does the Patrón give you an afternoon off?" Eufemia asked her son.

"Sí, and tomorrow also. I thought I would stay in town tonight with you, Mamá."

"And your friend also?"

"Oh no," said Carolyn. "I just came in to do a little shopping and have a look around. Thanks, anyway."

"You will have something to drink?"

"Now, that I'll accept gratefully!" said Carolyn. "It's hot enough to wither a fence post out there."

Eufemia led them to the bar. "Al," she said to the barkeeper, "do you have something for the youngsters?"

"How 'bout some ginger beer?" He took a couple of tall glasses and filled them from a jug under the counter.

When Carolyn and Ramón had taken the frothy drinks with thanks, Eufemia asked them to follow her. She took them through a door adjacent to the bar, which led into a short corridor where there were two or three other doors. She opened one of these onto a small parlor that was simply but nicely furnished.

"I think you will be more comfortable here than in the cantina," said Eufemia, motioning for the two young people to sit on the divan. She sat in a red velvet wing chair opposite.

"Thank you," said Carolyn. But as she looked around, she sensed the same ambiance in the room as she had in the woman—tasteful, lovely, cool, and guarded. She didn't feel very comfortable at all.

"So, what brings you to our little community?" asked Eufemia.

"You mean the town rumors left that part out?"

"No. It is said you are the Patrón's long-lost granddaughter; it is speculated that you are here on behalf of your mother, perhaps to prove her innocence of a crime committed many years ago."

"Well, that's partly true. The last thing my ma wanted was for me to come here. She'd rather see the courts prove her innocence. But I want to do what I can to help her. Mostly, though, I just wanted to meet my grandfather. It's a strange thing to learn you have a family that you don't even know. I couldn't rest until I'd done something about that."

"I imagine the Patrón was shocked when you showed up. Or did he know about you?"

"Not a thing. I reckon he was just as shocked as me."

"But you have had a good reunion?"

"Mamá," Ramón put in, "you should see; the Patrón has given Carolyn her pick of the horses and allows her to ride freely all over the ranch. She even rode out to the roundup camp and roped a calf."

"That is astonishing. It is well known that the Stoners have no use for women except as pretty parlor baubles." Eufemia's right eyebrow arched once more, but her demeanor remained cool and unperturbed.

"Have you known the Stoner family long?" asked Carolyn, unable to restrain her driving curiosity in this area.

"I have lived in this town many years, and there is no one here who doesn't at one time or other come into my cantina."

"Then the cantina belongs to you, señora? That's very impressive."

Eufemia shrugged. "Impressive, if not respectable, eh?"

"I wasn't raised to judge folks, señora. I reckon you've done the best you could. And you must have had to work hard to get this place."

"In that, I must disappoint you. I bought this with a small inheritance I received about eighteen years ago when I was very young."

Ramón said, "My mother's family in Mexico is one of some stature."

"But my son is only a stableboy." The rancor was evident even if Eufemia's tone remained as cool and controlled as always.

"I don't mind so much," said Ramón. "And I will soon advance to a higher position."

"We all have ambitions," Eufemia said rather vaguely. "Nevertheless, I didn't earn the cantina at all. And perhaps I could have used the money in a more worthy manner. But it isn't easy for a woman alone to make a living."

"Then your husband is dead?"

Eufemia's eyes darkened as if a cloud had passed overhead; then they cleared and she answered, "Ramón's father is dead."

In those words Carolyn detected the first note of emotion in the woman's voice or expression—bitterness. But that passed as quickly as the cloud, and her cool wall was shored up and secure once more.

"He died before I was born," added Ramón.

"I'm sorry, Ramón," said Carolyn. "I know what that is like."

"What is to miss about what you never knew?"

"That's a good question. I guess it just leaves a little bit of emptiness inside, no matter what you do to ignore it. A person's parents are an important part of who they are and, at least for me, having one absent like that is kind of like getting a piece of me cut off. I reckon that's another reason why I'm here; I want to try to get to know my father even though he's long dead."

"That would be Leonard Stoner?" asked Eufemia.

"Yes, señora. Did you know him?"

"Of course."

"Did you know him well?"

That eyebrow shot up once more. "As I do most of my regular customers."

"Regular?"

"Carolyn, I do not wish to tarnish any esteemed notions you may have of your father."

"It's not that, señora. I realize many men in the West frequent saloons. There ain't many other social outlets for them. He wasn't a drunk or something, was he?"

"You need not fear that. He was a respectable, upstanding citizen." There was an edge to Eufemia's statement Carolyn couldn't quite identify, a hollowness.

"What was he like?"

"Surely your grandfather has told you all about him."

"According to him, my father was nearly a saint. I know that can't be true."

170

"Because of your mother?"

"Because no one's that perfect. If only half of what my mother says is true, then there's a lot more to know than what either Caleb or my mother says."

For the first time a touch of amusement sparked in Eufemia's dark eyes. It lingered only a moment before that, too, was reined in behind her protective wall.

"I do not wish to become involved—" Eufemia began.

"Mamá!" Ramón broke in.

"No," said the woman. "It is never wise to become involved in other people's family disputes."

"I respect that, Señora Mendez. I'm sure there'll be other folks in town who will talk to me."

"Do not count on it, Carolyn," Eufemia said. "Caleb Stoner's picture of his son Leonard is the official town view. There are no others. *There can be no others.*"

"I can't believe that a whole town can be so controlled by a single man. There must be someone willing to tell me the truth."

"Do you truly wish to know the truth?"

"I *have* to learn the truth."

"Then I pity you, Carolyn Stoner."

Mouth slightly gaping, Carolyn stared speechless at this peculiar woman. But before Carolyn could form a proper response, Eufemia rose.

"It has been a pleasure meeting you, Carolyn," she said without enthusiasm. "I must now return to work."

"I—I . . ." Carolyn stammered. "Thank you." She rose also, followed by Ramón. "I hope I can visit with you again." All the manners her mother had drummed into her finally came to her rescue. In reality, though, Carolyn was not anxious to see Ramón's mother any more than was necessary. She was an extremely unsettling woman.

Ramón walked with Carolyn back out to the street. The bright light of day was oddly comforting to Carolyn. She took a deep, cleansing breath.

"I'm sorry about all that," said Ramón.

"There's no need to apologize. Your mother was just being honest, and I appreciate that."

"She has her reasons."

"What do you mean?"

"She has no great affection for the Stoners, that's all."

"Does anybody?"

171

"This town owes the Patrón a lot. Loyalty speaks louder than liking or disliking."

Carolyn shrugged. Then how would she ever find what she needed to know? Frustrated and discouraged, she bade Ramón good-day and walked down the street to the general store. Ramón returned to the cantina.

37

Eufemia had returned to the piano and was just seating herself on the bench when Ramón returned.

"Mamá, I don't understand why you treated Carolyn that way. She is a friend of mine—"

"She is a Stoner—don't forget that, Ramón."

"If you hate the Stoners so much, it's that much more reason to help her. She's trying to free her mother, and that is the last thing Caleb Stoner wants."

"You don't understand."

"No, I guess I don't. You were around when her father was killed. You might be able to help her and her mother."

"Why should I help them? What do I care about them? And for all I know her mother is a murderer. Would you have me help a murderer?"

"What if she is innocent as Carolyn believes? I'll tell you this, that Carolyn won't give up until she gets to the truth."

"How could she learn the truth? She is nothing but a foolish girl."

"I wouldn't underestimate her, Mamá. That's what Señor Stoner is going to do, and it will be his undoing."

"That is even more reason for us to stay away from that girl."

Ramón shrugged. Maybe he was making too much of this. But so was his mother, and that puzzled him. Perhaps it was best to not get involved.

"What truly worries me," Eufemia said in a cool, stern tone, "is your concern about all this. I don't want you getting involved with that girl, do you hear?"

"And why shouldn't I?" he retorted, irked at his mother's attempt to interfere in his life. "She's an attractive girl, and I like being around her—"

"You are a Mexican, she is white."

"Bah! Carolyn was raised among the Cheyenne, and her own brother is half Indian. She hates bigotry."

"I tell you, stay away from her!" Eufemia's impassioned words drew the attention of the bartender and another customer who had just come into the cantina.

"Well," Ramón said, "there's no need to worry. She's all taken with Toliver, the Bar S foreman."

"Then that is for the best."

"Toliver will use her, then cast her aside. He cares only about himself."

"It is not your concern. You are not for her and she is not for you. That is all that matters."

"And what other choices are there for me around here, Mamá? Two or three old, ugly señoritas. Maybe it's time I found a better place with more choices."

Eufemia's hard features softened momentarily. "Ah, my Ramón! Maybe it has been wrong of me to keep you here. And now that she has come . . ." She paused and seemed to retreat inwardly for an instant. She then spoke as if verbalizing half-formed thoughts, "It is something to think about, son. Perhaps that is our only choice. Unless . . ."

"What, Mamá?" Ramón prodded when his mother's comment trailed away, unfinished.

"Nothing. And now I must return to work. Ramón, could you go to the back and bring in some clean dishcloths? There are glasses to be washed."

After a few moments Eufemia set her fingers on the ivory piano keys, producing a melody both sad and haunting. A tear escaped the corner of her eye, but she did not stop to brush it away.

38

By the time Carolyn finished her shopping, it was getting near supper and time to be returning to the ranch. She could not help feeling the excursion had been a waste. She had hoped to question the townsfolk about her father. Señora Mendez had definitely put a damper on that.

She made a few small purchases at the store and was heading to her horse, debating whether to speak to the sheriff, when several riders came galloping down the street toward town. She recognized them immediately as Bar S men. Sean Toliver was in the lead.

He reined his mount in front of her. "Good afternoon, miss!" he said in that odd British-Western accent. He doffed his hat and swept it toward her in a wide arc.

"Hi, Sean! What brings you fellas riding into town in such an all-fired lather?"

"It's Saturday night," said Sean, "and the end of roundup, to boot. The boys want to kick up their heels a bit."

"I guess they've earned it."

"And what brings you to our fair city?"

"Just shopping. I reckon I mostly wanted a change of scene."

"Why don't you join us?" he asked with an amused glint in his gray eyes.

"Even I'm not that progressive, Sean," said Carolyn with a laugh. "On the range I'll hold my own with any cowboy, but that's as far as it goes."

"Why, I'm shocked, Miss Stoner, that you'd think I'd even suggest you accompany me to a house of ill-repute!" His amusement pulled at the corners of his lips. "I had more in mind something respectable, like a church social."

She eyed him with mock suspicion. "What church social? Where?"

"The ladies of our town—that is, the respectable ladies—host a little soiree every year at the end of roundup. They hope to provide an alternative to the saloons for the local ranch hands after a month of hard labor. They put on a fine spread for supper that draws the lads, and then a bit of dancing with the pretty daughters of our more upstanding citizens keeps 'em entertained for a few hours. It doesn't exactly put the saloons out of business, since most of the lads find a way to get in both forms of entertainment. Anyway, I'd be honored for you to accompany me."

"Well, gosh, Sean, it sounds great, but I ain't hardly dressed for something like that. And once I returned to the ranch, changed, and came back—"

"Buy something at the store and change right here."

"Something new? But it seems so extravagant. Besides, I'd have to tell my grandfather where I was."

"As far as extravagance goes, when was the last time Caleb bought you a new dress?"

"Never."

"Well, it's about time. Don't you know that grandparents love doting on their grandchildren? And, concerning the other matter—" He stopped and shouted to one of the cowhands, "Hey, Joe, you're going back to the ranch, aren't you? Well, tell Mr. Stoner his granddaughter is attending the barn dance with me."

Joe looked a bit puzzled, and Carolyn wondered if he had really planned on returning to the ranch. But he said, "Okay, Boss."

Sean swung back around to Carolyn. "There, it's all settled! Now let's go see about that dress."

"Both of us?"

"Of course. I happen to have impeccable taste."

He was right about that, but his choice was not exactly what Carolyn would have picked. It was a pale yellow gauze frock with a belt that tied in a big bow at the back, and yards of white eyelet lace trimming the hemline—hardly Carolyn's style. She preferred something a bit simpler and understated. All that flowery-flummery made her feel just a little silly.

He silenced her protests. "I'm the one who will be looking at you, Carolyn, so it makes sense that you oughta be wearing something I like."

The thought of him looking at her the way he so often did made her tingle all over, making it impossible for her to refuse. Besides, she was lucky the store had any ready-made dresses at all. The only other choices were a couple of calico skirts and blouses. This particular dress had been special ordered by the banker's daughter, but when it arrived it didn't fit—the girl had put on some weight in the

175

two months it had taken the dress to arrive from New York.

The dress fit Carolyn well enough, though she thought it could have used a couple of tucks here and there. She had just the opposite problem from the banker's daughter. She'd love to put on a few pounds, especially on her upper half. She hardly did the neckline justice, and stuffing a few pieces of cotton wool in strategic places in the bodice only slightly improved the fit. She felt like a child playing dress-up when she stepped out of the dressing room.

"Oh, Sean, I feel ridiculous!"

"You look splendid, my dear, simply splendid." But he cast a critical eye at her, and obviously wasn't completely satisfied. She self-consciously tugged at the neckline, but he wasn't observing that area at all. "The hair! That's the problem," he declared triumphantly. "Mr. Wexler!" he called to the storekeeper. "Call your wife."

Half an hour with Mr. Wexler's wife seemed to work a miracle, at least by Sean's reaction. Carolyn's dark brown hair, usually hastily pulled back in a single braid at her back, had been let down to flow freely about her shoulders except for the side curls, which the store-keeper's wife drew up with ebony combs. Mrs. Wexler used her hot curling iron to make ringlets in the drawn-up strands. The effect was fetching, lovely, demure, and sweet—all the things Carolyn knew she wasn't.

But Sean raved at the metamorphosis. And Carolyn tried to match his enthusiasm. She felt silly, but it was absolutely thrilling to have a man like Sean Toliver make such a fuss over her.

She felt like a different person as she left the store and walked with Sean to the big Cattlemen's Association Hall for the dance. In-deed, even her mother or brother would not have recognized her on first sight had she passed them on the street. She had been trans-formed into the kind of woman people like Sean and her grandfather were likely to admire. As she thought of her grandfather, she wished he could see her ... though, why it should matter, she didn't know.

39

The Cattlemen's Association Hall was decked out in colorful streamers, and there were already two dozen people milling around the two long tables that held a delectable variety of hot dishes, salads, and desserts. At first there was about an equal mix of ranch people and townsfolk in the gathering. Then ten or twelve cowboys entered just after Carolyn and Sean, and more filtered in throughout the evening. Soon the ratio of men to women was very high, and there was not a wallflower among the women present.

Carolyn had a good time, though at first she felt a little conspicuous, especially when it was obvious she was the object of everyone's curiosity. After all, she was Caleb Stoner's long-lost granddaughter. But once they got over their own awkwardness, they proved to be a congenial lot. The banker's daughter was glad her dress had found a good home, and even commented on the fact that it did Carolyn far better justice than it had her. She invited Carolyn to tea sometime, and Carolyn politely accepted.

There were five musicians, playing fiddle, harmonica, accordion, guitar, and banjo. They favored lively tunes, and Carolyn and Sean danced until they were breathless. Sean's excellent dancing made her feel clumsy—there had been few opportunities at the Wind Rider Ranch for learning how to dance. But he didn't seem to mind.

Even though the women were in great demand for dancing, Sean kept Carolyn to himself. Whenever another man asked her to dance, Sean turned him down. Carolyn began to get annoyed, for she thought it was unfair both to herself and to the partnerless cowhands. But she said nothing, had a couple of glasses of fruit punch to cool off, then let Sean swing her back out to the dance floor.

When the dancers paused momentarily to form up sets for a Virginia Reel, Carolyn felt another tap on her shoulder. She turned to see Matt Gentry.

"Find yourself another gal, Gentry," said Sean. "This one's taken."

"I don't mind, Sean," Carolyn said suddenly. "You're the only fella here who's danced every dance. It don't seem fair."

Sean scowled.

"Aw, come on, Boss," said Gentry. "Give us poor cowpokes a break."

Before Sean could reply, Carolyn linked her arm through Gentry's and moved into a set just as the music began. She was having a good time with Sean, but his attempts to control her rankled her. Best to let him know early that she was an independent girl.

Gentry, for all his gawky, coarse manner, was almost as good a dancer as Sean. He performed the reel flawlessly. When the musicians, hardly missing a beat between numbers, began their first waltz of the evening, Matt made the transition effortlessly. But Carolyn had some difficulty. A reel was one thing; if you just paid attention, you could get through without too much hazard. But Carolyn's upbringing had emphasized horses and cattle, not dancing—especially not waltzing. She just could not get her feet to move in sync with Matt's, and she tried several times to take the lead. Finally, after she had stepped on his feet a dozen times, the music stopped.

She smiled sheepishly. "After that, I reckon I owe you a new pair of boots."

"They ain't the worse for the wear. And, anyway, it was worth it to get a dance with the prettiest gal here."

Just as Carolyn opened her mouth to reply—though she hardly knew what to say to such an unexpected compliment—Sean appeared to reclaim her. She couldn't even say a proper thanks to Matt before she was whisked once more onto the dance floor.

After that dance, she found herself almost unconsciously looking around for Matt. Was she hoping for another dance with him? But he was nowhere in sight.

"Let's go get some fresh air," said Sean suddenly, forcing her attention back to him.

The breeze outside felt good. Carolyn took a deep breath.

"I'm sure glad you talked me into coming tonight, Sean," she said. "It's a real nice dance."

"Just so you don't forget who it was you came with."

"What do you mean by that? You're not riled because I danced with Matt Gentry, are you?" She couldn't help being flattered, even if his possessiveness did perturb her.

"One thing you'd better learn about me, Carolyn; I'm not big on sharing what's mine."

"*Yours?* I ain't sure I like the sound of that."

"Why not? Oh, I forgot, you fancy yourself one of them *independent* girls." He said the word as if he were speaking of a contagious disease.

"I wouldn't go that far, Sean. But I prefer to think a fella cares for me without having to control me. I still like to think for myself."

He gave a dry laugh. "Indeed you do, Carolyn! But you have a lot to learn about men. You are going to have a hard time finding a man worth his salt who doesn't like to be in control. That's just the male nature."

She narrowed her eyes at him. "Are you always so sure you're right?"

"Oh, I'm right. Trust me; I've been around a touch longer than you, dear girl."

She paused, studying him a moment, trying to fathom his eyes but finding them peculiarly expressionless. "What exactly did you mean about me being 'yours'?"

"I meant, I know a good thing when I see it, and I'm not about to let anyone else muscle in on my discovery. And that reminds me, Carolyn," he added quickly, obviously relieved to change the subject, "we have some unfinished business."

"What's that?"

Instead of an immediate answer, he took her hand and led her around to a secluded place behind the building. The hall was on the edge of town with the open ground surrounding it broken only by a few big mesquite bushes. A half moon illuminated the area a bit, but it was still quite dark. Except for the distinct sounds of the party filtering out from inside the building, it would have been downright eerie.

Carolyn's heart pounded. She remembered that day in the corral and knew she ought to tell him to take her back to the dance. But she couldn't get the words out. He stopped, pressed her back up against the building and, placing one of his strong hands on the wall and the other firmly around her waist, drew her to him. She knew she should resist, but his hand on her side was so warm, so urgent, so compelling. This time he made no attempt to tease or toy with her. His lips immediately sought hers, pressing against them with such passion that Carolyn could hardly breathe. His hot breath was nearly suffocating, and his hand groped for her.

She had never before been touched by a man in this way, and she knew it was wrong. But he was so forceful and strong, more than she could have imagined. His whole body pinned her against the wall again so that she could not move. She tried to speak, but his kisses prevented her.

179

She wrenched her head to one side. "Please, Sean!"

"You like it, dear," he said, misinterpreting her words.

"Th—that's not—I never—"

"Don't worry, honey, I'll show you what to do."

"But I—"

"Come on. I know a place—"

"No. I can't."

He leaned away from her, and his eyes bored into hers. "This was meant to be, Carolyn. And you know you want it as much as I do. You can't be the innocent cowgirl forever, you know."

"Sean, I really like you, but I'm not ready for . . . well, *that* kind of relationship."

"Oh, you're ready, all right. You wouldn't have come back here if you weren't. But like most women, you have to play hard-to-get. That's okay, I can play along."

He pressed toward her once more. His lips engulfed hers and both his hands grasped her body. She squirmed and tried to move, but he was so strong. Again she twisted her neck, finally jerking her head free.

"No!" she cried, perhaps louder than she intended. "Please . . . Sean . . . !"

But he did not stop. He seemed only to take encouragement, even pleasure, from her struggles.

"Sean . . ."

His touch, which had once felt good, now hurt her. The sensations that had caused her to hunger for him now brought an ache to her stomach. She was no weak girl, yet she suddenly felt as helpless as a foal.

Was Sean right? Was this the way it really was supposed to be? Sean was so handsome, and being near him did such funny things to her, but—

"Hey!" came a voice out of the darkness. "What's going on?"

Abruptly, Sean let go of Carolyn and spun around.

"Toliver?"

"What're you doing here, Gentry?" Toliver's voice was filled with violence and menace.

"Well, I heard someone calling, like they was hurt or something."

"No one's hurt—except maybe *you* in a minute!"

Carolyn took the opportunity to slip away from where she had been pinned against the wall. As she moved free of Toliver, Gentry saw for the first time who the foreman was with. He took it all in with sudden understanding.

"I was only trying to help," he said.

"Well, go help someone else. I don't need it," said Sean.

Carolyn had an overpowering urge to thank Gentry for his timely intervention, but her pride—and embarrassment at being in such a position in the first place—forestalled her.

Instead, she said with as much poise as possible, "It's time we got back to the dance, anyway, Sean. I'm powerfully hungry."

Without looking back, she strode away toward the front of the hall.

40

Since Carolyn had only her horse for transportation, she went home from the dance with Mabel Vernon, the banker's wife, who insisted on taking her in their buggy. Sean did not seem too thrilled about this prospect; he no doubt hoped to get Carolyn alone once more on the trail to the ranch. But Mrs. Vernon argued that Caleb would not want his granddaughter traipsing about the countryside at night on horseback, and not even properly chaperoned. Sean had to relent.

The next few days were quiet ones on the ranch. Carolyn didn't see Sean at all because he had to go to Fort Worth on business and would be gone for a week. She and Ramón went riding a couple of times, and his presence helped alleviate Carolyn's loneliness for her brother. She missed having Sky to talk to, and before she realized it, she was talking to Ramón as if he were an old friend. She confided in him about her confusion over the situation with her mother and grandfather. He again offered to help.

"If only you'd been old enough back then," said Carolyn. "That's what I need—a friend who was around then, someone willing to talk to me."

"I'm sorry my mother was not much help to you."

"I can understand. Even I can see my grandfather is not a man you'd want to cross. She has to look out for herself."

181

"There must be something else you can do besides talk to people," said Ramón.

Carolyn immediately thought of her conversation with Maria. Before she realized it, she was telling Ramón.

"I kind of feel funny searching my grandfather's house, especially behind his back. But I know I can't tell him."

"Carolyn, I don't think you have any choice."

"But I need time, and my grandfather has been staying close to home lately."

"Tomorrow night is the Cattlemen's Association meeting. It's once a month, and Señor Stoner never misses."

"I don't know . . ." But Carolyn did know, and she couldn't put it off any longer. "I guess you're right, I don't have a choice. It's for my ma." *And for the sake of learning the truth,* she added to herself.

"I'll keep a lookout for you if it makes you feel better to have an accomplice."

She hated to involve Ramón, but the idea of his help made her feel immensely better.

The following night Caleb left for town shortly after dinner. Carolyn wanted to start her search immediately, but she forced herself to wait until Juana had cleaned up and left for the night. Ramón posted himself on the front porch of the house with instructions to whistle "The Yellow Rose of Texas" if anyone approached. He practiced a few bars, and though it was a bit off-key, it was at least good and loud.

Even with these precautions, Carolyn's heart was pounding as she began her task. She skipped the kitchen and dining rooms as unlikely spots and went directly to the front parlor. Here, the only piece of furniture that could possibly hold secrets was a side table with a single drawer. The drawer was unlocked and filled only with table linens. There was nothing else in the parlor, so she headed toward the back sitting room.

Her father had been killed here, and Carolyn had not been in this room since her confrontation with Caleb some days ago. She was apprehensive about opening the door, but she did so with firm resolve. It looked much different now than it had when the sun streamed in through the French doors. Dark shadows instead of rays of sunlight slanted across the room. Now it was not hard for Carolyn to imagine a dead body sprawled out in front of the patio doors. Unconsciously, she glanced in that direction, shuddering.

She lit the lamp in the room, turning up the wick just enough to see. There was a small desk with a locked drawer, but without a key she could not open it. Perhaps Juana had keys? There was also a hutch cabinet, but the top part had glass doors and displayed only pieces of fine china and glassware. The hutch did not seem in keeping with the sparse, masculine air of most of the household furnishings, but Carolyn did not give it more than a moment's consideration. Perhaps these things had belonged to her grandmother. One day Carolyn would look at them more closely, but she didn't have time now.

The bottom of the hutch had a couple of drawers and another cabinet with wooden doors. Carolyn spent about ten minutes looking through them, for there were papers and other odds and ends in the drawers. There was nothing of interest, only a stack of magazines, a few letters that were mostly business related, and several old newspapers that Carolyn scrutinized briefly, finding all were dated years after her father's death.

Carolyn's next stop was Caleb's study. She spent fifteen or more minutes in there. There were several locked cabinets and drawers. But now that she had taken on the role of a common prowler, she could not resist the temptation to look through the unlocked drawers. They yielded nothing interesting. She also shuffled through the few loose papers on Caleb's desk. He kept a very organized office, and almost everything had been put away in the drawers. One thing that did catch her eye was a bill from Dr. Barrows for two office visits, totaling seven dollars. Both visits had occurred before Carolyn had arrived on the ranch. It made no mention of the nature of these visits, and suddenly Carolyn thought: *It's none of my business, anyway!*

All at once she felt horrible for rifling through her grandfather's private things. She tried to tell herself it was for her mother's sake. But that didn't quell the shaking of her hands. She hurried out of the office and went upstairs.

Besides her room and Caleb's room, there were two guest rooms upstairs. Avoiding her grandfather's room after her attack of conscience in his study, she went to a guest room. The first had the sparsest of furnishings and didn't appear promising, but she doggedly looked in every drawer of the bureau and wardrobe. She sensed she'd also be wasting time with the other guest room. Caleb's room had to be next.

She forced herself to walk to his door. Licking her lips nervously, she just stood there staring at the wood as if it were some adversary waiting to pounce upon her. Ramón had told her she had no choice, and she had told herself that many times since. But to invade her grandfather's bedroom? That seemed even worse than rifling through his study, where at least he occasionally entertained guests.

Yet she knew that if the secrets Maria had hinted about were

183

anywhere in the house, this was the most likely place. If she intended to learn the truth, she'd have to do this. But it wasn't easy. Placing her hand on that knob was harder than grasping a hot branding iron. Nevertheless, she took a breath and began to turn the knob.

Suddenly the faint but distinct sound of "Yellow Rose of Texas" floated up toward her.

She froze, and her heart beat madly within her chest. She didn't know whether to feel relieved or disappointed. But she jumped back from the door quickly and ran to her own room, hurrying inside as if fleeing from the devil himself. Not until she had shut her door, leaning against it, panting breathlessly, did she realize that it was much too early for Caleb to be returning from the meeting. Where she came from, the cattlemen's meetings could last for hours, late into the night.

She waited five minutes. When her heart calmed and her head cleared, she went downstairs to see what had happened.

Ramón was nowhere in sight.

She found him by the back porch.

"I'm sorry, Carolyn. Someone rode into the yard," Ramón explained.

"But didn't my grandfather take the carriage?"

"I guess I jumped the gun. It was just one of the hands, but he was riding right toward the house. Turns out he thought it was mighty suspicious, someone hanging around the house like that. When he saw it was only me, he asked me what I was doing, and I told him I was looking for Juana. He reminded me, as if I didn't know, that the Patrón didn't like the hands hanging around the house. Told me to go around back. Did you finish your search?"

"No."

"I'll keep watching if you want to go back."

"Are you kidding? I aged ten years when I heard that song! Maybe some other time. Besides, you'll get into real trouble if anyone sees you out there again."

"But what'll you do?"

"I don't know. I got through most of the rooms and didn't find a thing. It's probably a wild-goose chase, anyway."

Back in her room that evening, all Carolyn could think of was that she was alone in the house and a prime opportunity was slipping through her fingers. About an hour after the scare, she had summoned up her nerve again and decided to give it another try, when she heard the carriage rumble into the yard.

Carolyn couldn't shake the sense that she had failed not only herself but her mother as well. She resolved that at the next opportunity she'd search her grandfather's room no matter what. This was no time for her to suddenly become fainthearted.

41

On Saturday, Carolyn and Caleb received an invitation from the Vernons, the banker's family, to have dinner with them after church on Sunday.

At breakfast on Sunday morning, Caleb said, "I'm not up to accepting the Vernons' invitation, but you go ahead."

He did indeed look tired, even a bit pale. He insisted that she go and enjoy herself, and she saw no reason to stay. She had Ramón get the carriage ready, because she could hardly go to church in riding garb, and she left immediately after the morning meal.

The Vernons were good people. Mr. Vernon was a bit stodgy, but he left the ladies alone most of the time after church. Mabel and her daughter, Barbara, were likable, talkative and friendly, and Carolyn enjoyed their company—especially since she so seldom had the opportunity to interact with women. It was even rarer for her to have a female acquaintance of her own age.

When Mabel left for a few moments to attend to some matters in the kitchen of their large and affluent house, Barbara eagerly lapsed into typical girl-talk—a new experience for Carolyn.

"That foreman at the Bar S is ever so handsome," Barbara said dreamily. "And he seemed absolutely stuck on you at the dance last week!"

"It must have been that pretty dress of yours, Barbara."

"No, it was the way you *looked* in it."

Carolyn squirmed uncomfortably. Today she was wearing only a simple skirt and blouse, and her hair was back in its single braid. "Well, I'm as unused to looking like that as I am to having a man like Sean pay such attention to me."

"Get used to it, Carolyn. Around here, with so few girls, there's bound to be scads of fellows after you. Even I couldn't shake them if I wanted—not that I want to!"

"What do you mean, 'even I'? You're a sight prettier than me. I'd give anything to have beautiful blond hair like yours. My ma's hair is that color, but I got this mousy brown stuff."

"I'd like to be a couple of sizes smaller, though."

"Oh, girls!" Mrs. Vernon said as she reentered the parlor. "There's not a woman alive who's satisfied with her looks. But you are both as lovely as any man could wish for."

"That's what mothers are supposed to say," said Carolyn. "My ma says the same thing."

Mabel Vernon sat down next to her daughter, but she looked wistfully at Carolyn. "Your mother was one of the most beautiful women I have known," she said, "and you resemble her remarkably."

"You knew my ma?"

"Yes, of course. My husband has been banker here since before the War Between the States."

"Really?"

"I can't say I knew her well. She kept to herself most of the time. But she was such a lovely, tragic woman. I have always felt so bad about what happened to her. And now, to have it happen all over again . . ." Mabel sighed, then reached over and laid sympathetic hands on Carolyn's. "I want you to know, Carolyn, that if there is anything I can do for you—or your mother—feel free to call upon me."

"You would help my mother?"

"Perhaps that is an empty statement, because I doubt there is a thing I could do, but, yes, I would if I could."

"Aren't you worried about getting my grandfather riled at you for even sympathizing with her?"

"Certainly he can't still hold a grudge. I assumed that because of you he would have softened."

Carolyn shook her head. "No, ma'am. He's just as determined as ever to see my ma hanged. The only way I can possibly change him is to prove that my ma is innocent."

"But can you? Is it possible?"

"It's gotta be possible because she *is* innocent."

"I know how you must feel, Carolyn, because she is your mother. But the decision of the court—"

"Don't you think a court can make a mistake?" Carolyn asked fervently. "Don't you think the court might have been a mite prejudiced because of Caleb's influence?"

"Well, I don't know about that. But why would Caleb try to influence the court against his own daughter-in-law?"

"You don't know much about what happened, then, Mrs. Vernon."

"I testified at the trial, but I must admit my husband requested that beyond that, I not attend the proceedings because he felt the nature of the affair was unfit for the ears of a genteel lady. I was much younger then and apt to be rather compliant to my husband's wishes." She smiled. "He says I've changed in my later years and can be downright headstrong at times!"

Carolyn hardly heard the last part of Mrs. Vernon's statement, and she could barely wait till the woman finished before anxiously asking, "You testified? Why was that, Mrs. Vernon? I thought you didn't know my mother well."

"I didn't. We had but one conversation which, it seemed, the court thought pertinent to the case."

"Can I ask what it was about?"

"Oh, dear me, it's been a long time . . ."

The banker's wife paused so long in apparent thought that Carolyn mistook her intent and said quickly, "Mrs. Vernon, if you feel you ought to be quiet, I'll understand. I don't want you to get into trouble with my grandfather."

"Caleb Stoner may own ninety percent of this town and at least fifty percent of the bank, but he doesn't own *me,* my dear! I'm afraid I am no longer the meek and obedient wife I once was. If Caleb would try to ruin us for telling the truth—not that he ever would, I am sure—then so be it."

"Can I ask you something, Mrs. Vernon?" When the woman nodded, Carolyn continued. "Now, please don't take offense, but I have to ask. Did you tell the truth at the trial?"

"I did," Mabel said, a bit defensively; then she sighed. "Well, I *told* the truth, but later I could see how my 'truth' could be taken in many ways. I always wondered if I did justice toward Deborah Stoner. But then, I couldn't see what I could have done differently."

"My ma said just about the same thing—that is, that even the truth was twisted so it made her look bad."

"I am so sorry for that."

"She's got another chance now, Mrs. Vernon."

"I still don't see how my conversation with your mother can help. It was so brief, really. I recall that when I met her that day, she looked so unhappy. I invited her to tea, and she didn't hesitate once in accepting, except to glance at the big cowhand who was with her. At my house she was very reticent and reserved, and I could tell it took all her nerve to speak of her marriage. She did so only in the most general way. I recall very clearly her asking if it was common for husbands to strike their wives—poor thing! I had the feeling she was entirely innocent of such matters. But I was shocked, of course, when I realized the implication of her question."

"Then she said he struck her?"

"She never actually *said* so; and during the trial, the court examined that point quite carefully."

"But why else would she have asked?"

"Unfortunately, the law requires facts, Carolyn. They said it was pure speculation to conclude that her question meant he beat her. Besides, even if they had proven she had been beaten by her husband, that is not an acceptable motive for murder. And male-dominated juries would not even accept it as a fault against the husband. The prevailing opinion of the day was that if a man struck his wife, she must have deserved it."

There was a moment of silence as the three women absorbed this unsettling fact. Then Carolyn asked, "Was that all there was, then, to your conversation with my ma?"

Mrs. Vernon didn't answer immediately. Instead, she looked down into her lap for a long time. When she glanced back at Carolyn, there was shame in her eyes. "I'm afraid that was all. I realized later—too late—that she was reaching out for my help, and I gave her none. She needed a friend, and all I did was tell her she had to try harder to please her husband—"

"Mama!" cut in Barbara with astonishment. "How could you? You don't believe all that about women deserving to be beaten?"

Mrs. Vernon's lips parted with a ragged, distraught sigh. "I was young myself then, and that's what I had been taught. I know now it's pure nonsense. And, Barbara, you can be sure that if your future husband tries to hurt you, he will have a very dangerous mother-in-law to deal with!" She tried to smile at her daughter. But the look of sorrow quickly returned. "Unfortunately, my hindsight was of no help to your mother, Carolyn. I failed her then, and my later testimony helped to put her on the gallows. That has been a burden I have carried with me all these years. You don't know how glad I was when I recently heard she had been arrested again—not that she had been arrested," Mrs. Vernon added, a bit flustered, "but that she was still alive and well. We had all given her up for dead."

"You can be sure, Mrs. Vernon, that my ma doesn't hold grudges against anyone in this town, not even Caleb," reassured Carolyn. "She's had a good life in all these years, and I'm pretty certain she'd say she's been happy. So you don't need to feel bad. Another thing my ma would say was that God used those things to make us all what we are, hopefully better people." Carolyn paused, thought a moment, then went on. "But, Mrs. Vernon, you weren't the only one to testify at the trial, were you?"

"I daresay not. The trial went on for three days. But I couldn't tell you who else testified. As I said, I came only to testify and left immediately. No one informed me about the rest of the trial—and no one talked about it later, not even the few women in the town. It was not an item permitted for idle gossip."

" 'Permitted'? You mean by Caleb?"

"That's right. And out of deference to his grief, we respected that. I must also admit that I felt so bad about the whole thing that I didn't want to ask. I just wanted to forget all about it—which, as you can see, was impossible."

"I really appreciate you telling me what you have, even though it must've been hard. Everyone else in this town is too afraid of Caleb to say anything. I have one more question."

"Go on, dear," said Mrs. Vernon gently. "If the only way I can help is through my memory, then I am glad to do it."

"What was my pa like? And—" Carolyn quickly added, "don't tell me he was handsome and smart. I want to know the truth."

"But that is the truth, at least part of it. Whenever I saw him, he was quite charming and the perfect gentleman. But ... well, there were rumors. Ladies were not privy to all the details, but I'd heard there had been lynchings of rustlers and Indians by the Stoners. They were ruthless men, I think. I myself was at the bank once when your father was dealing with one of the small ranchers who had fallen behind on a note held by the Stoners—even to this day, your grandfather holds notes on most of the ranches around here. I remember wondering how such a gentleman—and your father was always that in my presence—could wear such a terrible look of menace. It sent a chill down my spine—"

Mrs. Vernon stopped abruptly when she noted the taut pain in Carolyn's expression. "Oh dear!" she said. "I'm sorry ... I didn't mean—"

"No, Mrs. Vernon. I asked for it. I want to know." But then Carolyn added in a whisper, "I think ..."

Mrs. Vernon rose, bent down next to Carolyn, and put an arm around her. The motherly tenderness of the gesture felt good to Carolyn, who missed her own mother's comfort more than she realized. She leaned her head against the banker's wife and was surprised to feel a tear escape her eye and drip down her cheek. Another one followed. She tried to sniff them back but without success.

"Dear child, I am so sorry," said Mrs. Vernon.

"It's not your fault. I'm such a fool, that's all . . . I don't just want to prove my ma's innocence. I want to prove my pa's, too. But . . . I know that's gonna be impossible!"

"It will all work out somehow," Mrs. Vernon soothed, patting Carolyn's shoulders. But even as she spoke, the banker's wife remembered how she had failed Deborah, and she feared she was doing the same with the poor woman's daughter.

PART 10

CONFUSING ENCOUNTERS

42

When Carolyn returned to the ranch that afternoon, the house was quiet and still. She walked through several of the downstairs rooms looking for her grandfather and finally ended up in the kitchen hoping to find someone. Just as she entered, Juana, Maria's niece, was coming in through the back door.

"Oh, Señorita Stoner," said the woman, who was about ten years older than Carolyn and only vaguely resembled her aunt, "you have returned. Do you need something?"

"I was wondering where my grandfather was, that's all."

"He is in his bed."

"In his bed? In the middle of the afternoon?"

"He has not been well."

Carolyn remembered how tired he had looked when she left that morning. Now she felt awful that she had gone off, leaving him when he was sick.

"What's the matter with him? It's not serious, is it?"

"Maybe just a touch of the ague."

"Has a doctor been sent for?"

"Oh no, señorita. The Patrón will have no doctors."

"Well, I'm going up to see him. If he needs a doctor, he's gonna have a doctor!" Carolyn wondered only vaguely about the doctor's bills she had discovered on Caleb's desk.

Carolyn swung around and made her way back through the kitchen and up the stairs to Caleb's room. She knocked softly on his door, and when there was no answer she gingerly opened the door a crack, poking her head in. Caleb was indeed lying on his bed, covers pulled up to his chin, eyes closed. She was about to retreat, thinking he was asleep, when Caleb's voice stopped her.

"Who's that?"

"It's me, Grandfather."

"Carolyn?"

"Yes."

"What do you want?" His voice was somewhat hoarse, but more inquisitive than remonstrative.

"I heard you weren't feeling well, and I just wanted to see if I could do anything for you. Can I come in?"

"I suppose so..." Then more firmly, "Yes, I'd like that." When she was in, he gestured for her to pull up a chair and sit by his bed. "It was thoughtful of you to come," he said.

"Why, of course I'd come! Land, Grandfather, do you think I'd be able to ignore your being sick and all?"

For the first time, Carolyn felt relaxed in Caleb's presence. Perhaps it was because he looked so different like this, lying down, with pale skin and a weak voice. He wasn't as intimidating. On the contrary, he seemed quite vulnerable, and that natural part of Carolyn that had a heart for the helpless instantly reached out to him. It was easy to forget for a moment all the things she had heard in town—Mrs. Mendez's bitterness when she spoke of the Stoners, Mrs. Vernon's guileless honesty and pain when she uttered the truth. It was easy because Carolyn wanted so desperately to cling to her tender hopes that she had found a dear and loving grandfather. It was simply impossible to think of him as the ruthless, threatening town patriarch, her mother's sworn enemy, when he was lying there looking up at her with such sad, pitiful eyes.

"You are a good girl, Carolyn, I must admit. It's been so long since someone has cared about me." He sighed, and his deep-set, dark eyes, now looking almost cavernous with fatigue, momentarily softened as if with some remembered joy.

"I *do* care about you, Grandfather, and I so want things to work out between us."

"I believe they will." He reached out and took her hand in his and they sat in silence for several minutes. Then Caleb said, "Carolyn, when I die, I want you to have the ranch."

"Grandfather, this isn't the time to talk about such things. You're not dying, for heaven's sake! There's plenty of time to think of that. Besides, it's Laban who should rightfully inherit your ranch—I wouldn't stand in his way."

"Bah! That bas—excuse my language, but that's the only way I'll ever think of him!—he doesn't deserve an inch of this place."

"You shouldn't talk of him that way, Grandfather. He's your son and ought to be treated better."

"Don't you side with him!" Caleb spat out bitterly. "I was resigned to my ranch passing to him, but now that you are here, things are

194

different." He stopped suddenly upon hearing a sound in the corridor; he didn't speak for a moment, but when the sound did not repeat itself, he continued. "I'd sooner burn the place to the ground than see him have it."

"That's not right, Grandfather, and I couldn't take it from him like that."

"Who says you'd have a choice? A man's will is sacred."

"Well, I'll be honest with you, then. If you left the ranch to me instead of Laban, I'd just turn it over to him. I would not be able to abide by a will like that."

"You are a stubborn girl."

"Laban has stayed here all these years and worked hard; it's only fair."

"He hates my guts! And if *he* had the guts, he would have killed me years ago."

"But he didn't."

"Not that he didn't think of it every day."

"Maybe if you were a little kinder toward him—"

"Bah!" Caleb turned on his side and, leaning on an elbow, he faced Carolyn directly. "Perhaps to save your mother you'd take the ranch?"

"What do you mean?"

"We can cut a little deal, that's all. You agree to run this ranch after I die—and we'd have it in writing—and I will do whatever I can to free your mother."

"What could you do, Grandfather? What do you know that could save her?" Carolyn asked, her hope rising.

"All I have to do is testify that Leonard was beating her—"

"Is that true? Was he?"

"That really doesn't matter. They'll believe what I say."

"You mean you'd lie?"

"Don't be so naive, Carolyn. That's the only way she will get off."

"You don't know what you are saying." Carolyn stared at her grandfather, appalled. Suddenly the helpless, fragile man disappeared, replaced by—she did not want to think what he had all at once become. "It's the fever talking, Grandfather. When you're better, you won't even remember all this."

"I'll remember, and so will you."

"Well, I wouldn't do it."

"Not even to save your mother?"

"My mother will be freed because she is innocent. I don't have to make any deals with—"

195

"With the devil, Carolyn?" Caleb cut in sharply. "Believe me when I say you will have no choice."

"Grandfather," Carolyn said as calmly as she could, "I'm going to leave now and let you rest. You'll think differently when you're better."

Caleb said nothing more, and Carolyn left.

It seemed that every time she was in her grandfather's presence, she left on the verge of tears, confused and frustrated. She needed to get away for a while, out in the open. She needed to think—or perhaps she just needed to *not* think, to forget it all. She naturally sought out the one place where she could do all those things best— the back of her horse.

As she hurried down the corridor on her way out of the house, she did not notice the dark figure lurking in the shadows just outside Caleb's room.

43

There was no one in the stable. Ramón had gone into town to visit his mother, and the other hands, having finished their necessary chores, were taking Sunday afternoon off. She went to Tres Zapatos' stall and quickly saddled her. But as she was leading the mare out, she heard the stable doors close. The bright light that had been streaming in from that source was suddenly cut off.

It took only a moment for the newcomer to make himself known. It was Laban Stoner.

"Good afternoon, Laban," she said in her most congenial tone. But he was the last person she wanted to see at that moment.

He said nothing for some time, just staring at her with his dark eyes that were so like Caleb's.

"Where are you going?" he demanded at last.

"Just for a ride."

"You think you are so high-and-mighty, don't you? The woman who has Caleb Stoner wrapped around her finger. He gives you a

196

horse, he gives you free rein on the ranch ... he gives you everything."

"I—I don't know what you mean."

"He's not going to give you this ranch—do you hear!" His eyes flashed, his mouth twisted with ire.

"I don't—"

"Don't play dumb. I heard your little conversation—my reward for coming to look after my poor, sick father."

"Well, if you heard, then you also heard that I wouldn't take the ranch. That wouldn't be fair to you."

He sneered at her, as if the idea of such an honorable gesture meant nothing to him. "You'd take it fast enough to save your mother."

"He didn't mean that; he was out of his head. None of that's gonna happen. There's no way he can make me take the ranch from you, Laban. You must believe that."

"You think, like everyone else, I am a spineless idiot, don't you?"

"That's not so!"

She wondered at the desperation in her tone. But a terrible panic had begun to creep upon her. She saw violence in Laban's expression, heard it in his voice. It frightened her.

"You would kiss the devil's feet to save your mother." He took a step toward Carolyn, and she stepped back, only to find herself up against the wooden stall. He reached up his hand—a large, calloused, strong hand—and circled her throat with it. "But what would you do to save your own neck? I think you would sleep with the devil for that!"

"Stop it!"

"I tell you now, Miss Carolyn Stoner, I will kill you if you stand between me and this ranch."

"Laban, please, don't say things you don't mean." When he had threatened her before, she had given it little consideration, but now, even as Carolyn spoke, she knew this was no empty threat.

"I could have killed him many times," Laban went on. "He thinks I didn't because I couldn't, but that isn't so. I thought I could be patient. Why risk my own neck when just a little patience would get me what I wanted? You have changed all that. *I am no longer patient!*" His hand tightened on her neck as he forced her harder against the stall.

"That hurts. Stop it!" She reached up a hand and shoved him, surprised at how easily he gave way, stepping back from her.

197

She tried to turn from him toward her horse, but he caught her arm in a vise-like grip.

"Like him, you think I am nothing, his bastard son. But I am a man, his true son!"

"I know that, Laban." But her voice shook as she spoke, lacking proper conviction.

"You don't think I could do it, do you? You believe I have no guts, or why else have I stayed here all these years under his thumb. You don't fear me enough, Carolyn."

"N—no, you're wrong. I—"

His hand shot up with a stinging blow to her face that brought tears to her eyes. Again he struck her, and again.

"Please!" she said, tasting blood on her lips.

"I have thirty-six years of hate in me. Don't ever underestimate it. I can kill. I will kill!"

His voice shook with that hatred, and Carolyn did not doubt his words for a moment. Then, as if something had snapped within him, he flew at her again, grabbing her bodily and forcefully pushing her against the stall. The horse snorted and skittishly backed off. Carolyn crumpled onto the straw-covered stable floor. Laban yanked her to her feet and was about to strike her once more, but his hand, raised in midair, stopped. He was panting like a crazed beast; his eyes no longer looked human.

Instead of hitting her, however, he flung her once more against the stall, knocking the wind out of her and sending her sprawling to the ground nearly unconscious.

"Don't forget this, Carolyn. Don't ever forget this!"

He spun around and stalked out of the stable.

Carolyn lay where she was for some time. Her body ached from the attack, and she was emotionally stunned, in shock. Such hatred, such evil, was simply beyond all her comprehension. Even Caleb had not looked that way when he spoke of her mother. It was almost as if Laban was the personification of all the things she had heard about her father and grandfather. Laban *was* those things—evil, cruelty, vindictiveness, bitterness. She had only heard about them in Caleb and Leonard, but she had seen them in Laban.

It took five minutes before she could pull herself together enough to stand, dust the straw and dirt from her skirt, retrieve Tres Zapatos' reins, and lead her outside. She swung up easily into the saddle in spite of her Sunday clothes.

She glanced around and, relieved that she saw no sign of Laban, rode off.

Perhaps it was foolish to take off alone like this, but she knew she couldn't return to the house right now. It would raise too many questions if anyone saw her bruised and bleeding as she was. It would be tantamount to disaster if Caleb ever found out what had happened in the stable.

She hated the idea that she was protecting Laban. Didn't he deserve to be punished for what he had done to her? Hadn't he threatened to kill her?

But would anyone believe her? He would certainly deny it, pitting her word against his. And he would no doubt accuse her of trying to discredit him to secure her claim to the ranch. It all could so easily be twisted against her—just as her mother's trial had been.

But almost worse than anyone not believing her was the possibility that they *might* believe, especially Caleb. After what she had seen today, Carolyn would not put it past either one of them to kill the other. She did not want to be responsible for that.

Thus, it was best, for now, just to keep this to herself. But that didn't mean that she was going to forget about Laban. She was going to keep after him, keep pushing him, one way or the other, until she proved that he, and not her mother, had killed Leonard Stoner.

And she would definitely guard against a repeat of that vile attack. She bent down and checked her saddlebag. In it was the Remington six-shooter that Caleb insisted she carry with her when she rode anywhere on the ranch. Laban Stoner would not vent his hatred upon her again. As much as she abhorred violence, Carolyn did know how to protect herself, and she didn't think she'd be squeamish to do so. She had killed rattlers and wild animals before. Killing a man, of course, was far different, but she could shoot well enough so that killing would not be necessary. Griff taught her never to point a gun at a man unless she was ready to kill him. Carolyn didn't think that was always true. A bullet in the arm could be enough to stop Laban if necessary.

But she prayed fervently it would never be necessary.

44

Two miles from the ranch, Carolyn stopped at a stream to wash her face. It brought fresh bleeding to the crack on her lip, but she tore a strip off her petticoat and pressed it hard against the wound for several minutes until it no longer bled. Glancing into the water, she saw her reflection and was sickened. A swollen lip, a cut over her eye, and a bruise on her cheek would never heal in time to keep others from seeing. She remembered something her mother had said about Leonard knowing how to inflict a beating without outward signs. Carolyn wished Laban had learned the same lessons.

No matter, she thought, *I'll just come up with a story. My horse spooked, and I fell off. That ought to do.* Then she added as if in self-defense, *It could happen even to a good rider like me.*

She mounted her horse again and continued to ride, losing all track of time. But at least three hours must have passed; night was beginning to close in. She didn't care. There was nearly a full moon and plenty of light.

Would Caleb ask about her or worry over her absence?

In spite of its inherent dangers, she loved riding at night when all the world was so quiet and peaceful. Under the twilight sky, studded with stars, she had a greater perception of the majesty of God, of His awesome power, of His presence. The intermittent flashes of lightning streaking the sky only heightened her spiritual awareness. She needed that now. She realized how much harder it was to focus on God without the gentle reminders of Sam and her ma. But Carolyn was an adult now, her own person, and she needed to be able to relate to God for herself. Her need for that was greater than it had ever been before.

"Lord, please direct me and keep me from behaving foolishly. You know as well as I that's kind of a fault of mine. That and thinking I can do more than I really can. Help me to keep looking at you, not only when I can see you best, like right now, but even at times like before in the stable, or when I'm with Grandfather. None of this is gonna turn out right unless you are in it."

In the moonlight, Carolyn came upon a little trail that led up a craggy rise. She could make out a profusion of trees and mesquite and brush at the top of the hill, which even in this Texas hill country was not very common. She had seen this ridge from the roundup camp, so she must be many miles from the ranch house. The trees at the top, however, drew her, for it looked like a nice place to sit for a while before returning home.

Suddenly clouds rolled over the sky, blocking out the moonlight. A summer storm was brewing, and even a proficient rider like Carolyn knew that a storm was no time to be out in the open, much less on horseback. If she didn't get back home soon, she wouldn't have to fabricate a story about her bruises.

A particularly jagged streak of lightning seemed to split the sky in two, lighting it up brighter than any moon. Tres Zapatos snorted and pranced nervously and Carolyn reined the mare to a stop. Then a sharp crack of thunder exploded above. The horse stomped skittishly. Carolyn tightened her hand on his reins.

All at once another sound rent through the night air. But this time it wasn't thunder. Carolyn recognized the sound immediately as the report of a rifle. She was about to dismount when a second shot came, striking the cantle of her saddle with such an impact that it nearly felt as if the bullet had penetrated her back. Tres Zapatos reared, and Carolyn jumped, landing without much mishap. She scurried on hands and knees to the cover of some brush.

Another shot quickly followed, but her six-gun was in her saddle and she dared not try to get it. Suddenly another gun fired from a different direction. Two more shots came in quick succession from the newcomer, then, after a short pause, the sound of a horse retreating at a full gallop.

"Hey! What's going on?" came a familiar voice.

"Matt? It's me, Carolyn. Someone's shooting at me."

"I think I scared 'em off." Matt came into view, leading his buckskin mount.

"Maybe we can still catch him." Carolyn jumped up, ran to her mount, and grabbed the dangling reins.

A flash of lightning stopped her, and then the rain came in torrents. It soaked Carolyn in seconds.

"This storm would have come sooner or later," Matt said, "and it would never have given us time to catch whoever was shooting at you."

"At me?" Carolyn thought—hoped—that perhaps the bullets had not been meant specifically for her.

"Who else?"

"Maybe it was Bonner's boys. Maybe they were gunning for you."

Matt drew attention to the shattered hole in Carolyn's saddle. "I doubt it. There was enough moonlight for a fellow to do better than this if he was after me. No, they were gunning for you, and they had to know you are a girl, too."

Carolyn swallowed. Although she wanted to deny it, she sensed all along that she had been the target. And all she could think of was Laban Stoner and the murderous look in his eyes when he had attacked her earlier.

"What in blazes are you doing out here in the middle of the night, anyway?"

"Riding, that's all. I wanted to explore that ridge."

"Are you crazy, girl? Don't you go near that ridge!"

"I'll go where I want," she said petulantly.

"Well, I ain't gonna argue with you here in the rain where we're likely to be struck by lightning. Come with me."

"Where?"

"Do you gotta question everything?" He rolled his eyes in frustration. "There's a line cabin not far from here where we can wait out the storm. We can get there in a few minutes." When she hesitated, he added, "I suppose you want to ride back to the ranch in this?"

Actually, she had been debating just that as an alternative to spending the night alone with a cowboy. But someone might still be out there gunning for her. And if that possibility wasn't convincing enough, another fiery streak of lightning struck so close by that they could hear the sound of a tree branch splitting in two from the impact. Tres Zapatos whinnied and reared slightly.

"Okay, lead the way," Carolyn said resignedly.

Five minutes later they were in the cabin and Matt was busily building a fire in the stone hearth. He had been wearing a slicker and, except for the legs of his Levi's, was fairly dry. Carolyn, on the other hand, had not even been wearing a coat, for it had been a warm summer evening. She was dripping and shivering. But before long the fire was blazing, and with much appreciation, she drew close to the flames.

"That feels mighty good!" she said, rubbing her hands together.

"You'll dry off real quick now. Maybe you won't catch the grippe, or something. It was pretty foolhardy, you out riding alone at night like that—I don't care how good you are." He added that last as she opened her mouth in protest.

"Well, I could say the same for you." Her reply sounded lame. She knew he was right.

"I was working."

As they spoke, he had continued to nurse the fire, not really paying close attention to Carolyn. Now that a good blaze was going, he turned and started to sit by her. He stopped suddenly as he caught a clear look at her face in the light of the flames.

"What happened to you?"

In the excitement of the night, Carolyn had forgotten her bruised face; now she groaned inwardly at her carelessness. But she had a story ready for Matt.

"Well, my horse threw me—you saw that hole in my saddle. I landed square in a clump of mesquite."

"Them mesquite thorns are poisonous," he said. "Let me have a look."

He moved toward her, but she pulled away. He was about to upbraid her again; then suddenly he stopped. She knew in that moment—she could see it in his eyes—that he had perceived the real cause of her wounds. With shame, though she knew she had no reason to feel so, she jerked her head away from him.

Carolyn was a little surprised at his gentle tone. "You didn't get that from a horse fall, did you?"

She knew it was no use lying anymore, and maybe she didn't want to. If Laban Stoner, or anyone, was gunning for her, she needed help. Perhaps, after all, Matt was a likely one to ask, for he was not directly involved in all this. She shook her head, but before she could explain, Matt jumped to his own conclusions.

"It was that Toliver, wasn't it?" Matt's gentleness all at once turned into hot anger.

"No, it wasn't. Now simmer down!"

"Come on, Carolyn. Why should you defend him? The other night you were struggling to get away from him, weren't you? That's what I heard. He came back later, didn't he?"

"That's the most ridiculous thing I ever heard!" Carolyn retorted. She didn't know why his accusations should rile her so; he was only concerned for her. "It's true Sean got a little carried away the other night, and I don't know what would have happened if you hadn't come along. But he'd never hurt me like this."

"Then who—?"

"Why should I tell you?" she said, feeling stubborn and defensive again.

"Looks to me like you're in a heap of trouble, Carolyn. First, someone hits you like that, then you're ambushed . . . and even if the two ain't connected, you got problems. Maybe you don't have to tell me, but if someone harmed you, then at least the sheriff should know."

"How do you know I didn't already tell the sheriff?"

"'Cause those wounds are fresh. You'd never have had time to ride to town and back out here." He reached up and, as if to prove his statement, dabbed away a drop of blood from her lip.

"All right, I didn't tell anyone, and I don't intend to. Now just forget it."

"You are the most stubborn person I ever knew!"

Carolyn was quiet for a minute. She began to feel bad about her insensitivity toward Gentry, who was only concerned for her welfare. That was no way to treat someone who had probably saved her life, then found her shelter from the storm, built a fire to warm and dry her, and tried to be nice. She hadn't even thanked him.

"Matt," she said in a repentant tone, "I'm sorry for being so or- nery—I guess it's just a bad habit with me. Thanks for your concern and for scaring off that varmint who was shooting at me."

"I'm glad I happened to be out there," he said.

She just nodded in reply. Her throat was getting tight, and she refused to start crying—that was happening much too often lately.

Apparently content that they'd made peace, Matt was satisfied with the quiet also, and they remained silent for some time. The radiating warmth of the fire was soothing, and Carolyn lost herself staring into the dancing tongues of flame.

In the silence, Carolyn had a chance to think about what Matt had said. She was in trouble, and she needed help. But she couldn't go to the sheriff for fear it would get back to Caleb or Laban. As with her mother, the town officials would probably believe Laban over her. Yet she couldn't just sit by and let Laban get away with attacking her.

"Matt," she said quietly, in an unusually contrite tone, "I'm just so confused, I don't know where to turn or what to do. You won't laugh if I tell you I am a little scared about it all?"

"Carolyn, you are really too much. Why, if I'd been through what you just been through, I'd be a heap of jelly. And for what it's worth, I wanta tell you that I'm here for you—I mean, if you want, you can turn to me."

"That's mighty nice of you, Matt, especially considering you don't know me much, and you don't know what it's all about."

"I reckon this might have something to do with your mother."

Carolyn nodded, and before she realized it she was telling him the whole story, including the most recent confrontation with Laban.

"That fellow deserves more than a thrashing—he deserves a rope!" Matt exclaimed when she finished. "But I guess I can understand why you're afraid to tell Caleb or the sheriff."

"If Laban killed my father, then it's best if we just watch him and hope he makes a mistake, or leads us to some evidence to convict him. I don't want him to get put in jail for hitting me and then escape punishment for his worst crime."

"What're you gonna do besides watch him?"

"I don't know."

"And the shooting tonight, Carolyn—you can't forget about that. Laban, or whoever killed your father, might be getting nervous, and might be trying to get rid of you before you can find any evidence."

"It might just have been those rustlers."

Matt nodded, but as they looked at each other, both knew that with all Carolyn was involved in, the chances of tonight's close call being merely a random incident with rustlers was remote. At least, they had to treat it as such and not get careless or lazy.

"Well, I'm gonna keep my eyes peeled and my gun handy," said Matt.

"Me, too, Matt. Thanks."

45

After about ten minutes of silence, Matt rose and stretched. "I'm kinda hungry, how about you?"

"They keep this place stocked?"

"Mostly in the winter for when a hand stays out here to keep an eye on the cattle grazed up here. But there oughta be something left over."

He walked to the cupboards in the kitchen area of the small, one-room cabin, glancing out the only window as he did so.

"It's coming down with a vengeance out there," he commented.

"That's Texas for you," Carolyn said. "Yesterday, it was dry enough to blow dust off the Brazos."

"I reckon General Sherman was right."

"That Yankee!" Carolyn laughed with mock disdain. "What could he be right about?"

"He said that if he owned Texas and hell, he'd rent out Texas and live on the other property."

Carolyn laughed. "That's good. But I wouldn't want to live any place else myself."

"Neither would I."

"Were you born here, then?" Carolyn asked.

"Yeah, over by Jacksboro. How about you?"

"I was born in Indian Territory, in a Cheyenne camp." She said it with some pride, even though she was always just a little disappointed she couldn't claim Texas as her birthplace.

Matt whistled. "You don't say? In an Indian camp? How did that come about?"

As Matt opened a couple of cans of beans and heated them over the fire, Carolyn told him the rest of her mother's story.

"Well, Carolyn," he said when she finished several minutes later, "I'm impressed. I guess you have been around some."

She smiled, pleased to have finally made her point with this cocky cowboy. Maybe he'd respect her more in the future.

Matt took the heated cans off the fire and set them on the floor to cool. Carolyn thought there was no better fragrance than beans cooked over an open fire when you hadn't eaten for hours. Though it was even better in the open air, this was almost as good. But Matt wasn't finished yet with their meal. He threw on his slicker and ducked outside for a few minutes with a bucket in hand. When he returned, the pail was half full of rainwater, and he proceeded to make a pot of coffee—the second best fragrance, in Carolyn's opinion.

She didn't feel at all uncomfortable that this cowboy was fixing their meal. She was so inept in the kitchen that she could hardly open a can without injuring herself.

When they sat down to eat, Carolyn took up the conversation where they had left off. "So, Matt, I told you my life story, now it's your turn."

"Aw, never mind about that. You don't want to hear it."

"But I do, and what better way to while away this storm."

"Well, it ain't a very good story, that's all. Not one I much like repeating." He paused a moment in thought, as if he was remembering something. When he began again, his tense attitude had softened. "I reckon it comes out okay, though, so maybe for that reason I should tell it. Anyways, someone once told me I didn't have to feel shy about boasting if it was about God."

"God?"

"Sure. The things you said about God, when you was talking about your ma and you . . . well, I can understand them a mite, though, I suppose, I don't talk about them out loud very much."

"What's in our hearts is more important to God than what we say," Carolyn said encouragingly. "Sam says some folks have the gift of verbally expressing spiritual things, and some don't. God don't expect us all to act the same, else He would have made us all the same. I'd like to hear what you have to say, Matt, but I'd understand if you don't feel comfortable talking about it."

"Time was, I *never* talked about it," Matt replied earnestly. "But, like I said, a couple of years back something changed for me and I was able to accept the past a little better. You see, when I was about ten years old, I watched my whole family get massacred by Comanche. I was down at the stream getting water when the war party came. I heard the shooting and ran up just as they was setting fire to our house. My ma and pa and two sisters were already dead. They'd have killed me, too, if I hadn't been a male. The chief's son had been killed by soldiers not long before their raid on us, and he figured I was young enough to take in as his own. So they took me captive instead of killing me."

"My ma told me that the Comanche were a cruel tribe, especially with captives."

"That's true, but mostly toward females. Of course, they don't take adult males captive—they kill them. But young boys had a little better time of it, I think. They beat me a lot, but I suppose no more than my own pa used to. It took me a long time to stop hating them for what they did to my family, but after a while I accepted my lot. I couldn't have survived if I had tried to escape; and there were some, including the chief, who were fairly nice to me. I didn't have no family left and no place else to go, so I just made the best of it. And, for a young boy, the life of an Indian is kind of idyllic—you know, riding, hunting, war parties. I learned a lot in the three years I was with them, and it was a good thing, because when I was thirteen, I struck out on my own. That was in seventy-four, when the last of the tribes finally surrendered to the whites. I could either join the renegades or go to the reservation if I wanted to stick with the Indians. But my loyalties weren't that strong—they were still the people who killed my family. So I lit out alone."

"At thirteen? That must've been tough."

"I knew how to take care of myself. The hardest part was the loneliness; not having any family or—well, anyone."

"Weren't there any families willing to take you in?"

"I reckon there might have been, but I was just too wild to care much about living a civilized life. The loneliness finally did get to me, and I fell in with a bad crowd—you know, outlaws. They gave me a kind of security without having to give up my freedom." He paused for such a long time that Carolyn thought he was finished and was about to prod him for more. Then he continued, though his reluctance was obvious. "I ain't proud of the rest. But I've told you this much, so I might as well continue. About three years ago I killed a man. All those years of riding with outlaws, and I'd never killed anyone. It shook me up, but mostly because I realized that it wasn't as hard as it should have been. It's kind of hard to explain, but I both liked the sensation and hated it all at the same time.

"Besides that, I got hauled into jail, too. It was a fair and square gunfight, so they couldn't hold me, but they suspected I was involved in the rustling in those parts and were trying to keep me in jail until they had proof. Well, I made the acquaintance of . . . a couple of fellas who, I guess, felt sorry for a kid like me being in such a heap of trouble. One of 'em convinced the sheriff to let me go, in his custody, promising I'd keep out of trouble, or else the sheriff could put *him* in jail. I'd never met anyone like that, who'd put himself on the line for a complete stranger. Well, what with feeling the way I did about the shooting, confused and all, I was willing to hook up with these two men for a spell. I had been about ready to leave the outlaws, anyway, and even had a promise of a job from a hand I'd met from the Stoner outfit. What I learned in a week from that fella—the one that got me out of jail, I mean—did more for me than I can rightly explain. It gave me the courage to change, to stop trying to prove how tough and independent I am." He stopped and grinned self-consciously. "Holy smoke! I ain't talked this much in, I don't know how long!"

Carolyn smiled, too. "It makes me appreciate it all the more." To lighten the mood, she added, "What I don't understand is how a fella with your background ever learned to dance so well!"

He chuckled. "Not long after I came here to the ranch and settled down to the 'civilized' life of the cowboy, I made myself learn."

"But why? Even I never had need to learn to dance."

"That's sure an understatement!" He looked at her slyly out of the corner of his eye, and when he saw her smile, he smiled, too. Then they both burst out laughing.

"So, why'd you learn?" asked Carolyn, ever persistent.

"Well, it's at dances like the one last Saturday that a fella meets girls—you know, nice girls like the kind a man would . . . marry." He fumbled a bit over the admission, and Carolyn wondered if she saw some red creep up his cheeks, although it might just have been the reflection from the fire.

"Why, Matt Gentry, are you looking for a wife?"

"Sure, what's wrong with that? I reckon after the kind of growing up I had, it's important to me to have a family and a home."

"Really?" His earnestness made her feel a little ashamed at poking fun at him. "But you've been at the ranch a couple of years now. How come it's taking you so long to get hitched?"

"Boy, you sure are full of questions, ain't you?" When Carolyn gave an apologetic shrug, he went on. "I ain't found the right girl, yet, that's why."

"You're the picky type, then?"

"Just because I want to get married don't mean I'm in a hurry to get stuck with just anyone."

"So, what're you looking for?" Carolyn's question was completely guileless. She had come to look upon Matt as a friend; having designs on him never occurred to her.

He seemed to feel the same way, for he displayed none of the usual reticence that was common between men and women when such topics were broached.

"I don't know," he said. "I don't think it's a good idea to get too specific. I think I'll know when she comes along, though. I figure that's where faith in God'll come in handy."

"Well, I wish you the best, Matt. Say, have you met the banker's daughter? She's a fine gal, a real homebody, too. She fixed that delicious fried chicken we had at the dance. I saw some of her stitchery, and it was beautiful."

"You ain't gonna start playing matchmaker, now, are you, Carolyn? That might put a real strain on our friendship. I'd rather just take things as they come, without pushing too hard."

"Okay, I'll back off. But she is a nice girl."

He smiled. "Well, I'll take a closer look at the next dance. What about you?"

"And the banker's daughter?" jibed Carolyn.

"You know what I mean. You ever want to get married?"

"You ain't proposing, are you?" Carolyn had begun to feel silly and couldn't imagine why.

"Be serious."

"To tell the truth, I ain't given it much thought—well, until recently."

"You mean, until you met Toliver?"

"He sure knows how to turn a girl's head," Carolyn said evasively. "But I got plenty of time. Besides, Griff says he pities the fella that marries me, that I'll probably drive the poor man to drink. I can be just a little headstrong at times—so I've been told."

Matt responded with a hearty laugh. Then he said with quiet sincerity, "I think there's a perfect match out there for everyone— even you, Carolyn," he added playfully, "though he would have to have the patience of Job, the serenity of Saint John, and the fortitude of the apostle Paul—"

"Oh, you!" Carolyn gave him a shove, then giggled when he shoved her back.

When the merriment had quieted, Matt said suddenly, "Hey, listen! The rain's stopped."

They both jumped up and looked out the window. Indeed, the storm had abated and the previous furor was replaced with a deep peace. Neither knew when during their conversation it had happened, but both felt more disappointment than relief. It had been a fine, relaxing time there in the line cabin. Carolyn couldn't remember when she enjoyed herself more, especially since coming to the Bar S Ranch.

"Guess we ought to head back," said Carolyn.

"It wouldn't do to spend the night here if we don't have to."

Carolyn had tried not to think of that possibility when they had first come. Now . . . it was just as well that the rain stopped. But she'd have more to fear if she had been with Sean; Matt had thus far been a perfect gentleman. In fact, anything beyond their friendly conversation had not seriously occurred to Carolyn, and she was certain it had been the same for Matt. Still, she hated to see the evening end.

"Yeah," she said, "we best get back."

46

They returned to the house long after midnight. Carolyn stole quietly up to her room, not encountering a soul.

She was so tired that she was asleep as soon as her head touched her pillow. When she awoke the following morning, she didn't have to remind herself about her beating. Her body ached all over, and the cuts on her face had bled in the night and were crusted and painful by morning. She had to avoid being seen somehow.

When she didn't come to breakfast, Juana came to her room.

Carolyn remained under her covers, her face turned and partially shielded by a blanket. "Come in."

"Are you all right, señorita?"

"I just ain't feeling too well, that's all."

"Perhaps the Patrón's sickness is catching, after all?"

"Oh no, I'm sure it's not that." The last thing Carolyn wanted was a doctor sent for and the house quarantined. "It's . . . just a girl thing, you know."

"Oh," Juana sounded relieved. "Can I do anything for you?"

"Could you get me a basin of hot water and soap and towels? I'll just wash up here. And, do you have any medicinal salve? I fell off my horse and have a couple of scrapes."

"Sí, señorita. I'll find something."

"Oh, and Juana, how is my grandfather today?"

"He is much better. He ate a good breakfast and perhaps will feel like getting out of bed later."

"That's good. Would you explain to him that I ain't feeling much like seeing anyone today? I'll just have dinner and supper here, if that's okay."

"Sí, Señorita Carolyn."

Feeling pleased with herself over her swift thinking, Carolyn lay back in bed and relaxed. Then it dawned on her that she was going to have to be cooped up in her room all day. A whole day would be lost! But she knew she had no choice. If Caleb found out what Laban had done, there was sure to be trouble.

By the next morning, the bruise on Carolyn's cheek was almost invisible. A bit of powder borrowed from Juana covered what remained. Her lip also was almost back to normal, although she had to take care not to smile suddenly or the crack would open again. The cut over her eye had improved a little with cleaning and salve, but was still rather nasty and might even leave a scar. However, she was confident that her fall-from-her-horse story would excuse that.

When she saw Caleb at breakfast, he, too, looked better.

"We have had a peculiar rash of illness, haven't we?" he said.

"Yeah, but let's hope there ain't no more."

"I agree." He paused, sipped his coffee, then added, "Carolyn, I want you to choose a different horse. The one you picked is a lively one and rather young."

"Because of the fall? That wasn't the horse's fault." She paused a brief moment to think of a plausible explanation. Sam and her mother would be glad to see that lying did not come easily to her. "I was just showing off in front of one of the hands. You can ask him; it was just my pure foolishness."

"Who was that?"

"Matt Gentry."

"I don't like you mixing with the hands. You are my granddaughter and ought to behave yourself accordingly."

"If I was your grandson, I bet it wouldn't bother you."

"But you're not, are you?"

"Just my dumb luck!" Carolyn grumbled.

Caleb made no response, and they ate the rest of their meal in silence. However, when they finished and were about to leave the dining room, Caleb paused at the door and said off-handedly: "I forgot to mention that there was mail yesterday while you were ill."

"For me?" Carolyn hadn't really expected anything, but the thought of hearing from her family was uplifting.

"No, but it might interest you, regardless. My lawyer has sent me a message to inform me that a new trial has been granted your mother on the grounds that she wasn't properly represented the first time and was tried in a hostile town. It's set to begin on Monday." He made no attempt to cover up his displeasure.

Had she been with anyone else, Carolyn would have jumped up and cheered at that news—her mother had a second chance, and there would be less than a week more to wait for it. Instead of cheering, however, she tried to be reserved for her grandfather's sake. She smiled, but even that had to be cautious because of her lip.

"She is my mother, Grandfather," Carolyn said, as if she had to defend herself, "and I do want to see her free."

"That's understandable; even I would not deny you that. But, Carolyn, a new trial does not necessarily mean freedom. In order to win their case, the defense would have to come up with new evidence."

"And what makes you so sure there isn't any?"

"Because all the evidence there is was presented at the last trial, and it convicted your mother."

"But that's what this new trial is all about," countered Carolyn. "Even the court feels the last trial wasn't fair."

"Don't get your hopes up," Caleb said flatly.

"And don't get *your* hopes up, Grandfather," Carolyn said with far more emphasis. Then she added with entreaty, "Grandfather, what if . . . what if a trial exonerated my mother? What would you do then?"

"It won't, so there is no use making idle talk."

"But *what if*! If the real murderer were found, would you stop hating her?"

"It will never happen."

"Oh, Grandfather!" Carolyn stamped her foot in frustration.

"Is that so important to you, Carolyn?"

"No matter what you say, Grandfather, I still want to have you both. And I think it's possible."

"I would like to ask you a probing question," said Caleb, his dark eyes intense. "What would *you* do if she were to be proven, beyond doubt, to have murdered your father?"

Carolyn licked her lips. She didn't like that question at all, and had tried hard to avoid it. "I just don't know." It was the only honest thing she could say.

"I give you the same answer, but I will add that regardless of whether your mother actually pulled the trigger of the gun that killed my son, she is still the one that destroyed my home and my son. I will never forgive her for that."

"Grandfather, I think you have hated my mother for so long you are afraid to give it up. And maybe, like me, you are afraid to accept the truth about just what kind of man my father was."

"Don't get cheeky with me, young lady."

"I'm not. I just want peace between us, but that will never happen unless we face the past."

"Don't talk to me about facing the past. I do so nearly every day as I mourn my dear son's loss. And every day I see your mother standing over him, holding his gun, and my Leonard lying there dead, a senseless bullet in his back."

Carolyn was thinking of the conversation she'd had with her grandfather in the room where her father had been killed; it was so similar to this, and she feared a traumatic repeat. Suddenly, one difference occurred to her. "In his *back*, Grandfather? Before you said there was a wound in his chest."

"Back, chest—it's all the same to me."

"But," persisted Carolyn, "a discrepancy like that could make a difference, couldn't it?"

"In the back of the chest, that's what I meant. You are grasping at straws, Carolyn, and that will only bring you disappointment."

Not wanting emotions to heat up any more than they already were, Carolyn changed the subject. "Will you go to the trial?"

"They will no doubt subpoena me."

"Can we go together?"

"If you wish."

In spite of her grandfather's intractability regarding her mother, Carolyn felt good as she left the house and headed for the stable. She had to believe that everything was going to turn out all right. Caleb was a hardheaded old man, but in only a few weeks she had gotten him to accept her. It might take longer, but there was no reason why he could not soften toward her mother also.

Caleb was justified in wondering why this was so important to her. She would have no problem maintaining a relationship with both, even if they were estranged from each other. She knew her mother would not prevent her, and Caleb had accepted her even with the questions of Deborah's guilt still unsolved. But turning the matter over in her mind, Carolyn realized that it was not for her own sake at all that she desired a healing between Caleb and Deborah. Nor was it for Deborah. Rather, it was almost entirely for Caleb. She had listened to Sam's preaching enough to know that forgiveness is one of God's great healers. And Caleb desperately needed healing from the hatred and bitterness he had been carrying all these years. Not physical healing—though, according to Sam, forgiveness often helped relieve physical ailments—but rather a mending of his heart and soul. There was no reason why Caleb Stoner could not spend his final years as a happy man. He was not incapable of such happiness. From what Carolyn had learned about his first marriage, he had been happy with his first wife, Elizabeth.

Thinking of Elizabeth Stoner, Carolyn's grandmother, made her cognizant of the fact that Caleb's bitterness had begun before Deborah ever came into his life. According to Deborah, the marriage to his second wife had been disastrous. Deborah hadn't said much about Caleb's two sons from this marriage, not even mentioned them by name, but she had said that they hated Caleb not only because of his demeaning treatment toward them, but also because of how he had made their mother unhappy.

Maybe I am being too idealistic, thinking that forgiving my mother will make everything better for Grandfather, Carolyn thought to herself. *There's probably something eating at him that goes far deeper than that.*

What could it be? And wasn't it possible for God to heal even that? Her faith was strong enough to believe God could do it. But Caleb had to pursue forgiveness himself, want it, ask for it—and that's where Carolyn's faith faltered a little. It was hard for her to picture Caleb a repentant man, on his knees crying out to God. *All things were possible,* yes—but Caleb, head bowed, hands clasped, beseeching God in anguished humility? That was not an image that could take any substantial form in Carolyn's mind.

47

In the stable, Carolyn encountered the two men she was most reticent about seeing. Sean and Laban were standing near the entrance talking together. She couldn't avoid them.

Sean's broad, handsome grin made her wonder why she wanted to avoid him anyway. "Hello, Carolyn!" he said cheerfully. "My morning is starting to look a lot better!"

"Hi, Sean." She gave him a smile that faded as she acknowledged her uncle. "And Laban."

"What happened to you?" Sean asked, noting the cut over her eyebrow.

She couldn't help a skittish glance toward Laban. "I fell off my horse."

"You?"

"Guess it could happen to anybody."

Laban gave her a scowl. "You should be more careful," he said, without sounding the least bit sincere. "Too many *accidents* can happen on a ranch."

"Reckon I learned that the hard way. You can be sure I won't let it happen again."

"So, what are you up to today, Carolyn?" Sean asked, apparently oblivious to the taut exchange, rife with double meanings, between niece and uncle.

"I just was going riding for a while. Want to join me?" Her invitation slipped out before she even realized what she was saying. When she was around Sean, all her good sense seemed to melt away.

Sean was about to answer when Laban broke in sharply, "Remember what I said, Toliver. You have important work today. I don't want you to be distracted."

"All right. But you take all the fun out of life."

Laban glared at Sean, then stalked away.

After he exited the stable and was out of sight, Sean shook his head. "That man is going to go too far someday. He thinks he's so high-and-mighty because he's the Patrón's son."

"I'd be careful around him if I were you, Sean," said Carolyn. "I think he *is* a dangerous man."

"Well, Carolyn, you only know the charming side of me, but I can be pretty dangerous myself when I want to. I'm not accustomed to groveling before any man."

"Why do you stay around here, Sean? You could probably get a good job at any other ranch."

"Won't be long before I'm not going to have to work for *any* man. I guess I can be patient a little longer."

"What do you mean?"

"Never you mind about that," he said cryptically. He grinned, showing a set of perfect white teeth. He put his arm around Carolyn's waist and drew her close. "Let's not waste the only minute we're liable to get together today on talk." He bent down and kissed her lips with passion, if not with the same force he had used before.

Carolyn melted into that compelling kiss and briefly returned it. Then, in a moment, she got hold of her emotions and pulled away.

"Sean . . ."

"Not again, love." There was more than a hint of disapproval in Sean's tone.

Carolyn tried hard to be firm. "Sean, I'm just not ready for this.

What you expect . . . well, I think it's something that ought to be saved for marriage."

"Marriage?" His voice was filled with amusement as he spoke the word.

"Yes, and I really don't think either of us are ready for that—at least I'm not. Is that what you want, Sean?"

She sounded so innocent, so naive, that even she heard it in her small voice. She hated being that way before a man like Sean, and yet . . . that's exactly what she was. Something deep inside—something that was at last beginning to awaken within her—told her that if Sean was any kind of a man, a suitor, a potential husband, he ought to be able to respect her in that way. Perhaps this sensitivity in her had been heightened during her evening with Matt Gentry, which had given her a standard by which to compare. Matt had indeed accepted her for what she was and hadn't tried to take advantage of her. And that was how most of the men in Carolyn's life had related to her: Sam, Griff, her brother, Longjim, and most of the other hands at the Wind Rider Ranch.

Perhaps Sean's very difference from the others had allured her in the first place. A girl does long for romance, and Sean Toliver was indeed the fulfillment of every young girl's romantic fantasy, so much so that Carolyn was often blinded to the glaring flaws in his character—his arrogance, his demanding nature, his insensitivity. She had a hard time seeing past the charming smile, the handsome looks, the smooth words; she hadn't seen that his smile was not often reflected in his eyes, or that there was a hard edge to both his looks and his silvery words. She hadn't seen, or perhaps didn't want to see, that the man's appeal went no deeper than his tawny skin.

Until now.

Her vision was gradually clearing. Her physical yearnings might still cloud her perceptions, but the long years of training during her growing up and the example of men she loved and respected were at last being felt. She was at least able to see that no man except a husband was worth giving up that most special part of her heart and soul.

"So, you want to get married, little Carolyn?" Even Carolyn could read the sarcasm in Sean's voice as it intruded into her brief thoughts.

"Not in the near future," she was able to say.

He took her chin in his hand and stared deep and long into her eyes. For the first time she saw more than cool cynicism there—could it actually have been real affection, or at least sympathy? Or was that only what she *wanted* to see there? Why did it puzzle her so?

"Who knows, Carolyn, I might still be waiting when you are all grown up and ready for me." He kissed her again, then said briskly, "Well, work calls. I'll see you later—and I mean that."

Before she could respond, he turned and strode from the stable.

48

Carolyn stayed close to the house the next day, partly hoping to avoid Sean, but mostly because she had awakened that morning impressed strongly by the urgency to help her mother. She had learned so little, and she now had less than a week to find the answers that would save her mother.

When her grandfather went out after breakfast, Carolyn forced herself to search his room. Her heart was pounding and her stomach was in knots as she entered what was like the "inner sanctum" of a shrine. Caleb's private domain. He'd no doubt skin her alive if he caught her. But after a brief search, she realized all her turmoil was for naught. There were no readily visible personal or sentimental items about. She had no way of searching the two or three locked drawers and cases in the room, but she'd have to figure out something.

She slipped from the room and quietly closed the door. She was turning from the door when a voice made her freeze, shocking her so that she thought her heart would stop.

"There you are, Carolyn."

She spun around, and her white face revealed her guilt for all to see. She was so shaken she could hardly feel relief that the owner of the voice proved to be Ramón.

"What are you doing up here, Ramón? You scared the dickens out of me."

"Juana was busy and she told me to find you. I think maybe I came at a bad time."

Carolyn lowered her voice as she spoke. "I was just searching in my grandfather's room."

"Any luck this time?"

"None. So why were you looking for me?"

"A fellow just rode in from town with a message for you. He said it was real important and you should let him know right away if there is a reply." He handed Carolyn a folded paper.

Carolyn opened it quickly and read: *I thought it best I not come in person, but want very much to see you. When would be a good time? Sam.*

"Get my horse, Ramón."

"What about your reply to the message?"

"That *is* my answer. I'm going to town."

———

Sam was sitting with another man at a table in the hotel lobby when Carolyn arrived. He barely got to his feet before Carolyn hurried to him and gave him a warm hug. What a joy it was to see a face from home!

"Your ma and I were worried about you, Carolyn."

"Oh, Sam, I am so glad to see you!" She had been close to calling him *Pa*. How she wished he *were* her father. Good, kindhearted Sam, who loved her in a way she was beginning to believe her real father never could have.

"I got someone for you to meet," said Sam.

Jonathan smiled. "My, Sam, you do get exuberant greetings from the prettiest young ladies." He held out his hand to Carolyn. "I feel as if I know you already, Carolyn. I'm Jonathan Barnum."

"This here's your ma's lawyer," added Sam.

"I'm very glad to meet you, sir," said Carolyn. The lawyer's woeful basset-hound features made her want to giggle. And they made him almost instantly endearing.

"Let's sit down," said Sam. "Do you have time to talk, Carolyn?"

"I sure do, but first tell me, how's Ma?"

"As well as can be expected. It ain't easy for her in that place, but you know your ma! She's strong, and the Lord is fortifying her. But we're doing everything we can to speed up her release."

"Is it looking good?"

Jonathan answered. "We were able to make a very good case for a new trial. However, we still have a lot of work ahead of us to make the most of that opportunity. I believe victory will be ours in the end, but it's not going to be obtained easily. We have one important asset in our favor, that is your mother's irrefutable innocence."

"I hope so, Mr. Barnum," Carolyn said.

"Carolyn!" Sam's voice rose in shock.

"I'm sorry, Sam. I believe she's innocent, too, but . . . well, I'm still not sure it wasn't self-defense."

"No, Carolyn!" It was one of the few times Carolyn actually saw Sam get riled. "Your mother did not kill your father, whether in self-defense or by accident, or in any other way. If you don't believe that, Carolyn, then—" Sam stopped suddenly as he noted the resentment creeping into his tone. He took a breath, and the taut lines on his face softened. "Forgive me. I forget that you must be having a hard time with all this, too, and you are doing the best you can to deal with it."

"I want to believe, Sam. But I've heard so many confusing things since I've come here." Carolyn, too, breathed in deeply to steady her rising emotions.

Jonathan spoke quickly to diffuse the tension. "We have work to do, folks, and very little time. Instead of debating what the truth is, let's *investigate* it. That's why you and I came here, Sam." When Sam nodded, Jonathan continued. "I know I am a perfect stranger to you, Carolyn, but I hope I can garner some of your confidence in all this. I need your support, as does your mother. Would you be willing to help me?"

"Of course! What do you want me to do?"

"I understand you've been here several weeks now. Can you tell me what you've learned?"

Carolyn's eagerness faded. "Very little, Mr. Barnum. And nothing new or revealing. My grandfather won't talk much about it except to say my mother is guilty and deserves to . . . to hang for what she done. I had a real promising discussion with the housekeeper. She hinted that there might be secrets of some kind hidden away. But she left town without telling me any more than that. I've searched most of the house, but so far I've found nothing helpful. I'm still thinking of a way to get into some of the locked places without getting caught."

"That's all?"

Carolyn rubbed her chin as she mentally reexamined all her interactions so far at the Stoner Ranch. She felt a little guilty about getting sidetracked with Sean, but she couldn't think how things would have been different otherwise. No one was telling her anything, no matter how hard she tried to probe.

"I've spoken to a few people," she said, trying to be helpful even if she realized it wasn't much. "But they've mostly just told me what I already knew. My ma and pa's marriage was in a bad way; there were fights, and there's a possibility that he beat her. Some folks say my pa was a fine, upstanding man; some say he was hard and ruthless. But not many will admit the negative very loudly because Caleb still controls this town." She paused, trying harder to think of something, *anything,* that was more substantial. Then she recalled her conversation with Caleb the previous morning. "There is one thing. It ain't much but—"

"Small things can turn the tide in legal affairs," Jonathan encouraged.

"Well, I was talking to my grandfather yesterday and he said something about my ma shooting his son in the *back*. The only thing is, another time he talked about a wound in my father's *chest*. I called him on the difference, and he said it was all the same and he'd meant 'back' all along. It would make a difference, wouldn't it, if he had been shot in the back or front?"

"Most definitely, yes," said the lawyer. "We'd be able to make a much better case for self-defense if the wound were in the front. Had that been the case in the first trial, I think your mother would not have been convicted. Shooting someone in the back implies that the victim had no chance to properly defend himself, and that the suspect could not have acted in his or her own defense. But, Carolyn, your mother wants to be exonerated of *any part* in your father's death."

"I know that." Carolyn sighed. She wanted that too, of course, but she was afraid that was hoping for too much, and she was subtly trying to brace herself for the other possibility.

Jonathan spoke again. "While Sam and I are here, we hope to interview anyone we can find who testified in the first trial. Perhaps, having been here for a time, you can help us locate them."

"I'll try. Do you have names?"

"Your mother provided me with a list as complete as her memory could compile. Let me see . . ." Barnum opened his leather briefcase and sorted through some papers. "Here it is." He began reading: "Caleb Stoner . . . well, we know where to find him, though little good to us. Laban Stoner—"

"Forget him, too," said Carolyn. "He's even more hostile than Caleb. But as far as I'm concerned, I think he killed my father and I'm gonna do what I can to prove it."

"Carolyn, don't you put yourself in any danger," said Sam.

Carolyn was saved from responding when Jonathan said, "I will look forward to getting both of them on the stand. Now, how about William Vernon?"

"That's the banker. I didn't know he had testified. I spoke to his wife, Mabel—"

"Ah, yes, here's her name."

"She's real sympathetic to Ma and will do what she can to help. And she's the only one in town who's not afraid of Caleb. Unfortunately, she didn't have anything new to say."

Jonathan read off several more names that Carolyn couldn't help with: Sheriff Pollard, Dr. Barrows, and two or three neighboring ranchers. "There was a storekeeper, but Sam learned the man died a couple of years ago. There was also the Stoner housekeeper named Maria—your mother didn't know her last name. But she was quite old back then—"

"She's still alive," said Carolyn. "She's the one who told me about the secrets, or whatever. But, like I said, she's gone to Waco to visit her sister. She left suddenly, and I suspect it was because she doesn't want to be involved in all this. She's real loyal to the Stoners, but I think she felt sorry for me, too, and so it was just better for her to leave."

"We can subpoena her," said Jonathan.

"She's a real nice old lady, and I don't think she's being purposefully deceitful."

Jonathan gave an understanding smile. "I will be gentle with her, Carolyn, if the need to call her arises." He glanced back at the list. "The last name isn't really a name at all. But your mother remembers a barmaid from the cantina testifying. Even at the time, your mother couldn't understand what she had to do with it all since they had never set eyes on each other before."

"I wonder . . ." Carolyn thought back to Ramón's mother, to her dark, cold eyes filled with both pain and bitterness. She obviously hated the Stoners. "Did my ma say if she was a hostile witness?"

"They were *all* hostile, Carolyn."

"Well, I just met a lady at the cantina—" She stopped as she noted Sam's raised bushy eyebrows. "She's the mother of a friend of mine at the ranch," she hastened to explain. "Anyway, she owns the cantina now, but back then she was what I guess you'd call a barmaid. I talked to her, but she didn't say anything about testifying at the trial, and she had plenty of opportunity to talk about it. She hates the Stoners. Still, she might have been hostile toward my ma just because she was afraid of Caleb."

"What is her name?"

"Eufemia Mendez."

"We'll make a point of talking to her. There's only one other person your mother could think of whose testimony might possibly help. Unfortunately, he disappeared nineteen years ago."

222

"Who's that?"

"Jacob Stoner."

Carolyn paled as she remembered what Laban had said about Jacob and her mother. "No one's ever mentioned him at the ranch, except once. I tried to question Laban and he said . . ." She glanced uncertainly at Sam.

"What is it, Carolyn?" Jonathan urged.

"It's kind of a delicate subject."

"We're all going to have to have pretty tough skins," Jonathan said. "This won't be the only time we'll have to broach difficult subjects. For your mother's sake, we must forge ahead."

"Well, he said that my ma and Jacob . . . that they—"

Sam mercifully broke in. "Your ma told us all about that, Carolyn. None of it was true. Your ma and Jacob were friends and nothing else—not that your ma might not have wished for more, but she was committed to being faithful to her husband."

"I knew it couldn't be true, but, Sam, why didn't she ever say anything to me about it?"

"There was so much for her to tell you, Carolyn; I'm sure it didn't seem as important as the rest."

"Laban said he testified about this in the first trial. Won't it hurt Ma if he testifies about it again?"

Jonathan answered, "We'll just have to present your mother's character as such that no one would ever believe it. That won't be hard to do."

Suddenly a terrible thought occurred to Carolyn. "What if Jacob killed my pa? What if he's dead now, and the real murderer will never be found?"

"Have faith, child," said Sam. "The truth will be victorious."

Jonathan nodded. "Even if what you say is true, Carolyn, we still ought to be able to prove your mother's innocence without this Jacob. We only have to prove she didn't do it; we don't have to find the real killer."

In spite of the encouraging words, they all paused in a brief silence. It was nevertheless a sobering thought, and, though Jonathan Barnum might be reticent to say so, it would be a lot easier to prove Deborah's innocence if they could produce the real murderer. If that murderer no longer existed, their case would be that much more difficult to prove, especially when all the clues had been buried for nineteen years. Carolyn had some hopeless moments at the ranch, but now, seeing how little she had gathered in these many weeks was truly defeating. Caleb said they would need *new* evidence in order to free her mother, the one vital thing they lacked.

Despite her discouragement, however, Carolyn knew she could not give up. She had to keep hunting, searching, asking questions. She would not quit until—

She just couldn't give up, that's all.

As if this resolve physically propelled her, she rose from her chair. "I'd best be getting back," she said. "There's lots to do."

"You ain't going back there?" asked Sam, incredulous.

"Of course I am. What else do you expect me to do?"

"I don't know. But—"

"Sam," Jonathan put in, "if Carolyn is willing, I think that's the best place for her. If no harm has come to her by now, I doubt any will."

Carolyn knew it was wrong to keep quiet about Laban's attack and the ambush, and she'd probably regret it, but she also knew that if she said anything, Sam would have her locked up before he'd let her return. At least she had Matt helping her. She could not retreat from the ranch yet. She might not have been very successful so far, but she still believed she was probably the only one who'd be able to unlock any of the answers hiding on the Stoner Ranch.

"I have to return, Sam. But I will be at the trial. Maybe I'll come up with something by then, who knows?" Then she turned toward the lawyer. "Mr. Barnum, I'm glad to have met you. I guess you know how much we're all counting on you."

"Yes, I do, and I truly hope to be worthy of that trust," said Jonathan with true humility.

"If anyone can do it, you can, Jonathan," Sam said. "Carolyn, you should have seen him with the judge the other day. When that fella found out this was the man who nearly won the Republican Presidential nomination a few years back, he was ready to jump through flaming hoops to get the wheels of justice turning for your ma."

"In the end," Jonathan said, "the only thing that's going to matter is how I perform on the courtroom floor."

"I'm sure you'll do just fine." Carolyn felt a bit awkward about giving encouragement to such an important man, but Jonathan accepted it graciously.

"And you will do fine also, Carolyn!" He took her hands in his and looked deeply into her eyes as if he really understood all the confusion and pain this was causing her. "Yes . . . just fine!"

PART 11

DAY IN COURT

49

Carolyn was glad to be able to immerse herself in her mother's trial. If nothing else, it distracted her from her sense of helplessness—at least for a while.

It began on schedule Monday morning. Carolyn awoke before dawn, dressed in a white shirt and plain dark blue cotton skirt belted with a wide leather belt. No matter what happened, she would be there for her mother, even if she could help her in no other way.

Caleb, too, was ready to go when Carolyn met him in the dining room for breakfast. Although he showed some signs of lingering illness this morning, there was a glint in his eye and almost a spring to his step. He ate heartily, while Carolyn picked at her food. His eager anticipation of what lay ahead and his certainty that it would go his way put her in a sour mood. She hardly spoke during the fifteen-mile ride, nearly three hours in Caleb's buggy, to the little town of Leander where the trial would be held.

As in many small western towns that had no other large meeting halls, the courtroom was set up in the town's saloon, with the judge's table at one end opposite the bar so as to minimize the impression of being in a saloon. To the left of the judge's table were twelve chairs for the prospective jurors. Two other tables faced the judge—one for the prosecution and the other for the defense. Beyond this, also facing the judge, were six rows of chairs. It looked enough like a real courtroom . . . if you pretended not to notice the smell of whiskey or the long, oak bar with its bottle-lined shelves and large oil painting of a beautiful, voluptuous woman dressed in a red gown that showed all her features to best effect.

When Carolyn and Caleb entered the saloon just before nine in the morning, about two dozen people were milling about. Most were men, but there were five or six women also. Spectators continued to arrive, and Carolyn was surprised that there were so many. She supposed that some had been called by the court for jury duty, but that hardly could account for the numbers that eventually filled all the vacant seats and left people standing along the walls.

"Why do you think there are so many people, Grandfather?" Carolyn asked, worried.

Caleb only shrugged and grunted, the gleam fading from his eyes. Carolyn decided that if the size of the crowd displeased her grandfather, it must be a good sign for her mother.

After ten or fifteen minutes, the noise quieted. A man entered the saloon from a back entrance so that his path led directly to the front without having to pass through the spectators. He was a tall, well-groomed fellow in a dark brown broadcloth suit. Carolyn, who had never witnessed any court proceedings, thought he might be the judge—he looked distinguished enough to be. But he took a seat at the front table to the right of the judge's.

A few moments after he was seated, several other figures emerged from the back entrance. Sam and Mr. Barnum came first, immediately followed by Deborah and the sheriff.

An ache gripped Carolyn when she saw her mother, looking pale and thin in her shapeless gray prison dress. Even more difficult was to see her hands handcuffed in front of her as if she were some dangerous criminal. Carolyn wanted to jump up and scream at the sheriff for being so cruel. Mostly, though, she longed to run to her mother and hug her and know that everything was really all right, that the serene look on Deborah's face truly reflected what was inside.

Carolyn sat motionless, but she gazed at her mother until she caught her eye and received an encouraging smile from her. Carolyn tried to smile back, but it was a forced attempt. The emotions churning inside her worsened when Deborah's gaze shifted slightly to take in Carolyn's companion; Deborah's smile faded, and the light in her eyes dimmed.

Carolyn could not help stealing a glance at Caleb. His eyes were fastened on Deborah, even after Deborah looked away and took a seat at the other front table. Carolyn could not believe what she observed in that brief moment. Caleb's normally stern countenance took on the quality of granite, and his eyes had the cold chill of ice. She had always realized that her grandfather hated her mother, but in that instant Carolyn saw what real hatred was. It grieved her deeply that the man she had grown so fond of had such a capacity within him.

She forced her eyes away from her grandfather, but it was an effort to concentrate on the remaining activities.

The sheriff, after seeing Deborah to her seat and removing her handcuffs, strode to the front of the room.

"Okay, folks," he said in a tone that indicated his discomfort at speaking before such a large group, "this here court's now in session with the honorable Judge Claude R. Wilcox presiding. If you didn't check your gun with my deputy at the door, you best do so now, 'cause there ain't no guns allowed in here while court is in session. Now, all rise for the judge."

Everyone obeyed, and Carolyn took the opportunity during the shuffling and momentary disorder to glance about the room. Then she saw the only other familiar face in the room. Sheriff Pollard, with a stubbled face and red eyes, was standing against the wall toward the back. It was the first time she had seen him since the day he had led her mother away at gunpoint.

The hours following the trial's dramatic first moments were painfully dull for Carolyn. She soon realized that her secret hopes of a speedy finish were in vain. By the lunch recess, only two jurors had been accepted—a process, Barnum explained, that sometimes was the most time-consuming part of a trial.

Caleb had exited the saloon the moment the sheriff announced the recess, so Carolyn was able to visit with her mother for a few minutes.

"Is everything all right?" asked Deborah, taking her daughter's hands firmly in hers.

Carolyn was touched by her mother's concern; after all, she had far more to think about than Carolyn's well-being.

"Yes, now don't worry," said Carolyn. "I'm getting on very well. But I'm afraid I haven't been able to get much out of Caleb yet."

"I could see that."

"But I don't think it's hopeless, Ma. I really believe he . . . well, that he has some tenderness deep down inside. He's just kept it bound up for so long that it's gonna take time to get it loose."

"You may be right, Carolyn." Deborah did not sound fully convinced.

Carolyn wanted to say something positive to show that her time at the ranch had not been entirely wasted. But what hope could she offer?

"Well, I'm not finished poking into things at the ranch," she said buoyantly. "There are still some rocks that I can look under."

"Just don't do anything dangerous." Sam, sitting nearby, gave Carolyn a stern look of fatherly concern. "Sometimes there's snakes under rocks."

Carolyn began to regret saying anything. "I'll be careful."

229

"Well, we can use whatever you find, Carolyn," said Deborah with a sigh. "We haven't been able to turn up anything new yet, and that's what Jonathan says we'll need to win."

"That's not exactly right," said Jonathan Barnum, striding toward them from where he had been talking with the prosecuting attorney. "New evidence—in our favor, of course!—would make it a sure thing. But we have other possibilities. Not the least of which is favorable public sentiment. That crowd in attendance today indicates we have people's interest. You may not have noticed, but there were several newspapers represented out there—besides three Texas papers, there's a reporter friend of mine here all the way from Philly. This trial is going to make national news; and believe me, none of the charges against you, Deborah, are going to hold up under that kind of scrutiny."

"I don't really like the idea of so much notoriety," said Deborah. "But I suppose things might have gone differently nineteen years ago had everything been more out in the open."

"Don't get me wrong. Publicity isn't going to win this trial for us, but I don't think it will hurt, either. We still need a strong defense. It helps that the prosecution's case is built mostly on hearsay."

The court session ended at three in the afternoon. Three more jurors had been selected, for a total of five. It was frustrating for Carolyn, but she reminded herself that the longer these preliminaries took, the more time she had to find something that could really help her mother.

50

The entire second and third days of the trial were spent in choosing a jury. It was such a tedious, nit-picking process that Carolyn could hardly sit still. Just as Barnum seemed to find a satisfactory man to fill one of the twelve seats, the prosecution would conjure up some reason to reject him; and several times the defense disqualified the prosecution's choices. Carolyn could understand that since the first conviction was overturned because of bias. Therefore, the attorneys were being especially prudent in their selections. But did they have to be that careful?

On Thursday, it seemed as if the trial would begin in earnest. The prosecutor, James Fuller, made his opening statement.

"Gentlemen of the jury, we are here today to confront a nineteen-year-old crime. You may wonder why it matters what happened so long ago. Isn't it time to put the past behind us and move forward? But I remind you that in our great country there is no statute of limitations on the crime of murder, and for good reason. We hold life to be so precious that the loss of a single human being diminishes us greatly. It is thus our sacred duty to see that any act of murder against another person is always confronted, even if it takes twenty years to do so."

He continued for ten more minutes, talking about the American justice system, extolling its merits, seeming to forget that even the court, in allowing this retrial, had admitted that the system had failed miserably nineteen years ago. His premise, of course, was that because the system was so great, it could not possibly have failed. He dwelt on that idea for a long time before once again reminding the jury about the value of human life. Finally, he concluded passionately:

"The accused, Deborah Killion, has spent the ensuing years since that heinous crime in freedom and comfort. We must now forget her previous trial, for the court deemed there were irregularities causing it to be nullified in the eyes of the court. But let us never forget that a life was lost; a young man was killed, murdered in the prime of life. He had no years of comfort and fulfillment, for it was all snuffed out one night by a bullet shot into his back.

"After twenty years, there is still only one suspect for that crime—the woman we now see seated in this courtroom. It will fall to the people of the state of Texas to prove beyond all reasonable doubts that she did in fact on the night of July 2, 1865, with malice aforethought, by her own hand shoot and kill her own husband, Leonard Stoner.

"And it will fall to you, the esteemed jury, to convict Deborah Killion of the crime of murder in the first degree. And in that way, justice will at long last be served."

Carolyn watched the prosecutor take his seat, but she hardly *saw* him. The man's words clouded her mind so that she could concentrate on nothing else. *Malice aforethought . . . by her own hand . . . murder in the first degree.*

Carolyn glanced at her mother and was able to focus on her for

231

a moment. *Oh, Ma, please let it not be true!* she cried out in her heart. Then quickly berated herself. It *wasn't* true. She had to believe in her mother.

Jonathan Barnum spoke next. "Yes, gentlemen of the jury, your prime objective here today is to serve justice. That is all the defense asks, because when that objective is reached, this woman, Deborah Killion, will be completely exonerated of all guilt in this terrible crime. Thank you."

Carolyn gaped with astonishment as Barnum sat down. The prosecutor had spoken for twenty minutes and, by comparison, it seemed that Barnum was slighting Deborah with such a brief statement. Carolyn liked Barnum, and he had seemed sincere. But was he really doing all he could for her mother?

Then she saw Sam, who was sitting at the table with Barnum and Deborah, lean toward the lawyer and whisper something to him.

Sam was disturbed by the lawyer's brief speech. He wondered if they were getting their money's worth.

"That all, Jonathan?" he asked Barnum.

"I learned long ago that a jury doesn't appreciate long speeches. They want this ordeal over with as fast as possible. I have a feeling they are now much more sympathetic to our cause than they were half an hour ago."

Sam smiled, his respect for Jonathan Barnum soaring.

Carolyn saw her stepfather smile and wondered what was going on. Had she missed something?

But the prosecution was calling its first witness. "I would like to call to the stand Mr. Markus Pollard, former sheriff of Stoner's Crossing, and arresting officer."

Pollard walked forward, and Carolyn thought he was swaying a bit on his feet. Had he been drinking? She remembered Griff mentioning that the man had become a drunk. He certainly looked it.

The bailiff, the sheriff of Leander, held out a Bible and proceeded to swear Pollard in. "Do you swear to tell the truth, the whole truth and nothin' but the truth, so help you God?"

"Yeah," said Pollard, but he didn't look the man in the eye as he spoke.

Fuller, the prosecutor, strode forward. "Mr. Pollard, it is true that you were the sheriff of Stoner's Crossing at the time of the crime in question, July of 1865?"

"Yeah, that's right."

"How long had you held that position?"

" 'Bout five years."

"Did you see yourself as an experienced officer of the law?"

"I was, and I still am. I've put plenty of criminals behind bars and know what I'm about. Why, I reckon I was instrumental in cleaning up the streets of Stoner's Crossing."

Next to Carolyn, Caleb made a quiet "harrumph" sound and rolled his eyes. His disdain went unnoticed by all but his granddaughter.

"Do you have a clear recollection of the events in question?"

"Objection, Your Honor!" Barnum interrupted. "The witness is being asked to evaluate a purely subjective matter."

"Objection overruled," the judge said. "The court will decide if the witness's memory is adequate."

"It oughta be mentioned," Pollard went on, "that 'cause of the suspect being a woman and all, most folks ain't gonna easily forget what happened."

"Mr. Pollard," said the judge sternly, "you are only to respond to direct questions by the attorneys or myself. Unsolicited comments cannot be accepted." He turned to the stenographer. "Please strike Mr. Pollard's comments from the record."

When the judge indicated for the prosecutor to proceed, Fuller tapped his lips thoughtfully for a moment, then said, "Mr. Pollard, you were the arresting officer the night of Leonard Stoner's death, correct?"

"Yeah," Pollard answered, with a sidelong glance toward the judge.

"Do you recall when you arrived at the scene of the crime? And, in your estimation, how long was this after the time of the murder?"

"Well, the coroner figured Leonard was killed around midnight, 'cause that's when the first shots were heard. Caleb Stoner found the accused standing over the body not long after that, and he then sent a rider into town to fetch me. It probably took 'bout an hour for me to get back to the ranch."

"And how did you find things when you arrived?"

"Well, Caleb said nothin' had been touched, except that Mrs. Stoner had dropped the gun she had been holding and was laying on her bed in what I guess was shock."

"Would you describe the scene?"

"Lemme see . . ." Pollard rubbed the stubble of beard on his chin. "The body was laying on the floor, of course, near the glass doors that led to a kind of patio outside. He was on his side, his back to them glass doors. So, when you entered the room from the inside door on the other side of the room, you didn't right away see that he was shot."

"Why was that, Mr. Pollard?"

" 'Cause the bullet wound was in the man's back, that's why. He was back-shot, he was."

"Were there any signs of other disturbances in the room, signs of a struggle, perhaps, or a burglary?"

"Nope. The place was pretty tidy—oh, wait a minute, I do remember an overturned chair right next to the body, like he had tried to grab it as he fell—"

"Objection," Barnum said. "The witness is drawing a conclusion there about the chair. I ask that his last remark be stricken from the record."

"Your Honor," argued the prosecutor, "the witness is merely drawing a conclusion about a field in which his expertise has already been established—"

"It's been *mentioned,*" said Barnum, "but I cannot agree that it has been *established.*"

"You are quibbling over semantics."

"Just because the man was once a sheriff and has arrested a few people doesn't make him an expert on criminology, Mr. Fuller."

"Around here, Mr. Barnum," interjected the judge, "it is often the closest thing we have. This isn't Philadelphia or Washington."

"I understand the limitations of the frontier, sir," said Barnum, "but I still wish to have a ruling on my objection. If it were a minor point, I might relent, but this is an important aspect of my client's case, since she contends that there was indeed an intruder in the Stoner house that night."

"I will overrule your objection, Mr. Barnum. Keep in mind that you will have ample opportunity to cross-examine the witness and explore the strength of his statements."

Jonathan nodded at the judge, submitting to his ruling. It was true, he'd soon have his chance at the witness.

But the interchange seemed to send the prosecutor in a different direction. Fuller explained that for the benefit of the court and to erase lingering doubts, he would gladly establish Pollard's right to testify as an expert witness. And the next two hours were spent at that task. Fuller questioned Pollard about other murder investigations he had participated in, and Pollard took the opportunity to ramble on and on about his colorful, and sometimes sordid, experiences as sheriff. His rhetoric made him sound like a dime-novel hero.

Finally, the judge put a stop to the torture. "You have made your point, Mr. Fuller. I think even our esteemed defense attorney will accept the witness's credentials."

"Most heartily!" Barnum nodded.

"We will take a recess for the midday meal," said the judge. "When we return, I hope we can resume a more pertinent line of questioning."

After lunch, the prosecutor took another two hours to question Pollard. How he thought of that much to ask, Carolyn couldn't imagine. Even she didn't have so many questions. He tarried endlessly on such insignificant points that Carolyn almost lost interest.

At three o'clock the court session had to recess for the day. The saloon owner needed time to clean up his place and get everything back in order for the evening's activities.

51

Jonathan Barnum cross-examined Pollard the next day. His goal was to cast doubt upon the man's previous testimony by discrediting him as a witness. He was greatly helped in his purpose by the fact that Pollard looked as if he had never left the saloon after yesterday's court session.

"Mr. Pollard," Jonathan said, "in your previous testimony you stated that you had a clear memory of the events of—"

"Objection," Fuller said. "Those statements were stricken from the record." The prosecutor folded his arms smugly across his chest.

"My mistake," Jonathan said. "Let me rephrase my question. Your previous testimony indicated that you had an exceptionally clear memory of the events of nineteen years ago, down to such detail as to how the victim's body was arranged on the floor. Surely, if your memory of nineteen years ago is so clear, you will have no difficulty in describing to me your activities last night."

"Objection," Fuller repeated. "I don't see where this is leading or how it relates to the case."

"I think it will become clear as I proceed."

"I'm curious myself," the judge said. "Objection overruled."

"Now, Mr. Pollard, please tell me about last night." Barnum folded his arms and waited.

"Well . . . um . . . lemme see, I reckon I spent a few hours right here in the saloon. I'm from out of town, you see, and I ain't got no place else to go."

"What did you do here—play cards, visit, drink?"

"A little of everything, I suppose."

"How much money did you win at cards?"

"Ain't that a private matter?"

"Yes, I see your point. Let me phrase it another way: Did you win over ten dollars?"

"I don't think so."

"You don't *think* so? It was only a few hours ago, Mr. Pollard. You have no idea of your financial standing following the card game?"

"Um . . ." Pollard scratched his head and screwed up his face in intense thought. He put a hand inside his vest and started to remove a wallet.

"No fair peeking, Mr. Pollard. Let's forget that for a moment and think of something else. Perhaps you can tell the court how much 'liquid refreshment' you consumed."

"Maybe a couple of glasses of whiskey."

"I will remind you, Mr. Pollard, that you are still under oath."

"Well, now that I think of it, maybe a few more than that."

"Five glasses? Six? Ten?"

"What in blazes does it matter?" a frustrated Pollard exclaimed. "Who counts, anyway?"

"I can tell you I had three cups of coffee last night at dinner and one glass of milk with an excellent slice of apple pie."

"Okay, I don't remember how much I drank, and I don't remember how much money I won at cards!"

"Just to set your mind at ease, Mr. Pollard, the bartender tells me you drank half a bottle of rye whiskey, and you played no cards at all."

"That still don't got nothing to do with the murder," Pollard muttered defensively. "I wasn't that much of a drinking man back then."

"You did indulge in alcohol at least occasionally?"

"Sure! I was never no teetotaler."

"Your Honor," the prosecutor said, "the defense is defaming my witness's character, and I demand that he show cause. If he wishes to prove that Mr. Pollard was not in possession of all his faculties on the night of the murder, then let him state it clearly *and* provide adequate proof."

"Point well taken, Mr. Fuller," the judge agreed. "Mr. Barnum, what do you say to that?"

"My intent is not to defame character, but rather to show that a man given to frequent association with strong drink loses a portion of his memory capacity. And for this reason, I must call to question Mr. Pollard's detailed recollections of the events in question. It is important that we discern between a man's actual memory and what he has been told about certain events." Barnum looked at Fuller. "As far as proof goes, I have several depositions from some of Pollard's acquaintances in the last twenty years." He went to his table, withdrew a folder of papers from his briefcase, and handed it to the judge. "I will submit these to the scrutiny of the court. In essence, they state that over the years Mr. Pollard has been far less associated with sobriety than with drunkenness. Two of those statements are from lawmen who had to fire Mr. Pollard because of intemperance. His memory of Leonard Stoner's murder may be clear, but as long as there is even a slight question of it being otherwise, then I must refute his testimony."

"This entire trial, by its very nature, is based on memory," Fuller protested. "How do you propose we judge between what you call actual memory and acquired memory?"

"In my opinion, the first step would be to call witnesses whose memories are generally reliable."

"Your Honor, that is entirely subjective!" Fuller complained.

"Mr. Barnum, you make an interesting point," the judge said, "but the prosecutor is correct in debating the issue. Our role in this court is to establish facts. As attorneys you may disprove the validity of such facts by cross-examination and by discrediting the witnesses' so-called memory. However, I believe it will be self-defeating unless we rule on an individual basis. Thus, all recollections of the events of nineteen years ago will be acceptable to this court unless you attorneys can rule out individual instances—but this will only be acceptable *with cause,* not as a blanket action. Now, since there is no objection before me, will you proceed, Mr. Barnum?"

Jonathan glanced at Fuller, who nodded for Barnum to continue.

"I have no further questions," said Jonathan, much to the consternation of both the prosecutor and the judge.

"Call your next witness, then, Mr. Fuller," said the judge.

Thus it went throughout that day, the next, and, after the weekend, into the next week. The prosecutor called several more witnesses—Dr. Barrows, Mr. Vernon the banker, and several other citizens of Stoner's Crossing.

It became increasingly difficult for Jonathan to discredit the memories of these more upstanding and credible witnesses. He was confronted with hours of testimony to the fine character of Leonard Stoner and the marital discord between him and his wife. In the matter of the discord, the witnesses described what they saw—even Deborah could not dispute the truth of their statements. And, mirroring the trial nineteen years before, Deborah somehow came off looking like the villain.

After days of such testimony, even Jonathan was stymied, though he continued to put a positive face on it. "We must remember that this is the prosecution's case. We will have our day in court and our own witnesses."

But nothing could hide the fact that they had little more now than Deborah had years ago. Mabel Vernon had agreed to testify for the defense, in stark defiance of her husband. But besides a few character witnesses, they had little else to present. Each day the lack of a new breakthrough in the case became more painfully evident.

An extremely daunting blow came when the prosecutor called his next two witnesses. The first was an elderly woman named Betty Jenkins, who was introduced as the widow of Bob Jenkins. Mr. Jenkins had been the proprietor of the Stoner's Crossing General Store twenty years ago. He passed away ten years ago, and his wife had moved back to her hometown of Houston. Jonathan was truly dismayed at his error in not investigating Jenkins' family closer after he had discovered the man was dead.

He had to admit the prosecution had done some fine footwork in coming up with the storekeeper's wife after all these years. But then the most crushing factor in her testimony came to light—she had brought with her a record of the transaction in which Deborah had purchased a derringer from the store. Her husband, she said, never threw anything away. She had cartons full of old ledgers and receipts from when he owned the store. She also testified that she recalled when "Mrs. Stoner" bought the gun. She had been in the store at the time, and later her husband had admonished her not to tell a soul because it was meant to be a Christmas gift for Mrs. Stoner's husband.

A few days after the Christmas holidays, Mrs. Jenkins saw Leonard and asked him how he liked his wife's Christmas gift. When Leonard had no idea at all what she was talking about, she assumed she had gotten the matter mixed up with something else and dropped it.

In cross-examination, Jonathan tried to cast doubt upon her statement.

"You must have met with many people every day in the store, Mrs. Jenkins?"

"Oh yes. The place was always busy."

"It probably wasn't easy to keep everything and everyone straight."

"That's just it," said the woman, "most folks were always amazed at my memory. I never forgot a name or incident or conversation. My husband often said it was uncanny."

Jonathan questioned her memory of other long-past events, and though some of it couldn't be corroborated at the moment, it did reveal a woman with a sharp, lucid mind. Jonathan finally dismissed her, and the ledger that recorded the gun sale was admitted into evidence.

The final witness for the prosecution was Laban Stoner.

Carolyn was shocked when he appeared in the courtroom, for he had not come to town with her and her grandfather. Caleb didn't seem surprised at all, but gazed at his son with a very rare approving look.

"What was the character of your relationship to the defendant?" asked the prosecutor.

Laban shrugged. "She was my half brother's wife. I seldom saw her because I stayed away from the main ranch house."

"Why was that, Mr. Stoner?"

"I did not like the company of my brother, Leonard, or my father. It was best, for the sake of peace, to stay away."

"But none of this ill-feeling carried over to your brother's wife?"

"No. I did not care one way or the other about her—that is, until after my brother Jacob left."

"She had something to do with his leaving?"

"She was having an affair with him, and when Leonard caught them, Jacob was forced to leave or—"

"Objection!" Jonathan said. "The witness's statement is pure conjecture. No proof has been given to establish this as fact."

"Objection sustained," the judge ruled.

"How do you know they were having an affair?" Fuller asked with a smug glance toward Jonathan.

"I saw them together often, riding, meeting in secluded places."

"You followed them?"

"I did a couple of times because I was worried about what was going on. I was afraid of what Deborah Stoner was doing to my brother—to both brothers."

Jonathan cross-examined Laban incisively, but could not get him to budge from his statements. He also questioned him regarding his activities on the night of the murder. Laban said he couldn't remember. Jonathan literally bombarded him over this point but could not get him to waver an inch from his claim. Nor could the defense attorney find any other chinks in Laban's armor. Finally, the prosecutor objected that Barnum was badgering the witness. He pointed out that Laban Stoner was not on trial, and the judge agreed. Obviously discouraged, Jonathan dismissed Laban.

Jonathan did cause some question to linger over the statements regarding the alleged affair between Deborah and Jacob because Laban had to admit he never actually saw Jacob and Deborah involved in anything "compromising." But the implication of the so-called affair could not be removed from the minds of the listeners.

Since her first conversation with Laban, Carolyn had wanted to talk to her mother about the accusation of an affair with Jacob Stoner. But after the court session, Sam and Jonathan were cloistered with her, and then the sheriff had to take her back to the jail. Carolyn lost her nerve, and Caleb was anxious to return to the ranch. Once again she felt like she had as a little girl—knowing something was wrong, but never wanting to force the issue because down deep she was really afraid to know the truth.

Since it was Thursday, court was recessed until the next week because the judge wanted to spend some time with his family at his home in another part of the state. Carolyn hated to see the trial delayed, but what good would it do to rush things if there was no real defense to present? Time could only work in Deborah's favor.

52

Time ... Griff McCulloch had a great deal of it on his hands lately, and it was driving him crazy. Not to mention what it was doing to poor Yolanda who had to put up with him every day. At least Sky and Longjim could escape a good part of the time because of the ranch work.

As soon as the doctor allowed Griff out of bed, he hobbled to the corral, saddled one of the mounts, and tried to ride. He had broken open the wound in his side and had been forced back to bed for several more days. No one was happy about that; Yolanda had threatened to handcuff him to the bed if he tried such a stunt again. And since that setback, he had been more reasonable about his treatment. Like a good patient, he built up his strength by starting with short walks, gradually increasing daily. Finally, to Yolanda's great relief, he was up to spending his days puttering around the corral and stable area. He still didn't ride, but he could groom and feed the stock, muck out stalls, oil saddles—all the menial jobs he had once sneered at. Now he was thankful to have something—anything—to do.

Still, having to stick so close to home galled him. He was glad for the distraction of the stable chores, but there was definitely not enough action and challenge in grooming a horse to satisfy a man like Griff. There was a ranch to run! Even if it was summer and the roundup was over, there were still more interesting things to do out on the range than in the stable.

No one was surprised when Griff saddled up to ride long before the doctor advised. But he had learned from his previous mishap, and he took it easy. Day by day he rode farther and did more, soon resuming some of his duties as foreman.

Griff had moved back to the bunkhouse, and Sky found him there one afternoon upon returning from town.

"Howdy, Sky. Everything go okay in town?" Griff was lying on his bunk taking an enforced rest from the day's work.

Sky sat on the edge of the opposite bunk, wearing a grim look. "Griff, I got some newspapers while I was in town." He handed them to Griff. "Ma's trial began."

"Yeah, Sam wrote that it was gonna start."

"Read this paper from Austin," said Sky. "It doesn't look good."

Griff took the paper and read where Sky indicated. He shook his head.

"This here article's got her tried and convicted all over again," said Griff. "But it says only the prosecution has presented its case so far. Your ma hasn't had her chance yet."

"Do you think they've found anything new to make a case with?"

"Sam would have let us know if they had."

"That's what I was thinking." Sky's lips were taut, and his deep blue eyes looked darker than usual.

Griff noted how Sky had matured since his mother's departure weeks ago. Running the ranch—doing a man's job, and doing it well—had given the boy confidence. But where his mother was concerned he was still, in many ways, a little boy. He was only sixteen, even if he looked like a full-grown man; and whether he could admit it or not, he still needed her and was afraid of losing her.

Griff was concerned about Deborah, too. Not a day passed that he didn't wonder what was going on, and many days he had to talk himself out of riding down there. He didn't know exactly what he could do for her, but he hated being so helpless and far away. It was only worse now that he was better.

Griff looked up at Sky. "I reckon you got something on your mind, Sky? Maybe it ain't no coincidence you got these papers."

"Work has slowed down here at the ranch," Sky answered. "You're back on your feet, and—well, I figure I could be spared around here."

"So you can go to your ma's trial?"

"Yeah. I don't know what I could do, but I hate being so far away while all this is going on."

"That don't sound unreasonable, Sky."

"It doesn't?" For some reason the boy thought he'd get an argument.

"Not at all. In fact, I think I'll join you."

"You, Griff? But that's a long ride."

"I can handle it."

Sky looked intently at Griff, not so much with suspicion but with curiosity. "You got something else in mind, don't you, Griff?"

"I'll tell you, Sky, I've been giving this a lot of thought, and this newspaper just confirms it all. I reckon you're old enough to know what I been thinking, and also to never say anything to your ma or Sam."

"I am, Griff. But whatever it is, I want to be part of it." Sky knew that what Griff had in mind would involve some action, not just sitting around accepting what happened.

"I suppose you're old enough for that, too. It's just this, Sky; I swore long ago that I'd never let anything happen to your ma. I'm willing to give the court a chance 'cause that's what your ma wants. But if this trial thing goes against her, I ain't gonna stand by and let them hang her or put her in jail. She don't deserve it, and it ain't gonna happen."

"What would you do about it, Griff?"

"I think you know, Sky. If I have to, I'll do what I done nineteen years ago."

"Well, I'm with you, Griff," Sky said without hesitation. "We ought to leave right away, then, shouldn't we? There's no telling when this thing could end."

"Let's go in the morning. Slim and Longjim can run the ranch, and maybe hire a couple of extra hands—"

"I already did that while I was in town," said Sky.

Griff chuckled. "You're pretty sure of yourself, ain't you, young fella?"

"I wasn't gonna take no for an answer."

"I got a sneaky suspicion Slim and Longjim ain't gonna take no for an answer either."

Griff was right about that. After all, Slim and Longjim had been an integral part of Deborah's escape from the gallows once before, and it did seem only right—as they both pointed out vehemently—that they be included this time. Griff had to emphasize that they might not be needed at all, that the trial might end successfully and they'd have ridden all that way just to celebrate.

"That still don't sound like a bad idea," remarked Slim.

"You're all like family," Sky said. "It's only right for you to be there, whether it's for a celebration or an escape."

Griff relented, though he didn't much like not having a senior hand or family member around to run the ranch. But Gip McCarthy was a good, reliable cowboy; he had been with the Wind Rider outfit for two years and was qualified for the job. It would only be for a couple of weeks, and during one of the slowest times of the year.

So at sunup the next morning, followed by a cloud of Texas dust, four riders galloped away from the Wind Rider Ranch. Three of those riders were thinking of the time two decades ago when they had ridden together on a similar mission. But then it had been to make a statement and foil Caleb Stoner; now they were riding to help a dear friend.

53

The next morning after the court had recessed, Carolyn went riding. After the stifling atmosphere of the makeshift courtroom, it felt wonderful to be out in the open air, on the back of Tres Zapatos, with the smell of leather and horseflesh in her nose and the grit of trail dust in her eyes.

When Carolyn returned to the ranch shortly before noon and rode up to the stable, she saw a knot of five or six of the men standing near the corral talking. She could tell by their agitated manner that it was not casual talk. Something had happened.

She dismounted, and Ramón came up and took the reins. "What's going on?" she asked.

"More Stoner cattle are missing; about a hundred head," he said. "All from the same herd. Señor Laban is in right now talking to the Patrón. He told the men to arm themselves and get ready to go when he returned."

"Go where?"

"To the Bonnell place. There's gonna be trouble, Carolyn."

"Are they sure Bonnell did it?"

Before Ramón could answer, Matt Gentry strode out of the stable, coming toward them. The men looked over at him, and Carolyn saw immediately there was something strange in how they stared at him. Matt, too, had an odd look on his face—intense, serious, and just a little nervous. He walked up to the group of cowhands, although it was obvious he would have wanted to be anyplace else. But he seemed especially determined.

"What're you looking at me like that for?" he said to his fellow cowboys. "I ain't done nothing."

"'Course you ain't, Gentry," a man named Pete said in a sarcastic voice.

Another man, who seemed far more in earnest, then said, "It's the last thing I woulda suspected, Matt, but the fact is this is the second time a herd you was watching has lost cattle."

"That don't mean a thing, Andy," said Matt.

"We all know what you was before you came here," Pete said in a rough, accusing tone. "Seems to me you're just doing what comes naturally."

"Why you—" Matt took a threatening step toward the man, but Andy quickly stepped between the two antagonists, laying a restraining hand on Gentry's arm.

"Don't get yourself in more trouble, Matt," he said. "We're gonna give you the benefit of the doubt till we have all the facts."

"It sure don't look that way to me," said Matt hotly. He wrenched his arm from Andy's grasp and spun around.

He strode past Carolyn without a glance in her direction. She hurried after him. Since that night of the storm, she had come to think of him as a friend. She hoped she could help him now as he had helped her that night. If nothing else, perhaps she could at least be someone for him to talk to.

He was walking fast, and she had to jog a few steps to catch up to him, but when she reached his side, he still did not acknowledge her presence even with a glance. His eyes were trained ahead, his jaw set and taut. They walked in silence for several minutes, Carolyn having to double-step every so often to keep pace with him.

He walked out behind the stable several hundred yards, to where the fence rails enclosed the back pasture. A dozen horses and three or four colts were grazing and romping in the distance. Matt stopped, but only because the fence forced him to.

Still he did not look at Carolyn. "What do you want?" he snapped.

"I don't know, I just . . ." Suddenly she felt rather silly. He probably preferred to be alone and considered her presence a nuisance.

"It ain't true what they're thinking!" he burst out defensively.

"What exactly are they thinking?"

"You heard."

"I know it has something to do with the missing cattle, but I also know there must be more to it than that."

Continuing to fasten his gaze upon the horses in the pasture, he said, "About a month ago I was grazing a small herd out by Stony Creek. I was moving 'em for the roundup, and since we were short-handed at the time, I was by myself. There were only about seventy-five head, nothing I couldn't handle alone, even over one night. Except that during the night someone jumped me, knocked me out, and when I came to, the herd was gone. You know, without a trace. A couple fellas, including Laban Stoner, were suspicious; they said I couldn't have been senseless long enough for the rustlers to get away with the herd. But no one listened much to them—then. But it happened again last night, and even Toliver is listening now."

"You mean last night someone attacked you and stole cattle?"

"It was different this time. I was riding a line north of here where the Stoners still have open range. I went up there right after the dance—that's what I was doing when I met you during the storm. I knew I should have ridden back to the ranch and told someone the minute I suspected something. I could have told you that night, but I wanted some hard evidence. Now, all I've done is got myself tangled up worse than ever!"

"Well, what happened?"

"I was up there about a week and a half checking the cows for screw worm and doctoring 'em if it was needed, bringing back strays, mending what fence there is up there—well, you know as well as I do what a line rider does. I saw some strangers riding up there—"

"That's up by the ridge, isn't it?" interjected Carolyn.

"Yeah, and it wasn't far from there that I last saw the strangers. That's why I didn't want you going up there alone, aside from the fact that it's a plain dangerous trail. The cabin we were in is two or three miles from there, and some ten from the cabin I was using. Mr. Stoner's got four line cabins up at the far boundaries of his land, each about ten miles apart. Well, I tried to track the strangers, but they gave me the slip. I took to scouting at night a couple of times to see what I might find. The night before last I was real tuckered out so I decided not to patrol that night—it wasn't part of my job anyway; it was just something I was doing for curiosity's sake.

"Sure enough, that morning when I went patrolling, there was cattle missing—a hundred head or more. I spent most of yesterday looking, just in case they'd strayed off, but I knew it had to be more than that. An Apache couldn't have tracked them cattle."

"They just disappeared?"

"That's what I been saying, but no one believes me. They think I'm in cahoots with Bonnell's outfit. And I can't prove a thing. Twice cattle under my care have been lost. And whoever's doing it is being real careful."

"You think you're being set up?"

"Of course!" he shot back as if her question meant she didn't believe him.

"But with no proof, it does look pretty bad for you, Matt."

"Yeah, and I'm probably gonna lose my job, too, and my reputation with it. I'll never work again."

"I'm sorry, Matt."

"Do you believe me, Carolyn?" His tone indicated that it really mattered to him.

She hesitated a moment too long.

"Why should you?" he retorted. "After all, I admitted that I used to rustle cattle. Why should I even try to live that down?"

"It's not that I don't want to believe you—"

"Forget it," he said sharply. "I was out rustling cattle."

"Come on, Matt. At least I'm willing to give you the benefit of the doubt. What else can I do?"

"Thanks a lot!" he sneered. "I don't expect you to believe me; you don't know me from Adam, anyway. Just take Sean Toliver's word for it—you know him *real* well!"

"How dare you!" Carolyn spun around and stalked angrily away.

"Carolyn, I'm sorry," he called after her.

But she was too furious to listen. She had only wanted to help him, to be a friend. He had repaid her by being rude. Maybe he *was* a cattle rustler. How should she know? She *didn't* know him. If he was innocent, he ought to be able to come up with some proof.

Then she immediately thought of her mother, falsely accused of a crime with no way, it seemed, to prove her innocence. Sometimes the truth was not as it appeared, no matter what others might say. Perhaps she was being unfair to Matt. True, she didn't know him well, but that night of the storm he had seemed a genuinely good man.

Perhaps she ought to give Matt more of a chance. He was probably telling the truth about why he was out that night of the storm. And he had been honest about his past, about the trouble with the law. The least she could do was listen to him.

She turned back toward the pasture, but Matt was gone.

54

Carolyn returned to the house. As she entered, she met Caleb, Laban, and Sean as they were exiting Caleb's study. Much to her surprise, Laban and Sean would be joining her and her grandfather for the midday meal. It was the first meal either of them had had in the house since she had been there. Apparently the men had not finished discussing the rustling problem.

At the table, the subject of Matt Gentry came up. Sean was willing to give him another chance, but Laban wanted to fire the man on the spot.

"I don't think he did it," Carolyn found herself saying, wishing she had exhibited similar faith within Matt's hearing.

"What do you know about all this?" asked Caleb, just barely covering his disapproval of her entering into male affairs.

"Just what I've heard here and there," she said. "And I've spoken to Matt a couple of times and he seems like a nice, honest fella."

"Maybe you don't know he was involved in rustling before he came here," said Sean, seeming to suddenly change sides. "I already gave him a chance when I hired him on."

"Without mine, or my father's, knowledge, I might add," said Laban acidly. "We ought to fire you along with him."

"Now, wait a minute!" protested Sean.

But Caleb broke in, his tone cool and even. "What's done is done. And there is no proof against the man."

"Since when do you care about proof?" sneered Laban.

"Watch your tongue, *boy*." Caleb glared at his son.

"Does your granddaughter call all the shots around here, now?" Laban shot back.

"Simmer down, Laban," Caleb warned. "I want to keep this man—Gentry, isn't it?—on the payroll. We'll keep an eye on him. He can't be working alone—" Then he added with a glance toward Carolyn, "If he's involved at all. If he is in on this, he can lead us to the rest of the gang, possibly to Bonnell."

"So, Boss," said Sean, "does that mean you don't want us to ride over to Bonnell's place and put the fear of God into them? I told the boys to be ready."

"This isn't the old days, Toliver." Caleb seemed disappointed at that fact. "We can't go shooting up a man's place, or hauling him out to be lynched anymore on pure hearsay. Bonnell is rallying many of the small ranchers around him. To them, he's a hero, probably a kind of Robin Hood."

"Call in their loans," Laban said. "You hold most of the notes. Put them out of business."

Caleb shook his head. "Don't be stupid, Laban! I don't want to turn this county into a battlefield, and that's just what could happen—a full-fledged range war. We've got to catch the rustlers red-handed. Then the other ranchers will be forced to desert Bonnell because they're not going to want to risk supporting a proven rustler. I want to catch the thieves and string them up, but not at the cost of the peace of this entire region."

"At what cost then?" Laban asked. "In the last six months we've already lost five hundred head of cattle. I say it's time Bonnell was stopped before *he* puts *us* out of business!"

"Keep that hot head of yours in check. We'll get the culprits my way, you hear?" Caleb turned to Sean. "You keep a loose rein on Gentry; give him enough slack to hang himself with, understand?"

"Okay, Boss."

"Aren't we about ready to move that herd we have grazing south of here up to the pasture in Buck's canyon?" asked Caleb.

"Well, Boss, Laban and I discussed that, and we weren't too impressed with the grass up there this season. We thought Duff's Valley east of there'd be better."

"All right, put Gentry on that drive. Make sure he gets plenty of time alone with the herd. Shorthand them if you have to. Let's see what happens."

After lunch, Sean contrived to get a moment alone with Carolyn when Caleb and Laban left the dining room ahead of them. Though he eyed her with his usual lust, there was something else in his eyes she couldn't quite identify—seriousness, perhaps—*deadly* seriousness. And it was accompanied by a hard edge to his voice.

"What's this sudden interest you've got in Matt Gentry?" he asked.

"I said before, he just doesn't seem like the dishonest type—"

"He admitted to quite a bit of dishonesty in his past."

"Can't a man change?"

"Sure, but that doesn't answer my first question—why it should matter to you."

"I just like the guy and I don't want to see him get into trouble, that's all."

"Are you sure?"

"Why, Sean, I think you're jealous!"

"Maybe I am. I just don't like anyone messing in my territory."

Being thought of as "territory" irked Carolyn, but she was nonetheless flattered by the notion that a man like Sean cared so much about her that he was actually jealous. Another girl might have played this interesting situation to its fullest extent, but such an idea didn't even enter into Carolyn's mind. And even if it had, she simply would not have known what to do about it, for she had never learned such feminine wiles.

"Sean, there's absolutely nothing like that between me and Matt—I'm not even sure if that's what there is between you and me."

"I thought we rode over this trail before."

"I guess nothing's changed."

He gave her cheek a pat. "You are something else, Carolyn. I might even say I've never met anyone quite like you before."

She couldn't tell if he meant it as a compliment or not. And Sean didn't give her a chance to ask, for immediately after speaking he turned on his heel and strode from the dining room. And, as usual, Carolyn was left with a slightly hanging jaw, and a confused mind.

55

Court convened Monday, and Doc Barrows was recalled to the stand and later cross-examined carefully by Jonathan as to the location of Leonard Stoner's wound. This went on for some time until the prosecution objected that the cross-examination was accomplishing nothing. Jonathan pointed out that he wished to establish before the jury that the assumption that Leonard had been shot in the back was just that—an assumption.

"It was considered a fact in the previous trial," argued the prosecutor.

"That was a *mis*trial," emphasized Jonathan. "The purpose of this trial is to right the wrongs committed then. There was never any proof on that point except the word of the good doctor here, and the testimony of the most hostile witness, Caleb Stoner. We cannot accept the location of the wound as fact without incontrovertible proof."

"There is the testimony of Sheriff Pollard," said Fuller.

"Yes, the sheriff . . . whose job depended on the good graces of Caleb Stoner."

"Now, wait a minute!" shouted Pollard from his seat among the spectators. "You calling me a liar?"

The judge pounded his gavel on the table. "We'll have order in this court," he said. "I will not have outbursts from the spectators."

Jonathan went on calmly, ignoring Pollard. "We cannot have a repetition of the travesty perpetrated nineteen years ago. The foundation of this trial must be based on facts, not merely the testimony of witnesses whose viewpoint must be questioned because of their close association to the principals of this case."

"Do you have such facts?" asked the judge.

"I must remind the court that the burden of proof rests on the prosecution," answered Jonathan with exaggerated respect.

"Then let us get on with our case," the prosecutor said snidely.

Without new evidence, it was the best Jonathan could do at that point to cast doubt on so-called facts from the first trial.

On Tuesday, the prosecution completed the presentation of its case with two surprises. The prosecutor presented its final witness, saying smugly, "She is someone who is in no way closely associated with the principals of the case."

It was Eufemia Mendez.

"Señora Mendez," asked Fuller, "can you tell the court what you do in Stoner's Crossing and what you were doing there nineteen years ago?"

"I own La Rosa Cantina. Nineteen years ago I was an employee of the cantina."

"An employee . . . would that be the same as a saloon girl?"

"Yes."

"Did you know the deceased, Leonard Stoner?"

"He was a customer at the cantina."

"A frequent customer?"

"No more than most of the men in town. Most of our customers

251

are the Mexican residents, but the gringos come, too, for a change of pace."

"So, you had merely a business relationship with him?"

"Yes, of course."

"He never spoke of personal things to you?"

"Occasionally he did, as did all the men who came. You know, sometimes strong drink loosens a man's tongue. Señor Stoner was no different."

"Do you remember any of those personal conversations with Mr. Stoner?"

"I remember because of all that happened later, and because I was made to testify in the other trial. For the most part he complained about his unhappy marriage. He said he'd never know for sure if her child was his. He was, of course, greatly disturbed by this. I don't remember all the details of what he said, but I had little doubt that the poor man had been cuckolded."

"Thank you, Señora Mendez."

Even Carolyn caught the prosecution's sly technique of dismissing the witness and allowing the final damning word, *cuckolded,* to be left ringing in the jury's ears.

And, because of Eufemia's cool, aloof demeanor, Jonathan could do little to discredit her statement. He decided to take a different tack.

"Señora Mendez, you stated that you were an employee at the cantina at the time of Leonard Stoner's death. Who owned the establishment then?"

"Alvarez Domingo."

"He paid you for your services?"

"Yes."

"Do you know what his financial situation was at that time?"

"I only worked there."

"You seem to have intimate knowledge of a mere customer's marital status, yet you say you had no idea that Mr. Domingo was on the verge of bankruptcy at that time?"

"Oh yes, now that you mention it, there was talk of that."

Jonathan smiled. "Must have slipped your impeccable memory."

Eufemia's color rose momentarily, and the prosecutor uttered a disgruntled groan.

Jonathan continued. "I have here documented proof of Mr. Domingo's financial state which I unearthed among some old, buried bank records." In lieu of anything more substantial, Jonathan and Sam had spent a great deal of time looking into the backgrounds of the wit-

252

nesses in the previous trial. "As a matter of fact, the cantina was about to revert to the holder of the loan note—one Caleb Stoner. You did not know this, Señora Mendez?"

"Everyone knows that Caleb Stoner owns or controls everything in and around Stoner's Crossing."

"Who holds the note on the cantina now?"

She hesitated before answering. "Caleb Stoner."

"No further questions," said Jonathan as he took his seat.

The final surprise of the day was that the prosecutor rested his case without calling Caleb Stoner. It at least was a surprise to Carolyn. Jonathan said he expected it because Caleb was too close to the events to be objective, and Fuller knew Jonathan would use that to refute Caleb's testimony. Jonathan was still undecided about whether he'd call Caleb as a witness. It was always tricky for the defense to use a hostile witness.

Although it was only Tuesday, the judge called a recess until the following week because he needed to attend other cases on his circuit.

When Sam suggested protesting the delay, Jonathan reminded them that a delay was an advantage for them.

"This is nothing unusual," Jonathan said, "especially when working with a circuit judge. Even in the city, our courts are faced with a multitude of delays. We will just have to be patient and remember the saying, 'Justice, even if slow, is sure.' "

"I reckon things like this teach patience," Sam said, "and I'm needing to learn it more than anyone."

Carolyn tried to keep that in mind as she kissed her mother goodbye and watched the sheriff escort her away. A delay might help the case, but it couldn't be doing much for her poor mother, who must spend night after night in a jail cell. And patience was simply not one of Carolyn's virtues.

PART 12

MYSTERIOUS ARRIVAL

56

Carolyn knew she shouldn't allow herself to get sidetracked from her problems or her mother's. Matt Gentry could not only take care of himself, but he'd probably be downright resentful of aid from a girl. Nevertheless, when she returned from Leander that day and heard that cattle were being moved to Duff's Valley, she had a strong urge to join the drive. And, since she was feeling absolutely helpless where her mother was concerned, she saw no reason not to.

Sam and Mr. Barnum had contacted everyone in town who had been even remotely connected with the murder, and Carolyn was sure they were far more competent than she in such work. She had tried and tried to get Caleb to talk to them, but he had refused. This recess would drive her crazy with helplessness and boredom if she didn't find something to distract her.

So the next morning Carolyn decided to ride out to the cattle drive. Caleb, of course, forbade her to do so, and even threatened to lock her in her room. But Carolyn proved her Stoner blood beyond all doubt when she stubbornly stood up to him.

"First, you talk about giving the ranch to me, Grandfather; then you act outraged because I want to be a *rancher*. I'm the closest thing you're gonna have to a grandson, so you better learn to appreciate me, and the fact that if I *were* ever to have this ranch, I'd take doggone good care of it."

That argument left Caleb speechless. He shook his head, threw up his hands, and made no more protests; however, he did insist on accompanying her as a chaperon.

"I really don't think that's necessary," she said.

"Don't tell me your mother allowed you to spend the night alone on the trail with cowhands!" He spoke as if this were nearly as heinous a crime as the one for which Deborah now sat in prison.

"No, I reckon not," admitted Carolyn. "I guess there was always someone like her or Griff along. But, Grandfather, do you think you're up to it? I mean, after being ill?"

"I am not yet a doddering old man, young lady."

The men, two others besides Gentry, were uncomfortable at having the boss and his granddaughter join them on the drive. It was absolutely unprecedented for them to have a female along on such an event, but Carolyn proved her usefulness by taking charge of the small remuda of twenty horses, thus freeing the men to keep better control of the herd.

The herd had been grazing near the dried-up riverbed, the very place Sam had discovered when trying to gain entrance to the ranch several weeks ago. Not only was the grass getting low, but the sole water source, a small natural pond, was nearly dried out. That last rainstorm had been the only rain in months, and it had not lasted long enough to replenish the pond. Duff's Valley, some thirty miles to the northwest, had not been used all season and still had a good water supply and plenty of grass. It was a three-day drive to move the cattle, and Caleb and Carolyn joined the herd on the second day out.

That night the herd was bedded down on a small rise a couple hundred yards from camp. The guard was divided into three three-hour shifts. They usually had more hands available, but for a small herd of five hundred head and only thirty miles to cover, it was manageable. Carolyn volunteered to ride "cocktail," that is, to guard the herd while the men ate dinner before the first night-shift began at around eight in the evening.

The men didn't know how to respond to this, but they conceded when Caleb rolled his eyes and said, "Don't try to argue with her, boys; she's got too much mule in her."

"Too much Stoner blood, you mean!" she countered playfully, then rode off to her task.

The men were glad to have the break; mealtimes had been especially difficult and usually meant that one man would have to have a longer guard shift. There was no chuck wagon on this short drive; each man carried his own hardtack and dried beef. Brewing coffee over the campfire was the only cooking done.

Just as the sun was dipping out of sight behind the ridge of hills Carolyn had tried to reach the night of the storm, she was relieved by one of the men, so she could have her own dinner. Matt greeted her at camp with a cup of hot coffee, and she hunkered down in front of the fire with the others. It was a warm night, and the fire was hardly necessary for warmth, but it lent a cozy, comfortable feeling to the evening and was allowed to flame at least until it burned itself out.

The men got to talking in low tones, mostly telling stories, lulling Carolyn along with a sense of delightful security. Caleb even joined into the storytelling with accounts of drives he had accompanied on the Chisholm Trail during the heyday of the big cattle drives in the seventies. He had stories of stampedes and Indian attacks that sent chills through even the seasoned cowboys.

"I'll tell you my most terrifying experience," said Caleb, "and it wasn't a stampede or an Indian attack—it wasn't even on a drive. This happened a good many years ago when I was much younger. One winter I was riding up near Buck's Canyon cutting ice out of the water holes so the stock could drink. One of the worst blizzards I've ever been in hit, and I couldn't beat the storm back to a line cabin. My horse froze out from under me, and I knew if I didn't do something fast, I'd die, too. So, I took out my long knife, slit that horse's carcass down the middle, glad to see his innards were still steaming and warm. I scooped what I could out and climbed in and waited out the storm, which, thank God, lasted only another hour or two. I was as snug as a babe in a cradle. No, there's nothing more terrifying than Texas weather when it decides to turn against you."

"That was some mighty fast thinking, Boss," commented Gentry.

"That's what survival is all about," said Caleb.

"Yep," said Gentry. "And, if I plan on surviving this drive I better get some shut-eye. My guard duty'll be here before I know it."

At last Gentry and the other cowhand bedded down at one end of the camp, and Carolyn at the other, with Caleb somewhere in between like a dutiful chaperon. Carolyn dozed off immediately, but in the night she awoke and could not go back to sleep. Rather than lie there feeling the hard ground beneath her, she decided to get up. She saddled her horse while Caleb and the two cowboys slept and rode out to the herd, taking it nice and easy so as not to spook the cows.

A quarter moon was up, shedding just enough light to illuminate the placid herd, while in the distance the peaceful, mournful strains of a little tune were being whistled.

Carolyn knew the tune; she'd heard it sung often at the Wind Rider Ranch.

Oh, the cowboy's life is the life of the wind
As he clatters across the plains,
With a laugh and a yell and a hearty word,
And a smile at the driving rains.

Then, as if harmonizing with her thoughts, Matt Gentry's voice caught up the words of the night-song the cowboys liked to sing to soothe and quiet the herd:

Oh, the cowboy's life is a life of flame
As he clatters across the plain,
While the coyote howl in the gathering night,
But the dreams he sees are vain.

Oh, the cowboy's life is a life of dust,
Though the cowboy laughs at fear,
But when he travels the last, long trail
Is there no one to drop him a tear?

No one could pity himself better than a cowboy, and perhaps no one had more reason for a little pity. A cowboy's life was, indeed, one of hard, grueling work. But most cowboys wouldn't trade it for anything, in spite of the fact that they could gripe and complain with more flair than most working men.

Carolyn smiled to herself as she thought of all the cowboys she knew—Griff, Longjim, Slim, Matt, Sean, and many others. Even Caleb had proved himself to be a cowboy at heart with his stories this evening at the campfire. And Carolyn couldn't help but envy them all. No matter how hard she tried, a woman would probably never truly fit into that peculiar and dangerous life.

Carolyn sighed, remembering how often her mother had tried to convince her that being a female had its own merits. "The men may seem to have all the fun, Carolyn," she'd say, "and maybe they get all the glory. But the women are the heart and soul of the frontier. The rooster may crow, Carolyn," Deborah would grin, "but it's the hen that delivers the goods. Maybe women are the *unsung* heroes, but the whole fabric of the West would unravel in a blink without them."

Deep in thought, Carolyn didn't notice the sound of the music getting closer. When she finally began to focus on her surroundings, Matt Gentry was less than fifty yards away.

"Howdy, Matt," she said quietly, just loud enough for him to hear, but careful a sharp sound didn't spook the herd.

"What're you doing out here at this hour?" Matt rode up next to her.

"Couldn't sleep."

"Now, I'm not only gonna be in trouble for rustling, but also for tarnishing a lady's reputation!"

"Don't be silly," said Carolyn. "Besides, my grandfather is sawing logs. I don't think a stampede would wake him."

"So, why are you here, Carolyn?"

"Told you, I couldn't sleep."

"I mean, why'd you join the drive?"

Carolyn looked out at the herd, reluctant to tell him the truth because it sounded so arrogant, so meddlesome. But since he already must think very little of her after their last meeting, she decided she had nothing to lose by being honest.

"I felt bad about the other day, Matt. I was hoping I could make up for it somehow, maybe help you some way."

"Out here on the drive?"

"Maybe you don't realize it, but there's a reason why you didn't get fired the other day."

"I figured they were keeping me on so as to lead them to the rest of the rustlers."

Carolyn nodded. "That doesn't bother you?"

"Maybe I *can* lead them to the rustlers—the *real* rustlers. Anyway, next time those varmints try to pull something on me, I'm gonna be ready for 'em."

"Well, it might help to have someone on your side when that happens in order to back you up and verify your story."

"You?"

"Is there anyone else around willing to take the job?"

Gentry chuckled, then looked at Carolyn frankly. "I ain't ever met anyone quite like you, Carolyn."

Sean had said almost the same thing to her the other day. Somehow it sounded different when Matt said it, more like a compliment.

"So, do you plan on nursemaiding me wherever I go?" he asked after a short pause. Then he smiled. "It's kind of ironic, now that I think on it."

"'Cause I'm just a girl?"

"Naw! Nothing like that. It's just that . . . aw, nothing, forget it. I'll welcome your help, only I don't want you taking away from what you really came here for. Your ma comes first."

"I know that, and I don't know how I'll be able to do both. But to tell the truth, I feel pretty helpless where my ma is concerned. Now that she's got that fancy eastern lawyer, I don't see where I can do more or better than him."

"I can use some help right now, watching over this herd. You ever do that before?"

"Yeah, we ride in opposite directions in a circle around the herd to catch any strays and to make sure they ain't getting restless."

"Okay. Let's go." He lifted his reins, then stopped and added, "It also wouldn't hurt to look out for . . . anything unusual out there."

"That's exactly what I was thinking."

Nothing "unusual" happened that night. Perhaps the rustlers knew that Matt would be extra wary now that he'd been duped twice before. Carolyn was disappointed, because she had hoped to settle the doubts about Matt once and for all. But there was still one more day and night left of the drive.

57

Carolyn slipped into her bedroll that night while everyone was still asleep. She and Matt decided it was best that no one knew she had joined him on his watch. The rustlers would never make a move if they thought he wasn't alone, so the quieter they could be about it the better. Not to mention the fact that Caleb would have a fit if he knew she was out like that unchaperoned.

The next day was fine for driving cattle. A stiff breeze diffused some of the summer heat, and coming out of the northwest, it helped keep the clouds of cattle-raised dust out of the drover's eyes. They bedded the herd down about half a mile from the foot of the ridge Carolyn had noted the night of the storm. It was a notable elevation in that flat country, but she'd learned that's about where the Texas Hill Country began.

"We use Buck's Canyon up there, off and on," Matt commented, noting the direction of her gaze as she staked out the remuda. "It usually has plenty of good grass. In fact, I don't know why we ain't taking this herd up there. We haven't used it for two seasons, and the grass has got to be better than at Duff's. The water, too. And it's closer."

"Sean said the grass wasn't any good there," said Carolyn.

"That's funny. Oh, well, he's the foreman."

This last night of the three-day drive, the men were dog-tired. No one had had a good night's sleep since it had begun. Caleb, too, was exhausted, for it had been years since he'd been in the saddle so long at a stretch. When Carolyn rode into camp from riding "cocktail," she met a quiet, glum collection of men. One of the boys played for a while on his harmonica, but no one was interested in singing and he soon gave up. Before long, Matt stood, stretched, and announced he was turning in. He had the last watch of the night and was looking forward to six hours of uninterrupted sleep before he had to guard the herd.

Caleb looked as if he wanted his bed, too, but he made no move in that direction until the other cowboy crawled into his bedroll for the night. Caleb was determined to be the watchful chaperon. But Carolyn was not in the least bit tired. In fact, she felt an odd sense of excitement stirring within her, an inexplicable feeling of expectation, anticipation. Was this going to be the night the rustlers would make an attempt on the herd? Or was it something else? She had to admit that this peculiar sensation had been gradually building all day. Maybe it was merely because she *wanted* something to happen.

Carolyn dutifully said good-night to Caleb and went to bed anyway.

But sleep eluded her, and the snores from the men only made it worse. Finally she slipped quietly from her bed. She wished Matt had his watch now. By the time his turn came, she'd probably be sleepy.

She saddled her horse, quietly led the mare away from the camp, then mounted. She started out toward where the cattle were bedded down, thinking to pass the time with the cowhand on duty. Then the ridge, bathed in silvery light from the rising moon, caught her attention. The sky was clear tonight, with no pending storm to darken the trail. In fact, the light from the moon almost beckoned her. What was it about this place that drew her? Was it only every Texan's fascination with high places and trees, so rare in most of this country? Or was it more?

It wasn't hard to find the trail that led up the ridge. She had expected the mesquite and underbrush to be thick from disuse, but she was relieved at the relative ease she had in traversing it. Perhaps farther on she would encounter obstacles, and so she picked her way carefully over the path. Her efforts would be rewarded, she thought, once she gained the top and commanded a view of the whole valley.

As she made her way something began to nag at her. Matt said they hadn't used this canyon for grazing in two seasons . . . why, then, wasn't it more overgrown? Not only that, but the trail was trampled. Almost as if—

Carolyn quickly dismounted. Going down on one knee, she had a closer look at the trail. This trail had definitely seen use, and very recently. And not from just horses, either. Cattle had been driven along this way, within the last week since the storm. The path was strewn with dung.

She jumped back on her horse. If her suspicions were correct, good sense would have told Carolyn to go back to camp and get help. But she was too excited to give much thought to wisdom and consequences. Besides, if the rustlers were using this canyon to get away with cattle, it would be stupid to alert them by bringing a bunch of cowboys clattering up here. It would be better if she quietly checked things out to see if her fears were founded before alerting everyone. If only Matt were with her!

She moved now with greater stealth than ever. Would the rustlers be here now? Did they have some kind of hideout here? Why hadn't anyone thought to examine this place before?

As she proceeded farther up the trail, she saw evidence of just what an ideal place this could be for rustlers. It did not appear to be a box canyon or a single ridge at all, but rather a series of rugged ridges with broad swaths of pasture and nicely concealed behind hills. It might not be the first place you'd think of, especially if you weren't familiar with the area. But surely the Stoners knew this ridge well.

Maybe she was wrong, then; maybe there was no outlet. The series of hills and pasture could come to an end, perhaps in less than a mile, and in the dark, she just could not see where. But why bother bringing the stolen cattle in here only to have to drive them back over the same trail and out again? If Bonnell were stealing the cattle, he could use the seclusion of the canyon to change the brands. Then he could lead the animals back to graze on the open range again and claim the cows fair and square.

That still failed to answer the most nagging question of all: How did they think they could get away with such an operation right under Caleb Stoner's nose? Surely this canyon had to have been investigated.

Carolyn's thoughts were suddenly cut short by a sharp sound. Tres Zapatos heard it, too, and pranced restively.

"Easy, girl."

Carolyn swallowed hard, her pulse raced. Someone was out there. And whoever it was had to have seen her, for she had hardly been trying to hide. The rustlers? Or whoever had tried to ambush her before? What had she gotten herself into? She could almost hear Griff groaning about her "blamed curiosity." There was no way she could make a run for it on this trail, but she turned her mount anyway. Perhaps whoever it was did not want to be discovered any more than she did. They might just let her go—

264

"Do not move!" The voice came out of the darkness like a muffled shot.

"Okay!" she answered. "Don't get jumpy now; I ain't moving." With great care, so as not to make a sound, she reached into her saddlebag for her weapon, hoping the darkness would conceal her movement.

"You don't listen very good." A gun hammer cocked, and Carolyn froze with her hand on the flap of the bag.

A figure stepped out into the open, but still shrouded in the shadow of a mesquite bush and out of reach of the moonlight. Carolyn tried to peer into the stranger's face but it, too, was in shadows under a big sombrero.

"Look, I ain't armed," said Carolyn holding her empty hands in the air. "So why don't you put that gun away and we can talk friendly like."

"Get off your horse—very carefully, now."

Carolyn obeyed.

"Yes," said the man, "I would like to talk to you also—like a friend. The gun was only to guard against your possible trigger-happy reaction. I thought you were someone else."

"Who would that be?"

"It's not important."

Carolyn jerked her head toward the man's gun. "So, you gonna get rid of that thing?"

He holstered his weapon, then moved a few steps away from the bushes. Carolyn still could not get a very clear appraisal of him except to note that he had dark skin, with black hair and a heavy moustache that nearly hid his lips. He was probably Mexican or maybe mulatto; it was just too hard to tell. But his looks were of less concern than one other important detail. Was he one of the rustlers?

"Who are you?" Carolyn asked.

"I go by many names; Santiago is one."

"What're you doing up here?"

"I might ask the same of you."

"I was tracking rustlers."

He looked askance at her comment, tilting his head back so that she got a better view of him. He was a swarthy, good-looking man, perhaps in his forties, and almost certainly Mexican. His moustache hid his mouth so that Carolyn couldn't read his facial expressions easily, but his eyes, dark and intense as they reflected the silver rays of the moon, were neither hard nor cold. They weren't exactly friendly, but they did not evoke immediate fear. Whatever else this man was, he seemed a man of reason.

"This is an odd country that sends a girl out after rustlers," he said.

"No one sent me, I just—oh, never mind, it ain't important. What's important is, have I found what I'm looking for?"

"Ah, you wonder if I am a rustler?" The man's moustache moved as if to accommodate a slight smile. "My answer might surprise you."

"Try me."

"You're a very brave girl to stand up against a strange man out here all alone."

"What choice do I have? Besides, I never learned how to whimper and get faint like some fragile lady. My ma taught me a lot of things, but that wasn't one of 'em."

"Your mother . . . ah."

Carolyn didn't know what to make of that statement, and since the stranger's eyes remained veiled, she couldn't begin to speculate. "What brings you up to these parts, mister?"

"Come with me, and I will explain all." He turned and took a few steps as if expecting her to follow. When she made no move to do so, he said, "If I had wanted to harm you, I could have done so many times in the last hour. On your horse you made a very big target."

That was too true. Besides, Carolyn had become intensely curious about this stranger who had appeared out of nowhere, made no dangerous moves toward her and, most surprisingly, in all their conversation had not once expressed curiosity about who *she* was. She found it hard to believe he was a rustler leading her to her doom. Nevertheless, as she grasped Tres Zapatos' reins and stepped out to follow the stranger on foot, she wistfully thought of her gun uselessly tucked in her saddlebag.

58

It was a narrow path they traversed, hardly wide enough for her horse to pass without brushing the thick growth of mesquite. They followed it on foot for about five hundred yards, taking a couple of turns. The moon still shone overhead, but there were enough big trees here, mostly oak and mesquite bushes as big as trees, to block out the natural light. Carolyn doubted she'd have found this trail even in the daylight.

After about a fifteen-minute hike, they came to a small clearing in the brush. A blackened area in the center indicated a recent campfire, but there were also other signs of occupation—a bedroll, a saddle sitting on the ground, and a horse, a chestnut with a black mane and tail, tied to a tree branch.

"In a few minutes," said the stranger, "we can return here, make some fresh coffee and talk. But first, I want to show you something."

"I ain't got all night, mister," said Carolyn. "I mean, I'm with a small cattle drive at the foot of this ridge, and they're gonna miss me pretty soon."

"I'll try not to cause trouble for you, Carolyn, but it would be in your interest to hear me out."

"How did you know my name?"

"That, too, will be explained. Leave your horse with mine; we can move faster without them."

"Who *are* you?"

"Come."

It seemed a terribly foolish thing to do, but, still sensing no danger, Carolyn followed the man.

It was another fifteen-minute hike through much of the same type of terrain, mostly uphill. Matt's guard shift should be starting about now. Would he notice her empty bedroll and rouse the camp in alarm? Her grandfather would be furious with her. He might never let her out of his sight again. Yet Carolyn was curiously compelled to take that risk. This stranger was just too interesting to walk away from. She had the odd sense that he had many secrets locked behind that veiled face of his. She simply had to find out what he was all about.

He stopped so abruptly ahead of her that she almost collided with him. When she drew up next to him, he parted some of the mesquite. "Look down there."

Carolyn gasped. They had come to a ridge that dropped about two hundred feet into a canyon that was almost twice that in width, rising on the opposite side to form a wall several more hundred feet in height. It was a long canyon, easily several miles in length, with a grassy floor. About a hundred cattle placidly grazed in that meadow. Two cowboys on horseback guarded the herd.

"The rustlers!" she murmured. "Does that mean these ain't box canyons, and there's a trail to get the stolen cattle through?"

"Yes, but it's a hazardous, narrow trail. You couldn't get a herd much bigger than the one that's down there through."

"I wonder if my grandfather knows about this?" she mused, mostly to herself.

"Of course he does. He's grazed cattle down there in the past. The trail you followed coming up here leads to the canyon, and it's not too bad. It's the trail leading out of the canyon, at the northern-most end, that's treacherous."

"How do you know about all this?"

"I think it's time for some coffee at my camp."

"What about them?" Carolyn jerked her head toward the herd, indicating the guards.

"I've been camped up here for two days, undetected. Believe me, I'm well-versed in stealth."

"You better have a mighty good story to tell."

"I don't think you'll be disappointed."

Back at the campsite, the stranger who called himself Santiago built a small, smokeless fire, filled a coffeepot with water from his canteen and several handfuls of coffee grounds, and set it over the blazing flames. After ten more minutes of silence, the coffee was ready and he handed Carolyn a tin cup full. Only with great effort had Carolyn curbed her natural inquisitiveness. She figured this Santiago wanted her full attention when he began his explanation, and so she tried to be patient. But once the steaming cup was in her hands, as if it were a signal, she fired her questions like shots from a Gatling gun.

"Now, how do you know about this canyon, Mr. Santiago? What's your interest in the rustlers? And how do you know my name? I know

I've never met you before. Where are you from, anyway?"

"We've never met, Carolyn Stoner," said Santiago. "But look closer at me. Am I not a little familiar to you?"

Carolyn was about to reaffirm that she'd never seen him before and had no idea how he could be familiar, when he pushed back his sombrero, turning his head slightly so that the flames of the fire illuminated his profile. He was a total stranger. How could she possibly—?

Then she saw it. She couldn't quite pinpoint where it originated. It was not really in the eyes, which were softer, wider set; nor was it in the silhouette of the face with its slightly humped nose and rounded jaw and full lips visible under the camouflage of the dark moustache. But somehow it was a combination of all these things, a bit here, a bit there, like puzzle pieces that fit together.

As her eyes widened with dawning enlightenment—and fear— Santiago's lips parted into a grin. And, oddly, this singular act seemed to break the spell, eliminate all her former sense of familiarity.

She frowned, puzzled once more.

"I feel the same way when I look at you," Santiago said. "Sure . . . and then not so sure; happy, and then . . . a little frightened. We're very much alike, you and I. We're made of two warring halves, good and evil, so to speak. And it's a constant struggle of one over the other."

"That's—that's the way it is with all folks, I think," Carolyn said in a broken, uncertain tone.

"More for some than others." He paused, studying Carolyn for a moment before continuing. "But you're not interested in philosophy or guessing games, are you? Your mother was like that, too. She never was very good at subtlety; perhaps that's why she was so miserable at the Stoner Ranch—"

"Who are you?" burst Carolyn out sharply, as surprised at her tone as she was at the sudden tremor in her hands. "What do you know of my mother?"

"She and I were very close once, though friends only. She had too much honor to run away with me and be my lover. I loved her, and I wanted her, in spite of the fact that she was my brother's wife—"

Carolyn sucked in a sharp breath. It couldn't be!

"Ah, you know now, don't you? She has told you about me," he said.

Carolyn nodded. "You're Jacob Stoner."

"Yes."

"Everyone thought you were dead. Where have you been all these years? If you cared so much about my mother, why did you never return to help her?"

"I have returned now," he said earnestly. "Whether I can help her or not is doubtful, but I plan to try."

"But where have you been?"

"Would you like more coffee, my dear niece? I have a long tale to tell."

Carolyn forgot all about the danger of being missed at camp and held out her cup.

What she heard in the next half hour was an adventure story like she had never imagined. It began several days after Jacob Stoner fled the Stoner Ranch, escaping the murderous wrath of his brother Leonard. He had headed for the West, for always in his mind was the dream of beginning a new life in California. He determined that someday he'd return for Deborah, but it would be too dangerous for him to do so in the near future. All those hopes and dreams, however, were crushed in the Staked Plaines. It had been foolish for him to travel across the plains alone, but he had no friends, no one he could trust to keep his whereabouts from his brother. A band of Apaches attacked him and, probably having been scared off by other hostiles, left him half dead on the searing plains. He was found the next day by a couple of buffalo hunters who gathered up his nearly lifeless body, took it to their camp, and nursed him. When he could be safely moved, they took him to Fort Belknap, in the northwest frontier of Texas, where he spent the winter months recuperating. In the spring when he was able to ride, he thought often of going back for Deborah. But could he be sure she'd even want to go with him? It had been months since his departure, and a lot could have happened in that time. He assumed she would have a baby by then, because before his departure she had revealed she was pregnant with Leonard's child. That alone would bind her tightly to her husband. Thus, he was dissuaded from seeking Deborah out.

He went, instead, to California. He never heard about Leonard's death, or Deborah's conviction for his murder. Jacob was of a bitter and resentful mind himself after the years of mistreatment and bigotry he had suffered at the hands of his father and brother, and many other white men. In California he fell in with a gang of Mexican nationalists—men who resented the United States for stealing, as they viewed it, so much Mexican territory.

Jacob made a life for himself in Mexico, a land where he for the first time in his life was treated with respect. He soon became leader of a gang—called nationalists south of the border, but north of the

Rio Grande, they were considered banditos. They all had prices on their heads. The name of Santiago became widely known and feared even by the Texas Rangers. Had Carolyn lived farther south, she no doubt would have heard of him.

"It was several years before I heard of my brother's death and Deborah's arrest. By then, of course, she had escaped and, I hoped, was safe. But she had disappeared and there was no way to find her, especially for me, also a wanted man. I knew it was best for both of us to remain as we were."

"Why, then, have you come back?" asked Carolyn.

"I've tried to maintain some contact with my father's ranch, though I knew it would be best for us, especially my brother, Laban, if I remained as dead to them. You'd be surprised how many Mexicans here are sympathetic with the cause of the banditos. Several friends have kept me up on happenings in the area. I learned of my father's illness—"

"Illness? You mean when he was under the weather the other day?"

"He has visited a doctor in Austin several times in the last year."

"What for? Do you know? Is it something serious?"

Jacob shrugged. "No man in the West goes to the doctor unless it's serious—*very* serious."

Carolyn recalled her conversation with Caleb that day he had been sick, how curiously intense his words had been. Was he afraid he was dying? Was he that ill? A sudden knot gripped Carolyn's throat as she considered this possibility. Would she lose her grandfather so soon after discovering him? But just because he had visited a doctor didn't mean he was dying; he might have a serious malady without it being life-threatening. It just couldn't be.

She tried to focus on her long-lost uncle. "So, you came back to claim your inheritance?"

"That would be impossible for me to do without also turning myself over to the authorities. No, that's not why I came back. I thought perhaps of attempting to see my father and making things right between us. But I put off that decision until I heard that your mother had been arrested again. I knew then that I must come."

"She's married again, you know," Carolyn said suddenly.

Jacob smiled. "I'm not surprised. A woman like your mother would have had many suitors to choose from. I, too, am married; my wife and five children live in Mexico. I did truly love your mother at one time, but more than that, we were friends. The love has faded over the years, but the friendship has not. We were very important

271

to one another at a time when we both desperately needed a friend."

"Most folks think you and my ma were . . . well, were much more than just friends."

"Who will you believe, Carolyn?"

That was a good question, and one Carolyn was faced with constantly. But she knew there was really only one answer.

"My mother," she said confidently.

Jacob's moustache moved, and his eyes reflected a smile. "A good answer, Carolyn. Always remember that."

Those words, more than anything else, caused a sense of kinship with Jacob to blossom within Carolyn. He was the only Stoner who showed any sympathy at all for her mother, and it was refreshing and encouraging. "But how can you help her now, Jacob? I'm sure she'll be glad to see you, but she has plenty of friends now, and she's still in trouble."

"I'd be glad to see Deborah also, but of course I can't even do that, at least while she's in jail. As I said, I am a wanted man."

"I thought Santiago was a wanted man," said Carolyn hopefully. "Isn't it possible that Jacob Stoner could appear and testify?"

"Not *impossible,* I suppose. Even lawmen might have trouble identifying me by my face. Still it's risky, especially to walk into a jail or courtroom where the law is especially wary."

Carolyn's disappointment must have been clearly evident on her face, for when Jacob spoke next, it was with deep sympathy.

"I have failed your mother in so many ways," he said, "and now I may fail you also. Let me give this some thought. I would do almost anything for your mother, but I also have my own family to consider. But, Carolyn, there may still be ways in which I can help. I know things, and I can tell them to you—"

"What good will that do? The judge wants to hear firsthand testimony—anything else, Mr. Barnum says, is called hearsay. It won't count."

Jacob shook his head. "There must be something I can do."

"Do you know what really happened with my ma and pa?"

"If I knew that, if I had evidence that would without a doubt free your mother, I'd be far more willing to risk my own freedom to help her."

"Would you, Uncle Jacob? I want to believe that—"

"But you can't keep from thinking that I had as much a motive to kill my brother as anyone."

"I reckon so."

"Do you think I came back and shot my brother?"

272

"I'd be lying if I said that thought didn't occur to me. Can you prove what you said about the Apache attack and getting wounded and all?"

"Probably not. The men who helped me are long gone."

"I'm sorry, Uncle Jacob. I want to believe you. If only you had something else to give us."

"I would never have allowed your mother to suffer for a crime I had committed," said Jacob earnestly. "But as with everything else, there is no reason for you to believe me." He sighed with discouragement. "It is time that we part. I've already kept you long enough. It would not be good if your companions started looking for you tonight and found you here with me. I'll meet you again soon, and we'll talk more."

"When?" Carolyn asked, not attempting to mask her impatience.

"How hard is it for you to get away?"

"I go where I please—well, most of the time. My grandfather is different with me than my mother says he was with her."

Jacob was genuinely surprised at this. "But then, you are Leonard's daughter, aren't you?" he said almost to himself. He eyed her carefully one more time.

"All right," Jacob said after a brief pause, "let's meet tomorrow night. Not here—that would be too risky. There's a line cabin about five miles southeast of the foot of this ridge. It should be deserted this time of year. I'll be there about an hour after sundown."

"Okay."

"Carolyn, it's very important that no one know I am here—not Caleb, or even your mother."

"I understand."

Carolyn stood and started toward her horse, but Jacob rose also and hurried up beside her.

"I'm glad I have come home, Carolyn, and found a niece like you here," he said, his dark eyes gazing earnestly upon her. "This ranch has needed someone like you for many years. You bring hope here, Carolyn."

She gave him a puzzled look, not quite knowing what to make of his statement. She only smiled before she said goodbye, mounted Tres Zapatos, and rode off.

59

When Carolyn slipped into her bedroll that night, the night was deep and still. Only the restive lowing of cattle disturbed the quiet air. She was glad to see no one had missed her; Matt was still asleep, but his watch was near. The camp was quiet except for the snores of the men.

Carolyn was tired and fell immediately asleep. And, although only ten or fifteen minutes had passed, she was in a deep slumber when she was awakened suddenly by a sharp snap. She jerked awake to the sight of a dark figure bent over her, and her eyes caught the dull glint of steel moving toward her throat. She gasped out a cry as a big, rough hand clamped over her mouth.

The steel object, now clearly revealed as a big Bowie knife, had come within a fraction of an inch of its target when a shot rang through the air. The knife fell on Carolyn's chest, followed an instant later by the dark figure.

"Carolyn! Are you okay?" cried Matt as he frantically hauled the dead man off her body.

"Yeah . . . I am. Who—?"

"Whoever he was, he's dead now." There was a deep regret in Matt's tone.

But before they could answer any other questions or Carolyn could comfort Matt with the assurance that he had acted out of necessity, another voice shouted, "The cattle! They're stampeding!"

There was not even a moment for Carolyn to thank Matt, or to discover who her attacker was. There was a mad dash for horses, a flurry of saddling up, and a race to where the herd was running madly out of control. Carolyn didn't even pay attention to Caleb's protests about her joining the cowboys. Everything was happening too quickly to think or reason. All was simply reaction, and Carolyn only reacted naturally.

The cowhands had grabbed their hats and blankets and were

waving them mightily to distract the herd which was fleeing in about as many directions as there were cows. Carolyn, Caleb, and two of the cowboys took flanking positions in order to turn the herd into a column heading in one direction. Matt guided the leaders, hoping to provide focus for the animals. Then, when the herd was more a rushing river than a scattering dust storm, Matt rode headlong into the herd, firing his pistol and turning them so they soon formed a U-shape. Their intent, after channeling the herd into some order, was to wait until the two "legs" of the U were even with each other; then the other four riders would "attack" the herd, yelling, waving blankets and hats, and shooting—forcing the herd to merge and, hopefully, to begin "milling," a stance that would eventually wear the cows out.

All was going according to plan, and Carolyn was impressed at how skilled the Stoner hands were. But the country was rough and uneven in places, and it was a major feat, even for an experienced cowboy, to navigate such terrain at the breakneck pace they were setting. When the flanks were fairly well under control, Carolyn was directed to ride ahead and give Matt a hand. Her eyes were on Matt as she rode forward. One minute he was waving his hat wildly in the air, then the next he suddenly disappeared.

"Matt!" she yelled as she dug her knees into her mount's flanks.

———————

Matt's mount had stumbled into a gopher hole, taking both rider and horse down to the ground. He managed to roll away from the weight of his horse, only to find himself right in the path of the stampeding cows. He dared not stand and run, for he'd be an even bigger target for the herd. He curled up, using his mount's fallen body as a shield. A steer flew over him, then another, but his luck couldn't hold out much longer. He thought about praying, but managed only a choked "God, help me!" before another steer's hoof clipped him in the head. The last thing he heard before all went black was the report of several pistol shots.

———————

Carolyn raced forward, Tres Zapatos' mighty strides out-distancing the careening herd only by a few feet, but it was enough to get ahead of them. She saw Matt's horse first and feared she was too late, especially when she didn't see Matt. But even if he was dead, she couldn't stand the thought of him being trampled by a herd of cattle.

She already had her Remington in hand with four shots in the chamber. She wouldn't have time to reload. But she raised it high and fired two shots in quick succession, then two more.

The herd seemed to visibly wince from the sharp sounds they so hated. Some turned, crashing into oncoming beasts, but breaking the flow. Another cowboy, seeing her problem, joined her and began firing until the entire body of stubborn animals were finally convinced to go the other way.

Less than two minutes had passed from the time Matt first went down. The ground around the fallen horse was now clear except for trampled grass. Carolyn's anxious eyes swept the area, and she was almost to the point of despair when she saw a booted foot sticking out from behind the horse.

When Matt came to, he was well out of harm's way, lying on the ground about a stone's throw from the now milling herd. His horse's carcass lay in a heap some distance away, and he realized what a close call he'd had.

He went back to camp with the intention of getting a new mount and rejoining the herd. But the hike to the camp had left him so dizzy and nauseous all he could do was collapse. An hour later, he felt a little better. He got up and built a fire, put on a pot of coffee, and rustled up a mess of beans. It was the least he could do for his companions who had been up most of the night tending an ornery herd.

The smell of fresh coffee was indeed welcome to the weary riders as they soon drifted back to camp. One man stayed with the herd, and his voice, raised in gentle serenade to the cows, wafted into the camp. Caleb, Carolyn, and the other hand, whose name was Rusty, collapsed in front of the fire and made no protest as Matt served them coffee.

"So, which of you galoots do I gotta thank for saving my hide?" Matt said after all were settled. His light tone in no way detracted from his earnestness.

Caleb shook his head in response.

Rusty said with a slight grin, "Don't look at me."

Carolyn said nothing but just stared into her coffee.

"Was it Potter, then?" said Matt.

Rusty laughed and said, "Nope."

"I guess it was me," said Carolyn sheepishly.

Matt laughed, too, until it made his head hurt and he stopped. "Well, I guess I ought to eat a mess of crow instead of these beans."

Carolyn shrugged. "It just makes us even—well, not quite, you're still one up on me. But I never did thank you for what you did this morning."

In the frenzy of the stampede, they had all but forgotten about the intruder.

Matt shook his head sadly. He had been aware of the body during his sojourn in camp but wished he could forget it. "I wanted to wing him," Matt felt he needed to explain. "But it was so plumb dark."

"No one's faulting you, lad," said Caleb. "You saved my granddaughter's life, and for that I'll be in your debt."

All heads turned to where the body of Carolyn's assailant still lay. It was full daylight now, and the man's face was clearly discernible to the small group that gathered around.

"Never seen him before," said Matt. "How about you, Carolyn?"

Carolyn shook her head.

"You sure?" said Matt.

"Why would a complete stranger want to harm my granddaughter?" asked Caleb.

Instead of responding immediately, Matt stooped down close to the body. He paid particular attention to the two guns the man wore strapped to his sides. They were expensive, well-made weapons, nothing that a regular cowhand could hope to afford. Matt searched the dead man's pockets and found a thick wad of cash.

"Must be two hundred dollars here," said Matt, replacing the money. "And them guns ain't your ordinary six-shooters."

"Yeah," added Rusty, "I ain't seen nothing like them since that shootist I met once in Dodge City."

Matt stood and faced Caleb and Carolyn. "I'd bet a month's pay this fella is a hired gun. And I'll bet he had a hand in that other ambush."

"Ambush? Hired gun . . . what is this all about?" questioned Caleb sharply.

Carolyn looked down into her lap. She feared her next words could ignite a terrible explosion that she did not want to be responsible for. Yet why should she protect Laban? If he had really killed her father, then he deserved whatever might happen to him for all the suffering his actions had caused so many others.

She lifted a steady gaze toward her grandfather. "I think Laban is responsible for this attack on me, and for an attempted ambush several days ago. A couple of weeks ago, when I said I had fallen off my horse—well, the truth is that he struck me several times, Grandfather. He hates me almost as much as he hated my father."

"He struck you?"

"Yes."

"I will kill him for that."

"Grandfather, no!"

"Why ever would you defend him?"

"I'm not defending him. It's just that there are more important matters at stake here than avenging what's happened to me. I think Laban killed my father, too. If anything happens to him now, the truth may never come out."

"Carolyn, be realistic," said Caleb. "You are so desperate to see your mother free that you refuse to accept the truth. It was she, not Laban, who was found standing over your father's body holding the gun that killed him. Laban was a mere boy back then—fifteen years old! He may be capable of murder now, but even I can't believe he was then. But besides all that, he was in town that night. He came with Sheriff Pollard from town. So, you see, it would have been impossible for him to kill your father, ride to town, then return with Pollard."

"You're sure of this? Even Laban said at the trial that he can't remember where he was."

"I remember every detail of that night, Carolyn, like it happened an hour ago. I will never forget."

"I still believe you're wrong, Grandfather, and I'm gonna prove it."

Caleb did not respond for a moment. Then he said, "I'm going back home. I want you to accompany me, Carolyn." Without waiting for her to reply, he walked to the horses.

Carolyn opened her mouth to argue about being told what to do. But she noted her grandfather's labored, unsteady gait. His recent illness and the strenuous morning was too much for him, but he likely was too proud to admit his fatigue and need for Carolyn to be with him in case the ride home became too much for him.

"Yes, Grandfather."

Matt smiled. "If I ever doubted that you two was related, I'd be a believer now. I never seen two more stubborn mules."

278

PART 13

GUILTY OR INNOCENT?

60

Griff and his companions arrived in Leander Sunday night. He had considered going to Stoner's Crossing but decided it would be wise to steer as clear of Caleb Stoner as possible. Griff had no great fear of the law as far as his past crimes went—that is, as long as Caleb Stoner did not press the issue. Stoner, of course, had no proof regarding Griff's past, but he could stir things up enough to get the law to investigate. There was also Pollard to consider, and he *could* identify Griff.

For those reasons, Griff, Longjim, and Slim were going to keep away from the trial, too. Sky would keep them informed about its progress while they maintained a low profile in town.

They did, however, risk visiting Deborah that night in jail. Sam was there, too, and it was a lively reunion. Deborah was so touched and happy they had come to support her that she didn't even mention her concern for the ranch. No one suspected that Griff had an ulterior motive for being there, and he left it that way. It might just get them all riled up for nothing if the trial ended successfully.

While Sky went to the hotel with Sam and Jonathan Barnum, the three ex-outlaws headed for one of Leander's four saloons. Sam had warned Griff that Pollard hung out in the town's saloons, mostly the one where the trial was being held and also one on the edge of town. Griff chose one of the remaining ones, a lively little place called the Dancing Tumbleweed.

They ordered beer and sat at the last empty table. It felt good to stretch out and relax after the long ride, especially for a saddle-weary Griff.

"Can't believe I was so anxious to get back on a horse," said Griff.

"Well, at least you made it," said Longjim, sipping his drink. "I was worried I'd have to be mopping up blood on the way."

"Naw, everything's just fine."

"And a good thing," added Slim, "'cause we was never much for doctoring."

Griff smiled. "That reminds me of years ago when we was with Deborah, and how worried she was that we'd have to deliver her baby."

"As if Carolyn ain't ornery enough!" laughed Slim. "Think what she'd be like if three sidewinders like us had brought her into the world."

"Well, if Deborah had wanted some fragile, genteel little lady, she was sure disappointed."

"She ain't disappointed one bit in Lynnie," Griff said with an almost fatherly pride. "You hear her talking 'bout how that girl has Caleb Stoner near wrapped round her finger?"

"You think Stoner's changed that much?" asked Slim.

But Griff looked away from his friend and hardly heard his question. An attractive woman who had been sitting at a nearby table had left her seat and was walking toward Griff's table. Her striking red hair had first caught his attention, but then he noticed that the rest of her was pretty striking also. She had pale, clear skin, though a thin layer of makeup attempted to cover scattered freckles. Her green eyes had kind of a sparkle in them, as if she was constantly laughing without making a sound or moving her lips. She wore the attire of a saloon girl—emerald green like her eyes, flouncy and bright, low-cut and well-fitted—and indeed, was lately employed by the Dancing Tumbleweed.

Griff gave her a big grin, never doubting that she had her sights set on him.

"Howdy, miss," he said, and, jumping up, grabbed a vacant chair and lodged it between his and Slim's. "Have a seat."

"Thanks," she said. "You gents are new in town, aren't you?"

"That's a fact," said Griff. "It sure is nice of you to welcome us lonely cowboys."

"You are welcome, no doubt about that, but I don't figure you to be just lonely cowboys."

Longjim bristled. "What's that supposed to mean?"

"Now, don't get me wrong. I'm not here to make trouble."

"So, what do you want?" Griff was deflated to think she might have something in mind other than just making his charming acquaintance.

"I couldn't help hearing your conversation a minute ago. I heard a name that was familiar to me, and I wondered if we didn't have a mutual friend. You were talking about someone named Deborah, and I happen to know a Deborah also. Could it be the same person?"

Griff decided he better be careful, at least until he found out who this stranger was. He did hope she turned out to be a friend. "Could be. Tell me about this Deborah you know."

"Well, Deborah Killion is my friend. She's over in the town jail right now and is on trial for murder. She and I were in the county prison together. I got out a couple of weeks ago."

"That so?" Griff took a keener appraisal of this woman.

"What was you in prison for?" asked Longjim bluntly.

"Now," Griff interrupted, "maybe that ain't none of our business."

"I guess I don't mind telling you. I mean, it's no secret, though I'm not exactly shouting it all over town. I was arrested for stealing money from a former employer. But I was just trying to get what was rightly mine, money he'd withheld that I'd fairly earned. He was a big man in town, and no one believed that for years he'd been cheating me and the other gals who worked for him. I'd finally had it and decided to take my share and leave town. I got caught and tossed in jail for two years."

"That must've been tough. How much did you steal?"

"Fifty dollars."

Griff shook his head, thinking of the inequity of the justice system, and he wondered how Deborah could place so much faith in it. But for now, he wanted to know more about this pretty woman who claimed to know Deborah. "So you and Deborah were friends?"

"Yeah. It's kind of amazing, isn't it? I mean, that a fine lady like Deborah could befriend a person like me who doesn't have all that much to be proud of. So, is it the same person?"

Griff, Slim, and Longjim all nodded with broad grins.

"Sounds just like Deborah," said Griff. "She seems to attract the oddest friends. But I like to think it's because she sees something good in them that most folks miss 'cause they ain't looking in the right places. Now, don't get me wrong, miss—ah, I didn't catch your name?"

"Lucy Reeves."

"Well, Miss Reeves, I know what I'm talking about, 'cause I happen to be one of her odd-ball friends."

Lucy chuckled—a hearty, deep sound. "I'll bet you're Griff McCulloch." She grinned at Griff's wide-eyed astonishment. She looked at Slim. "You must be Slim, and you gotta be Longjim."

"How'd you know?"

"There isn't much to do in jail but talk. I suppose Deborah and I know as much about each other as anyone, even you."

"So, I reckon it ain't no coincidence that you're here working in Leander," said Griff.

"No. I just couldn't take off before I knew how Deborah's trial turned out." For a moment the lightness of her demeanor was replaced by an earnestness. "She saved my life back there in prison. One of the inmates had it in for me and was trying to frame me for doing something that would have got my release canceled. Deborah took the blame and took seven days of solitary so I could get out on schedule. I owe her a bundle. I know it doesn't help her much, me just being here, but I couldn't walk out yet. And, if it turns sour on her . . . well, I still don't know what I'll do."

"Deborah's lucky to have a friend like you, Miss Reeves," said Griff.

"Why don't you fellows call me Lucy? I feel like I know you right well."

"That sounds just fine, Lucy. How's about having a beer with us?"

"Thanks, but I better be getting back to work. The boss don't like us giving too much attention to one customer." She pushed back her chair and stood. "By the way, if you need me for anything, just holler. I'll do just about anything for Deborah."

"I reckon I can't see what we could do for her at this point."

Lucy rested a hand on the table and bent low, speaking in an intense whisper, "If that's so, then maybe you three gents aren't the same fellows Deborah told me about."

"I don't rightly take your meaning, Lucy," said Griff innocently. He did understand, but he wanted to make certain that what she was implying was what he was thinking.

"From what Deborah told me, you aren't the kind of men to sit still and take a beating without fighting back—and the same goes where your friends are concerned. Well, I never did trust courts and lawyers and such like, and I got my doubts that Deborah is going to get a fair shake from them."

"And. . . ?"

"You are the three that busted her out of jail nineteen years ago, aren't you?"

Griff smiled and nodded.

"Well," said Lucy with the kind of grit Griff had to respect, "I'm here to help."

"Thanks, Lucy." Before she turned to go, Griff lightly took her hand. "I hope to see you again."

"I hope so, too."

When the three ex-outlaws were alone, Griff said, "Now, there's a woman!"

"Deborah sure knows how to pick 'em," said Slim admiringly.

"You think it's gonna come to that—busting Deborah out of jail?" asked Longjim.

"That's why we came, boys," said Griff. "I ain't looking for trouble, but I ain't gonna back away from it, either."

_____ **61**

Back at the Leander Hotel, Sam, Sky, and Jonathan Barnum were having what Barnum liked to call a "pow-wow." It was time, he said, to finalize their battle strategy. They were seated in Jonathan's room, which he had converted into a makeshift office with a desk and several oak chairs from the hotel lobby.

"I know we've debated about this before," Jonathan said, "but I've decided to put Deborah on the stand. I was waiting to make my decision to see if the prosecution would call her. They didn't, and I think the reason is that they feared she'd make too favorable an impression on the jury. Deborah simply does not come off like a murderer, and we must use that to our advantage."

"But once she's up there," said Sam, "the prosecution is gonna use her for target practice."

"You yourself said she's a strong woman, Sam. I think she can take it. So does she; I've talked to her and she wants to testify. Besides, if the prosecution does try to rake her over the coals, it will only make them look bad and get the jury's sympathy for Deborah."

"Maybe I'm just afraid *I* can't take it," Sam admitted.

Jonathan smiled sympathetically and patted Sam on the shoulder. "I am sorry, my friend. And there is no way to make this ordeal easier, except to be prepared." Jonathan glanced at Sky. "It won't be easy for you, either, young man. Some delicate subject matter must be dealt with."

"I know, sir," said Sky.

"I think it might be easier for your mother if you weren't present for her testimony."

"I came a long way to be here for her," Sky said, looking slightly rejected. Then he forced himself to respond more objectively and less selfishly. "Okay, I guess I understand."

"I'm going to put your mother on the stand tomorrow, and there's something you can do during that time, Sky." Sky nodded. "I want you to go to the bank in Stoner's Crossing and do some research for me."

"What do you have in mind, Jonathan?" asked Sam.

"I've been very unsettled about that Mendez woman's testimony. I think the jury is going to put a lot of weight on it because of her relatively objective position in all this. She obviously has no reason to be hostile toward Deborah."

"But I remember Carolyn saying how hostile she was toward the Stoners," said Sam.

"Yes, and it just doesn't add up."

"What'd you think Sky will find at the bank?"

"She owns the saloon now, and I'm curious about when she came into possession. We know that Domingo, the former owner, went bankrupt shortly after Leonard's death. The cantina then reverted back to Caleb. How long after that did Mrs. Mendez assume ownership? It would hurt the objectivity of her testimony if it can be proved that she came to own it as a result of her testimony at the first trial."

"You mean Caleb could have rewarded her for her testimony by giving her the cantina?"

"And this is what you wish me to find at the bank?" asked Sky.

"Exactly."

"I'll go first thing in the morning."

"Good. I'll prepare a letter of introduction for you. Mrs. Vernon has applied some pressure to her husband, making him fairly open with us. I don't think you'll have any problems." Jonathan folded his hands across his middle and leaned back thoughtfully in his chair. "There is one more matter we must discuss—that is, whether to put Caleb Stoner on the stand. The prosecution deftly avoided that also, and we must carefully consider the positives and negatives of such a move. It's late now, but give this some thought. We have a day or two before we must decide."

"I got a matter to discuss," Sam added. He pulled a paper from his pocket. "Just got this telegram from Carolyn. She says we ought to verify with Pollard the whereabouts of Laban Stoner the night of the murder. Caleb says Laban was in town and came back to the ranch with Pollard."

"Do you think Pollard will cooperate?"

"I reckon, if we're subtle. I'm for finding him tonight and questioning him."

"It might only prove more firmly the innocence of our most viable suspect. However, as it stands he's as good as innocent, anyway."

"It's worth the risk," Sam persisted. "But, Jonathan, I think you ought to do the talking; you got more practice at this sort of thing than me."

"Lead me to him!"

They left Sky behind, for he was too young to go to the kind of places Pollard frequented. Pollard was easily located in his favorite watering hole, and it was early enough in the evening so that he was still fairly sober.

"What do you two polecats want?" he asked, not masking his hostility. "Ain't I talked to you enough?"

Sam and Jonathan drew up two chairs at the table where Pollard sat alone, a glass of whiskey in front of him.

Sam sat back and watched while Jonathan said in his smoothest, candidate-of-the-people tone, "I hope you don't take personally all that posturing that goes on in the courtroom, Mr. Pollard. It's all in the way of business, and I surely hold nothing against you."

"It sure didn't seem like it." Pollard gulped down his drink.

"I have been told that lawyers are nothing more than highly paid actors. Well, sometimes, in that vein, I have a tendency to bury myself in my part."

"Hey, is it true you was a U.S. senator up there in Washington and that you was nearly president of these United States?"

"I am both proud and humbled to say yes."

"Well, I'll be! And you're trying to apologize to me?"

"If an apology is necessary, yes indeed! I am very interested in keeping our lines of communication open."

" 'Lines of communication'? What's that mean?"

"Talk, Mr. Pollard, nothing more. You'd be surprised how much more we can accomplish outside the confines of a courtroom."

"Is that legal?"

Jonathan smiled. "The law is my life, Mr. Pollard. I hold it in the highest esteem. And there has come to my attention a small matter, not really worth clogging up the trial time with. Would it be too much of a bother if I asked you to help me out?"

"I reckon I could."

"That's fine, just fine! It's simply this: I am a bit cloudy about when you came to the Stoner ranch the night of the murder. You didn't ride to the ranch all alone, did you? I can hardly believe even a notorious lawman like yourself would ride into such unknown danger all by yourself."

"Well, I did, 'cepting for the Stoner hand that came to fetch me—he rode back with me."

"That was a brave thing for you to do."

"All in the line of duty, I reckon."

"I'm sure I would have rounded up an entire posse to accompany me."

"Well, I didn't."

"No one else came with you? Caleb's son, perhaps?"

"You mean Laban? He wasn't even in town."

"Oh, somehow I got the impression he was with you at the scene of the crime."

"I met him at the Stoner place. As I was riding up to the gate, he was coming from the opposite direction. We rode to the house together."

"You're sure?"

"Yeah, that important or somethin'?"

"Just curious," said Jonathan.

Sam could hardly restrain a grin as he listened. He felt he had just watched a master fisherman reel in a big one.

62

When Carolyn went to the line cabin on the appointed night to meet Jacob, she wondered if she was in reality going to meet her father's murderer. If that were so, then she might well be riding into considerable danger. Yet there had been something about Jacob that made her want to believe him, to trust that she was not heading to her doom.

She was disappointed when Jacob failed to appear. She waited for over an hour before returning home, then went back the following night in the futile hope that he might show up. Her dismay was all the greater because on Monday, Mr. Barnum was to begin his case for the defense, and she had hoped Jacob would be able to provide the answers that would free her mother.

Monday came, and Carolyn felt just as helpless as she had been before. Jonathan began his defense with Mabel Vernon's testimony. She spoke her piece and felt immensely better for doing so, but because she had no hard proof that Leonard had been beating Deborah, the prosecution fairly discounted her entire testimony. Then Jonathan called Sheriff Pollard again.

He got Pollard to admit that Deborah had walked into an already volatile situation at the Stoner ranch, and he manipulated him into stating that he had, during the first trial, suspected self-defense. Then he questioned Pollard about the discussion they'd had regarding Laban. When the prosecution protested that Laban Stoner was not on trial, and thus his whereabouts were not in question, Jonathan argued, though he knew it would do little good, that not having a proper alibi could make Laban a suspect. The man had a definite motive and could well benefit from the victim's demise. But again, Jonathan's statements were pure conjecture, as the prosecutor was quick to point out. Without putting Laban on the stand, he could make little more of his suspicions. Unfortunately, Laban had disappeared. He apparently had heard of Caleb's threats and had made himself scarce.

Sky arrived during Pollard's testimony, and when Jonathan was finished he asked for a brief recess, during which Sky apprised him of his discoveries. Jonathan wanted to question Eufemia Mendez before he put Deborah on the stand, but having no warning that she was to be called, Eufemia was not present at the trial on that day. He asked for, and received, a recess until the following day.

Tuesday, Eufemia had been notified and was present. Jonathan got right to the point.

"Mrs. Mendez, how long have you owned La Rosa Cantina?"

She hesitated as if mentally tallying the time. "Eighteen years, señor."

"So, you came into possession only a year after Leonard Stoner's death?"

"Yes, about that long."

"I would like to remind the court that the last time Mrs. Mendez testified, it was established that Caleb Stoner held the loan note on the cantina." Jonathan turned back to Mendez. "You must have been saving your money a long time to go from saloon girl to saloon owner?"

"I'm sorry to disappoint you, señor, but it was an inheritance."

"From whom?"

"My relations in Mexico."

"Do you have proof of that?"

"I'm sure there are records in Mexico."

"You have none in your possession?"

"No."

"I would think you'd want some evidence for your own protection, since some might question such a sudden—how shall I say?—windfall."

"Objection!" said Fuller. "Counsel is drawing conclusions."

"Objection overruled," the judge said. When Fuller started to protest, the judge added, "I think it's in the interest of the court to see where this is leading. Proceed, Mr. Barnum."

"I have a ledger here from the Stoner's Crossing Bank recording several deposits in Mrs. Eufemia Mendez's name for the period of June 1865 to May of 1866. There are two deposits for one hundred dollars each in June of 1865, and one for five hundred dollars in July 1865. There is no more activity in this account until May of the next year, when a deposit of five thousand dollars was made. Are we to assume this money was from your wages?"

"Why not?"

"Come now, Mrs. Mendez, even I, greenhorn easterner that I am, know that a saloon girl doesn't earn that much money."

"This is a personal matter."

"And I am sorry to have to pry into such things, but my client's life may be at stake here, so I must put that before propriety. How did you come by this money, Mrs. Mendez?"

"It was from a business I had on the side."

"What business?"

For a moment Eufemia's hard face took on the quality of sharp, jagged rock, lethal and dangerous. Jonathan fixed a steady gaze on her, not turning from her uncomfortable ire.

"Some people refer to it as the world's oldest business," she said icily. "I had clients who were willing to pay well for such services . . . and for the discretion that accompanied them."

"I see." Jonathan did not blink, even though he had no idea he would stumble onto such a delicate matter. "What about this five hundred dollar deposit that was made less than a week after Leonard's death?"

"Life does go on, señor. The Stoners were not anything to me that I should stop my business to mourn them."

"And the five thousand dollar entry?"

"That was the inheritance."

"Did no one at that time comment on the coincidence of you receiving such an inheritance so shortly after Leonard's trial?"

"No. Why should they?"

"A very good question, Mrs. Mendez. But if you can't answer it, then neither can I."

"I cannot answer it."

Jonathan paused, glanced at the bank ledger, then asked as if it were an afterthought, "I notice there were no deposits made between July 1865 and May 1866, a ten-month period. Was business . . . uh . . . simply slow during that time?"

"I was traveling," said Eufemia coolly. "I went to Mexico. I married there, had a child, and also received the inheritance."

"Quite a busy trip, I should say."

"I suppose so."

"When, exactly, did you return to the States?"

"In May of 1866."

"And you immediately deposited your inheritance?"

"Yes."

"You are a widow now, Mrs. Mendez?"

"My husband died shortly before our son was born. That's why I decided to return to the States."

"I'm sorry; that's very tragic."

"I need no one's sympathy."

"Thank you, Mrs. Mendez. No further questions."

There was no cross-examination, and Eufemia Mendez stepped down from the witness seat.

Listening to the testimony, Carolyn was disappointed. She had spoken to Sky for a few moments after yesterday's session and had hoped Barnum would be able to make more of the money issue. Even after Barnum had said he would probably only be able to cast some doubt on Eufemia's credibility, she still thought more would come of it. The timing of the money was just too coincidental for it to be unrelated. Yet the fact that some of the money had come before Leonard's death did cloud the matter. Why would Caleb give Eufemia money *before* the murder? It made no sense. And there was no way to connect the five thousand dollars to Caleb. A trip to Mexico to verify Eufemia's claims would involve too much for the probable use it would have. Had the questioning at least given the jury food for thought? Carolyn glanced that way and could read nothing on the twelve impassive faces.

But she couldn't dwell on all this for long. Her mother was about to take the stand.

63

Deborah had told herself many times that everything was different now. In fact, there could hardly be any comparison to her situation nineteen years ago. She had been completely vulnerable when she had testified in her first trial. She'd had no hope; she didn't even care whether she lived or died. When they had asked if she was innocent, she had not spoken with conviction because inside she felt like a murderer, filled with guilt and filth.

Now she was an entirely different woman, full of hope and assured of her innocence. But she was still conscious of her vulnerability as Jonathan Barnum called her to take the stand. Could there be a small speck of uncertainty within her? She had held back that tiny inner doubt from everyone, hoping that by ignoring it, it would go away.

The night of Leonard's death had been spectral, like a waking nightmare. Some things were still hazy, depending upon how strong she seemed at a given time. Usually she felt as if her account of the events as she told them to Jonathan were the absolute truth.

"I was awakened by a nightmare and was terribly shaken. I went downstairs, intending to fix some warm milk to calm my nerves. I heard a shot and went to the room from which the sound had come. Leonard was sprawled out on the floor. But almost at the same instant that I noticed him, I saw the French doors click shut. Believing whoever had shot Leonard was making an escape, I started toward the doors, stumbling upon the gun as I went. Without thinking I picked up the weapon, believing I might need protection, and then I opened the doors. I saw a shadow disappearing around a corner of the house. Before I could think of going in pursuit, Caleb's voice stopped me. 'What in God's name have you done? You murderous tramp, you have killed my son!'"

She told the same story now as Jonathan questioned her on the stand. But in her mind even as she spoke, the old doubt reared its treacherous head. The nightmare that had awakened her had been so real! In it she had confronted Leonard and, with great satisfaction, shot him dead. She had heard of cases of temporary memory loss where people had done extraordinary things without even knowing it. Had she been so traumatized while shooting Leonard that she blacked out, not waking to reality until Caleb made his jarring accusation?

Why couldn't she be certain? Especially now, when those twelve faces were examining her so intently, looking in her eyes for the very speck of doubt she now wrestled with.

"Mrs. Killion," asked Jonathan gently, "we have evidence that you purchased a small handgun about six months before your husband's death. Can you explain your reasons for this?"

"I thought I might shoot him the next time he beat me. I . . . I also thought about using it to kill myself."

"You must have been very desperate, then?"

"I couldn't go on like that much longer."

"You didn't use the gun in that six-month period; does that mean Leonard did not strike you again?"

"No, he . . . he mistreated me several times after that. I just couldn't bring myself to use the gun."

Jonathan had her describe what her life was like married to Leonard Stoner, and she found it no easier to speak of such things now than it had been when she had been a naive young woman. Though Sky had left the courtroom for the testimony, Carolyn was still there. Deborah had not had the heart to insist that the girl leave. She had as much right as anyone to hear Deborah's answers.

And her testimony did make an excellent case for self-defense. Maybe that was as much as she could hope for. Maybe she should be glad to accept that. Yet, two things haunted Deborah's mind and drove her to fight that possibility. One was Carolyn and the fear of what the true facts might do to their relationship. Carolyn would always have to live with the knowledge that her father had been killed by her mother. It was an awful reality for a child to deal with—not only that her mother was a killer, but that her father had been the kind of man who could drive a woman to such extremes.

But there was something even more personal eating at Deborah's conscience. In her nightmare—or, what she desperately hoped was a nightmare—she had felt such satisfaction, such delight at seeing Leonard fall lifeless before her. And that had always troubled Deborah. Self-defense was one thing, but could it really be self-defense if she had pulled the trigger with such willing malice?

The next day, these thoughts still clouded her mind as the prosecutor began his cross-examination.

"Deborah Killion, would you consider yourself to have been a compliant wife during your marriage to Leonard Stoner?"

"I'm not sure what you mean by compliant."

"Did you try to do his bidding, care for his, ah, needs?"

"I wanted to, but his demands were often more than I could obey."

"Such as?"

Deborah described several instances, and Fuller questioned her in greater detail about each.

"Tell me again about the horses."

"He forbade me to go to the stables. I was raised with a love for horses and found great pleasure and satisfaction from working with them. It was a hard thing to give up."

"But, at his wish, you did give it up?"

"No, I went to the stables anyway. When he became furious with me for doing so, I told him I'd do anything else for him if I could just do that."

"And did you follow through with that promise?"

"You don't understand, Mr. Fuller; no one should have to beg—"

"Please, just answer the question."

"No."

"What did you do?"

"I tried to be the kind of wife he wanted, but he continued to mistreat me, even though he did allow me to go to the stables and ride when I wished."

"He granted your wish, and you repaid him by using that new freedom to begin an illicit affair—"

"Objection!" exclaimed Jonathan, leaping from his chair as if he was ready to do battle.

"Objection sustained," the judge said. "Mr. Fuller, you are drawing a conclusion and using it to badger the witness. Please keep your remarks in the form of a question."

The prosecutor was in no way abashed by the objection, for he had known full well it would be called. He had gotten his point across to the jury nonetheless.

"Mrs. Killion, did you at any time deny your husband his conjugal rights?"

"Yes."

"Did you lock him out of your bedroom?"

"Yes, but only when—"

"If you were so mistreated, why didn't you tell anyone?" the prosecutor broke in quickly.

"You must let me finish answering your first question," Deborah pleaded. "I desperately wanted to be a good wife. But he forced me—"

"I must insist that you answer only the questions asked of you. If

I wish further explanation, I will ask."

"But—"

"Why did you tell no one about what was happening?"

Deborah took a ragged breath. Jonathan had warned her it would be like this. The prosecutor was going to allow her to say only enough to hang her. He was going to do all he could to twist and confuse the truth. At least she'd already had the chance to tell her side of it under sympathetic conditions during Jonathan's questioning. She just hoped that testimony and not this would be what remained in the jury's mind.

"I tried to tell the banker's wife, but—"

"She didn't believe you, Mrs. Killion?"

"I don't know. Leonard was such a gentleman in front of others."

Fuller questioned her for some time about hers and Leonard's relations with friends and neighbors.

Deborah finally said, "But they were all his friends. They were all loyal to him and saw only what they wanted to see."

"You mean only you knew the real Leonard Stoner?"

"I suppose."

"How convenient, Mrs. Stoner. But that hardly is much of a foundation on which to build a case."

"There were his half brothers," Deborah said. "He treated them like dirt, and they hated him."

"Ah, yes, his half brothers," Fuller said smugly. "We have already heard from Laban."

"He didn't tell everything."

"Mrs. Killion, are you suggesting that he lied—perjured himself?"

"No, there is just more to it than what he said. Jacob told me things that had happened in the past, cruel things Leonard did to them as children."

"Unfortunately we cannot accept such third-hand testimony."

"I saw things, too."

"Mrs. Killion, why don't you tell me about Jacob Stoner?"

"Jacob and I became friends," Deborah answered as calmly as she could, but she could feel her nerves unraveling. "We often rode together. After the misery I'd experienced with Leonard, it was a comfort to be with someone who treated me like a human being."

"You were only friends?"

"Of course."

"Why did you meet in secret?"

"Leonard would never have understood such a friendship."

"Did you ever broach the subject with your husband?"

295

"No, I—"

"Then, how did you know he wouldn't understand?"

"It was just the kind of person he was."

"Wasn't the true reason you never told him about Jacob because you feared he'd understand only too well, draw the only conclusion one could draw from such a situation in which a young man and woman met secretly in secluded places?"

"I . . ." Deborah was so confused she wasn't certain how to answer that question.

"Answer my question, Mrs. Killion," Fuller persisted.

"Yes. But that's what—"

"Thank you, Mrs. Killion. Would you please tell me about the derringer you purchased?"

"But you don't know what I meant before—your question was exactly what I said. He'd draw those conclusions—"

"The gun, Mrs. Killion."

"No! I won't have you twist what I say. We did not—"

"Your Honor," interjected the prosecutor smoothly, "due to the lateness of the day and to Mrs. Killion's obvious distress, I recommend that we recess until tomorrow."

"A very good suggestion," said the judge.

"You can't do that!" protested Deborah.

"Your Honor," objected Jonathan, "can't you see the prosecution's obvious ploy to discredit my client?" Jonathan realized he had phrased his question poorly the moment it came out of his mouth.

"Mr. Barnum, are you questioning the judgment of the court?"

"No, I'm not, but—"

"Then in the judgment of this court, I consider Mr. Fuller's suggestion to be a wise one." The judge slammed his gavel on the table and was about to speak again, but the sound of the gavel seemed to make the whole courtroom erupt.

Deborah broke down in tears, and Carolyn rushed from her seat toward the front. Sam jumped to his feet with protests, and only Jonathan could keep him restrained.

"Sam, it's not worth it," Jonathan said. "I don't want you in jail, too."

Sam wrenched his arm from Jonathan's grasp. "I'm just going to Deborah!"

Jonathan let him go.

"I will have order in this court!" ordered the judge.

But no one seemed to be listening. Newspaper men were surging forward; others of the spectators were talking in a loud babble, commenting on the fairness or unfairness of the court. And many of the spectators, thinking the session was over, began to talk among themselves.

Deborah was aware only of Carolyn kneeling before her with tears in her eyes, hugging her.

"Carolyn, it's not how it sounds; you must believe me."

"Oh, Ma! I know that," sobbed Carolyn.

"Thank you, my dear."

"I wish you didn't have to go through this. If only Jacob could testify."

"Jacob?" Deborah studied her daughter and knew it was more than just a passing comment. "What do you know of Jacob, Carolyn?"

"He's back, Ma. I haven't said anything because . . . well, there's lots of reasons. This ain't the place to talk about it."

Sam and Jonathan were with them now and Deborah looked up at them. "Did you hear that, Sam?"

"Well, some of it."

"I heard enough to know we need some more time," Jonathan said. He swung around to face the judge, who was pounding his gavel again.

"Order! We have not been recessed."

"Your Honor," said Jonathan. "I agree with the prosecutor. A recess is a good idea. And, due to my client's extreme distress, I would like to request a two-day recess."

Carolyn wanted to stop him. She had little or nothing to offer them. She didn't even know if she would see Jacob again. But the gavel was striking the table as the judge dismissed the court until Monday morning.

64

Carolyn told Jonathan about her meeting with Jacob. She knew she was breaking her word to Jacob, but on the other hand, he had let her down by not showing up at their appointed time. What else could she do, especially after her careless statement in the courtroom?

But, as Carolyn feared, there really was nothing Jonathan, or even Sam, could do about her revelation. Even if Jacob did agree to take the risk and testify, his testimony might be as easily disputed as had Mabel Vernon's or even Deborah's.

"Hard evidence is what we need," said Jonathan. "I do think we are stirring things up enough so that the jury will not be able to convict Deborah beyond a reasonable doubt. But we may have to settle for self-defense."

Since Carolyn had wanted to spend some time with her family, Caleb had returned home on his own. When she was ready to leave after a brief reunion with Griff, Slim, and Longjim, Carolyn rented a horse at the livery stable, and Sky accompanied her back to the ranch.

It was late when they arrived after the long ride from Leander, but Sky declined Carolyn's invitation to spend the night at the ranch.

"I'll stay in town tonight, but if you want I can come out tomorrow if you think I can help with anything."

"I've missed having you around, Sky. But it might only muddy things up for someone new to enter the scene. There is one thing— no, it would probably just be wasted effort."

"What is it? We better not discount any possibilities at this point."

"I don't like Laban being missing. How are we ever gonna prove he did it if he's not around? I think we should find some way to flush him out so at least we know what he's up to and can't disappear completely. Also, I was just thinking that maybe you could nose around town and maybe even question some of the Mexicans around here to see if we can find Jacob. He mentioned that they sometimes helped him and gave him information, and they might speak more freely to you than to a white person."

"I'll see what I can do. You'll be all right here?"

"Of course."

————

Caleb had been exhausted after the long day. It amazed him that sitting in a hot court could be so tiring, but the emotional strain of the trial alone was probably enough to knock him off his feet. Nevertheless, when he returned home that day he could neither rest nor relax.

After the court session, he had spoken to a lawyer friend who was attending the trial in order to see the great Jonathan Barnum in action. Caleb had wanted a professional viewpoint of how the proceedings were progressing, and during the conversation with this lawyer, he realized for the first time that there was little hope of the earlier conviction, much less the sentence, to be repeated.

"It'll be next to impossible to get the death sentence for a woman in this state, Caleb. It only happened before because you were on the edge of the frontier. It wouldn't have happened in a city."

"What's the most she could get?" asked Caleb.

"Life in prison for murder in the first degree. But I just don't see that first-degree murder can be proven. Perhaps manslaughter, which would garner a shorter prison term, ten years perhaps. But, let's face it, Caleb, self-defense will be the probable outcome."

"That can't be!" Caleb pounded the table.

"I know it will be a hard thing to take, Caleb, because of the implications it will have regarding your son. But the burden of proof is on the prosecution, and they really have no hard evidence that Mrs. Killion was not abused, nor that she was having an affair."

"I will not have my son's character sullied like that."

"What else can you do?"

That question had hounded him constantly since hearing it. It goaded him that he was so helpless. It had been different during the first trial, when he had bullied and bribed the townsfolk to slant their testimony to favor Leonard. It hadn't been hard to do because most of them leaned in that direction anyway—they did if they knew what was good for them!

But the passage of time had taken much of the edge off that testimony. And Jonathan Barnum was a shrewd character; he knew just how to manipulate things to favor Deborah.

But it would indeed be a hard blow for Caleb if Deborah should walk away free. And worse, if that should happen at Leonard's expense. He simply refused to allow that to happen. Nineteen years ago he had been robbed of his revenge. He had been so close to seeing her pay for his son's death. She deserved to pay because she had killed Leonard, and she still deserved it because, in addition to her first crime, she would also kill his reputation. It was not right that his dear son should be accused of such things. What would his mother think? Leonard had been so dear to her. And Caleb would not see her son's memory besmirched. Caleb owed Elizabeth that much.

Pacing in his study, agitated and restless, Caleb paused at his desk. His gaze lingered a moment on the daguerreotype of Leonard; then he sat in his desk chair and unlocked a drawer from which he withdrew another picture frame. This photograph showed a woman with dark hair and eyes and skin as pale and pure as fresh cream. By the look of her clothing—a high-necked, dark dress with puffy sleeves, trim waist and huge, hooped skirt—the photo was many years old. In fact, it was almost forty-four years old. It was the last photo of Elizabeth Stoner, Caleb's first wife.

"I won't let you down again, Elizabeth," Caleb murmured to the picture. "It's too late to make up for all my wrongs, but this, at least, I will promise you. Even in his death, our son will not be dragged through the dirt by Deborah."

The lawyer friend had asked what Caleb could do, and the answer was simple. This sham of a trial had gone on long enough. No man could be expected to continue to watch such a travesty. There was not a man in that courtroom who'd stand by while his son was made to seem a monster. Maybe they wouldn't exonerate Caleb for what he had in mind to do, but was that really important? His life had ended nineteen years ago when that woman's despicable crime had left him with no one but a half-breed greaser to carry on his name.

No matter what they did to him, no one could hurt Caleb anymore.

PART 14

SECRETS REVEALED

65

Caleb was gone all the next day. When he returned home after dinner, he was exhausted, but he did not respond to any of Carolyn's queries about his activities. He went directly to bed.

After her brief conversation with Caleb, Carolyn returned to her room for want of something better to do. She was tired—mostly from frustration and helplessness—but she felt too restless to go to bed. It did not take long for her to decide to try to make contact with Jacob Stoner again.

She was descending the porch steps when a rider came into the yard. It was Sean Toliver. He saw her, stopped in front of the house, and dismounted.

"Well, well!" he said. "I wondered if I'd ever see you again."

"My ma's trial has been taking all my time."

"I suppose I can understand that. I've been away, anyway."

"I'm sorry, Sean, I didn't even realize it."

He laughed. "I'm crushed. I expected you'd be crying your eyes out missing me."

She saw he was being sarcastic; she also realized that she hadn't missed him at all. Yes, she had been preoccupied with the trial, but she had not even thought to seek him out when she returned home in the evenings.

What had attracted her to him in the first place? His kisses? His handsome looks? Surely if there had been more, she would have wanted to be with him every chance she could. But was there any more to Sean Toliver? What had they ever talked about or done together? The only thing he had seemed interested in was kissing her and such. But had she even tried to develop a deeper relationship with him? She knew much more about Matt Gentry, and he had not so much as touched her, much less kissed her.

Carolyn knew enough about love to know that there was more than kisses to a good relationship between a man and woman. She had her mother and Sam to look to for an example; they simply enjoyed each other's company and were always talking and sharing things. They had so much in common.

Did she have anything in common with Sean? She had never bothered to find out. Perhaps she owed him that much.

She decided she could look for Jacob another time. "Sean, I was just going to go for a ride under the stars. Would you like to join me?"

"Well, love, I'm just getting back from a long ride, and I'm not particularly eager to get back on my horse for a spell."

"Why don't we just sit here on the porch and talk for a while then?"

"Talk, eh?"

"Sure. We hardly know each other."

"I know all I want to know about you." He stepped to her, put his hands on her waist, and ran them up and down. "Like how good you feel, Carolyn, how soft and inviting." He pulled her close and brought his lips down on hers hard and passionately.

She tried to pull away. "Sean, not now."

"You're right. This is hardly the place." Keeping an arm firmly around her, he started to lead her around to the side of the house that was out of sight of the gate and the bunkhouse.

"I just want to talk, Sean," Carolyn protested. But she stumbled along, unable to break away from his grip without considerable effort that she was not yet ready to expend.

"Talk, yeah . . ." But he wasn't listening. When he got her into the shadows he came at her again. Talking was the furthest thing from his mind.

Then Carolyn got mad. He didn't give a hoot about her except as some female he could seduce. He didn't want to know who she was, or what she liked, or about the pain her mother's trial was causing her. Sean had shown no interest at all in her mother's trial—or anything about her life. He was totally self-absorbed.

"Sean, I don't want to kiss you." She pushed him, but he didn't stop.

"You don't know what you want, Carolyn."

"If you don't stop, I'll scream and bring out every cowboy on this place."

"I told you once before, Carolyn, I'm a man who gets what he wants."

"Well, you ain't getting me!" She gave him a mighty shove and, because he was not prepared, he stumbled back from her.

Before she could get away, he grabbed her arm and forced his kisses on her as he had the night of the dance, ignoring her struggles. But Carolyn was more angry than helpless now. When she freed her mouth from his she didn't scream, but instead taunted him bitterly. "Is that the only way you can get a girl, Sean, by forcing her?"

"I can get any girl I want."

"Don't look that way to me."

"Why, you—!"

For a brief moment, Carolyn felt a wave of fear. His voice had been like a frightening growl, filled with ire and sudden hostility. He could hurt her if he chose to. He had stopped kissing her but continued to grip her arms in a painful grasp.

Then he let her go. Panting and glaring at her he said, "You're not worth it." And he walked away.

Carolyn felt more relief than sadness at his departure. She could finally admit to herself that she felt no remorse at all, except the brief thought that it was too bad Sean didn't have character to match his looks. What were looks, anyway? Well, maybe they played a tiny part in these things, but hardly enough to sacrifice everything else for. She was just glad she'd had enough sense to realize that before it was too late.

Carolyn laughed at herself. "As if I have any sense at all, except what God's given me! Thank you, Lord, for opening my eyes. I don't know what I'd do if you weren't around to get me out of these scrapes I get myself into."

Then, hardly connecting her next decision to her so recently uttered prayer, Carolyn decided to go ahead with her plans to find Jacob.

66

A dark, moonless night greeted her as she rode away from the stables. At first, she was glad she hadn't run into Sean in the stable, but then she realized how late it was and began wishing she wasn't alone. She thought of Sean and quickly realized that the kind of companionship he offered was definitely not what she was looking for. Too bad she had sent Sky away. Even Matt or Ramón would be better—just a friend who truly cared about her. She glanced over her shoulder toward the bunkhouse, where a light still shone in the window. But it would cause too much of a stir for her to go after Matt or Ramón now. Besides, Sean might be there.

On reaching the line cabin, she found it deserted. She supposed she really didn't expect to find anyone there, especially since it was a good two hours after sundown, the time Jacob had said he'd meet her there many days ago. She headed for the ridge.

The trail to Buck's Canyon proved to be tricky to negotiate under the dark sky. She took it easy, for she was in no particular hurry. By the look of the path, she decided that the trail had not been used for cattle since she had last been there. She dismounted and gave the terrain a closer scrutiny to confirm her suspicions. There were no fresh signs of major activity. It was too dark to discern more than that. Jacob might have traveled back and forth on this path, as the rustlers also might have done, but no cattle had been herded along here. She mounted and rode about two hundred yards to where she had first met Jacob. That spot did not yield the same reward this night.

Where could Jacob be? Could he have had a run-in with the rustlers? Had he been forced to flee back to Mexico, or met with an even worse end? Perhaps she would never see him again.

Once again her hopes had been raised, only to meet with disappointment.

Lord, how could you do this to me, to my ma? Why are you making this so hard? You know my ma is innocent; why can't she be set free? I just don't understand.

Deep down she knew it wouldn't help to get angry at God. All He did had a good reason, even if she was just too dense to see it.

"He's probably only waiting for me to grow up and to depend on Him more," she sighed to herself.

Everyone was always saying how stubborn she was—well, maybe she'd just use that stubbornness for good this time. She wouldn't give up; she'd keep plugging away until she got it right. She wanted to depend on God, to trust Him. Her ma always said that was the way to real strength and independence. But she had such a strong urge to jump in and do it herself—to save her mother, to find the real killer, to change her grandfather's heart.

Now that she thought of it, it seemed more ridiculous than ever. As if she could do any of those things, much less all of them! She needed help, and she needed it desperately. And God was ready and able to help her if only she'd allow Him to.

She was surprised when, a few minutes later, she spied a figure on the trail a hundred yards ahead of her. Instead of welcoming it as help from God, her first instinct was to cringe, thinking it must be one of the rustlers. She never dreamed it was the answer to her prayers until, drawing closer, she recognized the shape of the man's hat and the color of his mount. It was Matt Gentry.

But before she could call out to him, he turned sharply in his saddle, a six-gun aimed right at her heart. Shock at seeing her registered on his face, quickly followed by anger. "What're you doing up here?" he demanded.

The relief that had started to form in her was quickly dispelled by the sight of his gun. And she suddenly remembered the night of the storm when she had seen him right at the foot of this trail in the dark of night. Was it just coincidence that he was here? What was he up to? Had her trust been misplaced? Was their friendship really meaningless? It was, she supposed, if she couldn't trust him when it really counted.

"I ain't answering any questions until you put that gun away," she said.

Gentry looked at the gun almost as if he had forgotten he was holding it, then quickly slipped the weapon into its holster; he knew better than to argue with Carolyn. "Sorry about the gun," he said. "I didn't know who was following me."

"I wasn't following you, but maybe I should have been."

"What does that mean?"

"Come on, Matt. I've tried real hard to believe in you, but what am I supposed to think, finding you here—"

"What do you know about this place?"

She saw no reason to lie. "The rustlers are using Buck's Canyon. I saw a herd of about a hundred cattle hidden down there."

"When was that?"

"When we were on that cattle drive."

"And you said nothing?"

"There was a bit going on then to distract me."

"I reckon so." He paused before adding more to himself than her, "Then they've moved them out already, and I've missed them." He pounded his fist against his thigh.

"You didn't know about that herd?"

"Of course not!" A sudden smile slipped across his face. "I see what you're thinking. I guess it would make me look kind of suspicious."

"Okay, Matt, I think it's time you told me what's going on—"

But before she could finish, a sharp snapping of underbrush caused her to stop abruptly. She looked at Matt as his hand went once more for his gun. But another sound stopped him—it was the cocking of a weapon less than two yards away.

67

A voice spoke before the figure emerged from the brush. "Raise your hands high so I can see them."

Both Matt and Carolyn obeyed, although Carolyn recognized the voice and knew there was no immediate danger. Still, in the West it never paid to argue with a cocked gun, even if it was held by your long-lost uncle.

"Uncle Jacob."

Jacob stepped into the clearing where Carolyn and Matt sat mounted on their horses. He continued to train the rifle on them.

"Carolyn." He nodded in her direction, then looked at Matt with the rifle still pointed at him.

"Uncle Jacob," Carolyn went on, noting his hesitation, "this is a friend of mine."

"Are you sure?"

For all Carolyn knew, both Matt and Jacob could be rustlers. Yet she felt fairly confident that these two men weren't about to gun each other down without first talking.

"Yeah, I'm pretty sure," she said. She glanced at Matt as if to warn him he better not let her down.

"All right, for now I will defer to Carolyn's trust. Dismount, and let's find a place to talk."

"Well, maybe I need a reason to trust *you,*" said Matt. "Who are you, anyway? And what're you doing here?"

"That's what we'll talk about."

Carolyn said, "Matt, would you just come on? I think we can get somewhere with what's going on at this ranch if we take a risk or two. I'll be here to protect you if my uncle tries anything."

"Ha!" Matt said. But he dismounted and followed Carolyn and Jacob.

Jacob led them to the same clearing where he had camped before. It was darker tonight, and even the small fire Jacob soon built gave only shadowy illumination.

"What happened to you the other night?" Carolyn asked Jacob after they had settled down around the campfire.

"The rustlers moved out that herd," said Jacob, "and I followed them to see what I could learn. They took it on that trail I told you about, and when they got on the other side of the canyon, they met up with four other men who took over from there. They drove the herd to a spread about two days' ride west of the transfer point."

"We've got them, then," said Carolyn. "We just have to get the law to that ranch."

"It's not so easy," said Jacob. "The brands have all been changed, and it'll be their word against ours. I'm sure whoever is running this operation has got their tracks covered pretty well."

"Did you find out who owns that spread?" asked Matt.

"I'm not in the position to make such inquiries."

"Did you recognize any of the rustlers?"

"No, but then, I haven't been associated with the Stoner outfit for many years. I did ride up to the ranch and, pretending to be a cow-hand out of work, I spoke to a fellow there about a job. Like I said, he didn't look familiar. He was about six feet tall, a handsome man for a gringo, brown eyes and hair, probably a few years older than you. Oh, and he spoke with an odd accent."

"An odd accent, you say?"

"Yes, kind of western but at the same time foreign, too."

Carolyn and Matt exchanged a significant glance.

"I know what you're thinking, Matt," said Carolyn, "but it can't be."

"Sean Toliver wouldn't be the first foreman to build his own ranch off his boss's herd. Besides, something you said a while back made me first suspicious. You remember on that cattle drive you said Sean didn't want to go up to Buck's Canyon—"

"Sean and Laban said that," Carolyn corrected.

"Well, I don't know about Laban, but it sure looks like Sean is mixed up in this—unless you think it's a coincidence that he was at that ranch?"

Carolyn shook her head. She couldn't argue that point, and she remembered that Sean himself had just told her he had been on a long ride. Could it have been a two-day ride? But something else also puzzled her. "Matt, what's all this to you? I mean, is your interest just because you want to clear your name?"

"Ain't that enough?"

"What is this about Laban?" Jacob asked.

Carolyn answered, "He and Sean Toliver told Caleb they wanted to drive the cattle to Duff's Valley instead of Buck's Canyon because the grass and water weren't good up here."

"But they obviously are," added Matt.

"And with the foreman *and* the owner's son organizing the rustling, they could pretty much have a free hand," said Jacob.

"Do you realize what you are saying, Uncle Jacob?"

"Yes, but doesn't it make sense?"

"I guess I wouldn't put anything past Laban after what he's done to me," Carolyn replied.

Jacob raised a questioning eyebrow. Carolyn just shrugged. "He attacked me once; then there were two other attempts on my life that I'm almost certain he was involved in. But why would he want to steal Caleb's cattle?"

"He is a desperate man, especially now that you have come on the scene, Carolyn. He's waited a long time to get this ranch, but now he sees it slipping through his fingers. Poor Laban! No matter what he's done, I still feel sorry for him."

"That don't change the fact that we gotta bring him and Sean in for what they're doing," said Matt.

"First, we have to find Laban," said Carolyn. "When Caleb found out Laban attacked me, he swore to kill him," she explained to Jacob. "We haven't seen Laban since."

"I'll find him," Jacob said grimly. "Matt, you will ride with me?"

"I reckon I'd first like to know who I'm riding with. I figure you must be related to the Stoners and all, but no one's said anything about you being here."

"I am Caleb Stoner's son. I've been away for the last twenty years," he answered. Then, hesitating only a moment, added, "I suppose if we are to ride together, you have a right to know the truth about me. I am also known by the name Santiago—"

Matt gasped, obviously aware of the significance of that name.

Jacob went on, "So, you will be associated with a bandito . . . do you object?"

"I've ridden with worse," said Matt. "The way I see it, you are looking out for Carolyn right now and that's what matters."

"Yes." Jacob glanced affectionately at Carolyn. "It's time many wrongs were made right. And it's time the Stoner clan began to stand for more than violence and misery. Carolyn is our only hope."

"I'll buy that, especially since Carolyn seems to believe in you," said Matt. "But I'll keep my eye on you, too, if you don't mind."

"As I will on you." Jacob grinned. "We'll keep each other honest."

"Let's hope so."

"Uncle Jacob," Carolyn said anxiously, "what about my ma?"

Jacob glanced at Matt and hesitated. "It's okay to talk in front of him," said Carolyn. "He knows just about everything, anyway." She didn't want to send Matt away because she had a feeling she'd want some companionship on the long ride back to the ranch. "Please go on, Uncle Jacob. We've got to have something new to present to the court. The trial is going nowhere as it is and, whatever her lawyer says, I think it ain't gonna go well without new evidence."

"I can only tell you how I saw things, Carolyn. None of it, especially coming from a third party, will be admissible in court."

"Mr. Barnum, my ma's lawyer, says that even if you testified—"

"You told them about me?"

"I had to, Uncle Jacob! You had disappeared, and I thought I'd never see you again. Anyway, Mr. Barnum said that if all you could do was support my ma's claims that she was abused, it probably wouldn't dramatically turn things around. The prosecution would even it out by saying you're not objective because you and ma were having an affair."

"I would have testified, Carolyn, and I still will if it would help."

"No use taking that risk right away."

"Then why have I come back? I thought I could do some good."

"You don't know anything else that would help?"

Jacob focused an incisive gaze upon Carolyn. "There was never any love between your father and me, Carolyn. Do you understand this? I hated him and did not mourn his death. I would have killed him myself had I remained at the ranch a moment longer. But I was miles away, so what could I know?"

Carolyn nodded, but she felt a quaking inside. Would she ever grow accustomed to hearing how everyone hated her father? Still, she had to face it—all of it. She could not protect herself any longer.

"Please tell me what you know, Uncle Jacob," she said stoically. "Whatever you have to say can't be worse than I've heard already. It may not help my mother, but I need to know these things."

"Do you really need to put yourself through this?" he asked tenderly.

When she nodded, he continued. "I can think of no easy way to say this, but I believe your mother had every right in the world to kill Leonard Stoner. I believe her life was in danger and I told her that when I tried to convince her to run away with me. My half brother was just like my father—'cut from the same cloth,' as it is said. And what was happening to your mother was a repeat of what had happened to my own mother. Caleb abused my mother as Leonard abused yours. I saw with my own eyes the physical pain my mother suffered at his hand. Seldom were there outward signs, but often I saw her bent over in pain or limping after she had been with him. But mostly I remember seeing the tortured, devastated look in her eyes, and finally an emptiness, as if the light of life had at last been extinguished. Life had become unbearable for her. I truly believe she died inside long before she took her own life."

"Your mother committed suicide?" Shock and horror registered on Carolyn's face.

"Yes, and your mother was traveling down that same road. I feared that if Leonard's beatings didn't kill your mother, she'd give up and do the job herself."

"But still you left her?"

"I'll never forgive myself for that, but at the time, there seemed to be no other choice. Your father caught your mother and me together—it was all perfectly innocent, but he thought the worst and threatened to kill me if I didn't leave. Deborah convinced me it was the best thing to do. As I said, I knew I'd kill him if I stayed."

"You didn't come back and kill him later. . . ?" She had to ask, though she was growing certain it could not be so.

Jacob sadly shook his head as if he wished he *had* come back. "Do you think I would let her be punished for a crime I had committed?"

"I don't know what to think."

"I understand," he said quietly, gently.

A long pause followed. Carolyn stared into the fire; Jacob sighed heavily and rubbed his hands over his face. Matt shifted his position, obviously awkward at being present during this personal conversation of which he was not a part.

At length, Jacob spoke again. "Perhaps if you had proof of the dangerous situation your mother was in, the court would find that she acted in self-defense."

"That would be something, I suppose," said Carolyn, "but what we all really want is to find the real murderer, to prove she didn't do it at all." Carolyn fell silent in an inner debate. Finally she said with resignation, "What proof is there?"

"My mother left a suicide note; Caleb never knew about it and I always kept it hidden. In it she tried to explain to Laban and me why she did what she did. We were young—I was only eight—and she did not go into details a child could not understand. But it was clear she did what she did because of Caleb's treatment of her. And she felt horrible guilt for leaving Laban and me alone with him."

"Do you still have that letter?"

"No. I wanted Deborah to have the letter; I hoped seeing it would bring her to her senses. So before I left, I went to the line cabin where Laban and I lived. I wrapped the letter up and had one of the Mexican hands whom I knew to be sympathetic to me take it to Maria, with instructions that she give it to Deborah. I feared it would look too suspicious if a mere hand, especially a Mexican, were to give anything to Deborah directly, but Maria saw her daily and it wouldn't look unusual for her to do such a thing."

"My mother never mentioned a letter. It's possible she never received it."

"But why—?"

Suddenly Carolyn remembered what Maria had told her, and she remembered the housekeeper's deep loyalty to Caleb and Leonard Stoner.

"Jacob, I don't think Maria ever gave that letter to my mother. Maybe she destroyed it. Maybe . . ." Could that be what Maria was hiding, the secrets she said were best left buried? "Jacob, do you know of any place in the house—a chest, a drawer, some hiding place—where a paper like that could have been hidden?" Carolyn explained about Maria's comments. "I think Maria feels guilty about withholding that letter, so she left town rather than face me asking any more questions."

313

"I doubt she could answer your questions and face my father at the same time," said Jacob. "The poor woman is torn between doing right and betraying the family she has served for so many years."

"I guess I understand how she feels," Carolyn said thoughtfully. "But the only thing that matters now is that the truth comes out. We have to find what she has hidden."

"Such a letter is still not direct evidence," said Jacob.

"And it probably won't do any good either, but what else do I have? I guess, if nothing else, it'll establish in me the reality of the kind of men my father and grandfather were. I no longer want any false perceptions."

Jacob fingered his moustache thoughtfully. "There are many hiding places in the house."

"I've looked everywhere, even Caleb's room. There are some locked drawers and such, but only Caleb has the keys, and I know he won't help me."

"Well," Matt put in matter-of-factly, "if Maria had that letter, don't it stand to reason she would have hid it at her place?"

"Of course! Matt, you're a genius."

"I been trying to tell you that," he replied with a sloped grin Carolyn suddenly found very endearing.

"I guess I was so intent on one track that I just couldn't get back far enough to see anything else." Carolyn replayed in her mind that conversation with Maria before her sudden departure. Had she, in her loyalty, hidden away the family secrets—"buried" them in a place she was sure no one would think to look? In her own home?

Before parting that night, Carolyn had one more question to ask Jacob.

"Uncle Jacob, do you think Laban could have killed my father?"

"He was only fifteen at the time."

"That's what Grandfather said, but is it possible?"

Jacob recalled his moody, sullen younger brother and nodded. "Perhaps he could have. I never knew what he was thinking about. He was a very closed person. I suppose with me gone, he had a great deal to gain by Leonard's death. But for a boy so young to kill . . . I don't know."

Jacob and Matt made arrangements to meet the next day. Matt was not to confront Sean, but if he saw him, Matt was to give him a message. Jacob hoped that Sean would know where Laban was and could somehow lead him and Matt to him. They discussed the plan Jacob had in mind, and then Matt accompanied Carolyn down the mountain.

Carolyn was glad for the company, and even more so for Matt's presence in particular. He wasn't as handsome as Sean, or as charming, and flattering words did not flow easily from his lips. But unlike Sean, Matt was genuine and trustworthy. She was still in shock to think that Sean had been charming her while all along he was stealing Stoner cattle—in a way, *her* cattle.

"So, do you think your ma is gonna be in the clear after you show the law that letter?" Matt asked.

"It's got to help her. I only wish we could find the real killer so she could be cleared completely."

"Who might have done it? Maybe you could figure it out by the process of elimination."

"That's the problem. I've eliminated everyone but Laban, and I don't know how I could get anything out of him if Jonathan Barnum couldn't. The only other possibility is that a thief broke in that night and my pa, catching him in the act, got killed. But, if that's the case, then the thief is long gone, along with my ma's hopes of complete exoneration."

"If you don't mind me saying so, Carolyn, it sounds like your pa might have had a lot of other enemies. Any number of folks might have had reason to kill him, from greedy ranchers to disgruntled renters."

"It'll be hopeless to try to come up with people like that from twenty years ago."

"Maybe, maybe not. I'd say when you get home, just sit down and think about it for a while."

Carolyn smiled. Such reasoning was not exactly her strong point. But that's the one thing she hadn't really done yet. If the murderer was not some random thief who had disappeared long ago, then there ought to be some way to discover who it was. She had to find that way.

"Matt, would you help me?"

"Sure. I guess two heads are better than one."

"First, I want to search Maria's place."

"I wish I didn't have to leave—just when you can really use my help. But I'll give you a hand with anything else as soon as I get back."

"Don't you give it another thought. Finding Laban and clearing up this rustling business is as important as what I'm doing."

"I did promise to look out for you."

Carolyn was more touched than irked by his protective concern. She knew he respected who she was and wasn't trying to make her seem helpless in order to make himself look strong. She had saved

Matt's life, and he had no false conceptions about his own infallibility. "I'll be all right. I won't take any chances."

"I'll get back as soon as I can," he said.

"I'll look forward to that." And Carolyn found she meant those words in more ways than one.

68

First thing next morning Carolyn went to Maria's cottage, about a mile from the ranch house on the road to town. Juana was staying at the cottage now, but at this hour she would be working at the main house, and Carolyn would be free to search uninterrupted.

In the one-room cottage, it wasn't difficult to find an old steamer trunk sitting under the only window. It seemed the most likely place to begin her search. Carolyn chided herself on how easy this was, and on how much time she had wasted simply because she hadn't taken time to think—to reason—all this through. Matt was right; it might be just as easy to find the murderer by such reasoning.

First, however, she'd see what secrets Maria's trunk held.

Inside was the kind of memorabilia one would expect to find among an old woman's things. An old wedding dress that Carolyn had to move very carefully out of the way because it was so fragile; a few letters from Mexico; two beautiful rosaries; and an old and exquisite carved wooden crucifix were among the most notable items.

Then Carolyn found a buckskin pouch. She carefully opened the yellowed paper inside the pouch and read:

My dearest sons, Jacob and Laban,

This letter will be the last you hear from your mama. I am sorry I did not have the strength to continue living, if only for your sakes. When you are older and understand such things you will know me for the coward I am. If only I had my faith, that might sustain me, but your father has robbed even that from me. He is completely opposed to the Catholic faith. Once, I carelessly

316

left my rosary out and he made me pay for that mistake later. I must leave you two alone, and that breaks my heart, but the thought of facing another day of life in this house is too much for me to bear. I must depart this life, and, as I hope God will forgive me, I also hope you my sons will forgive.

I don't know why your father hates me so. I have tried to be a good wife. And now I have also failed at being a good mother. Oh, God! Have mercy on my poor soul, and especially be merciful to my dear little sons, for the only wrong they have committed was that of being born to a violent and hateful father.

In the name of a Merciful God,
Manuela Stoner.

Carolyn folded the letter and slipped it back into the pouch. For a brief moment she entertained the idea of putting it back into the trunk, burying it once more. Could this letter really help her mother? It said nothing about Leonard Stoner. It had nothing to do with Deborah's life at the ranch.

Carolyn knew the source of her hesitation and knew she should rebuke herself for it. Deep inside her remained a need to protect both her father and grandfather, but especially Caleb, whom she had come to care about—perhaps even to love. Not only would it destroy him if such secrets were revealed about him, but Carolyn had a feeling it would be equally devastating to him for Leonard's memory to be publicly tarnished.

But how could she defend Caleb when he, of all people, knew what Deborah must have suffered during her marriage? He chose to cover up those truths and allow Deborah to be wrongfully convicted of a crime that she either did not commit or had no choice but to commit.

If only Caleb had been cruel to Carolyn, she might be able to hate him. But he had been fairly decent—stern, but not violent.

Yet Caleb *was* a cruel man. The proof was in her hands even if she chose not to believe her mother. He had driven his second wife to suicide and had completely alienated the two sons by her. So what if he had a rare tender streak for Carolyn? She could only guess at the kind of treatment she would have received from him if she hadn't been his beloved Leonard's daughter.

Carolyn began to replace the other items when her glance happened upon an old book with the word "Diary" across its front. Maria hardly seemed the type to keep a diary. Curious, Carolyn lifted it out of the trunk. Inside the front cover, she found, to her astonishment, the words, "The Diary of Elizabeth Stoner, begun in May of 1841 as

317

we embark on our journey to Texas."

Eagerly, Carolyn read her grandmother's account. The ink was faded, but the woman's handwriting was extremely legible and Carolyn had no trouble. Elizabeth Stoner described the trip from Virginia, calling it "their great adventure." But rather than being excited about the trip, she seemed resigned. She had not wanted to leave her home and family, but she believed her duty was to her husband and so could not refuse him. The journey, much of which was over unsettled territory, was not easy for the woman who had known only wealth and luxury all her life as the pampered only daughter of a Virginian plantation owner. And there was no reward at the end of the trail, because Texas was a wild and dangerous place. Indians and outlaws were a constant threat. And the inhospitable Texas climate alone had proved daunting to many a hearty pioneer, much less a frail southern lady.

Pages and pages described her misery in Texas. Many times she begged Caleb to take her and their son home, but he would not listen to her. He was in his glory, carving out a living in this virgin land. She made no mention of any abuse by Caleb. In fact, even Elizabeth commented on how he doted on her and Leonard as much as his funds would allow. He built them a cozy house and had many comforts shipped at great expense from the East. But Caleb himself seemed to spend little time in that house. He was gone, sometimes for days at a time, exploring, hunting and, in Elizabeth's words, "doing whatever it is that amuses men and keeps them from their families."

Elizabeth mentioned many times how lonely she was. They were miles from another white family. And though Caleb had one neighbor look in on her periodically when he was away, it was little comfort to Elizabeth ... he was an old, toothless man and a poor conversationalist. She had no idea if there were any other women in the entire land. Most days she was in tears, and she wrote that she didn't know why she continued with a diary that had become so dismal and melancholy. But often the diary was her only source of communication with another adult, even if it was only herself. Leonard was too young to be much of a companion for the lonely woman.

Toward the end of the diary, the tone seemed to change, become less depressing. A traveler happened by the Stoner cabin. Caleb was gone on one of his "expeditions," but Elizabeth welcomed the stranger eagerly. It had been over a week since she'd had contact with an adult, and she was starving for the companionship. She never mentioned the man's name, but she described him as a well-bred young man of about her age, and handsome. It was obvious they soon became quite intimate. She reasoned in her diary that for all she knew Caleb might be dead, anyway, so what she was doing might not even be such a terrible sin. She was happy and cheerful, going so far as to comment on how much better Texas seemed when one was in love.

The diary ended abruptly. She wrote how she planned that day to go out gathering some of the lovely wildflowers with her friend; then there were no more entries. Carolyn noted the date of the final entry was April 11, 1843—the year Elizabeth Stoner had died. Could that have been why the diary ended? With her death? But it must have been an abrupt death, for there was no mention of any sickness. There had been some comments on Elizabeth's fears about being left alone so often out there in the wilderness. Caleb left her with a couple of rifles and plenty of ammunition, and he had taught her how to shoot. But could some disaster have suddenly struck the cabin? An Indian attack, a fire, wild animals, or outlaws?

Carolyn closed the diary and began rummaging once more through the trunk. She found Elizabeth Stoner's death certificate, but it was dated May 15. Perhaps she fell ill and was too sick to make any further entries. Then Carolyn saw the other date on the certificate— April 11, 1843. She scrutinized the document closer. It was basically a handwritten note written by a Rev. A. Partain on May 15, officially witnessing to the fact of Elizabeth's death the previous month. Carolyn knew that out in the frontier such lapses of official records was not unusual. The presence of ministers and doctors was so rare that one had to do what needed to be done without waiting for official sanction. Marriages were often legalized months, or years, after couples began living together, because no church officials were around. Bodies had to be buried without official declaration of death. Even to this day Sam testified to such occurrences. How much more frequent it must have been in Texas of the 1840s.

So Elizabeth Stoner had died on the day her diary had ended. What had happened to cause her sudden death? If only the death certificate could have held such details. Carolyn came upon one rather curious statement by the minister: *I hereby give evidence that I have viewed the graves, and testify to the word of Mr. Stoner that his wife is therein interned.*

Graves? Was that a mistake? Did he really mean there was more than one grave? Carolyn held the document in front of the window where the light was much brighter. It did indeed look like an "s" at the end of the word "grave."

What had happened to Elizabeth Stoner, Carolyn's grandmother?

She was certain the woman must have suffered a violent death. Its suddenness could indicate nothing else. Carolyn sighed. Why should that surprise her? Wasn't the entire Stoner legacy mired in violence and tragedy?

The discoveries in Maria's trunk were important ones. Yet Carolyn questioned if they held any importance to her mother's plight. She had seen enough of courtroom proceedings thus far to have a fairly good idea of how this so-called evidence would be received. None of it pertained directly to Deborah and Leonard. Carolyn could almost hear the prosecutor:

Objection, Your Honor. All this evidence does is call to question the character of Caleb Stoner—but I must remind the court he is not on trial....

Whatever Caleb had done in the past was not a matter for this trial, though Carolyn knew it was something *she* must sooner or later have to confront him with.

Maria probably knew less about legal proceedings than Carolyn, so it was possible she had, in her ignorance, thought these items might be valid. No wonder she had not been willing to face the results of the revelations the letter and the diary contained. But that didn't help Carolyn or Deborah. This was a terrible disappointment, to have placed such hope in Maria's "secrets," only to find them useless.

With a sense of futility, Carolyn returned her attention once more to the trunk and took all the remaining odds and ends out. Then, replacing each item carefully, she examined them for some greater significance. She was left with only the written material lying on the floor where she sat—Jacob's letter, the diary, the death certificate, and Maria's letters.

Carolyn had at first discounted the letters from Mexico because they were addressed to Maria and were obviously personal, seeming to have nothing to do with the Stoners. Yet it occurred to her that possibly Maria had written to her relatives in Mexico about the events surrounding Leonard's death. These letters that Carolyn held in her hand would only be the replies to Maria's comments, but Carolyn had no other resources, and nothing better to do with her time. Besides, there were only half a dozen of them to read.

"Doggone!" she said as she removed one from its envelope. They were written in Spanish.

Yolanda's lessons had given Carolyn a passable ability to speak the language, but reading was a different matter. She was familiar with a few words on the page but not enough to make sense of the whole.

With a frustrated sigh Carolyn hitched herself to her feet, gathered together the significant items from the trunk, including Maria's letters, and headed back to the house.

69

She found Ramón mucking out the stable. He made no protest when she suggested he take a break from his work. He washed up; then they climbed a ladder to the hayloft. There they would not be disturbed, and there was plenty of light streaming in through the loft window.

She told him about Matt's suggestion regarding searching Maria's house, and she showed him the letters

"So, all you found are a few letters from Mexico?" he asked.

"A few other things, but nothing that'll help my ma. These letters are the only other possibility."

"From Maria's relatives? How?"

"I thought maybe she might have mentioned something about my father's death, or maybe even about my parents' marriage. I know it's a long shot, but it's all I've got."

Ramón shuffled through the letters. "They're all from the same place and, by the look of the handwriting, written by the same person."

"Would you read them?"

"Sure." He took one from its envelope and scanned the pages. "This doesn't seem to have anything useful—"

"Could you read it out loud? It's not that I don't believe you, but I can't stand just sitting here waiting."

Ramón smiled, then read that letter and two more out loud. They were from Maria's brother and mostly concerned the health and well-being of his family, with a few added tidbits of local gossip. It seemed the purpose of each letter was to inform Maria of either a birth or a death. Carolyn noted the dates on these letters were spaced several years apart. Checking the dates on the remaining three letters revealed the same pattern, the final letter having been written in 1874. But it was the fourth letter that caught Carolyn's attention—it had been written in 1866.

"The timing is off," said Ramón before he started to read.

"I know, I know. Why should I even waste my time?"

"Well, it beats cleaning out smelly horse stalls." Ramón held the letter up to the light, and began to read:

My dear sister Maria,

I am glad we stay in contact, even if it is just on paper. I would not like to think that we could disappear from each other, never knowing if the other lived or died. It happens too often to our neighbors who have family in America. I thank God every time I hear from you that we learned to write at the church school. You should have seen the excitement in the village when I received two letters from you so close together. I am sorry the first had news of tragedy in the family you serve—ah, but it is a hard land we live in, is it not? Your next letter coming so soon after the first, and having such an odd request, made me very curious. Too bad we cannot talk face-to-face like we used to as children. The Mendez family you asked about was not known to me, but since it seemed an important matter to you, I spent a day or two seeing what I could find. What else is a man to do when he is too old to work? There were, as you guessed, many people from our area who have moved to your part of Texas, the Mendez woman among them—

Ramón stopped reading and looked at Carolyn. She shook her head and shrugged ignorance, as surprised as he that his surname should be mentioned. He continued, now with keener interest:

The family lives in another village, but they were not too hard to find. They are shopkeepers in their village and so of a little better station than those of us that work the dirt. They did not much like me asking about the daughter, Eufemia, and it was hard to get information. Then I met a cousin who is not on good terms with the family and was willing to talk. It seems Eufemia Mendez did come to the village last summer and stayed for almost a year. She never married here, but did give birth to a child. The cousin swears that the Mendez girl was in a family way before she came to the village. He says the child, a boy, was born in January of this year. You, of course, can cipher these things better than I. I checked at the church, and no marriage is recorded. The baby was baptized on February the third.

Ramón had a difficult time reading the last part of the letter, and when he finished he stared at Carolyn as if he hoped she'd assure him that none of this had anything to do with him. But when Carolyn made no such assurances, he said, "This can't be my mother. How could she have a baby in January and then another in April, when I was born?"

"I don't know, Ramón. But you didn't hear your mother's testimony in court. She said she had a child in Mexico, but that she also married."

"Then there is some mistake!" Ramón argued. "I won't believe the word of some stranger over that of my own mother."

"Why would he lie?"

"He just got wrong information, that's all."

"He got this information from a church—they are very careful about such things." Carolyn sighed, hating to see the distress this was causing in her friend. From her own experiences, she knew exactly how he must feel, and felt terrible that this news should come through her. "Ramón, I don't know what it all means. I don't want to see you or your mother hurt. But can you try to understand how this might be important to me."

"I don't see."

"Your mother lied in court. She said she had been married in Mexico—it's only a small thing, but one lie could discredit her entire testimony."

"Why should her testimony be so important?"

"She was the one witness whose clear objectivity would have a lot of weight with the jury." Carolyn paused and eyed Ramón curiously. "But, aside from all that, Ramón, don't you want to find out why your mother lied about such a thing? Don't you wish to know the truth about yourself?"

"I'm not like you, Carolyn; I think sometimes the truth is best left alone, hidden—like Maria wished."

"I've got to show this letter to Mr. Barnum. It might be nothing, but—" Suddenly Carolyn broke off, her hand going to her mouth as a new and shocking idea occurred to her. "Ramón, if your mother was in a family way before she left Stoner's Crossing, aren't you curious about who the father might have been? Your father, Ramón! Perhaps it was someone right here in town."

"I don't care. That is past and has nothing to do with me and with now."

"Perhaps none of that needs to come out. But that is where you and I differ. I must know everything." She thought of her grandmother's diary and Jacob's letter. "I'm tired of secrets."

"What will you do, Carolyn?"

"I'm gonna tell Mr. Barnum about this, and I suppose he will question your mother again. I'm certain he'll do so with compassion, because that's the kind of man he is. But first, I am going to see my grandfather."

"What has he to do with this letter?"

"I found some other things at Maria's, and I want to talk to him about them."

Ramón shook his head. "Sometimes, Carolyn, I don't think you know what's good for you."

"Probably not."

70

Carolyn found her grandfather in his study, sitting in one of the leather chairs and smoking a cigar. He told Carolyn to come in and offered her the chair opposite his.

He held a nearly empty glass of whiskey in his hand, and he looked tired and pale. Why didn't he look like the monster all the evidence painted him to be? Why did he have to look so vulnerable?

"Grandfather, I found some things that I have questions about," she began in a gentle tone.

"You always have questions, don't you, Carolyn? It's your greatest fault, even more so than your infernal independence." There was affection in his voice, and Carolyn felt even worse about the subject she had to broach.

She held up Elizabeth's Stoner diary. "Do you recognize this?"

He nodded. "Where . . . where did you find it?"

"Maria had it. I think she had wanted to hide it, with some other things."

"I remember telling her, years ago, shortly after Elizabeth's death, to get rid of everything. I don't know why she didn't."

"She's a funny lady," said Carolyn. "She's so loyal to you, yet I suppose she feels a certain duty to the truth, also."

"What truth?"

"What happened to my grandmother? What is Maria trying to hide?"

"Your questions, Carolyn . . . will be the death of us all." He drank the rest of his whiskey, then with a tremulous hand, refilled his glass. "Did you read the diary?" After Carolyn's affirmative nod, he went on. "I loved her dearly, but life on the frontier did not always allow a man to properly display such love. She was a self-centered girl— oh, I don't blame her. She was from a very wealthy family, and always had her way. The rigors of the frontier were too much for her, and she complained so much; never a day passed without one complaint or another. It drove me to work harder to raise our income. I had to go farther and farther afield to hunt and trap. I desperately wanted to give her the things she desired. When I returned that day and found her with another man—in his very arms!—I went crazy. I never meant to hurt her. Do you understand, Carolyn? It was an accident. I was firing at him—the stranger in her bed—but she threw herself in the way."

"Oh, Grandfather!"

"I loved her and would have done anything for her. But I hated her also for what she did to me, to our son. He saw it all, Carolyn."

"And because of that, you both came to hate all women?"

"Not all—"

"Only the ones who would have loved you," Carolyn said bitterly.

"Your mother did the same to your father as my Elizabeth did to me."

"That's what you wanted to believe. My father never gave her a chance, any more than you gave your second wife. You both assumed from the beginning that they would be faithless, and you held them like prisoners in your awful jealousy. It was almost like you were doing everything you could to prove over and over again that all women were like Elizabeth."

"No! They are all faithless creatures; there is only one way to deal with them."

"To beat them, grind them into submission?"

"We had no choice."

"And what of me, Grandfather? I'm a woman, too. Why don't you beat me into submission?"

Caleb looked deep into his glass of whiskey. Then, as if the answer he found there was too much for him, he brought the glass to his lips and in one swift motion drained it. At last he seemed to have the courage to look into his granddaughter's eyes.

"You were different," he said softly. "You were Leonard's child. How could I hurt you without hurting all that was left of him? It was always about Leonard, you know . . . protecting him, supporting him, avenging him. I will never be able to do enough to wipe from my memory the sight of that little child watching his own mother being shot to death."

Tears streaming from her face, Carolyn took Caleb's trembling hand in hers. "Hasn't it gone on long enough?" she entreated.

He shook his head. "It cannot end until I am in my grave."

"Grandfather, do you ever wonder why Leonard's only child was a girl?"

"A cruel joke of the fates, I suppose."

"No, I don't believe that. It think it was the merciful hand of God. Don't you see? Only a daughter, a girl, could break the terrible grip of the past. A son you might have taught the same errors; but what can you do with a daughter? You can't hate your own flesh and blood."

"You are right about that. I don't hate you. I hope you can believe that no matter what happens."

"I do, Grandfather."

A long pause followed. Caleb puffed on his cigar; Carolyn wiped her tears with the back of her hand. She wanted to believe that a breakthrough had been made with her grandfather, yet she could feel that tension remained. She knew there was more to be said, and she feared it would not be what she wanted to hear.

Caleb broke the silence. "You said you found 'things' you had questions about. What else did you find?"

Carolyn held out Jacob's letter. "This is a suicide note from your second wife to Jacob and Laban."

"I never heard of such a thing."

"She left it for Jacob secretly, and he hid it away."

"How do you know of these things?"

"Jacob is back, Grandfather. I have seen him and talked to him."

"So, he's not dead after all." Carolyn could not believe his dispassionate tone. "And what will you do about all this, Carolyn?"

For a moment Carolyn lost all her sympathy for the man. Apparently he was cold and heartless after all. "I'm going to give all this to my ma's lawyer," she said as harshly as she could, "and he'll use whatever he can to get my ma free."

"You don't care what this will do to your father's reputation?"

"Why should I? What did he ever do for me?" she retorted angrily.

"None of it will be admissible in court."

"Then you don't have anything to worry about."

"You will be destroying your own name, Carolyn Stoner."

"I don't care anymore. It's not a name I'm much proud of. All that matters is my ma."

"None of these things will help her."

"How can you still be so blind?"

Caleb poured himself another drink. "Did you think any of these discoveries of yours would change the truth? Your mother killed Leonard. Nothing has changed that. And even if I should risk losing you, Carolyn, I cannot waver in supporting that fact. And I will not rest until she is properly punished for that crime. I owe that to my son."

"Then I have nothing more to say to you, Grandfather. I'm going to pack my things and leave."

"I'm sorry to hear that."

Tears once more flowed from Carolyn's eyes. "I wanted it to be different. I wanted to be your granddaughter."

Carolyn stumbled almost blindly out of Caleb's study. Within fifteen minutes, she was packed and in the stable saddling Tres Zapatos.

PART 15

FRONTIER
JUSTICE

71

They gathered in Deborah's prison cell. The sheriff didn't normally let so many people visit a prisoner at one time, but Mrs. Killion and her family seemed to be good folks, even if she was accused of murder.

Jonathan, Sam, Sky, and Deborah listened attentively as Carolyn told them all that had happened since she had last seen them at the trial. Sam was upset that she had taken so many risks and kept the knowledge of her danger from them. But Deborah took his hand, shrugged resignedly, and smiled.

"She is a grown woman, Sam. And God has protected her."

Her mother's words resounded in Carolyn's heart. For the first time she realized that despite all the frustrating and discouraging things that had happened since her arrival in Stoner's Crossing, she had learned much—and, according to her mother, perhaps had matured a little. That helped to salve the hurt she felt from the severed relationship with Caleb.

Meantime, Jonathan was examining the articles from Maria's trunk. When he finished, he passed them to Deborah. It was several minutes before everyone had a chance to appraise the content of the items; then Jonathan opened discussion.

"I'll comment on each item, if you don't mind," Jonathan said. "They're all significant, in their own way, but I'm sure, Carolyn, that none is in itself conclusive. Actually, I doubt any item could be used as evidence in the trial. However, they raise questions and give me some new directions to pursue. The diary, of course, will not be useful at all, but I'm sure that's not why you included it. Jacob's letter is most interesting—it indicates a history of violence and danger in the house, but still it is not going to be accepted by the court. I, however, am going to rack my brain to think of some way at least to present it to the jury, even if the prosecution has a fit and throws it out the window."

He paused, took a breath, then opened Maria's letter. "This is the most intriguing bit of . . . if not evidence, then information. It raises questions about Eufemia Mendez's testimony. But at most, we will only be able to show that the poor woman lied about the marriage in Mexico out of shame. To make too large an issue of this might only serve to alienate the jury from us."

"You mean you won't use it even for that?" asked Carolyn, somewhat deflated.

"I really don't think it will do us any good," answered Jonathan. "It appears she only lied to protect an illegitimate child. But there is a question raised by this letter that bears investigation."

"What's that, Jonathan?" Sam asked.

"Simply this: What prompted Maria to write the letter in the first place?"

"I never thought of that," said Carolyn.

"Ah, and it's the key consideration!"

"What do you mean?"

"Tell me about Maria," Jonathan said, directing his question to both Deborah and Carolyn, who were the only ones who knew the housekeeper.

They both agreed that Maria was kind and sincere; however, neither could say they knew her well.

"She does her work in the house," said Carolyn, "but in a quiet way. Most of the time I don't even know she's around; she sort of minds her own business, I guess."

"Yes," said Deborah. "In all the time I was there, I don't recall having a conversation with her of a personal nature. She did her work and kept to herself."

"She doesn't sound like a busybody," Jonathan said. "Like the kind of woman who indulges in gossip or interferes in other people's affairs."

"That was never my impression," said Deborah.

"Do you see what I'm driving at?" asked Jonathan. "Take these letters—none are filled with answers to her endless inquiries of all the village goings-on. Granted, they are only replies, and written by a man, who might tend to ignore gossip, yet this mention of Eufemia Mendez has the sound of being out of the ordinary. The brother takes it quite seriously, not just the request of an overly inquisitive woman.

"Also, look at the date on this letter—September of 1866. We know that Mrs. Mendez returned to the States in May, four months earlier. Let's assume for a minute that Maria wrote her letter inquiring about the Mendez woman after she returned to Stoner's Crossing.

332

Something about her return must have triggered such an inquiry."

"Something about the baby," mused Deborah.

"Why do you say that?"

"Besides the money, her so-called inheritance, that would have been the biggest difference in the woman. And a woman like Maria would most likely be able to tell the difference between a four-month-old and a month-old child."

"So Maria suspected a discrepancy in Eufemia's story about marrying and having a child and being widowed during her trip to Mexico." Jonathan's eyes flashed; he obviously loved the detective aspect of the legal profession. "But Maria isn't a busybody that she'd bother to write all the way to Mexico to clear up a matter of sheer gossip."

"Why, then?" several voices interjected at once.

"That's what I want to know," answered Jonathan. "We could speculate until the cows come home, but there is only one way to know for sure, and that is to question Maria."

"Then let's get her here," said Sam, eager to do something immediately.

"We could send a telegram and subpoena her to come, but that could take several days, taking into consideration that she is an elderly lady—"

"I could ride there and back in less than two days," put in Sky.

"That would be the most efficient way," agreed Jonathan. "You could get a written statement. Of course, that alone would not be admissible unless the prosecutor were present. But, if I feel her remarks will have a bearing on the case, I will request a lengthy recess so Maria can travel here to testify. The written statement will give my request more weight, and we won't have to get the woman here in such haste for nothing. But, Sky, I think it would be best if your sister went along." Barnum looked at Carolyn. "You know the woman, Carolyn, and, as you have mentioned before, she does sympathize with you. I would prefer taking a gentle approach with her."

"Yes, I think you're right," said Carolyn. "Maybe I can do better this time than when I spoke to her before. I spooked her off then."

"I have every confidence in you, Carolyn, and I think your going would be better than if a stranger approached her."

Since it was late in the evening, they decided to leave for Waco at dawn. Carolyn knew she wasn't the only one praying that this would not be another wild-goose chase. It was their last hope, it appeared, to untangle the deepening mystery of Leonard Stoner's death.

72

The last thing Matt Gentry wanted to do was to be subtle around Sean Toliver. The man was a scoundrel, a rustler and, worse than anything, a philanderer. Matt could forgive the first two offenses, but the last took more Christian virtue than he had. It never occurred to Matt that Sean might really care for Carolyn. He had seen the foreman in action around other women and knew his motives to be less than sincere.

When Matt finally laid eyes on Sean, his first instinct was to send a fist into the man's oily grin. But since he had been unable to locate Sean immediately, he'd had some time to cool off. Moreover, Jacob had a plan, and it involved keeping Sean ignorant of their knowledge until he led them to Laban.

Matt, scratching his head and looking deeply puzzled, sauntered up to Sean in the stable that afternoon as the foreman was unsaddling his horse.

"Howdy, Boss. Nice to have you back."

"I can't exactly say the same," replied the foreman, "especially if that look on your face means more trouble."

"Naw, I don't think it's anything like that—just kind of peculiar is all. Funny thing just happened as I was riding in. This here stranger— a Mexican fella—rode up to me and asked if I'm with the Stoner outfit. When I told him I was, he gave me a message."

"Yeah? For who?"

"For Laban Stoner. The fella said to tell Laban that if he'd like to see his brother to come up to Buck's Canyon tomorrow at sundown. Ain't his brother dead, Boss?"

"That's what I thought."

"So, what do you think I ought to do about it? I can't very well give Mr. Stoner the message. He's been missing since that ruckus with his pa last week."

"Give his father the message."

"That fella was real careful to insist I tell nobody else about this, especially his pa."

"Then forget it."

"Mr. Stoner ain't gonna be none too happy if he comes back and finds out no one told him."

"That's his problem." Sean heaved his saddle off his mount, lugged it to the saddle rack, then strode away, not giving Matt a backward glance.

———————

Toliver waited until a couple of hours after sundown to make his move. Matt and Jacob were ready for him.

It looked as if Jacob had guessed right. Before Laban disappeared, he must have given Sean instructions on how to reach him in an emergency. They had a rustling business to run, and Laban couldn't just abandon that. Of course, there was still the possibility that Laban wasn't involved in the rustling. It had just been Jacob's assumption. In which case, Sean would not lead Matt and Jacob to Laban. But no matter what, Matt was determined to put an end to Toliver's schemes tonight.

Sean took the trail south of the house that followed the dried riverbed. But just at the point where the trail veered toward town, Sean cut away north instead of south to town. It was hard going, trying to follow a man in such open country. Matt and Jacob stayed back, figuring they probably wouldn't lose Sean because there were few places for a man to go. In fact, after two hours of trailing Sean, Jacob felt fairly certain he knew just where the man was heading.

"It comes back to me," Jacob said quietly to Matt as they rode. "There is a pretty ravine about ten miles northeast of here. When we were boys, my brother and I used to go there to catch wild horses. No one knew about it but us, not even our father. We loved having a secret from him. Once he beat us trying to find out where we captured the fine horses we brought home. But Laban and I had made a pact that we'd die before we'd tell."

"And you never told?"

"No, and we still live! My father gave up eventually. It was one of our few victories over him."

"You know any other ways to get there without following Toliver?"

"Yes. But if I'm wrong we'll lose Toliver and my brother."

"We're bound to lose him anyway at the pace we have to go to keep him from spotting us. I say it's worth the risk."

335

They made better progress after that, not having to be so cautious about Toliver, but the trail Jacob cut was a lot rougher than the other. It was longer, too, perhaps adding an hour to their trek. The flat, open country around the dry riverbed became hilly as they reached the eastern end of the ridge where Buck's Canyon was located far to the west. The ravine turned out to be the source of that river, dried for eons. It had steep walls and only a few acres of grass at its bottom.

Wild horses no longer grazed here. Either they'd found new territory, or, more likely, someone else had discovered the ravine and captured the animals long ago. To Jacob, who was thinking of happier times there with his brother when they were young, it had an eerie, disquieting appearance.

"There's a cave down there," Jacob said quietly, "where my brother and I used to camp, sometimes for two or three days. No one at the ranch ever missed us," he added with a hint of melancholy. "They didn't care much what we did."

"I see two horses down there. If that's it, it's a good guess one is Toliver's. We have a couple hours till sunup. Maybe we ought to wait till then."

"Let's leave our horses here, get down closer to the cave, find some cover, and keep an eye on things. Unless they make some move before, we'll wait until dawn and then try to talk them out."

"You think it'll be that easy?" asked Matt skeptically.

"I hope so. That's my brother down there."

They tethered their horses to a clump of mesquite where they would be well hidden by the tree-size bush, then started on foot down the steep side of the ravine.

———

Sean Toliver had debated about taking Gentry's message to Laban. It was a long ride out to the ravine. And he was still saddle-sore from the even longer ride to the ranch where he and Laban were keeping their stolen cattle until they could drive them to a fellow in Dodge City who made a habit of not looking too closely at brands. But the appearance of this stranger might be significant. Most certainly he was Laban's only full brother, who for the last twenty years had been thought dead. For one thing, this brother stood in the way of Laban's inheriting Caleb's ranch. Of course, Laban had never been sure of his inheritance anyway; that's why he'd gotten into the rustling business a couple of years before. Nevertheless, it might not be wise to sit on this kind of information.

All the way out to the ravine, Sean tried to figure a way to use his information to his best advantage. He had never intended to share half the proceeds of their business with Laban. He wanted it all, especially that ranch Laban had bought. Laban, of course, was expendable; Sean was only waiting for the best moment to take care of his partner, when he ceased being useful to Sean.

Sean wasn't a killer, at least not in the sense that he liked killing. But he was a man who insisted on getting what he wanted, no matter what it took. When Caleb's pretty little granddaughter showed up, Sean immediately saw an opportunity to come out way ahead on this whole deal. Besides the profits on the rustling, he figured he could marry her and one day get all the Stoner holdings as well. That was another very good reason for eliminating Laban. And the girl offered a very convenient way to do that, too. If Laban could get nailed for the murder of his half brother, that would effectively put him out of the picture without forcing Sean into more unpleasant tactics.

Then things began to get complicated. First, there had been a couple of attempts on Carolyn's life. Sean could never prove that Laban was involved, but it was a good bet, and that was another reason to get rid of Laban. Then Sean had to go north to supervise the receipt of the cattle from Buck's Canyon. When he returned, he found that Laban had disappeared, so he couldn't do anything about Laban right away. Laban had left him a note telling where he was hiding. Still, Sean did not want to act hastily, especially since the girl seemed to turn cold on him all of a sudden. If only he'd had more time to charm her . . . but a man did have to work, too.

Now this brother had to turn up in the midst of everything. Even if Sean killed Laban and married Carolyn, he'd have a slim chance of getting the Stoner place. Before the girl showed up, he hadn't given a thought to taking over the Bar S outfit. But in the last few weeks, he had come to like the idea. He liked it very much.

All he had to do was kill both brothers and marry Carolyn.

To someone with a self-image as lofty as Sean's, those were not insurmountable obstacles. And with these things in mind, he had made his decision to tell Laban about the return of his brother. He also considered the possibility that the brother sent his message with the hope of following the person who delivered the message to Laban's hiding place. So he wasn't surprised when he spotted the two riders on his tail. But it was disconcerting when he appeared to lose them after a couple of hours. It would have been very convenient to get both brothers alone in that isolated ravine.

Laban was at the cave at the bottom of the ravine when Sean

arrived. A pot of coffee was heating over a small, smokeless fire at the mouth of the cave. The coffee was more welcoming than Laban.

"What's wrong?" asked Laban without preamble the moment he saw Sean.

"I got a peculiar message for you," Sean answered. "But first, I'll have some of that coffee." He had to get a cup out of his own saddlebag, and by the time he'd poured his coffee and settled by the fire, Laban was fuming. "Now, don't get all upset, Laban; we have to have cool heads to figure all this out."

"Then get on with it. What message?"

"It's from a fellow claiming to be your brother; and if you want to see him you have to be up at Buck's Canyon at sundown tomorrow."

"What did he look like?"

"I didn't see him myself, but the man he spoke to says he was Mexican."

"That's all he expects me to go on?"

"I didn't give the message, I'm just delivering it. I thought it might be important, since your brother is supposed to be dead, or at least has been missing for years."

"I don't like this."

"I thought you'd be delighted to see your brother after all these years."

"Why should I? I mourned for him twenty years ago, and all would be better if he would stay dead. If it turns out he has been alive all these years without ever contacting me, why should I care about him?"

"That wasn't very thoughtful of him, was it? Won't make it any easier to share your pa's ranch with him."

Laban gave a derisive grunt. "What makes you think I would be willing to share a thing?"

Now, that was an interesting statement. Sean felt sure it was aimed as much at him as it was at the brother.

"I wasn't ready to share with that no-account niece of mine," Laban continued. "Why should I do so with a brother who walked out on me?"

"So it was you who hired a gun to take care of the girl?"

"Does that surprise you?"

"Not at all." It was quite obvious that Laban didn't have the guts to do his own killing. How could anyone believe that he had killed his half brother nineteen years ago? More importantly, how could Sean trust that Laban would actually follow through in killing Jacob?

Sean would just have to trust himself for that job.

In the few hours that were left before daylight, Sean slept with one eye peeled and a hand on his Colt. A gunshot wakened him as the first signs of sunlight streaked the sky. The shot blasted a hole in the rock that formed the lintel of the cave. Sean stayed down, and Laban, who had been on watch, sprawled flat on the ground.

"You idiot!" hissed Laban. "You were followed."

"What better place than this lonely ravine to meet your long-lost brother?" sneered Sean. "I think I've done you a favor."

73

If Laban had ever imagined seeing his brother Jacob again, it certainly would never have been this way—at the end of drawn guns. But if it *was* Jacob out there, Laban was not about to let sentiment cloud reality.

He drew his six-gun and carefully crawled to the mouth of the cave to get a look outside. He saw nothing but scrub and rocks and mesquite. Whoever had fired on them was well hidden, probably behind those boulders fifty-some yards from the cave. And, for the time being, they had the advantage because they could keep Laban and Sean trapped in the cave indefinitely, or at least until they died of thirst.

"What kind of favor have you done, Toliver, by getting us trapped in here?" asked Laban caustically.

"I think we ought to be able to talk our way into a better position. If that is your beloved brother, he isn't going to be anxious to kill you."

That made sense. Jacob had no reason to kill Laban. That first shot was probably just a signal to let them know of new arrivals. Laban took a breath. He had to start thinking more clearly. Too much was at stake. He had already botched attempts to get rid of that niece of his. Now another barrier threatened what he had waited for so long. But could he kill his own brother? He had hired someone to go after the girl, and he cared less than nothing about her. But Jacob was different. He had meant something to Laban once.

"Who's out there?" Laban shouted, determining to take Sean's advice.

"Laban, is that you?" came a voice from approximately the direction Laban had guessed. "It's me, your brother Jacob. I've come home."

"How can I be sure of that?" But even as Laban asked, he could tell by the sound of the voice. It was Jacob's, though perhaps deeper and rougher than the voice of the twenty-year-old Laban had once known.

"I recognize your voice, Laban, although it's been twenty years. What proof do you want?" There was a pause, then, "I think I can tell you how you got that scar over your left eyebrow. You were riding Leonard's favorite horse—I think its name was Thunder—and our half brother knocked you off. You cut your head on a sharp rock as you fell. You were eight years old at the time."

"What do you want?"

"After twenty years, Laban, I'd think that would be obvious. I want to see you."

"Why do you suddenly have this urge? You let me think you were dead all these years—you should have just continued to do so."

"I'm sorry, Laban. My life has not been such that I could be free in all I did. I've been an outlaw, and I've been living in Mexico. It's not much of an excuse, I know. I guess once I was away from our father's place, I wanted to forget all about it. Forgive me for doing that to you."

"Why do you come now, shooting?" asked Laban, purposely ignoring Jacob's request for forgiveness.

"Just to let you know we're here. No more shooting, I promise."

"You're not alone."

"No. I'm with a Bar S hand named Matt Gentry. He's been concerned about the rustling at the ranch."

Sean cursed and whispered, "They're on to us."

But Laban said to his brother, "What has that to do with me?"

Gentry answered, "I know for a fact Toliver has been receiving Stoner cattle at that ranch north of here. And I don't think it's a coincidence that he knew right where to find you, Mr. Stoner."

"You'll have a hard time proving any of this," said Laban.

"Laban," Jacob said, not realizing the implication of his words, "right now only Gentry and I know about this. You can quit the

340

rustling, return the profits to the Bar S Ranch, and avoid all consequences."

Sean smiled and whispered to Laban, "All we have to do is eliminate these two, and we'll be in the clear."

Laban's choices were evident. He could trust his brother, who had always been a man of his word, give up, and try to wait patiently for whatever his father willed to him. Or, he could follow Sean's urging to gun down the only two men who stood in his way of getting what he wanted.

Well, he'd been patient long enough. How many times in the last twenty years could he have killed his father and received his due? But he had waited, hoping it would come to him eventually. And now Jacob was back, and Leonard's child. His hope was gone. Caleb would probably kill him on sight for what he tried to do to Carolyn. As far as an inheritance went ... it was foolish even to entertain the idea any longer.

"Jacob," Laban spat, "you always were a fool. I have no more hope of mercy from our father than I have of ever getting his ranch."

Sean whispered to Laban, "Keep him talking. I'm gonna slip out and try to circle around them." He checked his six-gun to make sure it was loaded and his belt had plenty of ammo; then he filled his pockets with extra cartridges and cradled his Winchester in his arms.

Laban didn't like being stuck in the cave with Sean out free, but he figured Sean had as much to gain from getting rid of Jacob and Gentry as he did.

"Caleb was seen just a few days ago talking to his lawyer," he went on, "and I heard with my own ears that he plans to leave the ranch with Leonard's runt."

Sean had reached the mouth of the cave and was inching out on his stomach. Some brush and a few large rocks stood nearby for cover, but after that he would be pretty much in the open, especially as the morning gray began to lighten. He'd need more of a distraction than mere talk could provide.

"You don't need his ranch, Laban. You can make a life for yourself without him. That would be the best thing you could do. Break away from him before it's too late."

"It's already too late. I've invested too much of my life in this place to give it up."

"And what will you do about those who stand in your way?"

For an answer, Laban fired toward the boulders.

"Laban, you don't want to do this," pleaded Jacob.

"I'm through with waiting; I'm through with talk. If you stand in

341

my way, Jacob, then I am through with you." Laban fired again, this time his shot shattering an edge of the rock.

———

Matt knew Jacob didn't want to shoot at his brother. He understood his hesitation, but he also knew that their own lives would be forfeited if they didn't fight back. He was also beginning to wonder where Sean Toliver was. The presence of Toliver's horse indicated the foreman was around someplace. But where?

Matt tried to look over the top of the boulder that provided some cover, but as he moved, a bullet zinged by much too close for comfort. Another bullet followed in quick succession as Matt ducked back to safety. Then there was a brief pause. Perhaps Laban hadn't started with a full gun and was now reloading. Matt didn't wait to consider all the possibilities. He raised his head like a startled jack rabbit and quickly craned it around. The instant he spotted movement in the brush about a hundred yards to the left of his and Jacob's position, he ducked back to cover, but not before another bullet sliced the air an inch from his head.

He nudged Jacob and pointed to the left. "They're gonna try and keep us busy," he said as he fired at Sean. He was too far away to hit his mark, but he hoped to draw Toliver out.

He immediately got his wish. Toliver returned fire with his Winchester. The bullet struck only a foot in front of Matt, spitting the dirt up in his face. Matt shouldered his own Winchester and fired back. He kept this up for several minutes, while Jacob, next to him, exchanged shots with his brother in the cave.

Soon Matt had to pause to reload his rifle. In the brief moments while he was thus occupied, Sean must have changed positions, for when Matt looked up he could not see Toliver. He carefully scanned his flanks and rear but saw no sign of movement. Toliver probably planned to sneak up behind them. Matt held his carbine taut and ready, eyes alert.

He saw a slight movement in the grass forty feet away; it could have been only the rustling of the wind. Then he saw the muzzle of a rifle as it was raised to aim. Matt fired. The weapon flew into the air, accompanied by a sharp curse of pain from its owner.

But Toliver was too experienced to let a little pain distract him; he recovered quickly, diving to his left to retrieve his weapon. Matt leaped up and crossed the ground between them in a heartbeat. He bodily slammed Toliver back to the ground before Sean could get a firm grip on the rifle. The impact dazed Toliver for an instant, and Matt got in a solid right hook to Sean's jaw.

Toliver shook the fog from his brain and retaliated with three or four painful body punches that left Matt gasping for air. The two were evenly matched, even if Toliver had more brawn, for Matt was quick and strong. They scuffled on the ground for a few moments until Sean gained his feet, but he made the mistake of attempting to kick Matt in the face. Matt caught Sean's foot and twisted it away. Then, while Toliver was off balance, Matt jumped up. They sparred like two angry boxers, each making substantial contact with his fists.

In the meantime, Jacob and Laban continued to exchange shots, both seemingly oblivious to the battle some yards behind and to the left of Jacob. Laban's bullet, then, must have been a stray as it flew over Jacob's head just as Matt came into its path. The lanky cowboy had just raised his fist to deliver what might have been a finishing blow to Toliver, who was nearly spent. But he never made contact; Laban's shot creased Matt's skull two inches above his left ear and sent him sprawling senseless into the dirt.

———

Panting, Toliver lunged for his rifle, grabbed it, and got off a shot before Jacob even realized there was danger from that direction. But Toliver was too quick to be accurate, and his shot only dislodged Jacob's six-gun from his hand. Sean aimed his Winchester again, this time with deadly accuracy. He squeezed the trigger at a helpless Jacob.

The Winchester jammed.

Before Jacob could recover his weapon, Laban came out of the cave, gun still drawn. The stand-off seemed to be over. Jacob saw that his partner was down. He had little chance of surviving the next minutes.

"Kill him, Laban!" shouted Sean. "There's no other way now."

Laban came within a few feet of his brother, still aiming his gun at him, but with a look of ambivalence clouding his hard visage. Sean saw immediately that Laban wouldn't have the guts to do what had to be done. He slowly made his way to where Matt had dropped his carbine.

"Why couldn't you stay away?" said Laban to his brother. "I had it all planned out so perfectly."

"Rustling our father's cattle—that was your plan?"

"The rustling was nothing—it was what I had hoped would come of it. This whole region was on the verge of a range war because of that rustling. The small ranchers wanted blood for all the grief the big outfits have caused them, especially our father. He was going to catch a bullet sooner or later—"

"And you planned to make it sooner? With a range war as a perfect smoke screen?"

"Why not? What did our father ever do for me?"

"You couldn't wait just a little longer?"

"That was my worst mistake—waiting. Now I've waited too long."

"It's still not too late to repair things, Laban," said Jacob.

"And it's not too late for you to join me. We can both have it all."

"We only have to kill our father and our niece. I can't be a part of that. I have lived the life of an outlaw for many years, but I have not forgotten about honor."

"Then you leave me with no choice," said Laban. He raised the gun, but his finger seemed to freeze on the trigger.

"You can't kill me," said Jacob.

It was true. Laban's father had always told him he was gutless; this was proof.

The next shot seemed to come out of nowhere. Jacob watched, stunned, as his brother lurched with the impact of the carbine cartridge, then crumpled to the ground. Then the weapon cocked again, aimed this time at Jacob.

————

Matt regained consciousness just as Sean picked up his carbine. He shook away his dizziness and tried to stand, but the ground seemed to rise with him, all sense of equilibrium gone haywire. He only made it to his hands and knees. Through blurry vision, he saw Sean aim the carbine and, assuming it was aimed at Jacob, he knew he must act quickly to save his partner.

But he wasn't fast enough, and he was certain he'd failed when the shot was fired unobstructed. Out of sheer fury, he gritted his teeth and made a lunge for Toliver.

Matt hit Toliver waist-high and leveled him. The blow caused his head to reel. When he regained his senses, he saw Jacob, very much alive, standing over Toliver, pointing his six-gun at the foreman's head.

74

On Sunday night while Jacob and Matt were trailing Sean, Caleb sat in his study stewing over the quickly unraveling events. He was in no way repentant of his actions. He thought Carolyn was a fool for leaving like she did and for hanging on to the fantasy that her mother was innocent.

He'd had enough of the lot of them, and he'd especially had enough of that sham of a trial. If it continued Monday morning, it would do nothing but ruin his and his son's reputations. Although none of those papers Carolyn had found could possibly be construed as viable evidence, even by the most incompetent legal official, Caleb knew that Deborah's lawyer would bring it all to light out of sheer spite.

But no one knew the spite game better than Caleb. And he had been waiting too long to be outdone once again by a snip of a woman—two women this time!

In the old days, it had not been unusual for a man to take justice into his own hands. Caleb himself had several times executed that so-called justice with the help of a rope and an oak branch. It had been purely stupid of him, nineteen years ago, to try to lend an air of civility to the proceedings by orchestrating that trial. It had been weak of him—just as gutless as he was always accusing Laban of being. There was only one kind of justice—the kind of justice he had given to that scoundrel who had stolen Elizabeth from him.

It was time—well past time!—that Leonard's death be avenged.

Caleb stormed out of his study in search of Toliver. At the bunkhouse he learned that the foreman had left a short time ago, saying he would be back in the morning. Caleb wanted Toliver's help, for he was a competent, formidable ally. But there were others who, for the right price, would do Caleb's bidding.

Within the hour he had gathered three such men together, each one a hand from the ranch. In Leander, he planned to add another man to his party—one-time Sheriff Pollard. Caleb didn't like the broken-down old drunk, but the presence of a lawman would lend a semblance of legality to Caleb's plans.

Pollard was at the Dancing Tumbleweed. He didn't frequent this place, but he was out of money, and his other regular saloons in town were no longer extending him credit. That was about the only reason he was glad to see Caleb Stoner that evening. Caleb still owed him the reward money for turning in the Killion woman.

"We got some unfinished business, Stoner," said Pollard.

"Let's talk about it in private," said Caleb, indicating for Pollard to follow him to a back room the bartender of the Tumbleweed had said he could use.

As soon as the door closed behind him, Pollard demanded, "So, when am I gonna get my reward?"

"You figure I'm going to give you a cent before justice is served on that woman?"

"The reward was just for her capture, nothing else."

"If you want your reward money, all you have to do is officiate at her hanging."

"What do you mean? She ain't gonna hang—you better get used to that."

Caleb shook his head. "She's going to hang, just like she should have nineteen years ago. I'm going to see to it, and you're going to help."

"A lynching? You're crazy, Stoner!"

"No, I'm not."

"Well, what do you need me for?"

"I want a representative of the law there."

"You think that's gonna protect you from the trouble you're gonna be in if you go through with this?"

"I'll worry about that. All you have to worry about is your five thousand dollars. If she walks away free, you don't get a penny. Five thousand will buy you a lot of whiskey, Pollard, probably a lifetime's worth."

When Lucy Reeves saw Caleb and Pollard going into the back room, she knew something was up. Those two scoundrels meant nothing but trouble for Deborah, and the fact that they were together made it even worse. She asked one of the other girls to cover for her, then quietly went to the closed door, which was secluded from the main saloon by a short corridor. She pressed her ear to the door and listened.

The two men had not taken pains to lower their voices, and she could discern most of the muffled conversation. She heard it all to the point when Caleb was bribing Pollard with the reward money. Absorbed in the conversation, she simply had not considered there to be any danger except from the two men in the room. She didn't notice the approach of someone from behind her.

"Hey you!"

Lucy gasped and jerked up.

"What're you up to, lady?"

"I—uh—lost an earring," she said lamely, and to confirm her story, she quickly knelt down and began groping on the floor.

The intruder was one of Caleb's henchmen, and he wasn't buying her story. He grabbed her arm and pulled her up. Then he opened the door.

"Hey, Boss," he said upon entering with his catch firmly in tow, "look what I found outside your door. She was tryin' to get an earful."

"Really?" Caleb eyed Lucy. He recognized her from the trial; she had been among the spectators, and as one of a very few women, and an attractive one at that, she had been hard to miss. "And who might you be?"

"My name's Lucy, and I just work here. I thought the room was empty and wanted a private place to meet my beau. You know how it is—"

But Pollard broke in. "I seen her talking with Deborah Killion a couple of times, Stoner. I'll bet they're in cahoots."

"That true?"

Lucy hesitated, wondering if she could lie her way out any further. She was furious with herself for getting caught at the door and upset that she hadn't heard more details of Caleb's plans to execute Deborah. Lucy knew she had to somehow talk her way out of this so she could warn Deborah and Sam. But what could she say to allay her captor's suspicions?

"I guess I know her a little. But I mainly was hoping I could make a few bucks from this situation. You know, maybe I could help you somehow, seeing as how I know the woman."

"Don't believe her," said Pollard.

347

"I'm not that much of a fool," said Stoner. "Besides, I have all the help I need."

"Okay," said Lucy, casually, turning to leave.

"Unfortunately, I can't let you leave," said Caleb.

"But I—"

"Steve," Caleb said to his henchman, "tie her up and gag her securely. I'll see to it no one uses this room for the rest of the night."

"You'll be sorry, mister!" threatened Lucy. "You ain't going to get away with this."

"Who's going to stop me?"

Lucy struggled every inch of the way as the ropes were cinched tightly around her hands and ankles. But she knew Caleb Stoner was right. No one could stop him, especially since it appeared he planned to do his terrible deed this very night. She was the only one who knew, and she was helpless.

When she had been left alone in the room, she fought against the ropes until she was exhausted. Then she thought of the conversations she and Deborah had had many times in prison.

Listen here, God, she silently prayed. *If everything Deborah said about you is true—even if only half of what she said is true—you oughta be able to get Deborah out of this fix. It's up to you. Get these ropes off me so I can warn someone, or help Deborah in another way. But, God, one way or another, help her!*

75

It was easy enough for Caleb and Pollard to walk into the jailhouse in Leander. The sheriff knew the men and welcomed them, even at that late hour. He didn't even bother to strap on his gun.

Caleb's plan was simple and to the point. He intended to do what had to be done no matter what the personal cost.

After about two minutes of trivial conversation with the sheriff, Pollard casually lit a cigarette as a signal to the three accomplices waiting outside, telling them that the sheriff was alone and it was safe to proceed. Immediately the ranch hands entered, masked, and with guns drawn. They made as if to take Caleb and Pollard hostage, knocked out the sheriff, and locked him up in the spare cell. It was an obvious ploy to attempt to cover Caleb's guilt, and the sheriff might not believe it, but Caleb would worry about all that later.

Caleb himself unlocked Deborah's cell.

Deborah had been lying on her bunk dozing when the opening of the next cell awakened her. She looked up and thought she was dreaming when she saw Caleb standing at her cell, a ring of keys in his hand. She had not spoken to the man in nineteen years, and her voice failed her as she stared silently at him.

"It's time to go, Deborah," he said, sounding exactly the same as he had years ago when he had accused her of murdering his son.

"Where?" Deborah croaked past the terrible constriction in her throat.

How many times had she fantasized about what she'd say to Caleb if she ever saw him again? At first she had heaped recriminations and hatred upon him, accusing him of turning his son into a monster, of ruining her life, and every cruel injustice she could think of. Later, as God began to work in her life, she wondered about forgiving him and thought of grand and saintly speeches that would bring him to his knees in repentance and redeem his heart for Christ.

Now, as she stared into his cavernous, cold eyes, her mind went blank.

"You had to know you couldn't get away with it," he said.

"No . . . I don't know what you mean."

"It's time to pay for what you did to my son."

Deborah shook her head. "You can't do this, Caleb."

In response, Caleb turned the key in the lock and pulled open the cell door, then stepped aside as Pollard entered with a length of rope in his hands. He tied her hands behind her and placed a secure bandanna around her mouth. Then they led her outside and took a short walk to where the horses were tied out of sight behind the jail. They rode quietly out of town.

Deborah thought of her escape from Stoner's Crossing so many years ago. How different it had been, in a flurry of galloping horses and clouds of dust. Would there be a rescue this time? How would anyone find out what had happened until it was too late? The sheriff could be unconscious for hours, and Caleb did not have to ride far to find an appropriate tree.

She prayed for grace and strength to accept whatever came, but a quiet sense in her spirit seemed to assure her that she was not meant to die at the end of a rope. That helped to calm her and relieve some of the shock over what was happening. It also cleared her mind so that as they rode, she began to think of her family. If Caleb's plan was successful, what would become of Carolyn? The others she didn't worry so much about—Sky and Sam were strong and would be able to overcome their grief. But Carolyn never had been as tough as she wanted people to believe. Losing her mother would be hard, but even more difficult would be bearing this cruel, hateful blow from a man she had placed such hope in.

How could Caleb be so spiteful and heartless? Didn't he realize how much Carolyn wanted to love him? Was revenge more important than that? Deborah began to berate herself for not speaking these things to Caleb while she'd had the chance. Now it was impossible for her to say anything because of the gag on her mouth. Feeling helpless, Deborah began to pray. She wanted to pray for Carolyn and Sky and Sam, but instead she prayed for Caleb alone.

————

Caleb knew it was risky, but he was going to indulge himself in one thing. There was a stout tree by the place where Leonard was buried, and it seemed appropriate that his son's murderer be hanged within sight of his grave. In a symbolic way, Leonard would watch the death of the woman who had ruined and ended his life. A more practical aspect was that the execution party would be distanced from Leander and, hopefully, from being easily found should their deed be discovered.

But it was a hard ride back to Stoner land—an hour and a half, and that was after the ride to Leander earlier in the evening. Caleb was exhausted, and they had to take it easy for his sake. He tried to ignore the pains in his chest, but they had to stop several times to allow him to catch his breath.

During the second stop, Pollard urged Caleb to get it over with. "Come on, Caleb! This has gone on long enough." Pollard had been looking skittishly behind him during most of the ride, and Caleb knew the old goat was losing his nerve.

Just to spite him, Caleb pushed on. After all, Pollard had botched the first hanging. That wasn't going to happen this time; they had a healthy lead over anyone who might try to follow.

"I'll say when we're going to stop," said Caleb. "That woman's got more backbone than you, Pollard. Now shut up and get back on your horse."

Caleb noticed Deborah eyeing him. Was that pity in her eyes? Or fear?

He sneered at her. "You're dying to talk, aren't you? Well, you'll get your chance—and they'll be your last words."

Deborah briefly closed her eyes, and when she opened them, he knew it had been pity he had seen in them. It made him furious. He wanted to see her tremble with fear. He had been tempted to remove her gag so as to hear her beg for mercy, but he knew she was too stubborn to do that.

Even now, when she was so close to the end, the cursed woman was robbing him of the satisfaction he had dreamed of for so many years. Why couldn't he feel the sweet comfort of victory?

But even Caleb knew that he'd never be fully victorious. When he hanged Deborah, he would lose the only person who had shown any inclination to love him in many, many years. He tried to tell himself that Carolyn didn't matter to him. She had walked out on him, refusing to see the truth. It was her choice to take Deborah over him—to side with the murderer of her father. Why should he care anymore?

Yet he could not wipe from his memory the pain he had detected in his granddaughter's eyes as she had left the ranch. She had desperately wanted him to be her grandfather, to love her as she wanted to love him.

Vengeance is stronger than love, Carolyn, Caleb told himself as he mounted and urged his horse forward.

76

The ropes were too tight. Lucy had struggled and twisted so much that her wrists were raw and bleeding. She had lost hope that someone would miss her and come looking for her; Stoner had no doubt told the bartender she'd be gone for a while.

A good fifteen minutes had passed, maybe longer. Lucy had lost track of time. She had to get loose. But another wrench against her bonds only brought tears of pain to her eyes. She tried again to work at her gag. If only she could make some noise, draw attention to her plight. She pushed against the cloth with her tongue, moving her jaw frantically up and down until her mouth ached. Still, she didn't give up. She had to help Deborah.

Suddenly she felt her upper lip come free. With a silent cheer, she continued to work at it until the cloth was pushed down around her chin.

"Yes!"

Then she rolled across the floor until she was near the door. In another second, the people in the saloon heard such a bellow that no one could ignore it. Lucy yelled till her throat was as raw as her wrists.

One of the other saloon girls found Lucy in the back room. "What in tarnation happened to you?"

"No time to explain. Get these ropes off me quick."

Lucy had to wait five agonizing minutes before her co-worker came back with something to cut the heavy ropes. Then she dashed out of the saloon, down the street to the jail. But she was too late. Deborah's cell was wide open, and the sheriff lay unconscious in the other cell.

She felt each precious minute tick by as she went in search of Griff. Since Pollard had started to come to the Dancing Tumbleweed, Griff hadn't come around as much. She had to waste more time because she didn't think to look in the most obvious place—his hotel.

She ran into Longjim at one of the other saloons.

"He turned in early tonight, plumb tuckered out," Longjim explained. "You know, only a few weeks ago, he was at death's door," he added as if he had to make excuses for his friend.

"We gotta find him. Caleb Stoner's got Deborah."

Longjim, a man of pure action, didn't waste time with questions; they ran for the hotel at top speed.

By the time they had roused Griff, Slim, Sam, and Jonathan, and all had heard Lucy's story and sorted out everything, ten more minutes had passed. They took a few extra minutes to go to the jail to check on the sheriff and question him in the hope he knew Caleb's destination. The sheriff was just coming to, but he had no more information. It was decided that Lucy and Jonathan would stay behind to see that the sheriff got some medical attention and to be there to meet Sky and Carolyn, and to deal with the court in the morning, should Deborah still be absent.

On a hunch, Griff suggested they head out of town in the direction of the Stoner ranch; it would place Caleb nearer to home once his deed was done. Caleb had nearly an hour lead on them when they finally thundered out of town, but once they determined for certain Caleb was indeed heading back to his ranch, the preacher and three ex-outlaws rode as if they were being dogged by a prairie fire.

Nearer to the ranch, however, they had to slow considerably so they could read the trail more carefully and learn exactly where on the huge ranch Caleb was heading. Tracking at night with little moonlight was tedious, frustrating work—a match even for Sam, an ex-Texas Ranger, and for Longjim, who had learned tracking during his years living with the Crow Indians.

All Sam could think was that anything might have happened in the time since they had discovered Deborah missing. If Caleb Stoner intended on carrying out the court's sentence of nineteen years ago, they might already be too late. He thanked God there were few trees in that country, but every one they passed caused Sam's heart to constrict and his stomach to knot for fear of the gruesome sight they might encounter at any time.

———

Caleb looked pale and gaunt, with a tinge of blue around his tightly pursed lips. Deborah had never seen him look so vulnerable. She wondered that she could have ever been so afraid of him. She felt sorry for him now.

But some of her fear returned when she chanced to look into his eyes during one of their stops. She and Caleb held each other's gaze for a moment in that old power struggle she remembered from the past, and she saw that this was a dangerous man—and he was intent on executing *her*. Nevertheless, she wanted desperately to talk to him, to share her heart with him, to tell him that she did not hate him any longer for what had happened when she was married to his son. She wanted to tell him that she did not see him as her enemy, and that for Carolyn's sake she truly wanted to reconcile with him. But the gag kept her silent. She wondered if Caleb kept it on her, now that there was no one to hear her cries for help, because he feared her words as much as she feared the death he had planned for her.

Soon they came to land she vaguely recognized as Stoner land ... at least she judged it must be because they had been heading in that direction, and enough time had passed so they should be near the ranch. When they came to a rise that gave them a view for some distance, she could see the ranch house about half a mile away, all dark and mostly in shadows. They made a wide circle, skirting around toward the back of the house.

Deborah wondered if anyone from the ranch would come to her aid if they knew what travesty was about to take place. She couldn't count on it; the place was, by appearances, deep in sleep. Even the cook was not yet awake to prepare breakfast. Dawn was still two hours away.

They traveled for another twenty minutes until they came to a little green patch of ground with a few cottonwoods and one big oak lining a small pond, or buffalo wallow. Three cows were bedded down near the water, but they were apparently strays because there were no herds anywhere near. The water source was hardly enough to support the three animals, much less a herd. But it must have had as its source an underground spring, for the trees were healthy and green even that late in summer. Deborah wondered that she had never discovered this little haven during her time at the ranch. Then she saw why Jacob had never brought her here.

On a mound a few feet from the oak were two tombstones, side by side. It was difficult in the dark to read the inscriptions on them, but Caleb made a point of drawing Deborah's mount close enough so that she was able to make them out. The first one read: *Leonard Stoner, Beloved Son. May he rest in peace. Born 1839. Died 1865.*

How inadequately those few words expressed all that was encompassed in that single span of life. The pain, the disappointment, the terror of a wronged and abused wife; and no less, the consuming grief of a father, filling him with hatred and bitterness that spanned a time almost as long as Leonard's entire life. But what struck Deborah even more profoundly as she gazed at the stone was that she felt nothing but a deep sense of irony toward this man who had once been her husband. There was no affection, no pain, no grief. She had never felt grief for Leonard Stoner, and that was the deepest shame, the deepest irony.

The second headstone read: *Elizabeth Stoner, Beloved wife and mother, Born 1821. Died 1843.*

Deborah remembered the diary Carolyn had shown her of Elizabeth's hardships and discontent. The woman had been only twenty-two when she died so tragically. Was it just a coincidence that her inscription said nothing about her resting in peace?

Deborah wasn't surprised that there was no grave here for Caleb's second wife, Jacob and Laban's mother. She wondered where the poor woman was buried.

Caleb motioned to Pollard to take Deborah's reins and lead the horse to the oak tree. Deborah hadn't noticed before, but there was a stout branch there that would withstand her weight.

Pollard removed the gag. "Okay," said Caleb, "you have five minutes for your last words." He was perhaps surprised at her first statement.

"I'm sorry, Caleb, for all the grief I've caused you. I wish it could have been different. But we can't change the past."

"Don't tell me how we can only affect the future," said Caleb caustically. "Don't preach to me, Deborah."

Deborah smiled in spite of herself, for she had been about to do just that. Instead, she said, her own bitterness lending an edge of sarcasm to her tone, "If I'm not to have the privilege of fashioning my own last words, then you tell me what you want me to say, Caleb. What do you want to hear? Shall I confess to the murder of your son? Would that ease your conscience over what you are about to do?"

Caleb shrugged. "It's about time, isn't it?"

"Oh, Caleb! No matter what I say, you are going to believe what you will. You've hated me so much that you have never been able to let yourself see that Leonard had many other enemies who would have loved to see him dead. But I don't want to talk about that now. If these are my last words, I want to talk about Carolyn. I want to tell you what you are sacrificing in carrying out this foolish vendetta you have against me. She wanted to be your granddaughter, Caleb. She wanted to love you, maybe even take care of you. She needed you in a way that a child needs an elder to look up to. She would have done anything for you until you forced her to make a choice no child should ever have to make. Leaving you broke her heart. But there's still time to win her back if only you'd see the foolishness of what you are about to do. For once in your life, look within yourself, Caleb! Ask yourself if your hatred and bitterness is really worth it. Try to find the man Carolyn longs to love—I know he's there, Caleb. You couldn't have loved Leonard so much if your heart was made entirely of stone."

"Is that all?" Caleb said when she paused. His voice was thin with strain.

Deborah nodded. She could preach for an hour at this man, but it would be to no avail unless he was ready to hear.

"All right, Pollard," said Caleb. "You got that rope ready?"

While she was talking, Pollard and one of the cowhands had formed a noose in a heavy rope and attached it securely to the limb of the oak tree.

"Get it right this time," Caleb said as Pollard raised the noose over Deborah's head.

"It looks like they stopped here," Sam said, kneeling down on the ground.

"Yeah," said Longjim, "but this rocky stretch pretty much covers up the direction they took when they started again."

Griff peered into the night. "It goes on for half a mile or so."

"We could lose a lot of time if we head wrong and have to double back," said Sam.

"Too bad we don't know the ranch better," offered Slim. "We might have an idea where they went if we knew where the best trees were—" He broke off when he realized what he was saying, and gave a skittish look at Sam.

"Why don't we split up?" suggested Longjim. "There's only a couple of ways you can go through here. Whoever catches up with their tracks again can fire a warning shot."

Longjim and Slim went northeast; while Sam and Griff went southeast. After half an hour of picking carefully over the rocky trail, Sam found the tracks again. Griff fired, and before long their two friends caught up with them.

Longjim took the lead, with Slim riding next to him. Griff fell back with Sam and rode up close to him, indicating that he wanted to talk.

356

The tracks were easy to follow now and Sam didn't have to give the task his full attention with Longjim leading.

"Sam," said Griff, "there's something I think we better talk about before we find Caleb."

"What is it?"

"I just want to know what you got in mind. You haven't said nothing and you ain't armed, so it just made me wonder. I doubt Caleb's gonna give Deborah up without a fight."

"I only hope we're in time to face that quandary." Sam's tone was dismal. He was trying to have faith in God, but what if God's will was to take Deborah home with Him this night?

"Does that mean you're gonna be willing to fight?" asked Griff ruefully.

"I don't know, Griff." This moral debate had been plaguing Sam the entire way. It frightened him, worried him, confused him. "Sometimes I feel as if I could kill anyone who tries to harm Deborah. But how can I be true to my God if there is a limitation on my commitment to Him, to my promise many years ago to never again draw my gun against another human?"

"I feel sorry for you in that respect, Sam. At least I ain't got no burdens like that to bear. I can kill to save someone I care about, and I *will* kill if I got to. It's simple."

"I guess in a way I envy that, Griff, but on the other hand, I pray it never gets that simple for me. I suppose you're a better man than me and that's why God's put these checks on me. I still remember what it was like to be out of control, to actually enjoy killing. I never want to go back that way again."

"Aw, Sam, I'll never be better'n you, and you know it. I was just blessed with one of them minds that sees things black and white, hot and cold, not getting all bogged down with them sticky gray places."

"So, Griff, where does that leave us?"

"I guess we're both gonna have to do what we gotta do. I only ask that you don't try to stop me."

Sam shook his head. "I'd be mighty hypocritical if I let you do my killing for me, Griff."

"Blame it! There you go with all that philosophizing. Maybe you ought to stay behind."

"I can't do that either."

"Let's just play it by ear then," said Griff.

"Maybe with a little prayer thrown in, too."

"That's your department, Sam, but I sure ain't gonna stop you!"

They rode on for a few moments; then Griff added in a grim tone,

"One thing, Sam. If we're too late, I'll move heaven and hell in order to kill Caleb Stoner."

Sam said nothing, but in his mind and heart he cried out: *Oh, God, please don't let us be too late.*

77

The ride to Waco had taxed Carolyn and Sky nearly to their limits. They had covered over one hundred miles in twelve hours, changing horses once. That was better time than many of the Pony Express riders had accomplished twenty years ago, and their rides had become a legend.

They arrived in Waco after midnight Sunday morning, dusty, hungry, and tired. It was too late to find a place to get food, so they ate the jerky and hard biscuits in their saddlebags. They had to wake the hotel clerk in order to get a couple of rooms for the night. As anxious as they were to complete their vital task, they just had to wait. They figured if they had no trouble finding the housekeeper and she was cooperative, they could get her deposition in the morning and ride back to Leander in time for the opening of the trial on Monday. They might even have time to sleep a few hours before the trial.

They awoke next morning, ate a quick breakfast, and after asking around, discovered where Maria's sister lived. Unfortunately, when they arrived, Maria had gone to attend morning Mass at the local Catholic church.

It dawned on them that it was Sunday, but it didn't look as if they'd be able to attend church. They didn't want to barge in on the Mass after it had started, and the Protestant churches wouldn't have services until after Carolyn and Sky were well on their way back to Leander—at least they hoped they'd be on their way by then.

While waiting for Maria, they went back to the hotel, had a more substantial breakfast, and tried, not very successfully, to relax. At nine-thirty, they went to the Catholic church to wait for Maria.

The old housekeeper recognized Carolyn immediately. "Oh no!"

exclaimed Maria, hurrying up to her. "What has happened? Is it the Patrón?"

"No, Maria, my grandfather is all right as far as I know," Carolyn said. "I'm here because of my mother's trial. I found your chest, Maria," she went on, getting to the point immediately. "I know that was invading your privacy, but I had to find some evidence that would clear my mother. I remembered you said something that made me think there were secrets locked away somewhere. When I looked in your trunk, I found Jacob's letter and Elizabeth's diary and your letters, but I still have questions."

Maria looked down; there was shame in her eyes. "Please, come to my sister's house and we can talk."

Fifteen minutes later they were seated in a simple parlor in a small house on the edge of town. Maria's sister served them coffee as they talked.

"The things in the trunk, Maria, answered a lot of my questions about my family," Carolyn said. "But they're not very helpful to my mother. That is, except for one thing—a letter from your brother in Mexico answering some questions you had about Eufemia Mendez."

"Ah, yes, that."

Sky was writing as fast as he could so as to have a document of the conversation, signed by Maria, to present to the court.

"You remember it?"

"Of course."

"I wish you had just told me these things," Carolyn scolded as gently as she could. "It would have saved a lot of trouble."

"I'm sorry, señorita. I am an old woman; I do not have much courage. It was too hard to stand against the Patrón who has been good to me and taken care of me these many years. But you—"

"Never mind, Maria," Carolyn broke in, perhaps a bit too harshly in her haste. "Let's just get down to what that letter is all about. It looks as if Señora Mendez lied on the witness stand about why she went to Mexico. But why did what Eufemia did eighteen years ago concern you? You don't seem like the type who gets involved in other people's business, yet Eufemia's trip to Mexico seemed to interest you. Why? And does it have anything to do with the Stoners?"

Maria sighed and slowly shook her head. "You have not guessed? I thought it might be clear to you when you saw the letter, but then I am seeing it as one who knew. Yes, I should have been brave enough to tell you more. You were not there eighteen years ago to look into the eyes of a little bambino and see reflected the resemblance to one you knew, one you had raised from a baby himself."

"What do you mean, Maria?"

"Eufemia's baby, of course. I saw him after she returned from Mexico. She said he was a big baby for his age, and perhaps that was enough for the kind of people she mostly associated with—the men who came to the cantina—who did not know better. Or perhaps no one cared enough to take note that the baby was not just big, but that he was mature in other ways, too. I might not have bothered either; it was none of my business that the poor girl got into trouble in her line of work and then went to Mexico to cover her shame. That's not why I wrote to my brother."

"Why, then, Maria?"

"Have you really looked at Ramón, Carolyn? Do you not see it? I saw it perhaps because I had raised three Stoner children already—"

"What are you saying, Maria?" Carolyn felt the color drain from her face and her stomach constrict.

"Ramón is Leonard's son—your own half brother!"

"Are—are you sure?"

"I have no proof, like what they might want in a court, but my eyes do not deceive me. If you look closely yourself, you will see."

Carolyn was quiet for a long time, trying to discern what this revelation might mean, but her mind was in too much disarray to make any progress on her own, so she continued to ply Maria with questions.

"Does anyone else know this? My grandfather? Does Ramón know?"

"I don't know, but no one has said anything to me if they did," Maria answered. "But Ramón has been working at the ranch for years. I know him, and I do not believe he knows."

Carolyn remembered Ramón's shock when he was reading the letters; that could not have been an act.

Carolyn continued to probe Maria for information. There were a few more questions Jonathan Barnum had asked Carolyn to question Maria about concerning the night of the murder; but after half an hour, it seemed apparent that she truly knew nothing about that night. She had been asleep in her cottage, she said. Carolyn berated herself for thinking that meant Maria was alone and had no alibi, but she was starting to suspect everyone. The housekeeper, however, did not find out about Leonard's death until she showed up for work the next morning.

It was almost eleven o'clock in the morning when Maria signed the informal deposition Sky had written of her statements. Carolyn and Sky bade her goodbye and went to the livery stable where their horses were ready for them—groomed, fed, and rested. On the way there Sky asked Carolyn, "Carolyn . . . this business with Señora Mendez; have you thought about what it all means?"

"It means I have another half brother," said Carolyn. "And, as shocked as I was to hear this, I really don't mind—I've fared right well with half brothers, Sky. Ramón is almost as nice as you; I think you'll like him."

"There's more to it than that." He paused and glanced her way to see if she yet understood. When she returned a somewhat blank expression, he continued. "Don't you see? What happened to the Mendez woman—getting into trouble like that, and then, more than likely, not receiving any satisfaction from the father. I think it could be a motive for murder."

Carolyn stopped dead in her tracks and gaped at Sky. "Not Eufemia Mendez!" she finally said when she found her voice. "Women don't kill for that reason. They go away quietly like she did, have their babies, and try to make a life for themselves."

"Yes, normally. But you said she was filled with an unaccountable hatred for the Stoners. Doesn't it seem possible that Leonard spurned her, told her to take care of herself, that he wanted nothing to do with her or her brat, that one troublesome woman on his hands— our mother—was enough? Isn't it possible that in a fit of desperate passion she shot him?"

Again, Carolyn was faced with the unsavory character of her father; and, again, she could not argue with Sky's reasoning. It wasn't hard at all to picture that man doing the things Sky described. But would Eufemia kill him over it? Carolyn shook her head.

"That's Ramón's mother, Sky," she said. "I just don't know. I still think it was Laban."

"Carolyn, sometimes you can be as narrow-minded as your grandfather," Sky said. "You pointed out that he's so set on our mother being the murderer that he refuses to see any other possibilities. You're doing the same thing with Laban."

"But he lied about his alibi—at least he tried to make everyone believe he couldn't remember. And he had the most to gain from getting rid of my father."

"What did he gain? He still hasn't inherited the ranch."

"Sky, if what you say is true . . . you are talking about Ramón's *mother*. And we both know how horrible that could be for him."

78

After the eleven-hour ride back to Stoner's Crossing, Carolyn and Sky were exhausted. But Carolyn could not go back to Leander before seeing Eufemia Mendez. It might have been more practical to wait until the law could accompany her, but Carolyn did not want Sky's new insight about Eufemia Mendez to wait until morning. The cantina was open late, and it was likely Ramón's mother was still there.

"What'll you say to her?" asked Sky.

"I haven't thought that far ahead. I appreciate you coming with me, though."

"Well, I reckon Sam and Mr. Barnum are sound asleep, so we can't do anything about Maria's deposition until morning, anyway."

Both Sky and Carolyn quaked upon entering a forbidden place like the cantina. Although it was late Sunday night, the saloon was fairly busy. Someone was playing the piano, a ribald, rousing tune, but it was not Eufemia. Sky went up to the bar.

"Your mama know you're in a place like this?" said one of the cowboys at the bar.

Sky ignored him and got the bartender's attention. "Is Señora Mendez around?"

"What's it to you?" said the bartender.

"We want to see her."

The bartender rubbed his chin and gave the two youngsters a quick once-over. He recognized the girl from when she had come before, but he had his orders.

"Don't know a thing," he said.

Carolyn shouldered her way forward. "It's important."

The bartender shrugged and returned to pouring a drink for a customer.

"Listen here!" Carolyn insisted.

"Carolyn?" came a voice from behind.

She spun around. "Ramón?"

"What are you doing here?"

"Ramón, we have to talk. And where's your mother?"

"Yes, we do have to talk. Come with me."

He led them to the back room where Eufemia had entertained them before. She was nowhere to be seen. They sat on the edge of their chairs, all of them tense.

"Carolyn," Ramón began, "before I say anything else, you must believe I knew nothing before yesterday. And what I've done, I did because I could do nothing else."

"I hear you, Ramón, but I don't understand. Are you talking about you being my brother? I found that out today from Maria. It seems like we should have known, sensed something, doesn't it? But I've got a pretty thick skull; maybe you do, too."

"There's more to it than that. More than just being brother and sister. I wish it were just that, for I'd be proud to have you as a sister. But now I'm faced with the same awful problem you've been struggling with all this time. I had decided to say nothing, to let the trial take its natural course. Maybe your mother would be let off, maybe it would come out as self-defense and no one would have to suffer. Maybe—"

"What are you saying, Ramón? Is it true about your mother? Did she—?"

Ramón bowed his head, tears seeping from the corners of his tightly closed eyes. Carolyn moved next to him and put her arm around him. She understood only too well what he was suffering; she even understood how he might be tempted to protect his mother even at the cost of another.

Ramón looked up, desolate. "When I saw you in the cantina, looked in your eyes, I knew I couldn't keep this secret, though my mother made me promise not to tell."

"Where is she?"

"She left town yesterday. She thought that if your mother had been successful in losing herself for so many years, perhaps she could, too. She signed the ownership of the cantina over to me, as if it mattered to me."

"Did she tell you what happened to . . . our father?"

He nodded dismally. "It was simple enough. She was in trouble, you know, with me. My father gave her some money and told her to leave him alone. My mother didn't want his money; she wanted him to acknowledge his child. She knew he would never marry her because he already had a wife. And maybe no one else would know I was his. But he refused to accept me. He said he wasn't going to make the mistake his father had made and accept a greaser offspring. She tried again, and when he turned her away, she went to Caleb—"

"He knows?"

"Yes, but all Caleb told her was to either leave them alone or get out of town. He also suggested that she could get rid of the unborn baby, but to my mother that would have been a mortal sin. Still, maybe Caleb has a small heart after all, for when she persisted, telling him she was ruined and had no way to support a child, he relented and asked her what she wanted. She said all she wanted was for her child to be recognized for who he was. Caleb offered her the cantina if she kept the matter a secret. She didn't accept his offer. Instead, she tried one more time to convince my father. She hoped that once her baby was born, his heart would soften toward both her and the child—me." He paused and shook his head at that still stunning realization. "She knew his marriage was a sham, and so she did have some small hope of that happening. She loved Leonard Stoner even after he treated her so. When she went to him, he only gave her more money—five hundred dollars."

"That would be the money in the bank account," said Carolyn.

"Yes, but as I said, she didn't want money. She begged him, told him all she wanted was to be his mistress and for him to accept his child, even if no one else knew. He laughed at her, Carolyn. And then he drew his gun." Ramón paused and swallowed. "He told her how easy it would be to kill her, how it would solve all their problems. He cocked the gun, and that's when my mother went mad. In a rage that she said only someone in love could know, she attacked him. The gun went off."

"Then he couldn't have been shot in the back?" said Carolyn.

"My mother figured that Caleb just concocted that to make certain there'd be no doubt about your mother getting convicted. He got the doc and Pollard to back him up."

It no longer surprised Carolyn that Caleb would go so far to avenge his son's death.

Ramón continued. "When my mother realized he was dead, she escaped through the patio door. By the time she got back to her room at the cantina, she had enough presence of mind to realize running would only make her appear guilty. Then, in the morning, the news came that your mother had been arrested for the crime. The best thing for my mother then was to stay put. It was hard for her to see your mother suffer for her crime, but she had her baby to think of, and, of course, no one knew your mother was also in a family way.

"When it was all over and your mother had escaped, my mother thought she could continue her life. She went to Mexico, and I was born. But she was shunned by her family. She decided it was better to starve in the States than in Mexico, and she could not forget that Caleb had once offered her the cantina. It was enough motivation for her to return. What else could a poor young woman with a child and no husband do? If Caleb turned her away, then she would do the best she could. And there was always the chance that one day Caleb would recognize me as his flesh and blood."

"It's hard to believe Caleb never suspected what really happened," said Carolyn. Then a little smile flickered across her lips. "No, I guess it isn't. We're too much alike. He got it in his mind my ma did it, and refused to look any place else."

Ramón voiced what both he and Carolyn were thinking. "I wonder how things would have turned out if I had never existed?"

"I've thought that about myself, too, a few times," said Carolyn. "But I'm glad I'm alive, and you should be also. What if our father had never been killed? I hate to say this, but both our mothers would have lived in misery. Yet even if he had lived, I think we would have been a comfort to our mothers. I don't think my ma ever regretted having me. And I know you must have been a comfort to your mother. Imagine how empty her life would have been without you."

"Well, it's no use to talk about what might have happened, is it? We are alive, and down deep, I wouldn't want it any other way." Ramón paused. "I haven't had a bad life. But now my mother is a fugitive. When what I've just told you is revealed, the law will go after my mother, and maybe she won't be as lucky as yours; they will catch her and she will spend years in prison, if they don't—"

"Wait a minute!" Sky, who had been listening with a clearer head than his companions, interrupted. "I've been listening enough to all this court rigmarole to know that your ma, Ramón, acted out of self-defense. No honest jury will see it any other way. You could ask Mr. Barnum to be sure, but I doubt your ma will go to prison or anything."

"That's right!" Carolyn's spirits lifted. "Do you know where she's gone, Ramón, so you can tell her?"

For a moment, Ramón looked suspicious.

"Come on!" said Carolyn. "You don't think we're trying to trick you?"

"The law isn't always the same for Mexicans as it is for gringos," he replied.

"Well, if it's the law you're worried about, I'll bet Mr. Barnum would take your ma's case in a heartbeat. He's the best lawyer in the country. He won't stand for any shenanigans from the law."

"Maybe it would be worth the risk, better than her hiding for the rest of her life," admitted Ramón.

These astounding revelations were too important to wait until morning to be told to Sam and Deborah. No one was going to mind getting awakened to hear news like this. Her ma could get out of jail tonight! There was no reason for her to spend another night locked up. That convinced Sky, and so the three saddled fresh horses at the livery stable and raced to Leander. They went first to the hotel so Sam could be with them when they saw Deborah and told her the news.

They found Jonathan Barnum pacing across the rug in the hotel lobby. He had even more shocking news for them. They had missed Sam and Griff by less than half an hour.

79

Even Carolyn, who loved being on the back of a horse second to nothing, groaned inwardly at the prospect of another breakneck ride. She had been in the saddle twenty-four out of the last thirty-six hours, but this time her mother's life truly depended upon her, and she was determined not to fail.

All three young people made the same assumption that Griff had made regarding Caleb's probable direction. They moved swiftly and came very close to catching up with Sam because Carolyn didn't have to pause at the rocky stretch. She remembered a small grove of trees a couple of miles from the ranch house and thought, with a shudder, that it was a likely spot. She had never been to the grove and had no idea of its greater significance, but because a hasty decision was needed, she chose that direction, praying it was right and rejoicing when trail signs proved she had made a good choice.

Carolyn was frightened for her mother, yet she felt a certain peace, too. The timing of when Sam had discovered Deborah missing had been too close to her abduction to be a coincidence. God could not have had it happen thus, only to end up snatching Deborah away from them. But besides the faith in God she was trying to cling to, Carolyn's innate stubbornness made her unable to accept the fact that she would be too late to save her mother.

———————

It was about two hours before sunrise. The night was chilly, but the moon had not yet set. Images were often deceiving at that hour; a fallen log might be mistaken for a stray cow, or a rock could vaguely resemble a stump. A moonlit shadow might be a cloud passing overhead, or it could be—

A clump of trees!

Sam had been searching the landscape, his eyes roving carefully over every inch on the horizon. He waited a moment when he first saw the dark splotch. But there were no clouds; it had to be trees. He trotted up to Griff, who was riding slightly ahead. Saying nothing, he pointed. Griff nodded. It was the first possible destination for the kind of deed Caleb had planned. Slim and Longjim gathered close.

"We better ride up quietlike," said Griff, "guns drawn. If they're there, we don't want to spook 'em."

"I think we ought to surround 'em," said Longjim.

"Okay, Longjim, you and Slim circle 'em in opposite directions. Sam and I will wait until you're in position; then we'll head forward. Ready?" He looked at Sam.

Sam nodded grimly, dreading what they might find in the midst of those trees.

There was no avoiding it. But he thought about the gun he always carried in his saddlebag. What kind of man was he that he let others do his dirty work for him? Is that truly what God wanted? He simply could not let his friends face dangers nor let them defend his wife while he stood by passively. Sam reached down toward his saddlebag.

"Don't do it, Sam," said Griff.

"I don't see how I can do anything else."

"Let me tell you, it takes more guts to ride up there unarmed than me and Slim and Longjim'll ever have. Besides, Deborah'll never forgive me if I stand by and let you throw out everything you've ever stood for. Maybe if we get desperate enough . . . but we ain't near to that yet."

Sam peered ahead. "Dear God, I hope that's true."

———————

367

Deborah was the first to see the riders approach the top of the rise overlooking the small valley of the trees and pond. Pollard stopped just as he tightened the noose around Deborah's neck, his eyes following the direction of her gaze.

"Not again!" he murmured.

Then Caleb and his cowboys also saw, and they drew their guns. But one of the approaching riders fired his weapon into the dirt about two inches from the horse Caleb sat upon. Another gun fired from about fifty yards behind. The horse Deborah was on, not held with any firm control, snorted and moved restively. Deborah thought she saw Pollard's hand grab the reins to steady the beast.

"You want a blood bath, we're ready!" shouted Griff as he and Sam rode near. "You'll be the first to die, Caleb."

"What do I care?" said Caleb.

"Maybe these other fellows ain't as ready to die as you," said Sam.

By now the presence of Slim and Longjim with strategically aimed weapons was apparent. The three Bar S cowboys looked uncertainly at Caleb, and he glared back at them with warning.

Caleb said, "Boys, if they make any more dangerous moves with their weapons, you shoot that horse out from under the woman." But just to be sure his men didn't fail him, Caleb pointed his gun at Deborah's horse. "You can shoot me, but I'll take her with me."

"Caleb, give it up," pleaded Sam. "No one wants to die out here. And you don't want to harm an innocent woman."

"Innocent? I'll never believe that!" Caleb shouted back, but the effort made his voice crack and brought on a paroxysm of coughing. His gun shook and for an instant was pointing away from Deborah.

Griff took the opportunity and raised his gun to fire at Caleb.

"Stop!" shouted a new voice.

Those gathered at the hanging tree had been so intent on their stand-off they had not yet heard or seen the rider crest the rise. It was Carolyn. She saw the gathering first and was shouting and spurring her mount into a full gallop as Griff poised himself to kill Caleb.

Two other riders thundered after Carolyn, but all the youthful riders were unarmed. None of the armed riders made a move. Caleb's boys would do what their boss told them, but they really had no taste for hanging a woman, so they were willing to give things a chance to unravel if they would.

Caleb recovered, fully aware that the new intruders had saved his life. He groaned inwardly when he saw Carolyn. She was the last person he wanted around now. He rubbed his gaunt and pale face, but he focused his gaze on her almost defiantly as she reined her horse to a halt near him.

"Get out of here, Carolyn!" he ordered.

"Why?" she cried, her voice laced with recrimination. "So I won't see the kind of man you really are? You're an evil monster just like my father! I don't know why I ever cared, why I ever tried to—" She broke off, emotion strangling her voice.

Ramón came forward. "Señor Stoner, you've got everything all wrong." They were the hardest words he had ever spoken; Caleb had been his boss, the *Patrón,* and he had always been afraid of him. He still could not fully accept the fact that this man was his grandfather. But he spoke as boldly as he could. "Carolyn's mother is innocent."

"What's this to you?" sneered Caleb.

"I think you know very well what it means to me," Ramón said, gathering courage as he spoke. Caleb looked guiltily away as Ramón continued. "You're going to have to accept me, Señor Stoner. I am your grandson, and I won't go away. But don't worry; I've gotten along without you all these years and that's the way I prefer it. All I want from you is recognition. That's all my mother ever wanted, too. You could have avoided so much tragedy if only you would have done that much for a poor Mexican girl."

"That's all you people ever want, a few crumbs from 'the Patrón's' table," Caleb said. "But given the chance, you'd take everything."

"That's not what this is all about, and you know it," Carolyn said, finding her voice. "You're just afraid to let anyone love you. You were hurt once, and now everyone who comes near you must suffer also— and, what's worse, you passed that sickness on to your son."

"Leonard's mother betrayed us!" retorted Caleb. "She made me kill her; she made poor Leonard watch."

"And every woman who comes close to you must suffer for that? And their offspring, too?"

"Your mother *deserves* to suffer!"

"You're wrong about that, too, Grandfather," said Carolyn. She looked at Ramón to see if he wanted to finish.

"It was my mother!" Ramón said. "She killed Leonard Stoner! He gave her no choice because she loved him."

For a moment Caleb tried to deny Ramón's revelation. He glanced at Deborah, and the hand that held his gun shook almost as if he would fire at her horse, anyway. But then Caleb looked back at Carolyn.

In that moment, he knew his defeat. He had wasted years of hatred, bitterness, and pain, while the true murderer of his son had lived under his nose in safety and prosperity, perhaps even happiness. A huge span of his life had been wasted, and he thought of Deborah's words spoken a few minutes ago:

"Ask yourself if your hatred and bitterness is worth it."

But now that his life was nearly over, could he accept that it had all been for nothing? Caleb Stoner was a proud, obstinate man. Damaged pride had caused the rage that made him kill Elizabeth and her lover. And even before that, hadn't pride driven him from Virginia rather than live under the condescending weight of his in-laws who saw themselves as his betters?

Was he ready to die with pride as his only comfort?

Skittishly, his eyes darted from Carolyn to Ramón. Dear God! Were these truly his dear Leonard's children? Leonard's *son*! How Caleb had wanted a male heir who had Leonard's blood in his veins. But a Mexican peon who would hate him as much as Laban and Jacob had always hated him? Yet, in the sudden rush of reality that threatened to overwhelm him, he had to ask if he deserved any better. Caleb's pride had driven him all his life; now he could clearly see that it had also destroyed him.

Leonard's children!

He had been willing to accept the girl; could he also accept the boy? He studied Ramón, and oddly, he did not see a greaser, the child of his son's murderer—rather, he saw Leonard. For the first time in eighteen years, he allowed himself to see . . . to really see.

The gun fell from Caleb's hand, hitting the dirt with a thud. Then he moved toward Deborah and with his own hands slipped the noose from her neck.

PART 16

TRUTH AND PEACE

80

Full daylight bathed the town of Stoner's Crossing as the party of riders rode at a slow and deliberate pace down the main street. The citizens had begun to stir, going about their day-to-day business. Several looked up and recognized their town's patrón riding in the center of the group. They had never seen him look so . . . broken.

Deborah could not help but think of all the other significant times she had ridden down this street. As a young, grieving girl hoping for a new life; as a prisoner despairing of life, hoping for death; as a fugitive galloping away with a gang of outlaws; then as a prisoner again, finally understanding what life was really all about.

It seemed to her now that this street had been like a stage in a theater where her entire life had been played out, where she had grown and matured into the final product of God's making. She could clearly see now how each of life's events is but a step closer to the Creator's ultimate design—if a person only chooses to accept God's way.

Deborah looked at her daughter and prayed she would also come to this spiritual insight. At least Carolyn was starting with a firm foot planted on God's path.

The riders stopped at the sheriff's office. There were no arrests to be made, but it seemed some representative of the law ought to be informed of the events of the morning.

Back at the hanging tree it had been decided to let Caleb's three cowboys and Pollard go.

But Sam told them, "If any of you ever come near here or any of my family or friends, I ain't gonna be responsible for what Griff McCulloch does to you."

Griff gave the man a dangerous sneer just to make sure the message was clear.

No one wanted to see any further suffering for events of the past.

But as they dismounted and entered the office, they did not realize one final scene still awaited them.

Matt Gentry and Jacob Stoner were having a cup of coffee with the sheriff. Caleb stopped, instantly recognizing Jacob. Their eyes locked together for a moment; then Caleb looked aside. He had no more stomach or strength for hatred.

Sam spoke first, and his words surprised everyone, especially Carolyn. "Matt Gentry! What are you doing here?"

Matt glanced sheepishly at Carolyn, then rose and shook Sam's hand. Griff stepped forward and pounded Matt on the back.

"Howdy, Sam—Griff," said Matt, with another glance toward Carolyn.

"What's going on?" demanded Carolyn.

"Matt here is a good friend of ours," said Griff.

"You never said anything to me," she said to Matt.

"Well, I—"

"They're not the ones you told me about, that helped you in that other trouble?" Carolyn asked.

Matt nodded.

"You done good, boy!" said Griff. "I knew I could depend on you."

"What do you mean?" asked Carolyn.

"I asked Matt to look out for you, that's all," explained Griff, "and from what I've heard, he's done a good job of it—"

"You what—?" She turned on Matt, glaring at him. "How dare you! You think I'm nothing but a helpless female who needs a man to keep her out of trouble? I *thought* you were my friend, but—"

"Aw, Lynnie," said Griff, "don't get your unmentionables all in a bundle. Are you gonna stand here and tell me you didn't need just a little help at the ranch?"

Carolyn narrowed her eyes at him. "You coulda said something."

Matt grinned and held out his hands in surrender. "I'm sorry, Carolyn," he said contritely. "It's true that Griff asked me to look out for you, but once I met you, well ... he wouldn't have had to ask. I reckon I just liked you, that's all. Besides—" He flushed and shrugged. "You saved my hide too, so I guess we're about even."

"I guess so," Carolyn relented. Then she quickly explained to Matt and Jacob all that had happened.

Finally, Jacob stood and, having gathered his wits and courage, approached Caleb. "Father, it's been a long time."

"Yes ... it has," Caleb said in a weak, quiet tone.

"I'm afraid I must deliver bad news to you. Laban is dead." He

374

briefly described what had happened in the ravine.

"I'm sorry," said Caleb.

"Are you really?"

Caleb only nodded. He began to sway on his feet, and when Carolyn rushed to his side to support him, Deborah smiled inwardly—yes, at least Carolyn would be all right.

"I'd better sit down," Caleb said. He crumpled into the chair vacated by Jacob.

Details of all the events were exchanged, but there was no jubilance or sense of triumph, for too much had been lost in the discovery of the truth. Even Deborah, who had once more been rescued from imminent death, felt drained and sad despite her sense of God's presence. The news about Laban only deepened her grief. He had been but a victim and deserved no recriminations for what he had done and tried to do. His earliest memories as a young child had been tainted by tragedy, rejection, and grief. Just like Leonard.

Poor Leonard! He had been cruel and hateful and violent, but Deborah found that she could at last fully forgive him. For now when she pictured Leonard, she did not see a monster but rather a chubby, innocent four-year-old watching his mother shot and killed by his own father.

Yes, these men were all products of one man's twisted soul; but Deborah could not judge Caleb, either. She felt sorry for him. She only prayed that the chain of family corruption would be broken now, once and for all. She looked at Ramón. Perhaps it was a blessing that Caleb had never accepted him. His grandfather's rejection had distanced the boy from the insidious and evil spell that had dogged the Stoner clan. And it had distanced Carolyn also.

Carolyn had never known the Stoner clan until she had the strength of character to withstand their influence. And after all Caleb had done, Carolyn was still able to serve him, giving him a glass of water and watching in case he should cough again.

————

Carolyn just followed her instincts. Perhaps if she thought about it more, she would have felt revulsion for Caleb. After all, hadn't he just tried to hang her mother?

But he was her grandfather, regardless of his demented deeds, despite all the people he had damaged along the way. And he was sick, helpless, alone. He needed her, someone to care for him, to love him, even if he was totally incapable of returning that love. She thought of the filthy lepers, the grimy beggars, the crazed demon-possessed souls that Christ had reached out to, had loved, had *touched*. She recalled as a child how when Sam or her mother had read those passages in the Bible to her, she wrinkled her nose with distaste. How had Jesus been able to do that when He had been so clean and pure?

She had a bit more understanding of her Lord now. He loved those people, those outcasts, no matter who they were, what they'd done, or what they looked like. When He looked at them, He did so with a love that somehow pierced beyond their ugliness. And though it surprised her tremendously, she found she could do that, to some extent at least, with her grandfather. She could love him no matter what. She could put her arm around him and rub his back soothingly as another coughing spell assailed him.

She hoped that for the first time, perhaps in his entire life, he could accept love from another person, especially a woman. But even if he couldn't, she could continue to give it. That was the only way the foundation of hate Caleb Stoner had laid could at last be broken.

Carolyn had another task that had to be tended to before she could help take her grandfather home so he could rest in his own bed. Matt led her through a door to the back of the sheriff's office where the jail cells were. Sean Toliver was sitting rather glumly on one of the cots.

"Well, well," he said sourly, "I've got a visitor."

"Hello, Sean," said Carolyn. Then she glanced at Matt, who took the subtle hint and left. "It's really too bad it had to work out like this," Carolyn said once Matt was gone.

"It doesn't have to be over, Carolyn. Even an old cattle rustler could use the affections of a woman."

"Not this woman, Sean," Carolyn said with confidence. "You charmed me for a while, but once I grew up a little, I just couldn't imagine how I could have been so gullible."

"You telling me you didn't like me a little?"

"I reckon I did a little, at least I could have if you had been sincere. But that's what you lacked, Sean. You're just too self-centered to suit me."

He chuckled. "I suppose you prefer that toe-in-the-dirt 'Aw shucks' Gentry fella."

Carolyn smiled. "You know something? I sure do."

She met Matt back in the office; all the others had gone to see about breakfast before they took Caleb back to the ranch.

"So, Matt, what's gonna happen to Sean?" Carolyn asked, then quickly added, "Not that it matters to me one way or the other; I was just curious."

"Jacob says Toliver killed Laban—aimed right at him and fired. Toliver denies that, insisting he was aiming at Jacob, and that he only did it in self-defense. The sheriff says that if Jacob testifies and his word can be established, Sean could hang. But Jacob can't do that. There's sure to be someone who'll recognize him."

"So Sean will just walk away free?"

"Looks that way. He'll have to face a court for the rustling—I'll testify to that—but you know how rustlers are handled around here. They'll run him out of the county, maybe out of the state, and he'll be black-balled from working at any reputable ranch. No self-appointed vigilante committee is gonna hang him, at least not unless Caleb instigates it."

"Grandfather won't do that."

"Then Toliver will walk."

"Well, in a way, I'm glad," said Carolyn with a sigh. "I just don't have the heart for any more violence."

"Come on," said Matt, casually taking Carolyn's hand, "let's go find the others and get some chow."

81

The constant prairie breeze was colder now than it had been a month ago. What few trees there were had begun to lose their leaves, and the changing of the seasons was clearly evident. Carolyn had come to Stoner's Crossing in the blazing intensity of a Texas summer, so it seemed appropriate that she should be thinking about leaving during the more temperate autumn.

It would not be a permanent departure; she had already decided that. She would return, but for now, she missed home—the Wind

Rider Ranch. She wanted to spend some time with her mother and Sky and Sam—normal, relaxing time that was not clouded with all the intense emotions that had hung over them these last several months. But she *would* return to the Bar S Ranch. She would have to—it was hers now, at least part of it.

Once all the legal dust had settled and she'd had these last weeks to explore in peace, she was able to appreciate Stoner land. It had been nearly two months since her mother had been officially acquitted of the murder charges, and she, Sam, Sky, Griff, and the boys had returned to the Wind Rider Ranch. Lucy Reeves had been convinced to go north with the Wind Rider folks, and Carolyn was sure she saw pleasure in Griff's eyes at that idea.

Jonathan Barnum had only recently left Stoner's Crossing. He had stayed to help Eufemia Mendez, and as they had expected, a hearing determined she had acted out of self-defense. The judge reprimanded her strongly for allowing others to suffer because of her silence, but he understood her dilemma because of her unborn child and her fear for him.

There had been no way to spare Caleb's and Leonard's reputations in all this, but the truth came as no surprise to the people in town who knew them. It wounded Caleb that his son's memory should suffer so; he would never be able to fully accept that Leonard was less than the image Caleb had built of him. It was almost as hard for Carolyn to let go of her childhood fantasies of a good and noble father. But at least she was learning that her father's character did not have to reflect on the kind of person she became. The example of Jacob and Laban stood out to her. Caleb Stoner was their father, but Laban had allowed himself to be hurt and crushed by Caleb's cruelty. Jacob had broken free and become his own person.

Carolyn was free now, too. Where she would go, what she would do might not be exactly clear, but at least there were no more shadows hovering over her.

She reined her mount to a halt on top of a rise from which she could survey several miles of Stoner land. It was good land—probably better, if not more beautiful, than the Wind Rider spread. But it could never be home. She had come here months ago seeking a family she had never known, and that search had more than ever made her appreciate the family she had left behind.

Her thoughts turned to her grandfather. He was dead now, in his grave a full week.

Physically, he had suffered terribly in those two months since the discovery of his son's real murderer. In the end he had finally come to accept the love Carolyn had for him, and Carolyn hoped that helped ease the physical pain a little. She still felt deep sorrow that so many years of his life had been wasted on bitterness and hatred. A few days of love seemed so paltry by comparison. But only Caleb could be blamed for his empty life.

Carolyn didn't want to dwell on that, however. She wanted to remember that last day before he died.

"You're still here, Carolyn?" he had called to her so weakly from his bed.

"I won't leave you, Grandfather."

"That's more than I deserve."

"It's not for me to judge."

"You always were a good girl. And I hate to admit it, but that's one part of you that is not from your Stoner blood. We were all a mean-spirited lot. If you think I was bad, you should have seen my father. As a child, I don't remember a day I didn't get a beating. And my grandfather was a captain of a slaver—the toughest, meanest man I ever knew."

"There were *no* nice ones, Grandfather?"

"The women—some of them were decent. I had a sister—you didn't know that. She was several years older than I was. She is long dead, but after my daily beating, she used to tend my cuts and sneak me food. Don't get me wrong, Carolyn, more often than not I deserved those beatings. I was an ornery child." He stopped for a while to catch his spent breath. When he began again, there was a more pleasant look on his wasted face. "I just remembered an uncle; I haven't thought about him in years, probably since I left home. His name was Thomas Stoner, my father's younger brother. He was a nice gentleman. He brought me presents and talked—actually talked!—to me, telling stories and such. I remember once when he was visiting, he grabbed the switch from my father's hand right as he was striking me. Uncle Thomas turned the switch on my father.

" 'See how you like that, Jed!' he yelled, hitting my father good. 'You're going to turn this boy into a devil if you keep this up.' "

Caleb smiled grimly. "Good old Uncle Thomas was right, eh, Carolyn?"

Carolyn didn't know what to say. A lie rose to her lips but it seemed so false, so transparent, it couldn't possibly be of any comfort to Caleb. Before she could form a better answer, Caleb interceded.

"Don't worry, Carolyn, I won't make you answer such a question. It doesn't really matter what you think. What you're *doing* is what I'll remember, what I'll take with me to my grave. No one, since my sister, has ever treated me with such care."

He reached up and took Carolyn's hand. His own hand was thin and bony, cold, with a bluish tone. She was glad she didn't have to say anything. Maybe he was a sour and misguided old man, but he was her grandfather.

"At least you can't say all Stoners were bad," she said at length.

"The bloodline is improving, I'll say that much," Caleb said. "That Ramón is a decent fellow. But I hope he can run a ranch. He'll need you around for a long while."

Caleb had stipulated in his will that Carolyn and Ramón would inherit the ranch equally. Jacob did not want the ranch, even if he could have risked his freedom by accepting it. Caleb willed him cash instead, which he accepted. Carolyn had decided that she'd stay on to help run the ranch until Ramón knew the ropes. After that, she wasn't certain what to do.

She wasn't ready to think that far into the future. There was still so much to deal with while her grandfather lived. His attitude toward spiritual things had troubled her deeply for a time. And on that last day with him, it was on her mind more than usual. She desperately wanted to see him die in peace—as much peace as a man like him could possibly know. He claimed he knew "his Maker," as he called God. But he didn't intend on making any eleventh-hour death scenes. Let God judge him for the life he had lived, not for a few moments of so-called "weakness" at the end.

Carolyn read to him the story in the Bible of the laborers who were given the same reward whether they had worked all day or just the last hour.

"I will cheat too many people if I die and go to heaven," he said with a dry chuckle.

"You never cared what people thought before," Carolyn told him with mock tartness. "Why start now?"

He laughed, though it brought on a bout of coughing that lasted for ten minutes.

"I'll think about it," he said finally.

Caleb had died before Carolyn could speak to him again. She would never really know if he had indeed made his peace with God. But it was not too difficult to leave his final fate in the hands of a merciful God.

At least she herself had peace, knowing she had done all for him that was possible. But Carolyn's peace went deeper than that, having to do with the struggles that had plagued her all her life. The things in her hidden past she had feared for so long had come true. They couldn't have been worse, she supposed, if she had dreamed them all up in a terrible nightmare. Yet by the grace of God she had survived—not merely survived, but matured and grown. Her mother's words to her before she and Sam had departed for home would always be a dear memory:

"I am so proud of you, Carolyn! To think, nineteen years ago I had been afraid I was going to give birth to a monster. But God surprised me, and blessed me! He gave me you—a vibrant and dear girl . . . a woman now! You have truly grown up."

Carolyn dug her heels into Tres Zapatos' sides, descending the low hill at a brisk trot. In another fifteen minutes she came to the gate that announced she was at the Stoner Bar S Ranch. Maria would have lunch ready, and Carolyn was hungry. It wouldn't be anything like beans and coffee from a chuck wagon, but the old housekeeper was a pretty good cook. Carolyn was glad Maria had decided to stay on to care for another generation of Stoners. With God's help, the woman's final years with the family would be more peaceful than her earlier ones.

Carolyn was greeted at the stable by Ramón.

"You're not going to take my horse, are you?" she scolded. "You're a rancher now, Ramón, not a stableboy."

"Old habits, you know." He grinned sheepishly. Carolyn dismounted and Ramón continued. "I'll take your horse anyway. The foreman wants to see you—there's a problem with the herd he's getting ready for market, and I didn't know what to tell him."

"Where is he?"

"Out back."

Carolyn gave Tres Zapatos' reins to her half brother and strode confidently away. She had been faced with many of her limitations and weaknesses these last months, but she still had no doubts about her knowledge of ranching.

Matt Gentry was in the back corral working a newly broken filly. She was a pretty little thing, kind of dainty, but full of vitality. She was going to make a good mount. Carolyn had thought about keeping the horse for herself, but she could see that Matt was quite attached to the roan beauty.

"Matt," Carolyn called after watching for a few minutes.

He looked her way, then strode to where she was standing at the rail. "Howdy, Carolyn."

"Ramón tells me you wanted to see me," she said to the new Bar S foreman.

"Just thought you oughta know I've found several dead calves lately. I'm afraid we got a wolf problem."

"A big pack?"

"Could be."

"You know any good wolfers in these parts?"

"There's a fella used to hunt wolves for the Bar S. He's kind of a character, though. I once saw him pick his cigarette makings out of a pocket full of wolf poison—mostly strychnine—and smoke all day and live to tell about it."

"Yeah, we got some dandies up north, too. If you think the problem's bad enough, we better take care of it." She paused. "I guess Ramón could have told you that."

"He ain't an old hand like you, Carolyn. Give him time."

Carolyn chuckled. "And how's it going with you, Matt? You taking to this foreman's work?"

"I reckon it's growing on me. It's more work than I thought it would be. You know us cowboys, always complaining about what an easy life the boss has."

"Well, I think we make a good team," said Carolyn. "I hope you stick around."

"I ain't going nowhere soon." Matt rubbed his chin and studied Carolyn for a moment. He didn't look at her in that frank way Sean had that was so disquieting, but it was with a kind of intensity that made Carolyn tingle. "I always figured this might be a good place to hang my spurs for a long spell."

"Hey, that reminds me," said Carolyn lightly, shaking away the odd feelings assailing her, "did you ever meet the banker's daughter?"

"Matter of fact, I did."

"You like her?"

"She was right nice."

"Really?"

"You sound like that surprises you, Carolyn. You told me yourself she was nice."

"I guess I did," she replied slowly, with regret she couldn't explain.

"Yessir!" Matt went on enthusiastically. "She fixed me chicken that melted right in my mouth; and can she dance! Why, it was like floating on a cloud."

"Good. I'm glad." Carolyn's tone seemed to indicate otherwise.

"One problem, though . . ."

"What?"

"She wasn't near as much fun as a gal I know who couldn't open

382

a can of beans properly even if a gun was held to her head, and who dances like a bow-legged horse."

"Why, you—" Carolyn began irately, until she figured out that Matt's words were as much a compliment as anything. "You really mean that, Matt?"

"Every word!" he answered with an earnest straight face, then grinned.

They laughed until their sides hurt. At last Carolyn said with complete sincerity and as much solemnity as she could muster, "I'm glad you're sticking around, Matt."

"Well, Carolyn, I know a good thing when it stampedes over me!"